We need a Revolution

David E. Merrifield

Published in 2012 by FeedARead.com Publishing – Arts Council funded

Copyright © David E. Merrifield

First Edition

The author has asserted their moral right under the Copyright, Designs and Patents Act, 1988, to be identified as the author of this work.

All Rights reserved. No part of this publication may be reproduced, copied, stored in a retrieval system, or transmitted, in any form or by any means, without the prior written consent of the copyright holder, nor be otherwise circulated in any form of binding or cover other than that in which it is published and without a similar condition being imposed on the subsequent purchaser.

A CIP catalogue record for this title is available from the British Library.

INTRODUCTION

The year is 2025 and this is really the story of just another normal everyday family, trying to live normal everyday lives in the current political situations that they find themselves in. A man with a wife and two daughters trying to do what was best for them all. A man who cared not only for those close to him but generally for everyone else he got on with. You can choose your friends. You can choose your partner and you can choose whether or not to have a family. There were in fact quite a lot of things that you did have the option to choose. But then there were many things that you didn't. You cannot choose what sort of political society they are brought up in. Everyone was mixed up in the politics of today in some form or another. You wouldn't find it that easy to just sit on the fence anymore you had to have an opinion and had to be prepared to voice that opinion. Socially the class divide had re-emerged but had not so much to do with money as to do with power, although one usually came with the other and in today's society you either controlled the people in some way or were controlled. You were either part of the establishment or against the establishment. It was practically impossible to live a nice easy life, or be middle of the road. Unemployment was also very high. Food was difficult to come by even if you could pay for it. Poverty extremely common! Trouble frequent! Luxury was almost unheard of. Death was quite a regular occurrence. Close family bereavement nothing unusual. Gary Newson at least has a job and a fairly good job at that. In fact a lot of people considered that he had a very important job. In many ways he was probably considered part of the establishment but that wasn't how Gary saw himself. He was trying to survive and he had to keep his job to help his family survive. A lot of people haven't got jobs so you would think that he would be happy or at least content. But he isn't.

Gradually things have got harder in the world. Things had in fact got a lot worse in Britain. More alarmingly, things had got worse in the village where Gary Newson lived. The village of Waydon, just about 6 miles outside of Kentley close to the east coast of England. It was a small village but growing very slowly. Gary had been born in Kentley and brought up in Kentley. Life in general was a lot harder than it used to be. Like most people though, Gary adapted with the times and did what he had to do to survive and bring up his family. Although he would probably find it very hard to admit, his family was very important to him. In fact they were the most important thing to him. He worked hard to make sure that his wife and daughters were fed and clothed and as often as possible treated to some fun times. Once, some while ago he had ambition he remembers. That desire to become rich and famous or at least get to a high ranking post in his job but not anymore. He'd always heard rumours of how ordinary people were being persistently forced further and further into poverty but he had dismissed most of those rumours as the exaggerations of some overactive minds. But now even he was tasting an element of what he recognised as poverty and reality for Gary was seeming to be getting much nearer to these rumours. A lot of things were changing. His home! His work! The whole way of life in fact!! Although there had not been any official statement as to why, the streets were now regularly patrolled by armed soldiers. They had practically taken over normal police duties. The police were very much non existent. The elected Government, as a decision making body seemed to have retreated into almost entire obscurity and there was almost a military rule. It wasn't a British military rule either. The regular Army nowadays was run from Strasbourg. The European Army was taking a stronghold over all the country. Locally even, a new military base seemed to have replaced the old school almost overnight just on the outskirts of the village and it was steeped in security by day and only seemed to be working by night. Nobody knew what was going on in the place, not even Gary. There was also the curfew that had been introduced almost without question which although a lot of his neighbours, friends and family had apparently taken to quite easily, Gary hadn't. He could still remember what life used to be like and he couldn't help thinking that things weren't what they should be. They certainly hadn't changed for the better either.

    Despite the fact that Gary had a job which gave him a fairly responsible position, he had decided that he was going to investigate what was going on at this new military site on the edge of his village. Even if all of his friends and colleagues were prepared to just sit around and let things happen he wasn't going to. But it gets him into trouble and makes him out to appear like a revolutionary even though he hadn't started with that intention. Although in the years gone past,

Gary had got mixed up with some anarchists he wasn't really a political animal and certainly no real threat to the days Government. However, incidents can change many a thing and Gary again gets involved with the revolutionaries which in today's political climate and especially for Gary, was quite a bad situation to find himself in but he was confident he would be able to cope with it. He might even be able to turn the situation to his advantage. Added to his problems, his wife Angela threatens to leave him if he doesn't stop looking for trouble or getting mixed up in things that shouldn't concern him. She keeps telling him she will leave and take their two daughters, Katy and Joan with her if he doesn't stop making all this fuss about the new military site but Gary believes she is bluffing. Anyway, it's a problem he is sure that he can handle.

Gary has also had quite some troubled times within his own family. Deaths in the family had caused a rift between him and his sister Sarah and although time had helped heal it, they were not ready to be as they were before, even though they probably needed each other so badly. They were both stubborn enough to get on with dealing with their own problems. It was only in the last year that Sarah and Gary had been speaking again on a regular basis and they had so much to tell each other.

But can he handle the secret undercurrents created by the new mess he has got himself into. Somehow he needs to find out who his friends are and who his enemies are without telling anyone exactly what his true feelings may be. There is revolution in the air and he seems to have got himself mixed up right in the middle of it. Who can he trust? Nobody but himself!

There is also an undercover Army agent working in the area. They seem to be quite close to Gary but who could it be. Their identity is not known. Not even by some of the higher ranking Army officials. It is most important that this agent keeps their identity a secret or else it could mean the end to their career. Not just their Army career but the one they had forged for themselves in normal everyday life. Exposure might also mean danger.

Over twenty five years ago the United Nations was a very busy organization which was given the task of trying to resolve as many of the worlds problems as it could. There were regular outbreaks of civil unrest in which the UN would play a leading role in keeping situations under control and then there was the occasional war for them to try and mediate between as well. Although the United Nations was seen as the only true representation of all of the worlds inhabitants, as always the leading military powers (USA in particular) seemed to get their way with decisions far more than some of the other countries involved. In particular, it was the Special Security Council that came under regular attack for being controlled by the Americans but nothing was ever done to disband the council so it was left to evolve in its natural way. What did happen though was that more and more, the Special Security Council had to form numerous sub-committees to discuss particular aspects of security. These were formed normally as small, short shelf life committees, usually due to be disbanded about a year after formation. They would usually meet in one of the main European buildings in Brussels, Geneva or The Hague but there was a newly formed committee that was about to meet in one of the many rooms in the UN building in Strasbourg.

The United Nations World Threat Committee was set up about three months ago to look at trying to identify what starts civil unrest and war so as to pinpoint future problems and deal with them at an early stage before they get out of hand. This committee was quite unusual in as much as there were no US representatives on it. At the previous two meetings only a few of the full electorate had met to try and sort out the various situations that they were informed about. It hadn't been a success as not too much had been achieved and the more senior members of the committee were convinced that they would all be criticized for it by the US and British members in the full house. As such it had been agreed that at this next meeting, that they would try a much more positive approach and tackle the situations with some aggressive and proactive solutions. The previous smaller meetings had always taken place at more secluded type places where watching eyes would not be able to work out who was meeting but again it had been decided that on this special occasion, something different was required.

It was Monday 10th. May 2004 and the sub-committee members were making their way to Room 729 for today's meeting. The meeting was due to start at 12.00hrs in order to give all members the chance to travel although many had flown in the night before. The room was on the seventh floor of course and the usual security arrangements were being enforced. Two Security Guards were on duty outside the room and they would have checked the room out for bugging devices and then waited for the committee to take their places. Once everyone that was expected had arrived, the committee would be locked in so that nobody from outside could disturb them. The door was of course able to be opened from the inside. There was no printed agenda and all members asked to keep notes to a minimum. Minutes were typed up by one of the UNs pool staff and copies given to each member before they were allowed to leave. No other copies of the minutes were filed or kept anywhere. The UN pool were probably the best paid workers in the country. They were expected to be fully conversant in at least four languages, able to both touch type and audio-type but not only via a tape machine. Shorthand was also a requirement as well as a totally trustworthy attitude towards the UN and all it hopes to achieve. Members of the pool were only allowed to work on two yearly contracts before they were moved on to other duties or another job. It was possible to apply to come back to the pool after three years.

The member of the pool staff chosen for today's meeting had only been decided that morning and it was Miss Anna Senior. She actually came from a small place called Forest Hill near Oxford, in England. Anna was not only senior by name but also one of the most senior members of the pool with only about three or four months of her second contract left to do. She spoke five languages fluently and typed up minutes of meetings with ease. Anna was very proud of what she did for a living and never told any friends about the exact nature of her work but there was always lots of speculation. She didn't have many close friends and most had been friends from old jobs she had worked in. She would usually meet up with some of them every now and then and they would have a little chat about what jobs each was doing now but not Anna. She had made one special friend though and often chatted about her work to him. Anna had spent many of her younger years living in Belgium before moving to Germany where she had applied for her first job. Anna had started work as an interpreter for an English Euro MP before very quickly moving to the Security Pool. She would be out of contract in four months and hopefully married in five. There was a lot happening in Anna's life.

The Chairman of the committee, Commander Eduard Montpellier was the first into the room and he took his place at the top of the circular table, or at least the part of the circle furthest away from the door. The Frenchman watched as his colleagues came into the room. Each one carried their little briefcase which would contain the important notes or figures they required for this meeting as well as their own name cards. These would be placed on the table in front of each member so that the secretary knew who was talking. General Martin Busch from the German Army sat next to Eduard and both sat in full military uniform showing off their many medals and commendations. Three others were in uniform as well. Major General Lassiba Prenisas from the Greek Air Force and the two naval officers, General Paulo Cassino from Italy and Captain Dario Vidmar from Spain. There were also parliamentary representatives from Holland, Switzerland and Denmark who were Mariano Zwolle, Bernd Jensen and Ingrid Frausen respectively. All had been carefully chosen by Commander Montpellier for their views on the role of the military within the UN and the committee as a whole had already shown that they were very much in favour of sending in UN troops at an early stage so as to stop a small situation growing into major incident.

Anna took her seat, set away from the main table and quickly wrote down on paper the names of all the members as they put their cards out. She got her keyboard ready before indicating to The Chairman that she was ready. With a nod of his head, the Security closed and locked the door and Eduard addressed the meeting. After a few words, Eduard got the meeting straight into the workload and asked the Dutch MP and the Italian General to give details of terrorist attacks that had been taking place in the specific parts of Europe to which great concern had been drawn. They both talked about well organized mobs attacking fields of particular crops and certain food processing plants within their own countries. Although a lot of research had been done by the Dutch MP, the Italian General went on about how these mobs needed to be taught a lesson and an end put to their revolutionary ways immediately. He invited the committee to send in UN troops to show the Italian youth in his country some respect. His comments were received with warm applause around the table but Mariano Zwolle was not as moved as the others. He had been made to see what the rioting was all about and although he had started things off with a description of the rioting, he had slightly different views on the actual problem and of course what he thought the solution should be. Mariano started to talk again as he wanted to have his say whilst at the table. He began with telling the committee that the biggest problem was that the fields of crops and the food processing plants which had been chosen to be attacked in his country all had something in common. General Martin Busch wasn't interested in listening to the Dutch MPs' views and interrupted the speech and said that everyone around the table knew what they all had in common. Not enough security. That was what this committee had been set up to put right and that is what this committee should do. The rest of the committee applauded again. Mariano Zwolle wasn't entirely convinced but was in favour of some sort of action. He felt that Busch was probably going to over react but thought he would wait his turn for now and see what suggestions were made before arguing against them. He had actually been to see one of the attacks on a vegetable canning plant just outside Arnhem where the local Police had managed to stop the whole plant from being destroyed. There had been a lot of violence and the police had actually lost the lives of two of their officers during the clash. What had really annoyed Mariano though was that out of the twenty or so rioters who had been arrested only two actually came from Holland. The rest were from England, Greece, Italy, Cyprus and then from countries like Armenia, Slovakia, Croatia and Bosnia. He tried again to tell the committee what he had learnt from the enquiries that had been made that all the food that had been targeted in his land was all destined to be exported to either France or Germany. Almost immediately Eduard questioned where he had got this information from which Mariano had to admit came from the terrorists. He had started to check it out but Eduard and Martin forced Mariano to keep quiet until he had proper evidence to give to this committee rather than terrorist propaganda that he was pushing around the table. Again this seemed to have the support of the rest of the committee and Mariano decided he should stay quiet for now.

Eduard Montpellier knew pretty well what Mariano was trying to tell the committee as he too had been advised by his briefing team as to what the terrorists were saying was happening. Basically more and more foodstuffs being grown around Europe were being earmarked for export to the more influential countries within Europe. This would normally mean either France or Germany but not entirely.

This was no real problem as they were the two richest countries and were prepared to pay over the odds for their imports and hence all things should balance themselves out with other parts of Europe getting more money for their exports and France and Germany getting less or nothing for theirs. Unfortunately things had started to change and a lot of Belgian farmland, for example, was being purchased by French farmers. They would then stop growing the sort of foods that the Belgians wanted and instead grow food that the French wanted and export their produce to them instead. It left countries like Belgium without enough food for their people whilst France and Germany had plenty to choose from. The population had had enough. Eduard had had enough. He wasn't going to let his country become the target of massive unrest in Europe so he addressed the committee with the result of his latest study.

Eduard told them about the fact that figures showed that major cities all over Europe were growing at such a rate that although it may seem that France and Germany were getting the best of things it was only a minor situation due to his countries financial strength and that his study went further to show that all of Europe would be starving by the year 2007 if something wasn't done about it. The population of Europe was going through the roof and there just wasn't enough land to grow enough food to feed everybody. We have been hoping all along that synthetic food would be the answer to all of our problems but recent reports show that this would only hold back the inevitable for a few months. Eduard brought the committee to a crescendo when he convinced them all with a date in 2009 when starvation would kick in. But he had the solution. The answer was within us and it was quite easy. We need a war in Europe. There was a stunned silence around the room at the suggestion.

The Swiss MP, Bernd Jensen was the next to speak and said that surely that was exactly what this committee was set up to prevent yet here we were suggesting that we do not stop or intervene in the next war. The military committee members all seemed quite pleased with the idea even if it meant their troops dying for the cause. He had expected the committee would be loud in support of his statement but he was disappointed with its quiet response. The Danish MP was next to speak and she did so in such a quiet voice that the rest of the committee immediately went quiet so that she could be heard. Her question was quite important as it got everyone thinking and it asked that if the next war to breakout was in, for instance Norway, would it actually help the overpopulation of Europe and if so how long would the war have to go on. This caused a lot of concern around the table but Eduard had an answer to everything. A war in Norway would not be the best place to bring a quick solution to our problem but it would help. What we really need is a war in a more populated part of Europe or at least try and drag such an area into that war. Now even better! If there was a war that we were actually in control of we could quite easily feed the war with troops from all over the UN until we had reached our desired population figure. It wouldn't be mass murder as everyone would have his or her chance. There would be rationing to help the situation in the early stages. Votes to carry UN Directive WTC 010504 were taken but only four of the military representatives voted in favour, the Greek Major General abstained and the three MPs all voted against. Another vote was taken after some discussion and the Swiss MP changed his vote to a Yes whilst the Danish MP abstained. Mariano still voted No and without him changing his vote the motion could not be carried. The meeting was eventually called to an end without any resolutions being finalised. The committee agreed to meet again to discuss different options in about a month's time but Eduard left them saying that he knew that this was the only avenue that would be able to bring about some control of the situation. Everyone was told to go away and think hard about his suggestion and he dared all of them to come up with an alternative workable solution. The committee waited for their copy of the minutes to be printed off and they were again reminded by Eduard that these minutes were to be strictly for this committee's eyes only. Nobody outside this room is to know what we have discussed today.

      The committee gradually left Room 729 and one of the first to go was Eduard Montpellier. He was not pleased with the way the voting had gone and was already working out how he would convince the committee at the next meeting to support him. Anna packed away her things and put away the computer and keyboard before taking out a floppy disk and putting it in her bag. She got ready to leave the room.
"Excuse me Miss Senior," General Busch said in his German accent as he grabbed her arm to prevent her from leaving the room. The two Security Guards stood to attention.
"I cannot let you leave with a copy of our minutes," he finished by

holding out his hand. A chill went up Anna's spine as if her grave was being walked all over. She kept her composure.

"You mean the disk?" She asked.

"Of course!" The General replied in a more aggressive tone.

"The minutes have been wiped from it. It only holds the face setting needed to take my next set of minutes." Anna said, swallowing hard.

"I'll take it anyway." Anna gave him the disk.

"And where is the paper that you took notes on?" The General had been keeping an eye on her and had counted at least three sheets of paper she had written on.

"There on the disposal pile as always Sir." Anna pointed to the little pile of papers at the end of the committee table. Martin looked at the papers and walked over to them counting out four sheets altogether. He nodded his head.

"She can go."

Anna was allowed to leave the room. The Security Guard still had to search her before she was allowed to proceed. Martin Busch was sure that the disk would contain a copy of the minutes but almost to his annoyance when he put the disk in the computer, all it contained on it was a template ready for the next set of minutes to be taken. She had been telling the truth after all. Martin Busch must have been losing it as he was rarely wrong about someone and he was certain she had taken a copy. He turned to the door.

"Has Miss Senior got any other disks on her at all?" He asked the Security Guard.

"Nothing, Sir!"

    Anna continued on her way out of the building and back to her flat where she was greeted by her partner and very close friend, Martin. As it was late he had cooked a dinner and had a drink ready waiting for her when she got in. She told him everything about the meeting but then she trusted Martin implicitly. To get these sorts of things off of her chest was brilliant. Martin would always know what to say to calm her down as well. After having a bath, Anna decided to make a computer record of what had happened at that meeting. Everything was still fresh enough in her head for her to record the fundamental aspects of the meeting. She listed some of the attendees and what was said in general before saving it to a disk. She wasn't quite sure of everything but had written down all the names and some key comments on the paper at the meeting. She had handed them all in to be destroyed but she always wrote with a heavy hand and there would be impressed papers she could pick up tomorrow that would remind her of everything. She never really knew why she wrote out these copies but she did and perhaps one day it might be useful. Anna knew well enough that it was practically impossible to take a copy of any minutes out on a disk but she had mastered the ability to keep a lot of the more important details in her head. As long as she wasn't asked to take any further minutes before committing them to paper or disk, she was reasonably happy that she would be able to get most of it down. Although the main subject of the meeting had been given an official UN Directive WTC number, both Montpellier and Busch regularly referred to 'their document of intent'. Anna used the same term.

There were further meetings of the UN World Threat Committee but most finished up pretty much the same way with no majority vote being reached. There was however a last meeting of the committee on 20th. February 2005. It was a 'special' meeting called very quickly and again held in a meeting room in Strasbourg. It just happened to be taking place just 2 days after the trouble started in Lesbos. The same eight members of the committee were present and Eduard Montpellier was in the Chair again. The meeting didn't last very long. The Greek Air Force Major General stood up and talked about the troubles in Lesbos and said that this was a great opportunity for this committee to try and help the population problem by removing some Turkish mouths. Martin Busch and Eduard Montpellier convinced Major General Prenisas that they would give Turkey to the Greeks and make them war heroes. Eduard still didn't get his vote but he'd got his war. The civilian recorder for this meeting went through the normal routines, taking nothing into the meeting with him and bringing nothing out. For this meeting they had chosen a Frenchman, Martin Giraund. He'd only been in the post about six months. He left the meeting and went straight home to his wife. Anna couldn't believe what she was being told. She asked Martin to tell her who was at the meeting and the list of attendees matched those who were at the meeting she had previously submitted to disk. The so called 'document of intent' was starting to grow.

One of the revolutionary secret undercover agents was sitting at his desk perusing his notes on the work that he had done in Motril just recently. It all revolved around instructions he had received from his contact known only as Robert Stevenson about six months previously. They were quite direct instructions. The details of how and when were left up to him. It was quite simple, there was a target to dispose of and it was his job to arrange it. No questions asked. The whole package had been sent to his operational name 'Doctor Livesey' as normal. The instructions were not posted in the normal fashion as this was too dangerous. There was an agreed method of getting this sort of package to where it had to go. It was almost military in the way it was executed. It contained brief details of a name and the likely address they lived at. He would know no more. He didn't need to.

The name was in fact, one of a number of delegates who attended two very important meetings of the UN World Threat Committee some time ago. There was a list of eight names. Bearing in mind that the list was over twenty five years old, most of the people in it were easily in their fifties and some even older than that but the leaders of The Revolutionary Party had all agreed that this was the real start to all of their problems and everyone on that list was guilty. A different name was picked from the list in order and the last known whereabouts of that member were sent with the usual instructions to one of the usual assassins. Very few people knew the full list of names and certainly none of the assassins knew.

It wasn't widely known but one committee member had already been assassinated and the list was down to just seven. The next target had been chosen and Doctor Livesey knew who it was. Dario Vidmar. He thought long and hard about his work so far and seemed happy that he knew what he would do next. There had been no word from his contact to suggest that anything was amiss so he began to bring his task to its conclusion. It was very rare that a mission would fail or that something might go wrong but Doctor Livesey was ready for any such eventualities just in case. If this were to happen, it might lead to the Military following the trail back. It might lead back to him. He never ever felt it would. Doctor Livesey folded up the notes and put them away safely in a specially constructed safe. It was unlikely that he would ever be identified but just in case, he didn't want any incriminating evidence found that easily.

Chapter 1 - EARLY INDICATIONS

It was the first of March and Sergeant Foulkes had been given his orders for this evening's duty. He was running through the final checks in preparation for a road check. There were numerous road checks being performed by The Army this afternoon as they were checking all the traffic leaving the town of Kentley. It was quite routine and the public were used to the ordeal even though it was intrusive and very much a hindrance. It didn't mean they liked it. As always, Sergeant Foulkes was only given as much information as he needed to know about the reasons for this particular check and that was good enough for him. Tonight they were looking for a man in his forties, without the proper papers to be travelling to wherever he might be going. Ed Foulkes was fairly used to getting these sort of orders nowadays and he was very good at organising his unit to carry out their duties efficiently. He had briefed them earlier and things had gone down well enough but he was a little concerned that there had been a question from one of his unit stating that there had been rumours they were looking for a revolutionary gunrunner. He had convinced them that he would have been told if that had been the case. He hadn't convinced himself though. Regardless, he knew his team would do a good job.

The roadblock started slowly as usual with the first few vehicles being stopped, quickly checked out and allowed on their way with nobody held up for very long. Unit Charlie 12 had been given the South Westerly exit out of Kentley. This would involve people travelling mainly to Bateley but it was also the outlying villages of Sutton, Greenfields, Lavenham and Waydon. As each vehicle was stopped the soldiers would make sure they looked at everyone's papers. This involved checking identity cards, resident's permits and vehicle ownerships as well but today was slightly different. The Army had also been instructed to confirm each person's reason for travelling. All of this had to be checked against Government and Military computer records and took a few more minutes than usual but the Unit were very disciplined and had a practiced method.

Everyone travelling by car nowadays knew the score and all would have their papers out ready. There would occasionally be the need to remind someone that one of their documents would be out of date soon but nothing more serious than that.

"Papers please!" The soldier asked the driver of the next car. He was polite but forceful and left the person in the car in no doubt what was required. The man sat there and just looked at him. "Papers. Now!" It was time to concentrate. The Private looked quickly in the direction of one of the more experienced soldiers, Private Kenton Bridge and he immediately tuned in to the fact that there was someone being unhelpful. Kenton checked there was only one person in the car so he moved around to the passenger side of the car and cocked his automatic to show support.

"Alright, alright, bloody papers. I have them here somewhere." The man in the car opened up the glove box in his car and rummaged around for a couple of seconds. He continued to curse whilst he searched. "Yes you see here they are, all in order." The man waved them in the general direction of the soldiers but never looked as if he was going to hand them over.

"Papers please. Now, Sir, before we have to arrest you." Everyone tried to remain calm. He guessed that the man was just having a bad day but he still had to comply with what he was being asked. It was a situation that could get out of hand if not handled properly. The man in the car sighed and dropped his shoulders then offered his papers out of the window.

"Thank you Sir. This will only take a couple of minutes."

"Get on with it then." The man replied. The soldier ignored the remark but wouldn't forget it. He took a couple of steps away from the car and looked at the information on all three documents. Robert Keith Benson he said to himself. His papers were all in order.

"And why have you been travelling today?"

"Why do you think?" This wasn't the sort of answer the soldier had hoped for and added to the man's previous answer his immediate future was very much in the balance.

"I'll ask you only once more. Why have you been traveling today?" As the tone of the soldiers voice gave off a warning, Private Bridge held his rifle a little harder. Both were aware of where each other was positioned and both were ready to react to whatever might happen next.

"Yeah I'm sorry." The man replied. "It's been a bad day." He started to sob. Again this was not what the Private wanted from him but the soldier kept his composure a little longer. "I've been shopping." The man pulled the lever inside the car in an effort to open the door and get out.

"Stay inside the car Sir." The soldier pushed his knee against the door to prevent it from opening. He then told the man exactly what he should do. "Put your hands back on the steering wheel." The man complied but not before he pushed his hands through his hair a couple of times and grabbed what little hair he still had in anger. The hands made a noise as he slammed them on the wheel.

"I'm just trying to get some food for my family." The man sobbed a little bit more.

The soldier dealing with the vehicle indicated to his colleague, Kenton to keep an eye on the man as he walked away from the car a little to hand the papers over to another soldier who in turn despatched them to the mobile office on the other side of the road for checking.

"Where is your shopping Sir?"

"In the boot." By now the man was too angry to move. His hands were turning white with the grip he had on the steering wheel.

"Just open it from inside the car so I can look at it." As the order was given, the soldier looked up at Kenton Bridge who was already on his way round to watch the man in the car whilst he checked out the shopping. The boot release lever was pulled and it sprung open. The soldier cautiously looked inside. It was a sorry sight as far as he was concerned. In the boot were a collection of just four vegetables. A medium sized turnip and a small potato with a half rotten parsnip and very old looking carrot. Sadly this wasn't an usual sight and he knew it was the sort of food that some civilians were forced to buy when times were hard. He guessed that times for Robert Benson must have been very hard. Under a piece of cardboard was a half eaten pigeon. Obviously the rats had got to it before its current owner but these were desperate times and the meat left on the bird would probably make a reasonable soup. This was not something that was available legally and he guessed that it had been acquired on the undermarket. Lots of illegal food was sold there. Desperate people never asked where the food had come from. They just paid with whatever they could to get it.

Officially, the Private should have asked a few more questions about the pigeon but he began to feel sorry for the man in the car. He was only trying to live. He thought quickly and made sure that nobody else had seen the pigeon before covering it back up and closing the boot.

"All okay?" Kenton asked. The soldier looking in the boot gave a nod of approval and Private Bridge retreated back to his original position. The soldier slammed the boot closed and made his way back to the driver's window where the man in the car was waiting for the outcome. He assumed he would be arrested and questioned but the soldier just stood there and looked at him. He looked deep into his eyes. Here was a man struggling to find food. It was pitiful. It was shameful. It was embarrassing. The driver turned and looked at the soldier. Nothing was said but the soldier just stared back at him.

"Yeah he's clear." The silence was broken by another soldier as she returned from the mobile office with the man's papers. She gave them straight back to the man in the car.

"Can I go?"

"Yes you can be on your way." Each soldier took a step back as an indication they were happy for the man to go but the soldier who had looked inside the boot held his stare. The driver felt the gaze as if he was using some superhuman ray. He fumbled with the ignition key and started his motor quickly. He continued on his way.

"Are you alright?" Kenton asked his colleague. The soldier stared at the car as it drove off.

"Yeah I'm alright."

Sergeant Foulkes kept an eye on proceedings and watched as his Unit carried out the questioning of the next car. A small queue had developed because of the delay with that last one but it wasn't too long at the moment and would quickly be reduced. Ed would also have to arrange for checks to be carried out on any busses taking these routes. That would stretch the Unit to its maximum but Sergeant Foulkes knew they would cope. They were professional soldiers who knew what was required. The whole of the team was at risk if anyone relaxed too much so there was no real time to be off guard.

A few minutes later the first bus was stopped at the roadblock. A soldier directed the bus out of the normal channels and over to a lay-by where all of the busses and lorries were being checked. It was a single decker bus. Two soldiers boarded it whilst two other Privates kept watch. There were only six passengers on the bus so it shouldn't take too long to check.

"Can you turn the engine off please?" The first soldier asked the driver as soon as they got on. The driver did as he was told. "You take the two at the back." The soldier indicated to a couple who had sat down on one of the seats towards the back of the bus.

"Right Sir!" He came to the first man on the bus. "Your papers please?" The soldier took the documents from the man and gave them a quick glance. Another uniformed Private was stood near to the door of the bus and he took the papers from him so they could be checked. He continued to question the man about his activities that day. Happy with the reply he moved on to an old woman and young girl who were sat two seats behind him.

"There we are Sergeant." The old woman already had her papers out ready. He took them and looked at them as usual.

"Millicent Wiltshire!" He said her name out loud. The old lady nodded in approval. As he looked closer at the papers, his colleague walked down the bus and passed him with some papers to hand to the waiting soldier outside of the bus.

"Are you just doing a normal check then Sergeant?" The old woman asked. The fact that she always called him Sergeant was already annoying him but he tried to ignore it.

"Yes madam. Where have you been today?"

"Just into Kentley!"

"And why?"

"Well my daughter went for a job interview so I went with her." The old woman seemed proud of the fact that her daughter had been given an interview. Not many people got interviews and most that did had absolutely no chance of getting a job at the end of it. It was done for statistics. To show that they at least offered any jobs going to the general public before giving it to a friend or someone who could offer something for it. There were no jobs open for just the best candidate anymore. The soldier looked at the little girl sat next to the old woman and judged her to be aged about twelve. This was obviously not her daughter.

"And you are?"

"I'm Hayley Parmenter." The little girl blushed as she answered.

"And do you have any papers with you?" He asked as nicely as he could. She reminded him of his young sister when he was growing up.

"Of course she doesn't have any papers with her Sergeant." The old woman answered with an indignant tone.

"I'm a Private." By this time the soldier's patience had reached its limit. "So please let me have her papers Madam."

"But she hasn't got any. She is included on her Mother's papers."
"But her Mother isn't travelling with her is she? Once again he started to get angry.
"Well no but her Grandmother is."
"Not for much longer." The soldier got ready to deal with this situation. "Private Smith," he shouted out.
"Here." Private Andy Smith was still on the bus but a couple of yards behind him.
"I have two people to be taken off of the bus." He had made up his mind that he would get both of them off. The little girl definitely had to be taken off as she had no papers but he felt it was right to take the Grandmother, if that was who she was, off as well. "Can you please get off the bus Madam?" He asked the old woman politely but firmly.
"I'm not getting off without Hayley." The old woman started to get a bit concerned. She grabbed her shopping bag and placed it in front of her on her lap in some form of defence against the soldier.
"I need you both off the bus." The soldier indicated with his gun which he had by this time brought back into a forward position. Both the old woman and the little girl were getting more and more frightened and less prepared to move. "Private Smith." He shouted out again.

Andy had alerted a couple of the other soldiers about a possible situation on the bus but one had gone off to the mobile van with some papers so only one Private was available as back up. He immediately looked around and caught the eye of Private Dobbs who had reacted to the situation and had also made her way over to the bus. Inside, the atmosphere was getting a little hot and the whole situation was beginning to get out of the Private's control. The old woman was sitting tight, the little girl was crying and the soldier himself was shouting out to the both of them to get off the bus. There were two other single males on the bus and both tried to get involved and stop the soldier from upsetting the little girl anymore. Private Rachel Dobbs hopped on to the bus quickly followed by one of her male colleagues. She immediately barked out an order above the commotion and called a halt to the shouting.
"Someone's going to die soon." There was a deafly silence. The bus driver turned around in his seat and looked back at the old woman.
"Just do as they say and get off the bus." He said in a frail nervous voice.

"Oh right." It was as if the old woman had not understood a single word the first soldier had been saying to her. Little Hayley started crying again as her Grandmother held her hand and started to leave the bus. A Private escorted them both off the bus whilst the two males muttered abuse at him.

"Shut up and sit down or you'll all be arrested." A soldier barked down the bus. One of the men sat down but the other remained standing in an aggressive pose. He was of Mediterranean complexion. Private Rachel Dobbs walked over to him in a most aggressive manner but he remained standing.

"You were told to sit down." She looked him in the eye as he remained standing. She was almost exploding inside with aggression. He began to look her up and down. In one quick action, Rachel moved her gun from an attack stance to an upright position before hitting him in the crutch with the thick butt end of it. The man bent over in pain. His eyes red and watering. He was gasping for breath. Rachel placed the palm of her hand on his head and pushed him back down on to his seat. "So fucking sit down. Twat." Rachel stopped herself from hitting the bloke again although she very much wanted to. She quickly composed herself and just calmly turned round and made her way off the bus. Her colleague watched her as she walked passed him. He nodded his head a few times in approval. Everyone on the bus sat in stunned silence.

As the two soldiers left the bus they were aware that their search had been far longer than usual. Not only that, the soldiers who were dealing with the private cars had also been hit with a few problems and there was an obvious atmosphere of discontent. Some of the more brave civilians had got out of their cars and as they both looked down the line of waiting cars, they noticed one or two were shouting obscenities in the direction of the roadblock. There were only a few words that could be properly made out like 'Wankers' and 'Bastards' but nobody was stupid enough to be seen to swear at the soldiers in fear of retribution.

Bateley Road was a main road out of Kentley and in the past would have been very busy but the decline in the number of people owning cars or, those able to afford to run them meant that traffic had reduced greatly in the last ten to fifteen years. The Bateley Road had only a few shops on it. Not many of them were actually open for business. Very few small businesses had managed to survive the decline in the last ten years and most had gone bankrupt. Most black market shops operated on the move or as and when they could and really only Government backed food outlets were up and running today. The road also had a number of small offices on it and then lastly a couple of bigger residential properties. Not all of the residential properties were lived in by just one family but a lot of them were now housing two or three generations of the same family. Some properties were empty and boarded up and others had been demolished to make way for small blocks of flats. The cost of repairing your own property was very high with very few builders still in business so most of the properties that had been kept going were worked on by family members. As the residential area came to an end, the Bateley Road opened up into a more open land area with mainly allotments to both sides of the road for about the next half a mile. Then there came a small wooded area beyond those allotments. There wasn't much more housing then until you got to the villages with most of the land being farmland in between. There was the irregular little yard or storage area but most of these had been vandalised.

It was in the area where there were allotments each side that Unit Charlie 12 had set up their roadblock. This was done for a number of reasons. One was the fact that there were very few legitimate turns a driver could take after the roadblock and still say they lived in town. Secondly, if anyone decided to do a runner from their cars there weren't really any alleys or streets for them to head for. The allotments were fenced off with six foot high fencing and then there was a small bit of rough land before another fence, about three feet high separating that ground from the pavement. The allotments were very keenly looked after as it was many people's only means of getting fresh vegetables and the allotments were well worked all year round. Many of them had erected sheds to house their tools and seeds but many people brought them with them from home in the fear that they would be stolen if left on the allotments. Not surprisingly many of the sheds were heavily padlocked and possibly housed all sorts of things. Mostly though they knew that the allotments were legitimately used by locals trying to grow a few extra vegetables. There wouldn't be much else going on.

Still there were no signs of traffic getting through the

roadblock that easily and a number of motorists who had got out of their cars had begun to bang their hands on the car roofs. As more joined in, the sound took on a timed drum beat as if it was some sort of war cry. All of the soldiers heard it and it annoyed them immensely. None more than Rachel Dobbs of course. She looked at the long line of cars waiting and the occasional driver stood on the road by the side of their vehicle and she became increasingly irritated by the drumming noise as it got slightly louder. Without warning she took a few large strides towards the line of cars and shot her machine gun into the air letting off a few rounds. The noise broke the tension a little. The drumming stopped and most civilians got quickly back into their cars.
"Private Dobbs." There was a shout from her Corporal. Rachel stood to attention and turned to face him.
"Sir." She replied as she stamped her right foot down hard into the ground.
"Don't waste valuable ammunition."
"No. Sir." She had got the message
"Is everything alright?" Sergeant Foulkes appeared from his mobile office after hearing the shots
"Yes Sir." Answered the Corporal. "All in order, Sir!"

  As far as Sergeant Foulkes was concerned, everything was going well. Despite a couple of problems there was nothing really to report and gradually the traffic started to build up as more cars were making their way home. From about five o'clock, there was a constant queue of traffic and people were getting more annoyed when they were being questioned. The Corporal had taken over on the car checkpoint and almost immediately found an occupant in a car with papers that were out of date. "Get out of the car sir." He ordered. With immaculate co-ordination is three colleagues all cocked their automatics and stepped up their attention.
"Is there something wrong?" The man in the car answered sheepishly. Pointing his own automatic towards the man, the Corporal just politely repeated himself,
"Get out of the car." He completed his sentence with a short sharp loud "Now."
As the man got out, he called across "Sergeant. One to be looked at!"
Sergeant Foulkes beckoned one of the resting soldiers to come with him as he made his way over to the car checkpoint. Taking the man's papers from the Corporal he noticed straightaway that the man was

about the correct age. His papers were about a fortnight out of date but showed that he had up to that date a fairly valid reason to be travelling along this road. It wasn't the most direct route to get to Chale but if you lived in the western or southern parts of Chale, it could sometimes be quicker to travel this way.
"You live in Chale?" Sergeant Foulkes asked.
"Yes," the man replied.
"So what do you do?"
"I have no job. I've been looking for work and trying to get some food today," the man replied.
"Take his details Private." Sergeant Foulkes ordered. He was quite happy that this was not the man they were trying to look for. Ed Foulkes looked hard and long at the man from the car. Brian Littlejohn he said to himself.
"Well Mr. Littlejohn, you'll be reported for having out of date papers and I would suggest that you get a relative to go to the issuing office to get new ones tomorrow." Sergeant Foulkes turned to the Corporal and ordered, "Let him on his way. Well done."

    This was about the fourth person found to be travelling on out of date papers. Not exactly what the unit were looking for. They hoped to find someone who was on papers relating to travel in a completely different area. Each stop meant another report Ed would have to file at the end of the shift and some trouble for the individuals who had been found out. They would probably think twice about travelling again with out of date papers in fear of being arrested. Ed thought it was all a bit over the top really as most of them were only trying to live their lives. Quite regularly people were just trying to buy or obtain some food but he had a job to do and wasn't going to let himself get into the position of having to worry about where the next meal was going to come from.

    The Corporal continued with his duties and got the line of traffic moving again. He was quite pleased with the way his colleagues had been right behind him. It was a very confident feeling. Members of his unit had been together for a few months now and they all worked well as a team. The next lot of cars were all quite in order and he had stopped the next car in line where a man and woman were the occupants. Just another man and wife trying to get back home. The wife was driving so he spoke to her.

"Papers", he ordered. The woman handed two sets of identity papers to him.
"Raymond and Susan Hobbs?" he said in a loud voice.
"Yes" the woman replied. "We're just on our way home to Waydon, officer," she added.
The Corporal took a look inside the car and he was about to ask another question when he heard one of his colleagues from behind him. He couldn't actually hear exactly what was being said but he was still listening. Although normally he would have ignored any noise from outside, he was trained to be able to listen for particular clues to potentially difficult situations. The tone in his colleagues' voice told him that this was just one of those situations.
"Stay in the car Madam!" A Private said in a raised voice.
Again as the words were being spoken there was the accompanying sound of automatic weapons being cocked. Corporal King looked up and saw that a woman in the waiting queue of vehicles was getting out of her car.

     From his brief glance he was quickly able to establish that she was in her late thirties or perhaps very early forties. She was obviously fit and had stunning long blond hair but seemed to be older than her fitness suggested she was. She obviously trained on a regular basis and this rang even more alarm bells in the Corporal's mind.
"Get back in the car." The Private shouted as the woman continued to walk away from the vehicle.
"Fuck you soldier," the woman shouted back. "I've had enough of these road blocks," she continued. By now there were at least three soldiers advancing towards her with loaded automatic guns aimed at her. The Corporal was aware that some sort of situation was developing nearby but he stayed in his position and told the occupants of the car he was questioning to stay where they were. He kept his gun trained on the general area of the woman. He looked from left to right in case there were other people ready to start a riot but was happy that she seemed to be working on her own. Within a few seconds, the rest of the Unit had switched on and were already training their weapons towards where the woman was. Under normal circumstances two soldiers would approach her from different directions and close in to arrest her but the woman was very swift and within seconds was out of easy reach of any soldier.
"Stop or I'll shoot", shouted the soldier who was already running after

her. He fired a couple of rounds over her head but it didn't seem to stop her. The blond woman had already made it to the side of the road where she quickly reached the small fence that was situated about a yard from the pavement. Behind the fence was some rough grassland and then another fence about six feet high. Beyond that was a field of allotments that were dotted with various garden sheds. Another soldier who had approached from further down the queue of traffic fired some more shots in the woman's general direction. She just stepped over the small fence like it wasn't even there and she was clearly going to be able to get over the next fence and into the field as the fence was in fact not that difficult to find a foothold on and had concrete posts to help. She had already shown that she was fit enough to climb over it but she stopped and started to turn back towards the soldier who was chasing her. It was almost a provocative type stance which teased him to try and prove just how macho he was. As she stopped, he immediately came to a halt. Without really realising it they had already covered about twenty yards and he was beginning to get sweaty palms. He didn't have too much time to think in these situations but knew that he would be backed up. As the woman turned, the Private bowed his stance and looked at her around waist level which was where he was trained to look. He was certain that he had seen her holding something in her hand. It looked shiny and perhaps metallic. It could have been a gun but he wasn't sure.
"Stay there. Don't move," he shouted but the woman continued to turn.
"Stop or I'll shoot!" He again shouted but she didn't stop.
Without hesitation, the soldier fired at the woman. He had only meant to fire to stop her from turning but the shots hit her straight in the back. The force of the shots twisted her body back the other way and the other advancing soldier reacted by also firing at her.

    Private Andy Smith had been one of the four soldiers stopping the cars at the front of the roadblock and keeping an eye out in case anyone had tried to attack the questioning team. With his colleague being the first to react, Private Smith had kept in the back up position expecting the woman to run towards the front of the queue of traffic. As she had ran towards the side of the road he had no option but to run level with her and be ready to cut her off should she decide to turn and run forward. He had heard every order that the soldier had shouted and knew in his own mind that she was not going to stop. As the blond woman reached the high fence he too kept his eyes trained on where her hands were positioned. She acted like she was ready to draw a weapon from her waist and as the first shot was fired by the Private who was following her, it was just instinctive for him to also fire at the woman.

Both soldiers reached the woman as she slumped to her knees by the fence.
"Fuck you soldier," she said as she died. Blood started to ooze from her wounds and very soon her knitted jumper was turning red. Her blond hair was also starting to turn a reddish tint from the blood.
"Keep alert." Sergeant Foulkes shouted as he ran over to the woman. He saw immediately that she was dead and realised that he would have to act quickly before there was any thought of a riot from other drivers.
"Get that car out of the way Corporal." Sergeant Foulkes ordered. The Corporal handed the papers back to the woman in the car he was questioning and told her to be on her way. The car behind had a single man driving it and he too was waved through. The other Private then helped him push the dead woman's car off the road and then they quickly got the next couple of vehicles through the checkpoint with a minimum check but stopped the third and continued with their questioning. Sergeant Foulkes ordered the two Privates to cover the woman's body with a groundsheet and then return to the rest area whilst two other Privates took their places in the roadblock. The soldiers both had the same burning question in their minds. What did she have in her hand? They both turned her over to see that she had only a leather wallet with an identity card in it. They looked at each other but said nothing.

-

The man in the car next in line was Martin Saunders. Although annoyed at the inconvenience, he had patiently waited for his turn at the questioning point. He knew exactly what he would be asked and he knew exactly what he was going to say. Although he had been out of the country for a couple of days there was nothing he had in the car that would indicate this. As the queue of cars had got nearer to the checkpoint, Martin had been keeping his eyes on the woman in the car behind him. She had tried to overtake him as they approached the queue of traffic which he had thought was rather rash but somehow professionally controlled. Not many drivers would have noticed what she was trying to do but he quickly spotted her intentions and this had brought his attention closer to the driver of the vehicle. He looked at her through his mirror admiring just how beautiful she was. As they moved nearer and nearer to the check point there was no suggestion that the woman was agitated at all, she just calmly opened the car door and sprang from the driver's seat. Martin thought to himself, 'what does she think she is doing?' 'What does she hope to achieve by running away.' As he watched her, he admired her athletic body as she strode across to the side of the road. He was able to see how fit she was and imagined the muscles in her thighs as she tore over the few yards of road. She had run a fairly short distance but it seemed like she was in slow motion, until the sound of the machine gun firing above her head snapped him out of it. She must stop running now he thought. He had already guessed that she was some sort of decoy. She had probably done her job. He was begging her to stop. Don't overdo it, he thought. She was a woman on a mission and nothing was going to stop her. He knew her sort.

Although he couldn't keep his eyes off of her he knew that something else was likely to happen soon. It could be a bombing of the checkpoint. He kept his eyes keen. He saw the first bullet rip through her jumper and into her back and then the second hit her in the stomach as her body twisted first one way and then the other. She danced from side to side like a puppet in the wind before she slumped to the ground. Martin knew she was dead. As he watched her lying indignantly by the side of the road he quickly realised that the checkpoint was in a state of temporary confusion and he started to drive towards the barrier as the car in front drove off. He was waved through as well. He was uncertain as to whether it would be better for him to stop and get checked but the soldier was most insistent so he drove through. Whoever or whatever the woman had been trying to cause a decoy for he didn't know, but he was quite able to deal with the situation. Nobody was going to speak to Martin Saunders tonight. As he drove off towards Waydon he took one last look back at the blond woman's body lying by the fence. Perhaps one day he would find out who she was.

Martin Saunders had watched the whole incident with ice cold indifference. He watched each and every soldier he could without them realising they were being watched. He kept a calm look on his face at all times which could often hide what was really going on inside. It was a look he had perfected over the years. The fact that he hadn't been questioned at the road block might come back to bite him so he would let one or two people know what had happened in case they heard anything. There was nothing he could do about it now he thought. He glanced at his watch as he drove towards his destination. He was slightly behind schedule for the start of his shift and he hated being late. He worked at the General Store in Greenfields where he had got himself a little part-time job. It didn't actually pay very much but Martin needed to work somewhere so he persevered with it for now but it was getting to the time when it would get in the way so he knew wouldn't continue working there much longer.

-

Sergeant Foulkes would get the body moved after the roadblock had been completed. His main duty was to make sure that the roadblock didn't fall apart and continued without anyone being missed. The dead woman's car was pushed out of the way and although the next two vehicles after the woman's car had only been briefly questioned the checkpoint was back in action properly by the time the third car got there. Within a minute and a half, things were back to normal and Ed Foulkes was happy he had missed nobody.

-

Gary left work at five thirty and got into his car. Most places were closing by this time of night but the Post Office carried on much later and Gary didn't have to worry about soldiers querying why he was travelling at this time. His job was almost like a military job and quite often considered as such. The car park was very much like a military zone with closed circuit cameras and barbed wire walls all around but it was something they were all used to. Gary drove to the automatic gate and swiped his card through the machine to make it open. As Gary drove out he made sure to miss the gaping great big hole in the middle of the road created by some bomb blast and yet to be filled in plus other obstacles like dustbins or bricks that may be lying about. The bonus about leaving at this time was the fact that there wouldn't be much traffic on the way home and so he would be able to get home a lot easier and so it appeared as Gary started the six-mile journey to his village. The first part of the journey was actually getting out of the town. This could be the longest part of the journey home if you were traveling at the wrong time. Pot holes and bits of rubble were the main problems to overcome but sometimes a turned over vehicle or a road that had become blocked. All of these things happened from time to time. The Army would eventually clear the roads again but it wasn't that quick.

It seemed like the journey was going to be no problem at all but Gary spotted signs of traffic ahead as he approached the outer suburbs of Kentley. Gary wondered what the hold up could be as by this time of the evening most people should have been arriving home. There was a quick burst of machine gun fire and Gary knew that the Army had to be involved. As he came up behind the last car in the line of traffic he looked to see if he could see any movement ahead. The man in the car in front got out and stretched up on to the tips of his toes in an effort to see what was going on. Like everyone else, he wanted to see what the hold up was but most knew that if you got out of your car you might be putting yourself into more danger. The man had the temerity to nod and look at Gary as if he was a close friend. He furtively approached. As Gary wound his window down the man quickly spouted, "Do you think there is an Army spot check?"

Gary knew he shouldn't have engaged into any sort of conversation but he didn't want to appear rude so he replied hoping it would only be a quick word. Gary wasn't too happy about the fact that the man's comments required a response but still replied, "Did I hear some gun fire?"
"Yes I think someone has tried to do a runner," the man answered.
The man suddenly looked around and decided that it would be safer to get back in his car. It was unusual for a stranger to come up to you and start speaking, as you had no idea what sort of person you might be speaking to. Simply telling Gary that there was an Army roadblock ahead could have been construed as an attempt to try and warn him and easily enough to be arrested on suspicion of being an anti-military activist. For Gary to have entered into the conversation could have also put him in a position of suspicion. There were undercover agents working everywhere to try and identify revolutionaries and they could be anyone. A simple stranger had often turned out to be a government agent trying to locate possible revolutionaries. Gary knew not to say

anything out of turn but the fact that this man had spoken to him caused him some concern. Gary was relieved to see him get back into his car.

After about five minutes the line of vehicles started to move and eventually Gary could see some signs of what had caused the hold up. There were two armoured vehicles and at least six Army soldiers with machine guns eyeing up the line of cars and to be more precise their occupants. To the left of the roadblock was an unoccupied car that seemed to have just been pushed out of the line of waiting cars. Two other soldiers were standing guard over something that was on the ground to the left of that car with another soldier crouching down carrying out some sort of inspection. As the line of cars drew nearer, Gary was able to make out that there was a body on the roadside. He tried not to make it obvious that he was looking and kept his head pointing forwards to where the Curfew Guards were carrying out document checks. Three cars in front of Gary, the single occupant was being given a bit of a hard time. It would probably be because he had no proper reason for being on this road, especially at this time. Gary thought though that any sensible person finding themselves approaching a line of cars waiting for a spot check who shouldn't be where they should be would have made a left or right turn and gone. It wouldn't have been impossible to make a turn and still be making your way to town accommodation or you could have some sort of cover story if you were stopped elsewhere. It would have been silly to have just turned around and driven the other way so you would usually drive to a friend's. Of course if you couldn't do that and still found yourself in a line you might be inclined to try and make a run for it. Perhaps that was what the body lying by the roadside had tried to do.

As Gary got nearer he could see that the body was a woman and it was pretty motionless. There was a mass of blood around the top half of her body and there was an Army tarpaulin sheet half over her head. It still allowed some of her long blondish hair visible and the sight made Gary sad thinking about the incident that must have just taken place. What a waste of life he thought to himself. As he stared at the body he noticed a soldier standing by the side of the body. His hands were also covered in blood. Already, another Officer was going through the woman's clothes looking for documents. 'Is this what we have come to?' Gary murmured to himself. Gary thought back to his

Army training. Everyone was conscripted into the Army for a minimum of a year if they were out of work between the ages of 17 and 21 or if they volunteered. Although technically part of the regular Army these recruits got very little in the way of privileges but were still expected to fight if necessary. It was known as the Conscripted Army, or the CA for short and was a very awful experience for the year most people did in it. About 40% of these recruits died before their year was up and many say they are the lucky ones. From the CA you could then go on to be part of the regular Army or if you were lucky, get another job. Gary had done his year conscription but had been lucky to get his job in the Post Office.

Gary realised he was staring at the soldier bending over the dead woman as he noticed that the car in front had moved through the checkpoint and that he was being beckoned to drive forward to be checked. Soldiers either side stood ready with fingers on the triggers of their machine guns.
"Papers!" A uniformed soldier barked through the car window. Gary handed him his identity card. "Gary Newson." The soldier said out loud. He said it as if he was just repeating the name but everyone knew that there would be another soldier out of sight but near enough to hear the name. The name would then be checked on the Armies computer system to see if he was a suspect. Gary was happy that he wasn't.
"And where do you live?" The soldier continued. Gary handed him his home permit that showed he lived in Waydon and had done so for about nine years. This would give him good reason to be on this road.
"And where do you work?" The soldier barked another question. On demand, Gary showed his Postal identity pass. Being a Government employee gave him a little bit of status even with the Army. Employees were meticulously checked out before being given jobs and all older workers were also checked for signs of revolutionary ideals or anti-government behaviour. They would be seen by most soldiers as being on the same side. On seeing the Postal pass, the soldier sent Gary on his way. He took one last glance at the dead woman as he drove on towards home.

How times had changed, Gary thought to himself. Road checks were far too common nowadays and he had got to the stage where it never bothered him. It was all part of moving around. He looked out of the side window as he approached the turn off to Waydon. He tried to weigh up his life. Are things that bad? As he drove down the long country lane towards his village he looked closer at the grass and weeds that formed the bank along the roadside. They were all grey and aged and showed many signs of wear as if they had been through more years than had been expected. They were overgrown, uncared for, oil stained and just generally filthy due to years of neglect. Gary sometimes felt that summed up life.

Finally Gary had arrived home. The shooting at the Army spot check on the way home was not a usual occurrence so it had given Gary something to think about. He also knew that the fact that he had been checked this late would be reported back to his Manager but this would not be a problem. He did wonder who the dead woman might be though and what had possessed her to make a dash for it. As he turned his car into the drive, Gary got out and unlocked the padlock, then opened the garage door. Whilst looking up and down his little road he drove his car safely inside. A lot of people with cars had remote control garages but Gary just couldn't afford one at the moment so it always meant that he had to get out of his car as he got home. Only the foolish left their cars actually parked outside in the road nowadays. Even in a quiet little village like Waydon, within a month it would have been set alight, rolled, nicked or possibly all three. He took another look around before going indoors but nobody was about. Everyone was safely locked indoors with their blinds or curtains drawn. As he put his key in the front door and pushed it open he gave his usual hail, "Hello, I'm home."

The family had been in the lounge listening to some old records but the sound of the front door opening had been the signal to charge down the hallway to greet the head of the family on his return back home. Joan and Katy both jumped into Gary's open arms and he hugged them as if he would never let them go. Sammy the dog was also pleased to see his master home as he too jumped at Gary's feet until he was given a welcome pat on the head. Finally Angela appeared from the lounge.
"Where have you been?" She asked sternly before continuing, "I've been worried about you."
"There was an accident or something on the way home, not my fault that I'm late," he replied.

"Were the Army involved?" Angela quizzed him.
"Well there were some soldiers about but I don't know if they were involved." He lied.

Although not entirely happy with the reply Angela kissed Gary on the lips, gave him a small hug and then went into the kitchen. The whole process was routine and wasn't a greeting full of love.
"The kids have had their dinner. Ours will be ready in about fifteen minutes." Angela shouted from the kitchen.
"That's good." Gary shouted back from the hall as he took his coat off. "That will give me time to take Sammy for a walk."
"But you've got to be joking!" Angela replied as she came back out of the kitchen to give Gary a disapproving stare, "It's already dark outside, and well passed..."
Gary interrupted her in mid sentence whilst putting his dog walking coat on. "It'll be alright, you see." Sammy was already jumping in anticipation of what was to come. "I'll be back before you can say Jack Robinson." Gary continued as he took the dog's lead down from the coat peg, attached it to Sammy's collar and was half out the back door before allowing Angela the chance to protest any stronger. He knew only too well that he was taking quite a risk and that Angela was genuinely worried. He had taken the risk so many times before though and had only really come across any difficulties on a couple of occasions and he was confident of being able to bluff his way out of anything that he might have to face. Fortunately, Gary's house backed onto a small country lane behind which were just fields. There was a big hedge separating the lane from the field but plenty of gaps that one could jump, walk or hop through to the other side.

Sammy knew the routine and pulled Gary into the back garden, across the lawn and between the brick shed and the vegetable plot to the hidden doorway in their back hedge. As Gary opened the door he stopped and looked around outside. As usual, nobody was about so off they went down the lane but Gary continued to look about just in case he could see or hear anyone moving. There was no actual lighting in the back lane but as Gary's eyes got used to the darkness it became easier to see any darker shapes ahead that might be another person. He was used to doing this and when he could hear some movement ahead he would jump into the field and keep Sammy quiet whilst whoever it was passed by. He never saw who it was that passed and guessed that it was most probably another neighbour walking their dog when they shouldn't be.

Things had changed quite a bit in the last few years Gary thought to himself. It wasn't that long ago that at this time of the evening he would pass at least three or four other people walking their dogs. Nowadays of course there was the six o'clock curfew and anyone caught out after that time was in breach of the law and risked arrest or perhaps imprisonment if they did not have a valid reason for being out. Being stopped driving home from work was okay as it could be checked on the system but out walking your dog was a different matter. Gary had heard rumours of people being interrogated about why they had been out after curfew although he had never actually spoken to anyone who this had happened to. He laughed to himself recalling how eighteen year old Billy Simpson, very impressionable and keen to be accepted by the rest of the staff, had been listening to them all talking about curious tales of arrest and interrogation and seeing his opportunity interrupted everyone to tell his own tale on the subject. He caught everyone's attention as he continued with the story of his friend who had said that his brother had been arrested whilst out after dark and just never returned. 'They executed him' Billy reported excitedly, at which point all the other staff just laughed at his supposed imaginary tale. Billy had tried to keep their attention by shouting 'It's true I tell you, it's true' and the memory of Billy's voice echoing out in vain whilst the staff ignored him stayed in Gary's mind for a couple of seconds. Poor young Billy! He found it hard to get on with the others. If only he were to be himself a bit more and not try so hard to impress they'd soon accept him but Gary could see that if things went on the way they were Billy would become a bit of a loner. I must try and do more with that boy, Gary thought to himself. His job was hard enough without having to cope with an unhappy member of the team.

Gary's job was another thing that had changed quite a bit in the last few years. He was a Postal Service Manager with full responsibility for all collections and deliveries in an area covering Kentley and the villages of Sutton, Greenfields, Lavenham, Norfield and Waydon. When he first took on the job it was mainly to make sure that things ran on time without any problems but gradually he had been given more instructions to check things out. Even the validity of delivery names and addresses was being checked nowadays and each day a big bag of mail would come in which his nine staff would sort check that mail was addressed to legitimate businesses or that post to individuals were to people on the residents list. They then arranged for the mail to be delivered as appropriate, reporting any irregularities to Gary who would then deal with them. Gary was expected to look into any unlisted residents by way of checking old lists or matching up names to wrong addresses. Each letter with a suspect name or address was normally made into a case. There were a few exceptions of course, when it was obvious that the letter was due to be sent to next door but all cases were recorded on both paper and the computer system.

There were large shelves full of old case files and it was quite normal for Postal Service Managers to go over old case files for various reasons. It would make sense to see if the same name had come up at another address, or if the address you were looking at had been checked before. A lot of PSMs would also use old cases to get ideas on ways to check things out. Gary thought of this as sort of cheating and never used old methods. He would always tackle a new case in a new way. Old cases were only good for old details Gary thought and he was innovative enough to come up with a new way of checking an address. In fact he could do any checks he wanted to as long as he didn't actually speak to the people at the address or even more importantly, open the mail. That was strictly a 'no go' area and he would be in trouble if this ever came to the notice of Gary's manager, the Assistant Postmaster. About seven months ago, Gary had delivered a report together with an open letter which Gary had admitted he had opened to look for clues as to who the letter was supposed to have been sent to. He had then spent nearly an hour being questioned by The Postmaster on what he had opened it for, what he had read in the letter, who he thought the letter was going to and lots of other such questions.

The Management would always give the reason for not opening post as an infringement of private rights but Gary was convinced it was more a case of staff of his level not being trusted. It wasn't that often that the Assistant Postmaster would come and query what Gary was doing so for The Postmaster to be questioning him he knew he had done something wrong. He never did it again! It was a natural step for the curious Postal Service Manager to open undelivered mail without reporting it to the A.P. Once again there had been rumours about the demise of the last Assistant Postmaster apparently opening some undelivered mail and finding just a blank piece of paper in it and within hours being taken away and never being seen again. Probably a made up story, Gary thought to himself but then again these rumours are often based on some truth. He remembered the fuss caused when the last Assistant Postmaster went. There was a special team who had come in and questioned various members of staff including Gary. Nobody really knew what had happened and the official story that he had been taken seriously ill was greeted with much scepticism. Gary had to stick to that story even though he didn't really believe it himself. Gary was pretty much his own boss as he could manage his own time and go off to check out an address whenever he felt it necessary but in the big picture of things his job was quite insignificant. Gary tried to recall the name of the old Assistant Postmaster. Mr. Longthorn? Mr. Longmore? Mr. Longshanks? It was definitely Mr. Long something. He couldn't remember properly but then he'd only met him a few times and he had only moved into his new job a few months before the incident.

Gary's mind had been wandering and he had forgotten that he was actually out after curfew. Sammy had just got on with his business and they had both continued along their normal path that they would take. Gary had not intended to go too far this evening as he was late but as his mind had been wandering they had both just carried along the lane as usual. To make matters worse, Gary suddenly came to his senses and realised that he was not keeping an ear out for any other curfew breakers. If Angela knew, she would be angry with him for being so careless. She was the sensible one who was always reminding Gary not to talk to strangers nor do anything that might be construed as being suspicious but as always Gary just did what he wanted. Gary's mind started to wander again but he quickly snapped out of it when he heard in the distance a repetitive mechanical noise that sounded like factory machinery. Gary looked in the direction of where the sound was coming from which happened to be in the same direction as the church. Behind the church was the school. At least it had been the school up until a few weeks ago when soldiers had come in and shut it down.

As Gary surveyed the darkness, he soon saw a glow that looked like floodlights. It seemed to be where the school was. Gary wondered what the hell could be going on at this time of the day. They wouldn't be doing building work this late. He soon put two and two together and thought that the Army must have taken over the school and there was some sort of military business going on. It must be very important work that was going on. This would also mean that soldiers would probably be patrolling the area as well. Almost at that very instant, he was fortunate to hear what sounded like footsteps ahead of him and it snapped him back into the realisation of the situation he was in. With a swift movement of his right arm, Sammy was picked up and held under Gary's arm as he nipped into the roadside and searched for a gap in the bushes. Only five yards ahead, Gary could see a small gap that would lead him into the field and being of thin build, he was easily able to get through it. He quickly put Sammy down and crouched down behind the bushes waiting for the sounds of footsteps to go passed. He would have to wait where he was until he was happy that it wasn't an Army patrol. Hopefully it was just a neighbour also out after curfew. Once they had gone passed he would start back for home. Seconds seemed like minutes as Gary waited to hear some indication of the stranger passing. He started to think what might be happening if it was a Curfew Guard. He would be armed and in radio contact with his base and would probably have heard Gary's footsteps as well. He would therefore be looking stealthily for signs of a curfew breaker. Gary wasn't quite sure what the guard would do if he did find him. Would he arrest him? Would he radio for back up? Surely he wouldn't just shoot at him? Gary was now thinking that crouching down behind the bushes in a field was probably not the best position to plead your innocence from should some curfew guards find him. It would be a lot better if they just found him walking along the lane but it was too late for that. Angela was right he thought. He had to laugh at his predicament and how embarrassing it would be for someone in his position to be arrested. Just at that moment he heard a noise from the lane which sounded like someone walking very slowly.

Gary then heard a voice, "Have you found something in the bushes?" His heart starting beating a little quicker when the voice continued, "Come on boy, let's get home." Gary realised that it was another neighbour walking a dog and that his dog had obviously smelt

Gary or more likely Sammy and that was why he had taken so long to go passed. It was a bit of a close shave but he could hear the hurried footsteps of a neighbour disappearing into the distance and Gary was happy that he was not in any real danger. It was two neighbours who had frightened each other because neither should have been out there at that time.

Gary picked Sammy up and made for the gap in the bushes. He looked left and right and happy that nobody was about put Sammy back down and made back for home. As he walked Sammy back Gary's pace quickened as he was still a bit annoyed with himself for having walked quite so far. He thought back to the neighbour and the fact that it was very risky for the neighbour to actually say anything. Had there been any informing minded people about, the incident could have been reported to the Army and the neighbour in trouble. Gary was not of a mind to inform on neighbours out walking their dogs after curfew. How could he when he did they very same thing himself. He was still surprised though as to how easily the stranger had put himself in danger. Gary soon approached the back gate to his house. He would not be able to tell Angela anything about the incident so he would just have to put it to the back of his mind if he could.

Sammy raced into the house through the back door and Gary followed a few yards behind.
"Where the bloody hell have you been?" Angela almost shouted at him as he came into the kitchen. Gary could tell by the look on her face that she was not very happy at all.
"Sorry." He replied giving a pathetic look as if to ask for forgiveness. He quickly added, "I'm sure dinner will not have been spoilt, I haven't been that long." Angela's eyes looked up at the kitchen clock and Gary did the same to see that it was just gone ten minutes past seven.
"Oh I didn't realise it was that late. I am sorry." Gary said quickly.

Gary and Angela had been arguing a lot more recently and were going through what most married couples did. Gary tried very hard not to but would still do things that annoyed Angela but then she did things that annoyed him. They had settled into a family existence and were both working hard to give their daughters everything they could. It wasn't easy.
"Did anything happen whilst you were out?" Angela asked with a

knowing tone in her voice.

"No nothing." Gary answered positively. "What made you think that?" He added.

"You had a phone call about two minutes before you got in." Angela said.

"Who was it?" Gary answered.

"Well that's exactly the point. It was a man who just asked if you were there. He asked for you by name, well at least Gary. When I said you weren't home he just said 'Are you sure he isn't out walking the dog. I'll ring again' then he just put the phone down". Angela was obviously concerned with the call and hoping for some sort of explanation from her husband that might put her mind at ease but it was not forthcoming. She had nagged him until she was blue in the face about getting involved with strange people but respected him enough to allow him to do what he wanted. The fact that strange people were now ringing worried her a bit more. It might put the girls at some sort of risk.

"Well I'm sorry but surely you don't expect me to know who it is, do you?"

"I don't expect to get those sort of phone calls."

"That's hardly my fault."

"Well it certainly isn't mine." Angela tried not to burst into tears.

"Somebody knows you were out walking the dog."

"Well I don't know who it might have been."

"It's your fault that someone knows what you are up to." Angela hadn't quite put her point over correctly but she didn't want to change what she had said.

"It's just ridiculous blaming me."

"So who should I blame then?"

"I don't know." Gary almost shouted.

Angela and Gary were both getting worked up. They just stared at each other neither knowing what to say next. They were both having worrying thoughts about someone else knowing more about their lives than they were comfortable with. Although it only lasted a few seconds, it was a deafening silence. Gary shook his head slowly from left to right whilst Angela bit her lip.

"So what is for dinner?" Gary changed the subject. Angela didn't reply but it cut the atmosphere.

Gary and Angela sat down at the dining table where she had already served their meal. It was a vegetable quiche with chips. This was a lot better than Gary had been expecting.

"Where did you get the quiche from?" He asked Angela.

"I managed to get half a dozen eggs from one of the women in the village who is short of potatoes," she replied. A lot of people swapped things nowadays as not much was ever on sale in shops even if they were open. The village shop only opened twice a week at the moment, on Mondays and Fridays and even then the price of any decent food was so high that not many people could actually afford to buy it. Gary had started his own vegetable garden, growing potatoes, carrots, onions and cauliflowers but he also had a sneaky greenhouse where he grew some tomatoes and cannabis. The produce was not just for their own use but was often used by Angela to swap with others for food that they didn't have, such as eggs and fruit. Angela was very good at bartering and doing deals and Gary was very impressed with the way that Angela was able to get hold of some excellent food every now and then so that the family could be reasonably well nourished. Eggs were very hard to come by and potatoes quite common so for her to find someone that desperate for potatoes and prepared to swap them for eggs was a real miracle. If they had had enough room, he would have liked to have bought some chickens so as to have their own eggs but it was out of the question with the small garden they had at present.

Gary put his knife and fork down and turned to look at Angela. "I'm sorry for losing my temper earlier." Angela looked at him without lifting her head fully.

"Forget it. We both lost our tempers."

The more Gary thought about it the more he realised just how much he admired the way that Angela kept the family going. He was quite lucky to still have a job so he was able to escape the boredom of home life most days. His income wasn't too bad either so the family could afford a lot of things that others couldn't, like soap, toothpaste and occasionally fizzy drink. The girls were really pleased when Angela bought some fizzy drink. They always looked forward to it. Angela was in charge of all the family money. They had managed to keep an approved finance account running and hence were able to go once a month to the private stores in town to buy new clothes. Usually only the rich and the longer serving government employees would be found buying things in these shops although the Army also got special privileges to use the stores. Gary's position in the Post Office wasn't exactly what he would call a higher ranked Civil Service post but he had applied a few years ago for an approved finance account and got it somehow. His salary meant that they were not able to shop at the private shops that often but with Angela's great bargaining ability, they normally went every month to buy both themselves and the girls some new clothes. The money was obviously from savings on food but between them they always seemed to be able to live well. Gary realised he had a lot to thank Angela for.

    The two girls had gone back to the living room and had started to play with the old records again. This was Gary's greatest contribution to the family for a while. His father had always kept a few old vinyl records dating back to the 1970's and as a boy, Gary had been shown how to use his fathers' old record player. Being interested in electrical things, when it had gone wrong Gary had tinkered about with it and had been able to get it working. About a month ago, Gary had seen an advert at work where a colleague had a broken record player to swap. Being a Postal Service Manager he was able to bargain some milk vouchers and the promise of some extra overtime for the record player. It had then only taken him a few days to get it working. He then got down some of his fathers' old records and had shown the girls how people used to listen to music in the old days. Seemed a bit funny but the fact of being able to put the records on yourself seemed to be much more fun than listening to music the conventional way which was through a computer of course. The girls would just sit and stare at the record going round and round and the fact that the quality of the sound was so poor didn't seem to matter at all. Gary also had some old cassettes and compact discs that he would have liked to show the girls but he had never come across anyone selling anything to play them on. The computer was the only current source of music today as radio stations were used to broadcast government propaganda. There were no musicians playing live concerts but it was all recorded in big private studios and put on the internet for people to listen to.

    The Newsons were also quite lucky as they owned a television. It didn't work at the moment and Gary was still trying to get a part to fix it but at least they had one. When it was working the shows that were on were not that brilliant. Most weekends there would be a spectacular show with comedians and dancers and occasionally a circus show but most of the schedule was taken up with news programmes, informative documentaries about how well off Britain was and then some old repeats. Sundays were again devoted almost entirely to religion but there would also be the peak viewing show when a Team Ball match was televised. Team Ball was a strange game devised for television where a team of six challengers, usually all family members, were expected to move a large heavy ball about fifty yards across an obstacle course of their choice. They had to do it in less than forty five minutes to win which seemed quite easy except that you were up against another team of six who were trying to stop you. It often ended with all six members of the losing side flat on the floor with broken arms or legs and both sides covered with bruises and cuts. The winners would then get the chance to try and push the ball across another obstacle course the next week. If you were good enough to win three challenges on three different courses you won a dream holiday for your family. The compere for the show was a zany character called Johnny Johnson. He was thin and gangly and wore very thick dark rimmed glasses. As he had a very pale complexion, the glasses seemed even darker and his spiky hair usually made things worse as it was often white in colour but would sometimes change to bright yellow or another crazy colour. Johnny Johnson would then wear a brightly coloured oversized jacket, often sparkly as well. Joan and Katy thought he was just brilliant but then they weren't allowed to watch all of the show that often due to its violent outcomes. Gary couldn't remember a team winning a dream holiday for a long time and viewing figures had dropped quite dramatically. He was sure that if someone didn't win soon that the game would be stopped being shown. His cynical view was that they would fix for a team to win quite soon and they would have a report of this team on their holiday. It would keep the programme viewing figures up and lift moral.

    Gary was in fact quite good at fixing all sorts of electrical things like radios and computers. Although in the past he had been given some training on how to make electrical circuits and basic radio units from scratch he didn't take up the profession. He saw it as a bit of a hobby that would take his mind off of other problems but Angela would often bring him a radio to fix. Gary didn't ask where they came from and guessed that they were friend's radios and he was also quite

happy for not too many people knowing that he could fix things. He was just pleased to be able to practice his skills. As with the family television, the only problems arose when he needed an actual part. Some parts he was able to improvise but not all parts. There was a strict military control over such parts and therefore they were quite hard to come by. Gary finished his dinner and gave a big sigh.
"Didn't you like it then?" Angela asked.
"Don't be silly, it was great. Long time since I've eaten quiche and you're the best cook in the world." Gary got up and hugged Angela very tight. It was more of an apology for being late back from walking the dog and Angela knew it.
"As long as you appreciate it," she replied giving him a sly look.
"Does this person you got the eggs from want anymore potatoes? Gary asked hopefully.
"She might do but it's unlikely that I'll see her again. I don't see her that often and was lucky to catch her wanting some today but I'll try and get some more if I should happen to see her again"
"Who is she?" Gary asked.
"I don't know her name. I just know her from the village." Angela replied casually.

Gary cleared the table and washed up in the kitchen whilst Angela joined the girls in the lounge. They continued to play records for a while longer until Angela ordered them to get ready for bed.
"Do we have to?" The girls groaned in harmony.
"Yes." Angela replied.
There was no hot water at the moment so the girls were expected to quickly wash their faces and hands before getting dressed for bed. Katy and Joan were very good really and despite always asking if they really had to go to bed pretty well always did as they were told. About an hour later, Angela made Gary and herself a cup of tea and they too got ready for bed. As they lay there drinking Gary asked, "How has your day been then?"
"Not too bad." Angela replied. "Yours?"
"Yeah okay."
Angela then continued, "The girls are hoping to go back to school in a couple of weeks. They are going to use the village hall or the old barn at Slater's Farm Restaurant."
"I suppose that will be good." Gary replied. "Has anyone heard what's become of that teacher?"

"Do you mean Miss Clark?" Angela joked. She knew exactly who Gary meant but also knew that he sometimes couldn't remember her name.
"Yes. Miss Clark." Gary said in a confident manner.
"No," replied Angela. "I'm told that she is still living near the village somewhere and will be allowed to come back and teach but I don't know if she will or not."
Angela had got on very well with the girl's teachers and Joan's teacher was a Miss Julie Clark.

She was at the centre of the incident when the Army came in to take over the school buildings a couple of months ago. She had attacked the Sergeant in charge scratching his face by all accounts but had then been knocked to the floor by the Sergeant and hit with the butt of his gun. This had all happened right in front of the children and Joan had got very upset. Miss Clark was then carried away by the Army and the rest of the teachers and children told to go home. The school was closed down the very next day. Angela had got to know a number of the teachers quite well recently and the attack by Miss Clark was considered to be well out of character but Angela had seen another side to Julie and wasn't as surprised as everyone else. She seemed to have noticed that she was more stressed out than usual and felt that she was under some increasing pressure. She knew that she had very strong anti-government feelings and obviously the Army moving in the way they did was just all too much for her and she had reacted without thinking. Nobody knew what would become of Miss Clark and Joan had got very worried having been told that she would be tortured and shot. Angela was very pleased to be able to tell her that Miss Clark was alright and put her daughter's mind at ease.
"Have you got ideas for what we might do this weekend?" Angela asked Gary but he had nodded off with half a cup of tea in his hand. She took the cup from his grasp and laid it on the bedside cabinet. She finished hers and then turned the light off. It would be another day tomorrow.

-

Sergeant Foulkes had finally closed the roadblock at seven twenty when most cars had finished moving. By now, people should be at home as the curfew had been in force for over an hour. He had called for another unit to come and get the woman's body but not before his unit had got her papers and checked out her car. Back at base he worked on his reports of the evening's incidents. He was very proud of the work the unit had done. The two Privates involved in the termination had been ordered to do reports themselves, as had their Corporal. When Ed was ready he knocked on the Major's door and awaited the command to enter.

"Come in!" Major Wooters shouted.

"My reports, Sir!" Sergeant Foulkes replied as he handed a number of documents to the Major who quickly went through the reports one by one calling out the names as he did so.

"Kiddel, Chamberlain, Miller, Littlejohn, Turner, Willis, Brown. Nobody really looks like who we were after Sergeant would you agree?" The Major asked.

"Yes sir. Just the one looked a bit interesting sir. That would be Brown," the Sergeant replied.

"Why is he interesting then?"

"Mainly because he has an ID card that had been issued just today, Sir! But then he also had an address permit that was a week out of date. Didn't quite seem right, Sir!"

The Major perused the names in front of him most intently.

"And what of the woman incident?" the Major continued.

"A Mrs Jenny Tetridge from Kentley sir! Known revolutionary sympathizer! She had a hand gun in the car and an overnight bag so obviously up to no good sir," responded Sergeant Foulkes.

"Any idea what might have spooked her?" asked the Major.

"Not really. I was unable to connect her to any other vehicle but it is possible that she was minding someone." Sergeant Foulkes replied.

"Do we know who was in the car at the check point at the time she ran?" asked the Major.

"Yes sir, the Hobbs. It is all in the report." "They were all perfectly in order." The Sergeant waited for the Major to take in what he had said then continued. "She did create a hell of a distraction and it is quite possible that someone in the next vehicle may have got away without us questioning them, Sir. The blond woman was a Mrs. Tetridge, aged 43 and trained to a good physical standard, Sir. Divorced and previously married as Mrs. Van Leer but she isn't Dutch. Lived in Kentley and has lived locally most of her life." The Sergeant took a quick breath. "Sir!"

The Major looked at the report and gave the facts some deep thought.

He looked up at Sergeant Foulkes. "But she was driving away from Kentley, Sergeant. Doesn't that seem a bit strange?"
Ed Foulkes hadn't thought to mention this and was a bit annoyed. He had recorded the fact that she was driving in the wrong direction to which she would have been expected to be travelling but had failed to mention it. He had at least previously mentioned that he had thought that she might have been minding someone.
"I have mentioned that fact in my report, Sir."
"Okay Sergeant. I'll go through these tomorrow and I'll see you in my office at fourteen hundred hours sharp tomorrow. Dismissed!"
Ed Foulkes saluted, turned and left the Majors office. He was a bit happier having been able to say that the fact was in his report and generally he was pleased with the way things had gone.

Although a very confident soldier and very good at his job, Ed took criticism quite hard and hated being pulled up on anything. He would always try and impress whenever he could but was keen to praise good work done by those under him. Edward Michael Foulkes was one of very few British born soldiers who had managed to get to the rank of Sergeant in the new European Union Army. Although there were quite a number of British soldiers in it, they were mainly at the ranks of Private or Corporal. Ed had got to Sergeant in the old British Army quite quickly and was one of those who did not speak out against the new regime when it came in and started taking over. He did have some views but kept them to himself. Many had not kept quiet but demonstrated and argued and finished up being forced to join the Euro Army at a lower rank or leaving the forces altogether. Ed volunteered to join the Euro Army at the first opportunity and although he was overlooked at first he was soon asked to join the ranks of Sergeant.

He knew that a lot of his former colleagues were still active in the underground and guessed that some were actively trying to bring the new Army down. There had long been talk about a revolution where the old Army would take control again but Ed wasn't convinced. He hoped that if they did they would realise that he was not really a traitor but someone trying to get the best out of life. He secretly dreamed of the day when he could rejoin the British Army but until that day came, he would get on with his job. Four years ago he met a local girl called Sally Jenkins at an Army dance. He was smitten immediately and in less than two years later, Ed and Sally were married. She now lived on the barracks and worked part-time as a shop assistant at one of the stores and the two of them couldn't be happier.

The Major looked at the report again and thought to himself that he needed to look a bit closer at this incident. It didn't seem right to him but this was definitely not the person he thought the Intelligence were looking for. Having been given only part of the story, as usual, it was always possible that this was their target but the description given to him over the phone was vague enough so that they could not identify the target but detailed enough so they would catch such a person. He would have to report to his Intelligence counterpart before leaving off. The one thing that he wasn't surprised about was how extensive a report Sergeant Foulkes had done. He knew how good the Sergeant was and in fact knew that he should have been promoted long ago but in today's climate, being English and ex-British Army it would take a long time for Ed Foulkes to get a higher rank. In the meantime, the Major was very pleased to have him on his team.

At that very moment the phone rang.
"Major Wooters." He answered. The person on the other end of the phone was his Intelligence counterpart. "Yes, that's correct, a Mrs. Jenny Tetridge." The Major was being questioned about whether or not his unit leader had got all the facts in a report yet or not and he was quite pleased to be able to say that it was already on his desk. "The report is here. I'm going to give it a closer look tomorrow and question him a bit further tomorrow afternoon but it seems to be in order." Major Wooters continued. "An Intelligence agent! When exactly? How will I know them? Of course!" The Major was given instructions and with no goodbye the telephone call had ended.

An Intelligence agent would be calling in for a copy of the report tomorrow. The Major now knew that this was a bit more interesting if they were that keen to get a copy of the report. It was quite unusual for any Intelligence person to make a personal appearance, let alone an agent. The Intelligence agents were usually under cover staff who basically worked out of uniform on top political cases. All would have been trained in Army basics but from a fairly early time in their career been earmarked as Intelligence staff. Some would have been integrated into normal jobs where they would stay until called upon whilst others would be out of work and would infiltrate revolutionary factions if they could. Nearly all of them had particular targets that they would be trying to bring to justice and the Major knew that it was quite likely that the name Jenny Tetridge had probably been a name that they were expecting to find. He had heard that some cases had lasted years. He had a lot of admiration for these agents and in fact was quite proud to think that he would meet one tomorrow. He was looking forward to meeting him in person. Tomorrow was going to be an interesting day.

-

The Intelligence Major who had been on the phone was very surprised at today's incident. The whole of Operation Hunting had appeared to have gone down the tubes a couple of months ago and the agent who was working on the case had been very disappointed. This operation had been running for quite a while now and came straight from the top. Everything had gone cold but they now had one of their best local agents working on it. Despite the bad miscalculation that had caused the early set back, they had thought that they were very close to achieving their goal and to getting the identities of some very influential local revolutionaries. An agent was still well under cover and working on other leads. The Major had received the report of the possible movement of the Operations main target from one of his other agents that afternoon but it was only an unsubstantiated report. Mrs. Jenny Tetridge was also mentioned as being the possible minder but this was not confirmed and the Major was pleased to receive Major Wooters report. He knew that his agent would want to see the report first hand. He was due to meet the Agent so things would be set up for them to pick up the report from Major Wooters directly. The identities of all the agents was a closely guarded secret and the regular Army would never really know if they were meeting an agent or not. Major Wooters would only know for sure that Major Tannier was part of the Intelligence Section. Jacques Tannier hadn't decided yet whether to send in his agent to collect the report or one of the office staff. He would decide tomorrow.

Operation Hunting seemed to most to be a very typical case. The Intelligence section would regularly gather information on likely suspects from various Army sources and then every now and then would come across information that pointed to a suspect being a bit more than just a sympathiser. This case was just like that. Once the agent who was running the case had got their teeth into things, more and more intelligence started coming through until Major Tannier had said it was time to pull the plug and arrest the main target. Something went wrong somewhere and the target fled before they were arrested. Not a very common occurrence but one that the Major had seen before. A brief inquest had taken place but the agent and the Major were both cleared of any suspicion of warning the opposition. Major Tannier knew though that the agent was now even more determined to get their man. They would be pleased to receive today's report.

In actual fact, Operation Hunting was anything but a normal case. Tannier knew that there were orders coming direct from Strasbourg on it but that wasn't completely out of the ordinary. The whole operation had been set up so that it looked like it was just another case. If only Tannier had known who was really pulling the strings, he would have known otherwise.

Chapter 2 - HOW IT GOT TO THIS

It wasn't long before Angela was asleep and the Newson household was at peace although there were in fact a lot of different noises in the house. Gary was snoring as was Sammy the dog as he lay on his mat in the hall. Everyone was asleep. It seemed like a house with no worries at all but Gary had a lot of things on his mind and his sleep was not that restful at all. His mind went back to the events of that afternoon and he pictured the blond hair of the woman who had been shot earlier that day plus soldiers everywhere going about their business. It all seemed perfectly real, just as if it was happening there and then but it was all happening in slow motion. There was no sound. A bit like a film report of a news incident. Gary was transfixed as he looked at the woman's blond hair. He seemed absolutely powerless to turn away. Although he didn't actually move any closer to the body he realised that he was able to see things a lot clearer, as if he was behind a camera zooming in for a close up. He stared closer at the covered body when it all of a sudden started to move. The woman's arm grabbed hold of the groundsheet and threw it back so she was fully exposed. Gary looked at her long blond hair which was covered in blood. Gary then looked at her blood soaked jumper. The woman started to get to her feet but it was as if not a single soldier noticed her. Although her face was visible it was also somehow blurred so that he couldn't clearly see it but had an image of her face in his mind. The woman started to walk over to Gary's car and she kept her stare fixed in Gary's direction. "Look out for her," she said.
"Watch out for her," she repeated. It suddenly dawned on Gary that the woman was in fact talking to him. She was looking directly at him and talking only to him. "Watch her. Watch her. Watch her!" The woman's voice kept repeating. Her voice was interrupted by a loud crack of gunfire as the woman was shot from behind. As the force of the shot made the woman stumble she was still able to keep on her feet. Gary saw the bullets explode out of the front of the woman's jumper as they tore through the front of her body underneath. It was as if he had been standing in the allotments towards which the woman had been running. There was a strange feeling that the woman was in fact only running in that direction in order to get to him. Gary hadn't noticed properly but before these new shots had been fired the woman's body already seemed to be covered in blood but with no

actual wounds. The woman tried in vain to get to Gary and seemed as if that was her only aim in life but eventually she started to fall to her knees and as she did Gary could see a soldier with a smoking automatic in their hands behind her. As the woman fell to the ground, more of the soldier who had shot her became visible to Gary. Gary looked at the woman as she lay on the ground and then focused on to the soldiers' boots. He then moved up the soldiers' body but his attention was forced towards the automatic machine gun that the soldier was holding. The soldier slowly started to lift the gun, it was moving towards Gary very slowly. Gary looked at the smoking barrel of the gun as it lifted. He could see the carnage on the side of the road. He could see the uniformed soldier holding the gun. Gary could see the allotments and fields in the background but he just didn't get as far as seeing the soldiers face before his attention was drawn back to the gloved hand holding the automatic. He saw the trigger being pulled and he was waiting for the loud crack of the exploding bullet. It never came.

He awoke with a start. He had been dreaming. As he looked around the room everything seemed normal and Angela was there asleep by his side. All of a sudden he realised he was sweating. He recalled the blond woman's voice again. What was it she said? 'Watch out for her'. He looked at Angela. She was safe. Gary knew that he would do anything to protect her.

Gary tossed and turned and punched his pillow in an effort to get back to sleep but it wasn't working. He tried to picture the face of the woman he had seen in his dreams but he just couldn't recall it properly. He then tried to remember what she had looked like when he had seen her at the roadblock. It was strange as he just couldn't recall her face. The long blond hair was clear but the face was not very distinct at all. He tried in vain as his mind switched to the voice of the man he had heard in the back lane. Again his voice was familiar but Gary just couldn't put a name or a face to it. And who was the man who had phoned Angela. Was it the person in the back lane? If so, what had Gary done to give himself away so easily? He went over his reactions to hearing the strangers' footsteps and couldn't understand how he had given away his identity. Gary passed thoughts around in his head for seemed like hours. He then thought about Billy at work and his voice telling the guys at work about people being executed.

And that wasn't all he thought about when work came to mind. Gary then tried to think of what might be going on at the old school. He considered taking a closer look although he knew it would be a dangerous thing to do. There was so much going on in Gary's mind, he needed to get to sleep but he couldn't. He looked at the clock. Twelve twenty. Was that all, he thought. Why did he have so many problems to worry about? How had it got to this?

Gary tried to think back to his childhood when everything seemed so much better. He pictured himself in the garden with his Mum and Dad and Sarah and David. Gary was the middle child with his sister Sarah only two years older then himself. He also had a younger brother David who was a good four or five years younger. He pictured the three of them playing in the garden without a care, Mum and Dad watching with happy faces. He could see them all playing with a football, kicking it around the garden and throwing it to each other. They were all very happy then but without realising it there were significant incidents that changed all of their lives and led to things going wrong. It seemed impossible that so much had changed in such a short time.

It all happened about twenty years ago when Britain became part of Europe's one big country. We had always been members of the European Union, his Father had told him that but we had always seemed to hesitate over taking that final step to join Europe completely. In the early years of the twenty first century things changed when there was a great economic revolution. Europe started to become a successful world power industrially with the driving force behind this being in Germany and France. These two great countries were able to produce far cheaper and better goods than most of the other countries and seized a stronghold on the markets, consequentially also becoming the political force governing the EU's wealth. At the early stages this was not a problem but in fact something to be envious of as the rest of Europe prospered whilst Britain remained more like outsiders. For a number of years Britain swayed back and forth undecided as to how far we should get involved in Europe. Whether or not we should join with France and Germany! In the end we joined quite easily. Although part of Europe we hadn't been prepared to give up our nationalistic stands completely in order to be fully part of Europe. We had always been a fairly self-sufficient country and not too concerned about not always getting the better deals from the Unions commerce but all the time we stalled, the Germans and French were getting stronger. As in most political situations there were endless squabbles and rows between the various countries but usually they would be sorted out through discussion and debate.

Then things got a bit nasty and there was a little war that broke out between the Turks and the Greeks. It was called the Aegean War of 2005 and it lasted for about three months until the rest of the European Union started taking sides. Gary would have been about 18 when the war first broke out and although the television was full of reports about fighting, air raids and battles he didn't really take much notice of it at the time. As the other countries in the Union started to get involved and the war started to escalate there was more talk of mates joining the Army. There was no compulsory conscription to start with and as Gary had not been that way inclined he was not quick to volunteer and join up. His brother David on the other hand was always talking about becoming a soldier but being only 13 he was too young. As the war started to involve other European countries it became obvious to Gary that he would probably get conscripted. He had spoken to his family about not wanting to go and fight in a war he knew nothing about and although his parents were in full agreement, younger brother David just didn't seem to understand. In 2007, when a lot of British men went off to fight, Gary would have been nearly 20 but had already managed to get himself a job with the Post Office. This meant that he was not expected to join the Army unless he particularly wanted too. It was the unemployed who were forced to join. Gary had already finished his year's conscription. It was called conscription but not everyone was made to join the armed forces. There was a year where you received basic training and prepared like the regular Army but if you didn't want to go and fight abroad and had a job that excused you, as long as you did your year that was okay. It was seen as enough preparation so that if in the future you did have to join the regular Army, your basic training meant it wouldn't take long to get you up to standard. Anyone who was a keen volunteer would join with the bulk of the fighting forces made up from the unemployed well before they finished their years training. To a lot of the older unemployed it seemed a totally unfair system but the younger ones seemed to relish the challenge.

By the year 2007 unemployment had started to become a real problem. Jobs were not that easy to find mainly due to the progress made in computerised machinery. Industry had become so labour economic that the factories that had employed hundreds of staff in the past were now being run by just 20 or 30 people. It also meant that because of the countries taxes going to the war effort, if you didn't have a job, life was quite hard. Times were hard during the war and sacrifices were made by most European countries but as always there were no real winners or losers. The war sort of fizzled to an end. Things got worse after the war had officially finished when the Union Army took control of the whole European forces in an effort to keep peace in Europe. Not only was there animosity between the two armies but as most of the European forces were paid better wages than anyone else most of those troops were able to live far better lives than the people in whose home countries they were living. Technically, the Union forces were only supposed to maintain law and order for a short period after the end of the Aegean War with the separate countries governments still running the everyday affairs but of course once established they remained. The Turks and Greeks were not easily able to get on with each other and in many parts of Europe there were little problem areas. Because of this the Union Forces were installed in each country, their main reason being said to be to control such problem areas but Gary's experience was that most now got on with each other quite well but the Union Army remained. There were rumours that the actual argument that started the Aegean War in the first place had all been sorted out years ago but the Union Forces insisted that there were still problems. Then the Union Forces moved into a large number of towns and cities that had never even seen a Turk or Greek person. There were a few terrorist type bombings taking place that were said to be part of the Aegean War problem but these were used as reasons to recruit new young soldiers to the Union Army. It just seemed that the Army was used in other European countries to keep control of the people. Probably very much like what was going on in Britain. They introduced curfews. They set up roadblocks. Gradually they became part of everyday life.

There was still a national Army in some countries but gradually they were disbanded or given purely traditional ceremonial duties. The only properly armed forces were the European Union Army, controlled from their main headquarters in Strasbourg. A lot of British men and women were part of that Union Army. There was a lot of ill feeling towards them from the original British Army as they were often seen as traitors or enemies. This resulted in the European Army staying isolated from their old friends and family. A few years ago you would still hear of British Army officers having a go at the Union Army but over time this stopped. The soldiers themselves had probably joined the new Union Army or the ranks of the unemployed. Gary didn't really know.

David had never quite been old enough to join the Army during the war years and when he was old enough he refused to join an Army controlled by foreigners. Gary remembered how surprised he was to hear David talking about his political feelings when he was arrested at the young age of 15. David had been with a group of his mates demonstrating outside a Union Army barracks when he had been arrested. Fortunately he was only charged with causing a public disorder but as Gary heard his Father trying to get him to explain why he was doing what he had been doing, he was very surprised as to how informed and intellectual his younger brother seemed. David never changed his political views and despite the efforts of his parents, never got a job either. He kept his head down for a few years but still mixed with the political anarchists who were regularly being arrested and charged with revolutionary intent and as the youth demonstrations got bigger, it was no surprise to see David on the front line complaining about having no job, no money and no food. By this time, Gary's parents had lost control of their youngest son and had been forced to accept his regular arrests. It was taking its toll on both of them as they were getting older. Gary also knew that David was more active than they thought. Gary had kept a sort of brotherly eye on David's actions, through a friend or some contact or other he would hear most of what David had got up to. He also knew that on a couple of occasions David had been caught by Euro Army soldiers in places where he shouldn't have been and had had some lucky escapes. Gary thought it was best not to tell his parents the whole truth and he often covered for him when he went missing for a day or two. Fortunately the friends that Gary knew trusted him enough to tell him where David was and Gary would go looking for him when he went missing to persuade him to come back home.

On the last occasion Gary went looking for him he thought the inevitable had happened. It was at a demonstration back in 2014. Quite a large demonstration compared to others his brother had been to and was well co-ordinated all around the country to cause as much inconvenience and trouble as possible. Gary had known for some time that a big storm was brewing. David had told him a little bit and he had gleamed more from his old friends but Gary had always thought that this big event would take place in the capital and not at all in a town like Kentley. How wrong he had been. All along, the revolutionaries had planned to cause lots of unrest at various towns all around the country and it was well carried out. You could say it was carried out to military precision. Not surprisingly as a lot of the old British Army were behind it. David had, as always, been heavily involved in the local planning of the demonstration and was not afraid to lead by example when the time came to march on the European troops. Maybe the revolutionaries had miscalculated exactly how many followers they would get but there seemed to be hundreds. Maybe the passion of the masses had been underestimated but reporters told of how on the day there was tension in the air. The atmosphere was heavy with anger. Just one careless flammable thought and the whole place would explode with Revolution.

The European Army's response had never really been considered as ever being a violent retaliation but reports in the news after the event told how European Army soldiers feared for their lives on seeing the crowds and felt it was a 'them or us' situation. David was shot by soldiers trying to disperse the crowd. Being at the forefront he made himself a target. The crowd reacted by charging the barracks but this only brought more deaths. Although the aftermath of feeling carried on for a few days, the demonstration itself only lasted about two hours in Kentley. Crowds ran from the barracks and started to damage anything they could get their hands on but the crowd was in disarray and without direction. The demonstrators soon started to make their way back home, half not completely sure what the original demonstration had been about anyway. Gary's brother's friends had dragged David back to their meeting place where they then left him to die, more concerned for their own lives. Gary found him and carried him home. Gary did what he thought best and took David's body back to his parent's house. It was a struggle but he got there. By this time, local news reports were on the radio with information that demonstrators had been killed. Gary felt that his parents should have had some sort of idea that David might have been mixed up in all the trouble, and possibly deep down they both did but as Gary returned that day they both acted as if it was a great shock that their innocent son should be killed. His Father blamed Gary, his Mother was heartbroken and the family was torn. Gary wasn't living at home as he had got married by this time but his Father still blamed him. They never talked again. Within a year, his Father wilted away to his death. His Mother had often pleaded with Gary to apologise to his Father just to get them talking again but Gary didn't feel that it was his place to take the blame and therefore not his place to take the initiative and apologise. He wished he had now.

This demonstration also marked the end of an era. It was the last one that was properly planned in advance on such a big scale. There was obviously a lot of bad feeling about the Kentley deaths and braver youths would still seek revenge on the Union Army. As more and more youths attacked soldiers, more and more soldiers shot in self defence and of course many of the youths were killed. A lot of youths were being shot by the Euro Army soldiers around the time of Gary's Fathers death a year or so later and this was when the youth riots really started. Jobless, angry youths would take it upon themselves and attack soldiers who were still not ready to open fire at will. They would use stones, sticks and anything they could get hold of to attack the soldiers and eventually the Army would get reinforcements to arrest those who were unlucky enough to get caught. Again rumours were rife to the effect that prisoners were tortured and shot but nobody really knew what happened to them. A lot of these rioters were unemployed youths. Although not growing up expecting to get jobs most had expected at least some sort of decent living. Unemployment was growing everyday and spiraling out of control. Food was very hard to come by and there certainly wasn't anything in the way of entertainment to keep the kids happy. They were just left to fend for themselves like a forgotten part of a nation. Many of them weren't prepared to just sit and take it. They saw the European Army getting nice food and living in lovely houses and felt very angered about their whole situation. Youths weren't the only people at these riots. Political anarchists would be there stirring up as many people as they could. Sometimes ordinary folk who were just angry would also attend these riots. Very few people had jobs so it was easy to hear of when there was going to be a riot.

Sarah was one of those other angry people. She had always blamed the Union Army for the death of her younger brother and consequently the death of her Father. Gary and Sarah were very close in those days and Sarah had mentioned it to Gary that she had attended a riot. Gary was surprised. They had often discussed their political views and Gary knew that Sarah was probably more pro European than most. In fact she had never really had any interest in political matters that much at all but the deaths in the family had fueled her anger. She had told him that she had met up with some of David's old friends and they had persuaded her to go to some of the underground meetings that were being held. It was here that she met up with other people like herself and she was keen to show her support by attending a riot. Gary had tried to talk her out of seeing David's old friends but Sarah kept seeing them. At least for another week or so!

It was about a week later that Sarah disappeared. Nobody knew exactly what had happened to her. Had she died? Was she in prison? Was she alive? She had just disappeared. For Gary's Mother it was the final straw and her health deteriorated very quickly and she died two weeks later. Sarah had apparently been shot during the riot and had been moved away to a safe house in order to get better. Unconscious for a couple of days the revolutionaries were not really able to look after her and she had been left at the safe house to either get better herself or die. Luckily she had made a friend at these meetings who cared enough to get her some medicine and help her recover to some extent. His name was George and he helped conduct the riots against the European Armies. He had seen Sarah on a couple of occasions and wasn't prepared to just let her die. He stayed with her through the first couple of days but knew enough about injuries and wounds to know that if Sarah was going to recover fully, that she needed proper rest.

George took Sarah back to his family home in Lancashire. It was a journey of some three hundred miles or so and one that couldn't be taken overnight. Nevertheless he managed to get hold of a car and got her to his home and nursed Sarah back to full fitness. All of this was done unofficially by George and the revolutionaries were not very happy at the fact that he had decided to take time out at a time when they needed him most. George was a very important part of local revolutionary plans at the time and his absence was seen as desertion. Sarah didn't contact her family during this period for this very reason just in case the news of her whereabouts should be heard by local revolutionary ears. Unfortunately it also meant that she was totally unaware of the effect her disappearance had had on her Mother. She stayed with George and his Mother for a couple of months before returning to Kentley. It was one of the worst times of her life. She had made the long journey back home only to find strangers living in her house who were just about able to fill her in with the details of her Mothers death. Sarah thought about making contact with Gary but something stopped her and she returned immediately to George.

Whilst she was away, she had realised that she had fallen in love with him. It was quite obvious that George had been in love with her for a long time. The two of them lived together for a few months whilst making plans to get married but things took a turn for the worse. George had known for a long time that he would have to return to the revolutionaries one day and try and make his peace with them. He knew that they would catch up with him and probably punish him for dropping out so when Sarah returned to Kentley, George felt that no more time could be wasted and that he should contact the revolutionaries.

If George and Sarah were to have any sort of future, he didn't want to be looking over his shoulder all the time or worrying about who the newcomer was in the corner of the café. This was of course all done without Sarah knowing and when she returned as suddenly as she did, George never really found the right moment to tell her what he had done. The knock came on the door one afternoon and George was taken back to Kentley a prisoner. Sarah learnt from her neighbours what had happened and she made her own way to Kentley to find George. He had apparently been tortured and beaten unconscious by the revolutionaries as a punishment. This sort of incident also served as a warning to other members not to betray them but George was a bit of a special case. Having been such a leading light it was expected he would take over his old role so that the revolutionaries did not lose face. When he refused, he was beaten again but this time George died. The word put out by the revolutionaries was that George had confessed to being a traitor and hence had to be put to death. Sarah knew this was not the case. She knew George wasn't a traitor. Sarah never spoke much again about how he died but the anger never left her and she now found herself in the very strange situation of unofficially inheriting the small fortune that George had. She returned to their little house in Lancashire but she never felt comfortable there. A few months later she returned to the Kentley area and had made contact with Gary. Sarah never told Gary the full story. It was a difficult time.

Gary had blamed Sarah for the death of their Mother and had showed a lot of anger towards her. Sarah was full of guilt for not being around when her Mother died. The early meetings between them were not nice but the years had helped mend things. Sarah still kept in touch but nothing was good about those years. Well not much anyway. Gary could look back and say that he had met Angela during those times but he couldn't really look back on those years as happy ones.

It was mainly because of David that Gary and Angela had met. It was at the time when David would go missing for a day or two. He was only fourteen and Gary was twenty one so he felt a bit of a responsibility to try and make sure that David wasn't getting into too much trouble. Although Gary had got himself a job with the Post Office he still had a few friends that were unemployed and a bit closer to the many anarchist underground movements that had steadily built up since the end of the war. It was quite unusual for someone to be seen as a 'government employee' to have such a close connection with the unemployed but old childhood friendships were sometimes difficult to break. Gary had heard a little bit from David about the sort of people he was meeting but David knew that Gary's sympathies were not fully in line with his own so as he got older he said less about what was happening with the movement. Gary was never sure if this was done because David couldn't trust Gary or more as his own way of protecting his older but less politically active brother. Gary would never know. In the early days David had tried to get Gary to come to some of the meetings so he could hear what was being said. Gary wasn't interested.

They were both still living at home when David was first found not to have come home for the night. Their Father had tried to lecture

David but it was falling on the deaf ears of a young rebellious youth who had no time to listen. David then started going missing for a day or so but then a couple of days and then on one occasion it turned into a third day. Gary decided he would try and find his younger brother to persuade him to come home. Gary wasn't really bothered if David stayed out all night or not but it was hell at home and best all round if he could get him back. That afternoon, Gary had made an excuse to get off work early and he made straight for the 'Social Centre' which was where the unemployed all congregated to get money, jobs hand-outs and political information. The Euro Army knew that the main activists would recruit their followers from these sorts of places and were believed to have a number of undercover people on the lookout for suspects so you didn't just go down there and ask outright.

Gary also found it a bit strange as he didn't really know the system for looking for work. He had never been in a position to have to look for work before so he entered the main building feeling that he stood out like a bit of a sore thumb. He imagined that he was being stared at by everyone else because he looked out of place but within seconds the next person had entered the main building and he realised that all eyes were just looking at whoever came into the building regardless. Gary soon saw a notice board titled 'JOBS'. He went over to it and saw that there were just two vacancies. One was refuse operative working weekends only and the other was for a welder. Neither paid very much! The welding job paid an hourly rate just over half of what Gary was already earning whilst the refuse operator was a slightly higher hourly rate but Gary knew that this was a job where you had to fight off families looking for freebies from other people's rubbish. It was a tough job and rumours had gone around suggesting that most of the refuse operators worked only as part of a gang and most carried weapons of some sort.

A feeling of despair came over Gary as he saw the lack of opportunities that were on offer. Europe had a lot to do with the situation with German and French industries getting the benefit of bigger investments from the European coffers so it was they who were able to provide cheaper and better goods compared to companies in the rest of Europe whilst keeping employment levels reasonably steady. It didn't take long for British, Dutch and Spanish companies to hit hard times at which time the German or French rivals would buy them out.

As industries became more and more computerised the need for large workforces became less and less and the old British companies were run by just a handful, mainly French or German. It obviously caused mass unemployment in certain European countries.

Gary stood at the board looking at the two vacancies when a voice interrupted him. "You're new here aren't you?" Gary turned quickly to see that he was being spoken to by another job-seeker. He was unshaven, scruffily dressed but seemed pleasant enough.
"No, well I mean Yes." Gary replied. Gary was disappointed with his own response for if he had been trying to blend in he had just fallen at the first hurdle.
"If you're looking for a job then don't bother to look on the board brother. The clerks have the jobs. If you pay them enough you'll get one." The stranger turned and started to walk away but stopped and turned back. "That is if you are looking for a job?" The stranger added before continuing on his way.

Gary wasn't quite sure what the stranger had meant by that last remark but he felt even more conspicuous after this small encounter. He looked around to see a number of people obviously just hanging around and talking in small groups. Gary spotted a counter with a number of leaflets and forms on so he headed for it pretending to be looking for a job. On the counter were a couple of pens which were chained to the notice board so that they could not be stolen. There was also a pile of blank forms. Gary took a form and held a pen in his hand. He looked for a face he recognised so that he could start to make his own enquiries but there just wasn't anyone he knew at all. He waited and pretended to complete one of the forms for nearly 40 minutes before he saw an old friend. Frankie Braidwood. They had been at school together and in the same year but Frank had been a bit of a troublemaker when he was younger so not someone who Gary could say was one of his best mates. Frank was unemployed. As far as Gary could recall Frank had joined the Army and had gone off to fight in the Aegean War but he wasn't certain. He walked across to Frank. "Hi how are you doing?" Gary patted Frank on the back.
"Well bloody hell. Fancy seeing you here!" Frank replied in surprise. "I thought you had got a job in the Post Office, Man! What happened?" Gary was a bit surprised that Frank actually remembered who he was let alone remembered where he had been employed but

Gary felt that he should stick as far as possible to the truth so he tried to explain his presence.
"Yes, I'm still with the Post Office but I'm looking for my brother David. Do you know him?"
"No can't say I do." Frank shrugged his shoulders. "What does he look like?"

Gary started to describe his brother David to Frank but the description could fit almost everyone who was in the 'Social Centre' that day. David was usually unshaven and dressed in worn out scruffy clothes. Not one of them stood out. Even Frank was the same except that he had some highly polished and good standard Army boots on.
"Didn't you join the Army Frank?"
"Yes I trained for 6 months and managed to join up with the regular Army so that I could go off to fight. I then spent a year watching the shores of bloody Lesbos from a small boat. I then got transferred to street duties in Portugal before getting attacked and almost killed by some youths and finally got sent back here."
"So did you leave the Army?" Gary asked.
"I don't talk about leaving the Army." Frank's mood changed and he grabbed Gary by the arm. "And you certainly don't ask those sorts of questions. Not here." Frank loosened his grip. Gary got the message. "Sorry I can't help you with your brother but I must be going." Frank swiftly departed from the building as if his outburst had caused a problem. Gary looked around but couldn't see too many people looking or concerned about what had just happened. He stayed for another 10 minutes before deciding that as it was already passed closing time it was unlikely that he would see anyone else he knew.

The 'Social Centre' was another one of those places which was said to be run by the British Government but was really controlled by the European Government in Strasbourg. All new jobs were scrutinised by senior management before being advertised. Most of the jobs would finish up being handed to one of the clerks to be filled but it was common knowledge that every now and then a job would be earmarked for some outsider who needed to work. If a job vacancy did get to the clerks, they would hang on to them until they had traded the job for some sort of deal. Food, electricals, clothes vouchers were often promised to clerks in return for a job. Cash would often change hands outside as well because although the management had to be seen to stop this sort of thing going on in the building, they didn't stop it outside. In fact they quite often would advise job seekers to hang around after the offices had shut to speak to a clerk.

Now here was a job that had power. If you had a job as a clerk, or should I say an employment registration officer, you not only got paid a regular wage of a reasonable standard but got lots of other illegal benefits on top. It had been known for the occasional greedy clerk to be given the 'gypsy's warning' but usually they were treated with what Gary saw as a misplaced respect.

Gary left the 'Social Centre' and thought about what sort of problems he would get in at home. His Father would rant and rave and his Mother would try to calm him down, all because David was missing. He stood outside the 'Social Centre' for a short while before making his way to the bus stop. The bus didn't leave for another 20 minutes or so. He looked in the hope that he might see a friend that might help him find David. The trouble was he wasn't too sure now, how he could ask for help. Everyone was suspicious of people asking too many questions. Gary being one of the employed was probably thought of as being even more suspicious. It was at this moment that his fortune turned. A voice spoke behind him. "Hey man. I hear you have troubles. Perhaps I know a place where you can get help. You might see people you know there."
Gary turned to see the stranger who had first spoken to him in the 'Social Centre' right behind him. Gary was aware that he was very vulnerable and that this man could have done anything. He took Gary's hand and placed a flyer in it before quickly walking off. Gary looked at the flyer and then looked to see where the stranger had gone but he was quickly out of sight. The flyer was brief. 'Unhappy with the world today! Want to know the truth! Meet at Paiges! 7 p.m.!'

Gary wasn't quite sure what to make of it to start with but went over what the stranger had said and hoped that this was a lead as to where he could find David. He went home and said nothing to either of his parents about what had happened but said that he was having to go into work later to do some overtime. It wasn't unheard of to get overtime and although there was a sort of curfew on, if you had a valid reason for being out it was okay. Even if you didn't have a reason, in those days as long as you looked as if you had you very rarely got stopped. At six thirty Gary got ready to go out. He tried to dress down a bit more than usual but couldn't quite get rid of that 'working' look. He knew where Paiges was. It was the old fish & chip shop on Aldersgate Street towards the northern part of the town. Gary was certain that it was closed and in fact all bordered up but couldn't think of any other place by the same name. Gary made his way from the town heading towards Monks Way which would take Gary in a westerly direction.

Half way down Monks Way were a couple of residential streets that cut through to Wall Street which would then take Gary to Aldersgate Street. As he walked down Aldersgate Street, Gary thought he would see a few people going into Paiges, or at least where the shop used to be but he was a bit alarmed to find the street practically empty. The shop was indeed bordered up and as he walked passed it he could see no obvious signs of how to get into it. Had this all been a joke? Was he being set up? Gary suddenly realised that he might be doing something really stupid and getting himself into a very awkward situation. He pondered on his predicament for a few seconds but then he knew he had to try and find his brother if he could. Gary walked right to the far end of Aldersgate Street and looked at his watch. It was five minutes to seven. He stood and thought for a while before turning around and making his way back to the fish & chip shop. Still there was no sign of anyone around so in desperation he turned down the side turning next to the shop and stopped and looked up the alleyway that went behind the shop. It was long and dark but Gary plucked up the courage to walk down it. He came to what he assumed was the back door to the shop and he tried the handle. The door didn't open to start with but with a little pressure it gave and easily swung open. Gary darted into the yard and closed the gate behind him. The yard was dark and bare with just an old dustbin in one corner to be seen. He looked towards the back of the shop and could see that a couple of the boards had been half opened so he pushed one back and stepped inside. Gary found himself in an old storeroom which had obviously not seen life for years. It was behind the front of the shop and was probably used also as a cutting room when the fish and chip shop was running. There wasn't much to it. Some large work tops, a door through to the front of the shop and then another door that presumably led to freezers in the old days. Gary looked around the room to figure out where he should go next.

"What are you doing here?" A voice came from the shadows.
"The meeting!" Gary gingerly replied.
"Where's your invitation?" The voice continued.
"Err invitation?" Gary was confused.
"Flyer!" The voice said impatiently.
Gary felt in his pocket and retrieved the flyer he had been given that afternoon. "Oh yes, invitation." Gary held out the flyer towards the voice. A hand grabbed it and checked it.
"You're late. Down the stairs to your right, second door on the left," the voice ordered.
Gary never caught a proper sight of the voice which by now had withdrawn back into the shadows. Gary turned to his right to the door he had assumed led to freezers and walked through it to find a set of stairs. Not very long, only about ten stairs in all and quite narrow. He went down them and at the bottom found that they led to a corridor. He walked down the corridor not too sure what to expect next but as he approached the second door on the left he could hear the muffled sound of voices. He opened the door and the voices stopped.
"Come in friend," said a voice at the end of the room. "You haven't missed anything."

    Gary found himself in a room with around twenty others all of whom were sitting on the floor or leaning against some old barrels. He couldn't make out everyone's faces as it was very dark. The person at the far end who was obviously giving the talk had a candle which gave out the only light available. "Please sit if you can," the voice said again. Gary felt a bit awkward and out of place but sat on the floor next to a young girl. The voice then went on to talk about the way that Europe was now being run by military agents of France and Germany. How most of the rest of Europe was being kept in the dark about what was really happening in Europe so that we starved and suffered whilst the French and German people lived lives of luxury. The voice talked about his days in the British Army when he was sent out to Lesbos on the instructions of the Union Army and was eventually part of a raid on the island. He had been shot at by what he had been told were Turkish armed forces and left wounded on the beach as his troop retreated back out to sea. A friend of his had been shot as well and had landed on top of him. He had seen another wounded soldier try to crawl for cover from where he lay on the beach only to hear a snipers bullet shoot him dead where he lay. As the night time fell, he saw soldiers come on to the beach from the land looking for souvenirs. They all looked like very young Turkish soldiers and some would cut off ears to keep. Anyone who they thought was still alive was shot again. The dead bodies were the obviously dragged up the beach and used as barricades. Before he or his dead friend was moved the Turks obviously thought that another fleet of boats was in its way in as they retreated back up the land. He talked about originally thinking of waiting before trying to make any moves himself and after seeing the land soldiers come out to kill off any wounded had changed his mind. He needed to act fast. He had been lucky enough to get shot near a deeper part of the beach and he took his chance back in the sea.

Expecting to get shot at as he dived, things seemed to be going his way and he swam along the sea bed until he could surface further along the beach. The story continued and Gary half listened to it but spent most of his time trying to make out who else was in the room in the hope that he might recognise someone. As his eyes moved around the different people he felt that he too was being watched. He was. It was the young girl he was sat next to. Gary looked at her and she smiled. Gary then saw his brother David. He was one of the three men stood at the far end of the room. The man giving the talk continued to tell tales of horrific executions during the war and how they could never really see their enemy as being the Turks. Not all of the soldiers they shot at seemed to be Turkish but more like other Europeans. The trouble was the only soldiers who actually saw who they were shooting at were those who landed on the beaches. As far as he knew, none of them survived to tell their story. The man went on to say that he gradually took his time to make his way from the beach inland with the idea of infiltrating the Turkish Army. It came as a big surprise to find that the first set of troops he set eyes on were all talking in German. His initial thought was that they had fought their way into Lesbos to defeat the Turks but then it suddenly struck him that none of the soldiers sent to fight on the beaches of Lesbos seemed to have any Germans amongst them. In fact there weren't many French soldiers on the beaches either. They would be in charge of operations alright but not actually doing the fighting. Or the dying! He finished off by saying that it had taken him a couple of years to get back to England and that he was in fact officially dead. The French and the Germans had cheated the rest of Europe. The Union Army had now infiltrated the British Government and taken over control of our country. It was doing the same in all the other European countries. We were slaves to the French and Germans. It was our duty to stop them. Revolution was the answer.

There was also a very big growing problem in the form of mass over population. Not just in England but over the whole of Europe. Over population brought with it many other problems like unemployment, lack of accommodation, poverty, starvation, disease and general unrest. All over Europe there were little problem spots. One of the big drives behind the computerisation of the food industries in the first place was in an effort to grow more food at lower prices so that people in Europe didn't starve. In the initial stages, French and German people got the main benefits of the new computerised systems whilst the rest of Europe waited its turn. There were a number of starvation and poverty traps around Europe which although I'm sure the Strasbourg European Government had originally intended to deal with in as good a way as possible became big problems. It is rumoured that the Lesbos War was then used to kill off a large portion of the population so as to reduce the starvation problem. Nobody will ever really know what decisions were made. Everyone had his or her own story to tell and everyone had his or her own view.

As the meeting drew to a close, Gary made straight for David. They hugged each other and quickly went into talking about how each other looked. Gary wasn't quite sure if he was going to be able to persuade his younger brother to come home with him but within minutes David had agreed. Over the next few months, Gary went to a number of other meetings but really only to bring David back home with him. Nevertheless, as he was there he would listen to what was being said and he formed his opinions of what he thought was going on in the world. Gary got to know others at the meetings and was soon seen as part of the group. Gary also got to know the young girl who had spoken on that first night and although it was very brief he eventually got to talk to her. Her name was Angela. Gary guessed she was only about David's age and he felt a bit protective of her. There was no mistaking the fact that her voice had attracted him the first time he heard it. He couldn't quite put his finger on why it was. It just was. Eventually they fell in love. Gary looked back on that first moment he set eyes on his future wife. Even then he knew she was something special but had never thought that it would lead to marriage and a family.

-

Gary woke to the sound of his alarm clock. It was six fifteen. Angela, although stirred by the alarm would stay in bed for another thirty minutes whilst Gary got ready for work. "Do you want any toast?" Gary whispered to his dozing wife.
"No," came the prompt reply. The bread was usually stale and Gary knew that Angela wouldn't want any toast but always asked. The response he got was miserable but perhaps one of these days she would surprise him and say yes.

Gary went downstairs and made toast. It wasn't very tasty. He let Sammy out in the garden and then got ready to leave for work. He continued to put marmalade on his toast working his way around the mould with the knife as he did so and thought to himself that was another thing that he remembered being good about the old days. Marmalade! In order to get this jar of orange marmalade, Angela had done a lot of deals and arranged for Gary to fix a radio set and he had made sure it was used. It was probably a year old by now. Gary was the only one who actually ate marmalade but Angela knew how much he loved it and she always tried to get him some if there was any available on the black market. Angela came into the kitchen. "Oh can you get me some black shoe laces today as I've broken this one again." Gary said without looking up.
"I'll try and get to the little market and see what I can do but I have that school meeting this morning so don't expect me to do it today." Angela replied. She felt that this was quite an inconvenience but knew she could do it if she had the time. She was good at bartering up and could easily get what she needed for very little if she took the time.
"Of course I don't expect." Gary replied with a sarcastic grin.
"Oh yes you do," she said with a knowing nod. Gary kissed Angela on her cheek.
"See you about six," and it was on with his coat and out of the door. Angela had a busy day ahead of her today with meetings and things. She couldn't think how she was going to fit in getting some shoe laces. She thought for a second or two and then got on with the more important task of getting the girls up and ready for school.

Gary suddenly remembered part of what he had been thinking

about the night before. The whole revolutionary movement that had featured so prominently in his life. Well at least in some of the more important incidents of his life. Gary found it a bit strange to think back just those few years and look at how much had changed. There had always been a number of people around who were discontent and shouting to bring the military down. It wasn't really acceptable but it still went on. Nowadays, nobody dared go to such meetings or voice their opinion in such a way for fear that the person next to you would report you to the military. They would soon come round and arrest anyone thought to have been voicing anti government feelings. Sometimes it would be someone in your own family who would report you. Wives, husbands, brothers or sisters. Nobody could be considered above suspicion. Because of this, the revolutionary movement had become a lot more professional in the way they operated. Gary knew that there was a growing feeling of unrest amongst the general public. They wanted action.

Gary continued thinking whilst he drove to work. He was at the Post Office at half past seven as usual and the incidents of last night were now the furthest from his mind. The team had already started on the early shift. Gary had got his team working pretty well unsupervised now, except for Billy of course who was the youngest and newest recruit to the team. By the time Gary had come in to work he knew that his team would have already taken delivery of the days post and be half way to having it all sorted. There wasn't as much post as there used to be in the old days as very little commercial post was sent out anymore. Most of the post was either personal letters or official Government post. The Army did most of the transportation of the post around the country and at six fifteen there would be an armoured delivery at Kentley Post Office ready for sorting and the Post Office team would of course have a bag of outgoing post all bagged up for the Army to takeaway with them.

Firstly the official Government mail would be sorted into the delivery boxes and then they would take piles of letters from the incoming sack and start going through it to check addresses. Micky Mercer was sorting codes KT1 to KT3 today. Each address had its official residents listing and provided the letter or parcel was addressed to someone on that list, the post was okay for delivery. If the name was wrong, it would be singled out for further checking. Gary relied on Micky as he was Gary's right hand man.

Micky sifted through his bunch of letters handing across any codes that weren't his. This would usually be the way that the team operated, all four sitting around a big table and sifting the bag of mail between them. It wouldn't normally take much more than an hour to get all the post to the right sorter and they were usually able to do this whilst chatting to each other about what they had done the day before. By seven thirty, they would hope to have all their respective codes in place and when Gary arrived it was time for the first tea break of the day.
"Good morning team. Are we all well today?" Gary called out as he entered the office.
The four of them would take it in turns to shout back the obligatory 'Yeah'. Gary would then put the kettle on before continuing on to unlock his own little office.
"Andrea, are you making tea this morning?" Gary said in a way that meant it was her turn.
"I guess so," she replied.

Gary put his brief case down by the side of his desk and turned his desk lamp on. It would still be darkish for another hour and he needed the artificial light. Gary looked on his desk for his cup and noticed a sealed envelope addressed to him laying there. He picked it up and gave it a quick look. It was from the Assistant Postmaster. Gary could tell from the writing. He couldn't be bothered to open it now so put it back down on his desk. Gary then went over to the safe and twisted the dial to feed in the code. The safe was used by most of the team as it was where most of the undelivered post was put if it hadn't been made into a file and any important notices were also stored there. Lastly, the roster and swap book was kept in the safe.

Gary picked up his cup and made his way to the kitchen where the other four were already sitting awaiting Andrea's tea. Gary plonked his cup on the side and sat at the table. Andrea Smith then brought through the first two cups of tea to everyone's delight. As the five of them sat around the table Gary tried to get them talking. "Did anyone see that old musical on telly last night?"
"Do you mean Cats?" William replied.
"That's the one. All dressed up in cat costumes and dancing around on

the stage. It must have been brilliant to have seen that in real life." Gary continued.
"I don't think I've ever heard of it," one of the others added.
"Not a surprise really," laughed William, "It must be nearly fifty years old," he confirmed.

The five sat and thought about it and then Andrea spoke. "Have you ever been to a live musical show William?"
"Yes, in the old days I used to travel to London to see them. Really fun and a great day out!" William almost cried out the last bit of the sentence as he remembered the old days.
"Did you go out at all yesterday?" Andrea asked.
"No not really. I went to the corner shop but it was closed. What about you?" William replied.
"No nothing." It was a typical morning's conversation.

As tea finished, the four went back to their respective sorting boxes and started work looking at the names and addresses on the post in front of them. It was hoped that all of the post would get put into one of the many boxes used for sorting but any post not properly addressed would have to be put in a larger transparent folder with a marked sheet ticked to show exactly why it had been found to be incorrect. Sometimes the sorter would know why it was wrong. For instance a letter addressed to 35, Downley Road for the Durkin family should be addressed to 55. This information would also be put on the sheet but the envelope still selected and separated. When the late shift came on at ten, one of the shift would open the public counter whilst the other three would take sorted post out and deliver it. There were many other tasks for the team to do during the day and Gary would allocate these to members as they became free.

Gary went back to his office and sat down at his desk. He got out his current work load of files from his drawer and then opened the letter from the AP. It was a normal instruction to intercept all post going to a list of various streets for the next five days. Gary would simply have to work out who was working on these areas on the shift roster and type out instructions to those sorters to pass all such mail to him. This sort of check happened about once a month and Gary would just pass it all on to the AP each afternoon and then the next day it would come back ready for delivery. Gary checked the list and nodded as he saw some common streets. Brook Road and Harmony Road in Kentley were quite often on the list and again Cambridge Way in Waydon was a regular. A few of the other streets mentioned were ones Gary had seen on lists before but those three were the real regular ones. No doubt they were expecting some sort of illegal post. The checks were to start from tomorrow so Gary had to get going on typing out his lists.

At ten o'clock on the dot, Major Jacques Tannier was informed that there was someone to see him. His agent had arrived as planned and as always was out of uniform. The Major's secretary didn't know that this was an agent but assumed it was just another person calling for an interview or an appointment as arranged. Major Tannier had about ten to a dozen visitors each day and most of them were general members of the public. He would be speaking to members of the public who wanted to come forward with information about their neighbours. Also there were people of influence who had been called in to arrange special deals whilst he also interviewed other workers who had been reported for showing revolutionary tendencies. If the Major felt it necessary he would just arrange for completely innocent people to be called. It helped confuse anyone who might be watching the visitors and kept everyone guessing as to who was saying what to whom. Lastly of course there would be agents who were undercover. The agent was shown in by the Major's secretary and Tannier starting talking.
"It's a real piece of luck that you were due today as I have confirmation of the death of one Jenny Tetridge," the Major started. The agent showed no emotion and said nothing.
"She was stopped at a roadblock out on the Bateley Road yesterday afternoon and shot whilst trying to make a run for it," the Major added. He looked at the agent keenly looking for a flicker of interest but like all trained agents there was nothing at all.
"I haven't got the report as yet but it is ready and waiting with a Major Wooters. Do you want to see him or shall I send someone for it?" The Major asked. The agent considered for a second before answering.

Twenty minutes later there was a knock on Major Wooters door.

until about an hour after Tetridge was killed. Is it possible that he had been in the queue further back and had tried to run for it. No this didn't fit in at all! The agent would of course give him the quick once over but Miller looked the best bet apart from the unknown bloke in the car.

The agent went back to Major Tannier's office having taken some notes.
"I'll leave the file here with you sir," the agent said.
"Of course! No problem. If you need to look at it again just let me know."
"Oh and thanks for getting one of your staff to go and get it for me." The agent added. Over the next ten or fifteen minutes the agent relayed details of who should be commended on the content and fullness of the report and Major Tannier concurred. Sergeant Foulkes would be thanked. They quickly chatted about how Operation Hunting was going but not ever mentioning the target by their name, only ever being referred to as 'The Target'. They talked about how difficult the operation had been at times but the fact that if they got the list of local revolutionary sympathisers at the end of it, it would have been worth all the effort. There were certain details that the agent required about the Millers and Nigel Brown as well as anything else that comes up from the follow up checks that would be done as a matter of course. Major Tannier would have this all in hand and organised for results to be collected from a pre-arranged collection point. This was all done so that the agent could go about their normal life whilst still keeping in touch with their cases progress.
"I gather you knew Mrs. Tetridge?" The Major asked.
"Yes I've come across her a couple of times and seen her in the field as well. That was a number of years ago now naturally. She was very good and obviously wouldn't have been expecting any of the road block to actually shoot but I'm surprised that she took such a chance on this one. It does hopefully go to show that the list is here and that it is that important," the agent replied.
"Did she know you?" The Major asked again.
"Well she knew me but I don't think she knew my background. We've only been on acquaintance terms very recently." The agent confirmed. The Major was again impressed to find that one of his agents had managed to get so close to a named sympathiser. There wasn't much else to ask really. The agent left. The Major awaited his

next caller.

-

Tonight's journey home was back to normal for Gary. No roadblock this evening and so it was a straight drive to Waydon. By six o'clock he was in the front door.
"Hello I'm home," came the usual shout from Gary as he shut the front door.
"Hello Daddy," came the reply from Joan and Katy as they rushed out of the lounge to greet him. They both took turns to jump up into Gary's arms and he gave them both a big hug. Sammy was also not far behind to greet his master and he waited for his regular pat on the head.
"And how was your day?" Angela said as she poked her head round the door from the kitchen.
"Pretty good!" Gary replied.
Angela went back into the kitchen to carry on with the family dinner. She was always glad when Gary was home on time so that all four of them could sit down together.
"What's for dinner tonight?" Gary asked
"Cottage pie!" Angela shouted from the kitchen. "It'll be ready in about forty five minutes so if you're going to be a long time taking Sammy out, go now please" she added. Without any further encouragement, Gary put on his dog walking coat and took the lead down from the coat peg at which point Sammy danced around in circles in anticipation of what was to come. Although it was six o'clock, it hadn't got that dark and there would be time for Gary to take Sammy for a walk down the lane and back. Gary let Sammy off the lead for a short while as they walked down the lane away from home. It was light enough to see where he had gone but dark enough to see the lights of any cars that might possibly be driving towards them. Gary would also be keeping an eye out for any soldiers that might be patrolling just in case. He knew he would be okay for being out with the dog but particular soldiers could always make things a bit difficult if they wanted to.

As they were walking Gary decided to take the leafy lane that headed towards the old school building and Sammy was clever enough to sense roughly where Gary wanted to go and take the same route. In the distance, Gary could make out the noise of drilling, which he assumed meant people were working at the school again this evening. His curiosity took him nearer to the school entrance. As he approached the school building, he could make out a couple of figures moving about at the front gate. They must be guards he thought to himself and this was the signal to turn around and make back for home. Fortunately Sammy came to heel very easily and Gary attached his lead so that the two of them could make quick ground back when he was ready but he wasn't going to leave without having a sneaky look through the hedge first. Only the main building seemed to have any lights on but there were a few Army vehicles parked down the side of the school and the sound of mobile generators ticking over. A bit like the sound of the old funfairs that Gary used to go to as a boy. He couldn't make much out but it looked like there were at least a dozen uniformed officers working on something in the building. He stared a bit longer but then decided that the time had come to get back. He could easily have another look tomorrow night and anyway he didn't want to upset Angela too much.

The walk back was fairly uneventful and Gary and Sammy were just about fifty yards from the back gate when the lights of a vehicle could be seen heading towards the bend in the lane ahead. Gary looked at how far it was to the gate and knew he would never make it. Best to be on the safe side and take Sammy through a gap in the hedge again. Here he stayed until the vehicle had driven passed. It was an Army vehicle as well and one that would have stopped and asked Gary what he was doing on the lane had it seen him. Gary again was confident that he wouldn't ever get into trouble whilst out walking the dog and he started to go through the gap in the hedge back out into the lane when he heard some footsteps.

Shit! Gary thought to himself. Had the Army vehicle been dropping off soldiers for patrol? He quickly darted back behind the hedge. The footsteps got louder as they got closer. Gary held Sammy close but as always, Sammy kept quiet. The footsteps stopped as they got to the gap in the hedge.
"That was a close one boy, wasn't it. An Army vehicle as well," said the voice. It was the same stranger as the night before who was obviously out walking their dog again. All of a sudden Gary wondered if the voice had in fact been talking to him knowing that he was there hidden behind the hedge. The thought was soon dismissed

as Gary felt certain that the stranger was in fact talking to his own dog. The footsteps started again and then faded away as they went into the distance. Gary picked up Sammy and they went back on to the lane and straight home through the back gate. As Gary got in, Angela was just serving up dinner.

"You're lucky!" she said. "Another couple of minutes and it would have been cold Cottage Pie for you!" Angela said in a discontented voice. "What's taken you so long again?"

"Oh I didn't go that far. Just up to the lane." Gary replied in a casual manner.

"You haven't been bloody trying to look at the school again have you?" Angela said in an accusing manner. Her voice had raised a little as she tried to curb her annoyance. She knew Gary only too well.

"No". Gary replied. He wanted to add a bit more but wasn't quite sure what else to say. As he tried to work out what else he should say to explain why he had been so long, the gap after saying 'No' had become so big he just left it at that.

"So go on then where have you been?" Angela's tone got tougher.

"Er. Er." Gary was a bit taken aback. "I've just been up the lane. I lost track of time."

"Lost track of where you were more likely."

"I didn't go anywhere near the school."

"The back lane takes you near to the school."

"Well…" Gary held his arms out in a questioning manner. What could he say?

"You know you will only get into trouble if you go up to the school." Angela said. "And then we'll all be in trouble," she continued after regaining her composure a bit. "Why can't you just leave it alone?"

She finished with a strong sentence that could have been taken both as a question and as a warning. Angela was not happy about Gary trying to find out what was going on at the old school and they had argued about it before. They both knew that the military had moved in but only she seemed to realise how dangerous it was to investigate. It was dangerous to just be seen looking let alone be going near the school. Gary had tried to explain that somebody needed to know what was going on at the old school but Angela couldn't understand why it had to be Gary. Gary wasn't really that interested in what the Army was doing but he was curious and annoyed that it had interfered with local life. Disruption of this kind was commonplace but it didn't make it any easier to take when it disrupted you personally.

They sat down for dinner and ate in a deafening silence for a while.
"You had another phone call whilst you were out." Angela said in an effort to cut the atmosphere.
"Who was it?" Gary asked casually.
"Same as the person last night who wouldn't leave their name. Just said they'd ring back."
"What tonight?" Gary asked as he looked at her in surprise.
"I don't know," she replied abruptly. "They won't leave their name, they don't tell me when they're going to call back." Angela sounded rather annoyed. She was annoyed. Not because of the phone call but because of the school. She needed to try and forget it but she couldn't. Gary thought he should change the subject.
"Did you get me any laces?"
"I said I didn't think I'd have time today. I'm sorry but I was busy and didn't have time to get down to the shop. I'll get you some tomorrow." Angela replied. Gary thought to himself. Perhaps not the best question to ask.
"Oh and Sarah popped round just before you got home. She couldn't stay but said she would see you next week. I think she has some news." Angela said.
"What sort of news?" Gary said quizzically.
"I don't know just some news."
"How can you say you think she has some news but then not know what sort of news she has? That's just daft." Gary said looking at Angela in a funny way.
"I felt she had something that she had specifically popped round to tell you but as you weren't here she didn't want to tell only me."
"Sarah would know I wouldn't be at home." Gary said defiantly.
"Perhaps because she wanted to tell you her news she had forgotten what time you get home from work. You mark my words. I think she might have another bloke." Angela finished.

Gary thought about it but then came back to the fact that Sarah was still so very much in love with George. Not that he had ever met the bloke but he heard a lot about him and he knew that Sarah was still mourning his death. Although she had been back in the area a few years now it had only been in the last year or so that Sarah had put so much effort into trying to communicate with Gary. She had made a real effort, popping round every couple of weeks. Gary still holding on to that hurt didn't respond very positively. Angela had got to chat to Sarah more often than Gary had in the early months but now the two of them were back to being like a real brother and sister. Sarah still came round to see Angela and the girls but now Gary and her were back on proper speaking terms again. Gary was of course very pleased to have made up with his sister after so much time and there was an element of jealousy leaking in at the thought that someone might take her away again. Sarah got a new bloke. I don't think so.

Chapter 3   -   AND LIFE GOES ON

It was the start of another day for Gary and by half past seven he was at work and in his office.
"Hello team," he shouted out as he raised his hand in the air. All four of the staff replied with their usual 'Yeah alright,' as Gary dropped his briefcase in his office and made his way to the kitchen. One of the staff followed Gary into the kitchen.
"How's it going boss?"
"Oh alright I suppose." Gary replied without seeming to have heard what the question was. He had his mind on so many things that he found himself drifting. Angela seemed more miserable than ever this morning and had not given him his usual kiss goodbye. He knew that she had been a bit upset last night but it was obviously worse than he had originally thought.
"Are you with us Boss?"
"Sorry, lots on my mind, you know how it is." Gary replied.
"Yes we all have our problems eh."

Gary snapped out of his drifting state and turned his mind to work. "Did you all see the new lists of suspect addresses this morning?" Gary made conversation.
"Yes, we've had a few and there are some in the box for you including a couple of strange ones for you to look at."
"Good." Gary replied. "I'll look forward to seeing them," he continued in a slightly sarcastic tone. Gary picked up his cup, paused briefly and then left the kitchen and went to his office.

He noticed a couple of reports in his tray. As Gary looked at the files he suddenly realised that he had forgotten to put them in the safe last night. This was very remiss of him and not something that he was known to do. He opened the first file. The file was in a plain brown folder and simply had the address written on the front. It read, 12, Lavender Lane, Greenfields. Gary read the report inside so as to recap what had happened. It was a personal letter addressed to a Mr. P. Smith. Not very adventurous for a made up name, Gary thought to himself. The house in question was apparently lived in by a Mrs. Rose Colney who was recorded as the only occupant. She had lived there for the last seventeen years although up to about five years ago she had been living there with a Mr. Alfred Colney. Gary hadn't bothered to check him any further at this stage and had assumed that he was Rose's late husband. There was no mention of any Smiths having ever lived at any address on Lavender Lane so Gary decided that the next action should be to knock on the door and ask some questions. He wrote up his thoughts, completed the action sheet and prepared the file for today's round attaching the sheet to the front of the file.

The next file was similar. An address in Greenfields and a personal letter to a Miss Wendy Garner. She had been had been recorded as living at that address with the current occupants recorded as having moved to Liverpool about two years ago. Again this would mean a knock at the door to ask questions. Gary quite liked visiting people in their homes to ask about undeliverable mail but his job kept him in the office more and more. He thought back to the days when he used to do the visits on his own and would come across many nice people during his work. The public were quite happy for the postman to ask questions about unknown names and Gary had never come across many real problems. Gary looked on the list to see who was down from the late shift to do the 7 and 8 codes deliveries today. Billy Simpson. Gary thought that this would be a great opportunity to get out and see how Billy was doing, have a little chat with him whilst also getting out of the office.

There was a knock on Gary's open office door.
"Come in!"
"We've done well today boss, all finished and ready for delivery and it's still not quite nine o'clock." The man handed Gary four transparent folder bags each containing a suspect piece of mail and a ticked check sheet. Gary took them and placed them on his desk to his left. "Do you want one of us to do any checks at all?"
"No not this morning. I'm hoping to take young Billy out with me to see how he tackles some of the checks. One of you can go down to the Information Centre and pick up any lists from there so they can be done earlier." There was a light pause as Gary expected an answer.
"Is that alright?" Gary added
"Yes, I'll go and do that." The man replied but was quite surprised at being given the task.

Each day a clerk from the Information Centre would supply a list to the Post Office detailing changes to resident's lists for the area the sorting office covered. New residents would be listed well in advance of them actually moving into housing and there were regular updates as to moving dates so that the Postal Service knew what was going on. There would then be various details of changes of residents. This would include, births, deaths, long term lodges etc. all of which might mean that another person might be receiving mail at that address.

There was no more post to sort and all the bundles were prepared so Andrea, Micky and William were able to sit in the kitchen and relax. William made his way to Gary's office and knocked before walking in.
"The safe is open William." Gary said as he saw him come in.
"Cheers boss." William bent down and took the swap book from the safe. Gary was busy looking at the four new pieces of suspect mail that had been brought in earlier. He would give each new suspect letter a quick look just in case he could finish it off fairly quickly and then leave time to ponder over the more serious looking ones. Quite unusually, all four were for the main town. The first one was a small sized personal letter addressed to nobody but just to the address itself. 29a, Wall Street, Kentley. The fact that it was not actually addressed to anyone would make it undeliverable mail straightaway as the Postal service required personal or business names to be put on all post. Micky Mercer had been doing area code 1 again today and it was his check sheet that was included in the file. He had very little to put on his check sheet but was able to write that there was no such address as 29a but that there was a newsagents shop at number 29. The 'a' on the envelope could have possibly been another number but Micky had also mentioned that the numbering on the street only went as high as 67 so it was unlikely to be a three figured number. Gary pondered for a minute before moving on to the next file.

The next one Gary would definitely have to deal with himself as it was a brown enveloped Government letter. It was addressed to a Mr. & Mrs. T. LOCKWOOD at 13, Riverside, Kentley and again Micky had intercepted it. His check sheet said that the house was occupied by a Tom and Lucy SHAW who had been living there for the last five years. With this being a Government letter, Gary would have to report the non-delivery of it before he finished this evening to cover his back. Every now and then a Government letter would get sent to a wrong address to make sure that the Postal Service Manager was working properly and Gary didn't want to get caught out. He knew that he would deal with this one first but before he tackled it he cast a quick eye over the last two files. One was a long thin windowed envelope addressed to FILBERTS LTD, Eastbank, Kentley. They used to run a furniture business but shut down about four years ago and as far as Gary knew had stopped trading altogether. The last one was a long personal letter addressed to a Mr. S. DAVISON, 1, Ferrybridge Street, Kentley. Gary was not too up to date on the housing on that road but Micky's report stated that the address did exist but was currently unoccupied.

Gary went back to the Government envelope and got out a new brown file and some writing paper. As always, Gary had to confirm what his team member had put on the check sheet and so he got his residents listings out and wrote on the report that he agreed with Mr. Mercers findings. Unlike with the personal letters, this was not one that Gary would be allowed to go and call on so he simply completed his report and put the file in the tray ready for the AP when he came down. The other three were also made into files and by eleven o'clock Gary had completed his work. The rest of the team had started their duties at ten o'clock and as usual Billy Simpson was a little late but he was still in the office by five past ten so nobody was really that bothered. Another member of the team was working the public counter today and by a minute past ten the public entrance door unlocked and ready for business. A lot of other towns had shut their public counter but Gary fought to keep theirs open. It was used for people who had larger packages to be picked up. The other four members of the team would be on delivery duties which was the first type of work you learnt to do as a Postal worker and a duty that nearly all the staff liked doing.

Billy Simpson was of course doing the deliveries for area codes 8 and 9 today. As he came in Gary called him into his office.
"Boss is there something I can do for you?" Billy asked as he poked his head around the door. Gary found that Billy was keen to get involved in almost anything.
"You're doing 7 and 8 today?" Gary asked in a knowing manner.
"Yes." Billy replied.
"I want you to do the suspect letters today when you've finished."

Gary told him. Billy was quite pleased as it was not usual for him to be given these sort of duties. "Try and get your round done as soon as you can and come and see me when you get back." Gary added.
"That's great Boss. I'll see you at lunch." Billy was full of excitement. He grabbed his bundle of post and made his way to his round in Lavenham and Waydon. It was usually the smallest rounds bundles of post but did require the need to drive to both villages.

    Billy was the youngest team member and had only been in the job about four months. He lived at home with his parents and was very pleased to be earning. He tried very hard to get on with everyone in the team and was always telling jokes or pulling someone's leg to help establish himself as one of the team. His father had always taught him not to take any shit off anyone and Billy felt that this was good advice at the current moment as all the other members in the team would try and make the jokes turn on him. Billy found that the same advice had done him good at school as he was never picked on by any of the teachers. He had been in a few fights but nobody got the better of him. His school mates felt it would be a natural thing for Billy to join up with the Army but Billy wasn't in agreement. His uncle had been a member of the old British Army and most of the family was against the current military set up. His uncle was a very fervent supporter of the underground movement and Billy knew he would take some stick from him when he had to do his conscription with the Euro Army. He would have to do it though and Billy knew he would survive it. Until that day came, he was quite happy working for the Postal Service.

    By lunch time, Billy had finished his round and returned to the Office. Gary wasn't quite ready to join up with him so he made his way to the kitchen to wait. Most of the team were also in the kitchen. Micky was reading the local newspaper. "I see the local yobs have been causing trouble again?" Micky read the report out loud. "It says here that a gang of youths attacked an off duty soldier down by the refuse centre. Were you there Billy?" Micky knew it would wind Billy up.
"If I had he wouldn't have been alive to tell the tale." Billy replied and then joked by clenching his fist and flexing his muscles.
"Oh aren't you just the hard man." One of the team said in despair. "You bloody kids make me sick," Andy continued.

"I'm no kid. You better just watch what you're saying." Billy stared back at Andy long and hard.

"Or else what? You'd give me what for?" Andy responded to Billy and stood up to stare back at him. Billy was in no mood to back down and stepped a bit closer to Andy.

"I'd show you right now but I don't fight cripples." Billy said with a brief laugh. Andy grabbed at Billy's neck and Billy grabbed at Andy's arms. The two of them were locked together and staring each other out as the rest of the team tried to split them up. One of the team pulled at Andy whilst Micky got Billy in a neck lock. Between them they pulled the two apart. Not happy with Micky having hold of his neck, Billy threw a punch at him. Micky let him loose but Billy then threw another punch in his direction. Micky ready to defend himself threw a punch back at Billy which connected with Billy's nose. There were a couple of seconds of brief silence as the whole incident shocked everyone in the kitchen and then Billy's nose started to bleed.

Billy felt the blood trickling down but refused to move from his stance which was ready to take Micky on should another punch come his way.

"You better watch your back Mercer. I'll get you back for this!" Billy stared at Micky.

"Come on boys there's no need for all this," said Dee and she looked at Andrea. Andrea took the signal and got up to stand in front of Billy.

"Come on let's get you cleaned up." Andrea said as she wiped some of the blood from Billy's nose. Billy at first moved his head out of the way in an effort to keep staring at Micky but Andrea was persistent and eventually Billy gave in and let her clean him up a bit.

One of the other female staff pushed Micky back into his chair. "Bloody sit down and act your age," she said to him as she shoved him.

"Billy, go and get washed." Gary ordered him. Andrea led Billy towards the bathrooms and offered to help him get cleaned up completely but he refused and went into the bathroom himself.

About five minutes later, Billy came into Gary's office. He was still holding on to a bulk of toilet paper and continually wiping away blood that was still trickling down from his nose. He stood there in a defiant manner and the atmosphere was obviously tense. Gary didn't want to appear to be against Billy but had to remain his boss.

"Are you alright?" Gary asked him gently.
"Yeah. They won't get the better of me," he replied in an aggressive manner.
"They are not trying to get the better of you. You must learn not to react so intensely to everything that is said." Gary tried to explain but it was obvious that Billy was not going to listen.
"I think perhaps you ought to go home and get your nose seen to." Gary told him
"What about the suspect letters?" Billy replied.
"You cannot call on houses with blood down your uniform. You can do some next week. Now go home and I'll see you Monday." Gary said in his managerial voice. Billy did as he was told.

It had been a stressful day for Gary and he was pleased to get home. He put away his brief case but not before getting out the local newspaper that Micky had left him. Gary thought he might get a chance to read it over the weekend. Newspapers weren't that easy to buy as only a few copies were ever printed and most would have been sold by about seven in the morning. Micky always seemed to get a paper from somewhere but Gary didn't usually bother. As always, Angela had dinner almost ready for when he got in so for once Gary took Sammy for a short walk and was back home in good time. Gary was a bit unsure as to how Angela was going to be but she seemed to have forgotten last night. Gary was not absolutely sure if she had forgiven him or not. He decided to do everything he could to make sure he didn't upset her this evening.

The conversation was about general things but soon got to the subject of the family's television.
"The girls were asking when it was going to be repaired Gary." Angela started.
"Well all I need is an Emitron and I could probably do it in a few hours. Most of the other things I need I have here." Gary replied.
"Do you know where you can get one of these……. things?" Angela asked him with a pause.
"There are a couple of places that might have one." Gary replied.
"Are these places in Kentley?" Angela continued.
"They are but then I wouldn't be that sure that they'd actually have one in stock. Mind you, a bloke I sort of know in Chale would probably be able to get his hands on one easily but he'd want a fair bit

for it."

"Let's go tomorrow and see if he has one." Angela said. Gary was quite happy to go as it would be nice to have the television back up and working again. He nodded.

"Yeah that would be a good idea. Perhaps the girls might like to go swimming?" There was a swimming pool in Chale which was open to the general public at weekends. The Army used it during weekdays but it got full at weekends.

"I won't tell them, we'll take their costumes and see if we can get in." Angela replied. "Oh and I got you the shoelaces you wanted," she continued whilst pointing to a brown paper bag on the sideboard. Gary got up and looked at the laces.

"Thank you darling," he said as he walked over to her and hugged her in the chair. Angela smiled and kissed him. Perhaps things were okay after all, Gary thought. He picked up the local paper which had dropped by the side of the chair and put it on the table to read it over the weekend.

The next day was busy and the Newsons were getting ready for a day out in Chale. Joan and Katy were excited as was Sammy although he had no idea what was going on.

"We're going to have to do some shopping girls." Angela tried to calm them a bit.

"Can we go to the park?" Katy asked.

"Can we go swimming?" Joan added.

"We have to go shopping. We'll have to wait and see what else we can do." Angela hugged them both and they were happy with what their Mother had told them. Fairly soon they were in the car on their way to Chale. The first stop was the little electrical store that Gary knew on one of the small back lanes of Chale. It was a dirty little shop with all sorts of bits and pieces hanging down from the ceiling or in boxes on shelves and most of it looking as if it had been there centuries, let alone years. Gary went up to the young man behind the counter.

"Have you got an Emitron to fit a Guvdot Model 5 television?" He asked.

"Bloody hell now, that's an old style television. You might be better off trying to buy a new one."

"No thanks. All I need is the part and I'll have it up and working in no time." Gary told him.

"Do you know how difficult it is to get such a part?" The man added.
"Look can you get me one today or not?" Gary was ready to leave.
"I can get you one in a couple of hours," the man replied.
"How much would that cost?" Gary continued.
"About seven E's I would think." The price was a bit expensive for such an item especially a secondhand one as it would probably only cost about three to buy a new one. If you could find somewhere where you could buy a new one that is. Gary looked at Angela and they stared at each other.
"We'll give you four." Angela said as she turned to the young man at the desk and stared at him.
"You've got to be joking Madam. It will cost me that much to buy it myself. If I'm putting myself out I've got to make a profit."
"If you can get one here in two hours you can't be leaving Chale so I think if we asked a few questions in the right places we'd also find where you'd be getting it from." Angela said in a very confident manner.
"Maybe you would but you wouldn't know what you were looking for," the man tried in vain to regain some ground.
"I would though." Gary quickly added.
"I'll take six then".
"You'll take five"
"Five fifty or it's not worth me leaving the shop," the young man said. Gary nodded affirmatively to Angela.
"Five fifty it is then but I know you'll send your boy. We'll be back at twelve." Angela concluded the dealing and they left the shop.
"It's great to see you in action." Gary said as they walked back to the car.
"You'd have bloody given him seven E's wouldn't you?" She gave him a strange look as she said it. The rest of the day went well. Some shopping for clothes and a short visit to the swimming pool plus they returned to the electrical shop to buy the electrical item as agreed. They returned home and almost immediately Gary started working on fixing the television.

Gary had already been close to getting the television working a few weeks back but the old circuit board he had just wasn't up to it anymore and he had realised that the only answer was to get a new one. The soldering iron was now what was required and Gary had a couple of them in his work room. A big one for the more major bits of soldering and a much more delicate one for the fiddly bits. Gary worked away for the next couple of hours whilst Angela got the girls ready for bed. She fed the two of them and bathed them so that they would be ready to go to bed as soon as Gary had finished showing them the working television. Angela was confident that he would get it working and sure enough by seven thirty Gary came struggling through from the work room with the set in both arms. The girls cleared a space where the television had previously been placed and then sat down in front of it wide eyed waiting for the magic show to begin.

"It won't be long now girls." Gary assured them as he wound out the mains lead.

"You better not let them down." Angela warned him.

"What's going to be on Daddy?" Joan asked.

"I don't really know." Gary replied.

"Didn't you bring home a newspaper last night?" Angela queried.

"Yes I did. Good idea." Gary answered. The local paper would have a section in it showing what television programmes would be on over the weekend so Angela and the girls gathered round the table and opened the paper to find the right page. It took a little while to find it but eventually Angela found the page in question.

"What's on Mummy?" Katy said excitedly.

"Don't get too excited darling as it will probably be news programmes." Angela replied. How right she was. All three channels were showing programmes during Saturday evening but between seven and nine o'clock only news was on. The main three channels were the only ones who were allowed to make proper national broadcasts. They were all strictly controlled by the Government so none of the programmes were ever controversial. Every now and then there would be a local television station trying to make broadcasts but they never lasted very long. Joan and Katy kept looking and hoping for details of some interesting programme but as the disappointment of finding just news was beginning to sink in, a noise was starting to emerge from the television set. It soon turned into speech from the newscaster who was giving details of the latest youth riots in some country like Czechoslovakia or Hungary. When you looked at the pictures it could have been any town in Europe and quite possibly was. British television rarely reported trouble on the home front. It all went towards making the British feel that they were better off than they really were.

The Newsons all sat down and listened with intrigue at the news report coming from a remote little Greek town called Ballikaida. Youths were protesting about poor living conditions and attacking Euro soldiers who had gone out there to distribute food parcels. The slant of the report was to suggest that our brave British soldiers were being unfairly attacked. It was all a load of bollocks. It was more likely that British troops had been sent out there to stop the Greeks from getting food rather than the other way round. Both Gary and Angela knew that this news report was likely to be far from the truth but it was difficult to tell a twelve and a ten year old that the report they were listening to might not be the truth. Both had tried before to explain about open reporting and the way that Governments altered information to make things sound different to how they really were but the girls could see the pictures that went with the reports and weren't quite properly convinced about their parent's views. Fortunately the news soon changed to a little report about migrating birds and showed some nicer scenes of flocks flying in the skies.
"How do they know where to go?" Joan asked whilst still watching the television.
"They have a clever one at the front who has been before and the rest just sort of follow." Gary replied. Angela looked at Gary with that disbelieving stare.
"They do it naturally Joan darling." Angela tried to put Joan right. "They have some sort of inborn sense that tells them what to do." Joan took it all in. Once again the mood of the news changed as an up to the minute report was received about an attack on a retired Spanish Navy Captain in a small little town of Motril in Spain.

His name was released as Dario Vidmar which meant very little to the folk of Kentley but in the halls of the European Army HQ it meant quite a lot. He had been taking his fishing boat out as usual when it exploded about half a mile out to sea. The local Police started to investigate the incident but within hours the Euro Army had taken over the case. Despite the fact that television reports called the whole thing a most unfortunate accident, initial enquiries by the Army showed that the boat had been tampered with and that the explosion was not an accident. None of this information was ever released to anyone outside of the Army hierarchy but an urgent report on the findings winged its way to Martin Busch. Dario Vidmar was a retired member of the European Army and had once been a very influential member of the United Nations World Threat Committee. He was in fact the second person from that committee to have died under mysterious circumstances in the last year. It was a fact that had not gone unnoticed by Martin Busch. There had been a number of rumours going around that certain ex-committee members had been targeted by the underground forces for assassination but Martin Busch made sure that these rumours remained just rumours. He knew otherwise of course.

A few months previously, the European Military had chanced upon capturing a rather high ranking activist in the Revolutionary Underground. He had been caught with his trousers down so to speak and the Military were going to take advantage of it. The revo was tortured for weeks and he let slip a number of vital bits of information relating to the identities of activists within the underground but he also let slip that the revolutionaries had compiled a hit list. Even the prisoner they had knew very little about how it had been drawn up but he mentioned a few of the names and they were all ex-committee members of the United Nations. Martin Busch had ordered the initiation of a full scale undercover operation looking into the accusations. He also kept his own file on the subject. A new page in that file would be started today with the death of Dario. None of this of course was known to the news station doing this latest report.

-

The revolutionaries were very well organised and had the expertise and assistance of many different countries old armies at their disposal. One of the most important things that the revolutionaries had put into practice was to get an elite number of assassins trained up ready to be called upon at a moments notice. They were highly trained, well motivated and very well funded. Each assassin was protected from being identified as they would have the names of about 5 contacts who they would be able to keep in touch with in order to obtain whatever they required. This included their monthly fees. The 5 contacts would only know the assassin they were empowered to assist by a verbal code name, usually named after a character from a novel. One such assassin was John Silver.

John Silver would of course be responsible for keeping his own identity a secret and he would have to do whatever was necessary to ensure that he kept one step ahead of the authorities. All assassins were given training in this respect and passed details or updates of the latest tools the Euro Army used to try and track down the revolutionary undercover agents. The net work was bigger than many guessed it was.

John Silver sat back and studied his most recent instructions whilst sitting back in his expensive leather upholstered armchair in the lounge of his little home in the UK. In his business it was often necessary to move home at short notice leaving behind most of the furniture but occasionally he would allow himself a little luxury. His armchair was one of those luxuries. Although a lot of his more recent work was taking place on the main European continent at the moment he preferred to keep his base in the UK. It was advantageous for him to work from the UK for a couple of reasons. Firstly, he knew he could get in and out of Europe under various false names and hence nobody could trace him that easily and also he had been born in the United Kingdom and didn't want to live anywhere else.

John Silver had no files or papers relating to Dario Vidmar and had never heard of him prior to tonight's news but it was a name he was aware of. It was the name, or more correctly the news of his death that triggered the start of a new case for him. Although he hadn't received the go ahead quite yet, John Silver would very soon be given the green light to go ahead with his next mission. This would mean he would have to leave his cover job in the near future so he worked on plans as to how this would happen. There were then other things to plan now and he had written down things he needed to do and quietly perused his list that he had made. There was a small file in his safe. A secret safe! It was one of four safes he had at his home but this was probably the hardest one to find. John Silver had alarms set up on the other safes so he would know if anyone had tried to tamper with them. There were only useless things kept in them. Nothing important! That was all in the secret safe.

The list that he had just written out wouldn't be going in the safe. He often wrote things out. It helped him to see things more clearly. This list needed to be burnt. Picking up the list he started to check what other papers he had in the safe that also needed to be burnt. He picked up a letter that was beginning to get a little dog eared. It was addressed to a David Thomas. David Thomas doesn't exist anymore he said to himself as he quickly opened the letter to remind himself of its' contents. It was a letter from a woman he had met about two years ago and had stupidly got involved with. He knew that he shouldn't get involved with anyone in his profession but he had found it so difficult to resist her. They got close rather quickly and he had done what he could to make sure that she knew very little about him but then this letter arrived at his home address at the time and the alarm bells rang. He was out of that place in less than a week and never spoke to or saw her again. He read the letter and his heart skipped a beat. He recalled the feel of her soft skin and the smell of her cheap perfume. He knew he had probably broken her heart. She had twisted his. It was for the best and it was time to get rid of all evidence of David Thomas. He added the letter to the list he already held in his hand and walked out through the front door before turning left and making his way down the narrow passage between the house and the garage to the back garden. Throwing the papers into a small incinerator, he set light to them and watched the flames as he dropped the lid back down on top of it. He returned back to the house and got on with the serious work of considering his next target. He had not been involved in the choice at all but he was given basic details of the next person to be assassinated. Mariano Zwolle would be next.

-

Martin and Anna Giraund were at home listening to the recent news on the radio. Anna's mouth was gaping in surprise. "He's another one of the names on that list Martin." Anna said.
"What list?"
"You know the one about the 'document of intent'." Anna got up and went over to the little writing desk in the corner of the room to check.
"Oh that list. Well he probably got all he deserved then." Martin answered in an effort to finish the matter.
"But don't you think I should do something?"
"What can you do Anna?"
"Well that's two people from those meetings who have died in the last couple of years, don't you think it's strange?"
"Possibly but then they were all military people weren't they?" Martin

was still unmoved by the death.

"I just think it is suspicious." Anna found her secret drawer with her disc copies in. She found the one marked 'document of intent' and put it in the computer on the desk. As she opened the disc the words 'Top Secret' could be seen printed in red. She quickly cursored down to a password input and she typed in her password. A list of names came on to the screen. "See here he is. Dario Vidmar."

"What's that darling?" Martin was engrossed in some other news item.

"That bloke in the fishing boat. His name is here on the list of people who attended those meetings."

"What meetings dear?"

"It says here…" Anna started to read aloud but Martin wasn't really listening. "Aspect 37c. If troops are needed to fight America or China then we will first send men from the more densely populated countries. Aspect 37d. If there are no wars to fight then troops will be sent to control civil unrest. Aspect 37m. If population did not fall by the required numbers then troops would be sent to fight other troops. Aspect 48g. Food will first go to The Army. Aspect 59a. Any areas seen to show anti-Army feelings will be rationed and food will be stopped from getting to those areas. You see Martin, the bloody General introduced all those aspects."

"It makes no difference Anna. Come and sit down and put those discs away. I wish you'd never made the copies."

"But perhaps I should take a copy to the Police so they will know who might be next."

"Someone else probably also made a list and all you will do by telling the authorities is put suspicion on yourself. Not only that, the Euro Army would find out that you actually have an illegal list. Let sleeping dogs lay." Martin gave Anna a big cuddle. She knew he was probably right but remembered that other people knew of the discs, not just her.

-

For the Newson family, Sunday was a family matter and the television didn't go on at all during the day. Again all three channels were running similar programmes which mainly consisted of sermons, hymns and various talks on different religions. Sunday evening however was different as Channel 1 had 'Teamball' on and the Newsons were all ready and waiting in front of the television when it came on at eight o'clock. This was a similar story in may homes around the country and many were at a loss when the programme was postponed for any reason. There had been no show for the last 2 weeks and many people were beginning to get angry with the Channel 1 employees because of it but the station were doing all they could to make sure it returned to the screen as soon as possible. This Sunday it was back and Channel 1 did all they could to let the public know. Angela had seen an advert for the programme whilst she had been out shopping this weekend.

Teamball was a strange programme as it was designed to keep the public entertained whilst also giving an opportunity to a family to win a nice holiday. The show tried to go out every week but it wasn't always possible as they needed contestants and sometimes these were hard to find. The prize was good but the consequences could be disastrous. Angela had allowed Joan and Katy to stay up and watch it as they hadn't seen it for a long while and there was anticipation and excitement as the programme was about to start. The recognisable music blared out and the voice began,
"I hope you are all sitting in your seats now as you won't be for long, It's time for another challenge of Teamball with your host Johnny Johnson." The voice said in various excitable tones. The camera switched to Johnny Johnson who was the compere and host of the show. He was about 5'6" and as thin as a rake but had the spikiest hair you'd ever seen. Today his hair was a peroxide blond colour but Johnny Johnson was also wearing his very distinctive heavy framed, black rimmed glasses.
"Hiya folks! Are you ready to be entertained? This is the country's most popular event and it is nearly time to start." Johnny Johnson continued in a similar excited tone to the previous voice.

Johnny Johnson was as always quite pale skinned and he moved his thin gangly legs around as if he was being operated like a string puppet. Every now and then he would also move his arms in a similar way but as he held on to his oversized microphone with one hand this movement never really looked quite right.
"Can you remember who our reigning family are?" Johnny asked,
"That's right, it's the Philpotts from Oxfordshire" Johnny said, raising his tone to say the 'shire' bit in a silly way. Whilst saying this little bit he constantly shook his head up and down in an affirmative manner.

The nod was very pronounced that you might have thought that his glasses would have fallen off but they didn't. Almost immediately the camera swung slowly round to the right and in shot came a family of six people togged out in dingy white tracksuits. This was obviously the Philpott family.

"And here they are." Johnny Johnson continued as the camera zoomed out to get all the family in focus. The whole of the family waved and smiled with great enthusiasm and they looked like a happy bunch.

"As you'll remember folks, they beat the last reigning champions, the Potters and now it's their turn to choose." Johnny Johnson walked up to the man in the middle of the family who was obviously the spokesman.

"And you chose where Oh mighty Philpott leader?" Johnny Johnson said in a silly voice.

"We chose to come here to Cambridge." The man replied.

"And why did you choose Cambridge?"

"We wanted a course with water and mud after last time." The family leader continued.

"Well we've got plenty of water and mud here." Johnny Johnson finished off the conversation. *"Okay let's meet the Philpotts,"* he said looking straight into the camera. At this point the picture changed to what had obviously been a pre-recorded slow sweep of the Philpott family. A voice gave their christian names, relationship in the family, age, height, weight and hobbies. As you looked a bit closer to the six of them you could see some signs of bruising and wounding from their battle against the Potters. Nobody seemed to have any limbs broken but a couple were showing obvious signs of pain nevertheless.

"And now we go and meet the challengers, the Howley-Smythes." Johnny Johnson said this surname with such stupidity that it was obviously going to get the audience laughing back at home.

Joan and Katy fell about laughing and even Gary and Angela chuckled away to themselves.

"They seem a bit too posh for this sort of programme" Gary said out loud.

"This is going to be easy." Angela started to reply. The camera went to another pre-recorded bit of film introducing the Howley-Smythes. They were all immaculately decked out in good quality polo shirts and were wearing what looked like top of the range training shoes and track-suit bottoms.

"I cannot believe that this family have entered this competition can you darling?" Angela said.

"No." Gary replied.

At this point, Johnny Johnson had a quick word with the family leader of the Howley-Smythes and finished with his usual, *"And you fully understand the rules?"* All of the challenging family jumped up and down and shouted *'Yeah'* whilst waving and sticking clenched fists in the air.

The rules to Teamball were reasonably simple and Johnny Johnson would now only explain a rule when one of the teams were pulled up on one of them. Firstly there was the large leatherish ball. Nobody actually knew what it weighed but it was of a very strange design and stood about six feet tall. Although the ball was made mainly of leather it has various holes and orifices some of which had various types of metal objects protruding from them. Nobody really knew the full design of the inside of the ball but there was a big hatch on one side of the ball that was padlocked up during games that could obviously be removed. It would appear that once removed, one could then fix whatever metal objects were required from inside the ball so that they stuck outwards. There would be a selection of spikes, knives and nails as well as other awkward sized objects that made moving the ball difficult and other rough edged implements that would tear skin if scraped across them. Then there were small holes all around the ball that seemed to leak different sorts of contents from itching powder to acidic substances but also other things like soap. All of these things made the handling and moving of the ball more difficult than it originally sounded although some families found that the protruding objects could sometimes be used in their favour.

Now as you might guess, the reigning family now had the task of moving the large ball up a marked out course from one end to the other. The course was fifty yards in length and about twenty yards in width which ever course you chose but the courses were all very different. Today's was on mud with some little streams across it but other courses would be on concrete with brick walls, or on ash with broken glass or tins on or grass with sand. Each one had its' particular difficulties. The Philpotts had probably chosen this course so that when being floored by their opponents the landing was much softer. It would make the moving of the ball a lot harder but they obviously didn't consider that a big worry. Now the other basic rule is that you had to move the ball from one end of the course to the other in under forty five minutes. The reigning family were then allowed to call as many time stops as they wanted but the total time stopped could not total anymore than fifteen minutes. As you can see we are now getting the recipe for the perfect one hours television show. The whole of the ball had to cross the finishing line to win. If you got the ball across the line in time the reigning family had won but if they failed then the challenging family had won.

Those were the basic rules. There were quite a few others though. Firstly each team had to consist of first generation relatives and had to have three males and three females. The reigning team were allowed to ask at anytime for up to five accessories from a list of about twenty. These would range from ropes to shovels to a plank of wood. Some families would get all of their accessories ordered before the game started which saved time but they were not allowed to change their mind on which accessories they got once the game started. It was a bit of a gamble sometimes. The reigning family also knew that they must not push the ball outside of the painted course. If they did, they would be disqualified. The mud course did bring another problem in as much as the painted course would often disappear during the game and teams would find themselves pushing the ball in the wrong direction and off the course. There were flag markers in each corner of the course but these didn't always help. If a challenging team felt the ball had been pushed off the course they could call for the referee who would stop play and make his or her decision. It wasn't very often that this happened.

And so to the challenging team or family. Their main objective was to stop the reigning family from getting the ball moved along the course within the prescribed time but they had a couple of simple rules to follow. They were not allowed to touch the ball itself nor any of the accessories being used by the reigning team. They also could not do anything that would force the ball to move back down the course. They had no accessories of their own to help them but could make use of anything that was laying around on the course except any discarded accessories asked for by the reigning family. Depending on what course the reigning family had chosen there would normally be some things laying around that could be used. If there was a brick wall, anyone could knock it down and then re-use the bricks or there might be a tree where branches could be broken off and used. Lastly there was a general rule that both teams had to follow which was no punching, kicking, head-butting, pulling of hair or gripping around an opponent's neck. Apart from that anything was allowed. As you can probably guess, there was a main referee whose job it was to see that none of the rules were being broken and he had the power to stop the game or send team members to the cooler. The referee could be a man or a woman, would have four others to help them. One would stay with each of the main parts of the teams whilst the other two would stay further out looking for any incidents that might be happening away from the ball. It all got very exciting and could often be fast and furious. As you can probably guess, some of the participants finished up rather badly injured. This made no difference if you were on the winning or losing side. This caused a few complications. Firstly some of the winning teams needed a couple of weeks in order to at least be fairly ready to play. Broken limbs, closed up eyes were always given a few weeks to get better. Then of course the organizers had to make sure that they could find opponents who were evenly matched. They didn't really worry if the teams won or lost as long as the match was entertaining. They usually were.

Gary and Angela had never known anyone that had taken part in Team Ball and guessed that there might someday be a course in Kentley or Chale where the programme would be filmed so that they could go and watch.
"There seems to be a large crowd there again," Gary said to Angela
"Can we go and watch a Team Ball game one day Dad?" Katy asked
"If we knew someone in it perhaps we could. I assume you have to be invited to go and watch the game." Gary replied.
"Surely these two families haven't invited all this crowd though?" Angela queried. As they watched the television and more specifically the crowd, it seemed less and less likely that they were all invitations only.
"No you're right. Nobody has that many friends."
"Well perhaps they do but not all that would go and watch them play Teamball." Angela felt she had scored a point.
"So how else do you get to go?"
"They must sell the tickets locally to where the game is being played."
"Dad could we go and watch one week?" Katy asked again.

"I will make some enquiries darling."
"Don't be silly Gary. Unless you live in the vicinity or know the families you won't be allowed."
"But surely if people want to pay to go and see it they will sell tickets."
"I wouldn't mind betting a lot of the crowd have been forced to go."
"If they have they're lucky." Gary wasn't convinced.
"It probably isn't such a good day out."
"What do you mean dear?"
"I bet the crowd are all under some sort of guard or control." Angela wasn't quite sure that was exactly what she meant. Gary thought for a moment.
"But the crowd are always so partisan," Gary concluded.

He was right. As the two teams lined up at the half way point ready for the starting whistle it was obvious that each side of the ground was full of supporters for the team on that side of the pitch. Angela laughed in agreement.
"You're right. There aren't that many people on the posh families side, look," she continued. As
she said this, the count down to the start of the game had begun. Today's Referee was Mark Harris and he had blown a whistle which meant that both families should get ready to start. They had to run down to their respective ends of the course and get themselves sorted out ready to either move the ball or prepare to stop the movers. Once the count down had finished a rocket was released which indicated that the match could start. The reigning family would start to push the big leather ball as soon as they could and get it as far down the course before the challenging family started to attack them and try and stop them from moving it.

The Philpotts had obviously worked on their plan of how to move the ball having watched how the
Potters had moved the ball the previous week. The two eldest and strongest males started by pushing the ball whilst the three females marched in front ready to tackle any of the challenging family. The last male was shouting out instructions to the two men pushing the ball and seemed ready to help with stopping any of the challenging family if needed. The Philpott men had got some good motion on the ball but the Howley-Smythes were no pushovers and the whole family raced

towards the three female Philpotts before breaking off into what looked more like an acrobat act just before they reached them. The Philpott females stood in bewilderment and confusion as two of the Howley-Smythes knelt down in front of them and two of the family were half catapulted over the Philpotts. It gave the Howley-Smythes a very quick advantage as there were already two of the family behind the Philpotts front line.
"Wow that was something special." Joan said in an excited voice.
"Are they from the circus do you think?" Katy added
"I don't know darling." Gary answered. None of the Newson family took their eyes away from the television. Within the first two minutes, one of the Howley-Smythe's had reached one of the Philpott males who were pushing the ball and he was able to interfere with their initial momentum. This was quite crucial as it was always necessary to get a good start before the ball was stopped by the challenging family and this was not a good start. Within a few more seconds, the rest of the Howley-Smythes had reached the ball and there were various tussles going on between the various members of the families. The Philpott male who had been removed from pushing the ball had now got back to his feet and despite having a Howley-Smythe consistently trying to pull him away, he was able to push at the big ball. It was very slow going and at the rate they had pushed the ball so far there was no way they would make the fifty yards in time. A quick change of plan had to be put into operation and the Philpotts started to use one of their ideas. The biggest of the Philpott males was about sixteen stone and looked like he could look after himself quite easily.

  The Philpott plan was not going to be used until later on in the game but things had not gone their way. The rest of the Philpotts held on to one of the Howley-Smythes males and forced him to the ground. There was a lot of grabbing, pulling and pushing and one of the referees looked closely to make sure that there was no punching going on. Despite this the Howley-Smythe male on the floor had blood dripping from a cut around the eye. Elbows were moving backwards and forwards and it was quite regular for one of these to make contact with an opponent. Having got the Howley-Smythe on the floor, the Philpott male came along and sat on him so that he could not move. The Philpotts then grabbed a Howley-Smythe female. It was an easy choice as to which one to go for. She was probably the youngest aged at around nineteen or twenty and a lot skinnier than the rest. Certainly unusual compared to the normal sort of contestant as she was more like a model than a fighter but she was obviously fit as well. She was dragged over to where the Philpott male was sitting on her uncle and the Philpott male grabbed her around the waist with one arm and held her. She pushed at his chest, pushed her head into his head and scratched at his arms but he would not let her go. This gave the Philpotts a one person advantage and they made the most of it by pushing the ball another ten yards quite quickly. The Howley-Smythes were not giving up though and one of the family went back to help release the two family members held by the Philpott male. This was the Mother of the Howley-Smythes and a lot heavier than her daughter who was being held captive. She took a running jump at the Philpott male landing her shoulder into his upper body. The Philpott used the daughter to try and protect himself but the damage had been done and his balance was lost and he was on his back on the mud. He held on to the daughter but her uncle was able to get free and with the aid of his sister-in-law, they freed the daughter and all run back to the rest of the family at the ball. Only half-way down the field with nearly thirty minutes gone the Philpotts called for a time out. They never really got any more momentum going and although the ball was moved another few yards, the Howley-Smythes had easily won the day.

-

It was Monday morning and Gary Newson was on his way to work as usual. The weekend had gone quite well and any thoughts that Gary had had of any problems between Angela and himself had practically disappeared. Gary had even forgotten all the other things that had previously been troubling him.

Gary walked into the Sorting Office to be greeted by one of the team. "Morning boss. Billy hasn't got in yet." Gary dropped his shoulders in disappointment at hearing the news.
"Has anybody rung his home?"
"No we couldn't get to the book."
The staff telephone and address details were in a book that was for security reasons, always locked up in the safe. Gary was of course the person with the safe combination so none of the others on the early shift could get to it.
"Nobody actually knows Billy's address." Dee added shrugging her

shoulders.

"Okay, leave it with me. How is the sorting going?"

"We've done okay. It just means that we'll do 7 and 8 when we've finished the others but it shouldn't make that round too late."

"Do you want me to get anyone in a bit earlier?"

"No don't think so."

Gary went to the kitchen and made himself a cup of tea. He made a pot so others could also pour themselves a cup. This was more to help out the three on the early shift but also because it was probably his turn to make it anyway. As it was made, Gary took his tea back to his office and got out the staff book. He looked up Billy's details which gave his home address and telephone number. Billy lived at home with his parents in Lansing Road in Kentley but they did not have a telephone number listed.

There wasn't a lot that Gary could do at this stage so he sorted through his post and files and made sure that there wasn't any really urgent work that had to be done. The time passed fairly slowly but Gary got himself ready to go out to Billy's. He walked out from his office.

"William, I'm popping out for about half an hour but hope to be back well before ten o'clock. If the AP comes down just tell him I'll be back soon." Gary shouted his message across the office. The team of three on today's early shift were already hard at it. William raised his hand to acknowledge that he understood and Gary went on his way. It was just before nine when Gary got to Billy's house. As he parked the car outside he looked at number 12 and saw what looked like signs of the household all being asleep. All the curtains in the house were drawn and there were no obvious signs of lights being on. The house was quite old and small and the paintwork was in urgent need of repair but this was quite normal for most houses in town. One of the upstairs windows was decayed so badly that it had been half boarded up but Gary knew that nowadays it wasn't easy to find someone with both the know how or the tools to do those sort of jobs. It was a typical town type house. The curtains didn't actually seem that much better either. All old and dingy and in urgent need of a clean. Gary rubbed his hands together and rang the front door bell. It gave out a loud continuous ring. Quite quickly the door was answered by an old man in old trousers, a very thick jumper and slippers.

"Hello who are you then?" The old man asked

"I'm Gary. Is Billy in?" Gary said in his nicest possible voice.

"The boys at work. He'll be home about four I spose," the old man answered with a strange accent.

"What time did he go to work then?" Gary continued.

"Woss it got to do wiv you?" The old man started to look Gary up and down in a suspicious manner. He obviously wasn't the Army as they'd have just knocked the door down. He wasn't revolutionary as they would have said by now so he guessed he was a reporter of sorts. The old man hated newspapers. Before Gary could say anything in reply, the old man had shut the door and left Gary standing there with his mouth wide open. Gary rang the bell again.

"Are you still ere then?" The old man said as he re-opened the door. "He'll be back at four I said," he continued as he tried to close the door again. Gary quickly spoke.

"I'm Billy's boss at work can I have a word?" The old man thought about the statement and considered it half plausible.

"So where he work then?" The old man asked quickly.

"Er… at the Post Office." Gary gave the answer automatically whilst confused as to why Billy's Dad wouldn't know where he worked. He started to take out his identification card to show the old man but it was unnecessary. The door was opened a bit wider to let Gary in.

"Come on then." The old man said shaking his head. Gary followed him through to the kitchen at the back of the house where his wife was frying an egg at the old stove.

"This is Billy's boss," the old man said to his wife. "He wants a word wiv us," he added. There was a brief silence as all three looked at each other and then Gary started.

"You said that Billy was at work". Both the old man and the old woman nodded. "What time did he leave this morning?" Gary put the question to nobody in particular. The old couple looked at each other for a couple of seconds and shrugged their shoulders before the old man answered.

"We don't know. He goes very early in the morning before we get up."

"But you know he went this morning?"

"Guess so."

"What time did he go to bed last night?" Gary asked both of them again. Once more they looked at each other before the old man answered.

"We don't know."

Gary was finding this all a bit awkward as he was having to question Billy's parents like they were suspects in a crime. He didn't want to tell them that Billy was not at work in case that caused them alarm but it was getting difficult to get any sense from them.

"Was Billy in the house when you went to bed last night?" Gary plucked up the courage to ask what he considered a very awkward question.

"No he got back later and was up and at work before we got up." The old man replied. He felt that anyone who was a manager in the Post Office was as close to authority as he was happy to accept before thinking that the person had sold out to Europe. Gary could have asked anything and the old man would have answered him as honestly as he could.

"Okay, I'll probably call back later then." Gary said as he turned towards the front door. He felt he had found out enough here and thought that to ask much more would only do more harm than good. The old man saw him to the door and let him out without saying a word. Gary got back into his car and pondered over what he should do next. It was quite possible that Billy was round some friend's house sleeping off a hangover. He couldn't really do much until he returned to work.

Gary returned to the Sorting Office and got on with working through his files whilst considering what his next move should be with regards to Billy. He tossed around in his head whether or not he should tell the Assistant Postmaster about Billy not turning up or not and concluded that he wouldn't. As if to speak of the Devil, that was the very moment when the AP walked into Gary's office.

"Hi Gary, just come to pick up the five day mail," the AP said.

"Yeah boss, it's in the tray there for you." Gary pointed to the AP's tray although they both knew exactly where it was. The AP picked up the few envelopes from the tray.

"Oh I've also got some ideas for a new roster that we might discuss," the AP continued. He held a black file up for Gary to see. "I haven't got time to chat about it now so I'll stick it in your safe until we can." The AP bent down and placed the file at the bottom of the safe.

"No cutbacks I hope," Gary said

"No just some new ideas," the AP smiled. "Everything okay?" He asked, almost knowingly.

"Yeah no problems at all." Gary said to try and convince him.

"I heard there was a little argument on Friday," the AP pursued his inquiry.

"Don't believe everything you hear boss." Gary now realised what the AP wanted to know and tried what he could do to divert the conversation from the incident.

"Oh I don't Gary," the AP replied as he winked at Gary. "But some things I feel are worth believing."

"Everything is in hand." Gary looked at the AP as he said this quite defiantly.

"As long as you're sure," the AP replied, with a knowing nod. "As long as you're sure."

Gary wasn't sure, but wanted to speak to Billy before he did anything else on the matter. Gary knew from old that although most incidents like this would blow over as if they had never happened, the odd one could sometimes escalate out of all proportion if not handled properly at an early stage. He hoped that this wasn't going to be one of those.

"Alright boss?" Micky said as he knocked and walked into Gary's office.

"Morning Micky. How was your weekend?"

"Yeah, okay! What did the AP want?" Micky was straight to the point.

"Nothing really!" Gary gave a short reply and looked up at Micky. "He's heard from someone that we have an old hooligan working in the sorting office and he wants me to tell him who it is." Gary said as seriously as he could. Micky looked at him unsure as to whether Gary was serious or not.

"Are you reporting me?"

"No I'm not reporting you. We're all a team here aren't we?" Gary reassured him.

"Yes boss. I'll try and sort it out with Billy." Micky said in an apologetic tone.

"He isn't in today but it would help if you could that would be appreciated." Gary was happy about Micky's response. "But also beware, somebody out there is talking." Gary completed his warning. Micky left the office.

Gary was annoyed that someone had managed to get the details of Friday's incident to the AP so soon. It must have come from one of his team, he concluded. It was probably someone who didn't realise what damage they might be causing by speaking out of the office but the AP was obviously getting good information from somewhere. Gary's thoughts were interrupted as he sensed that someone was at his office door. It was William.

"Excuse me but can I get to the roster book?"

"Yes William. Not swapping to another early shift by any chance?" Gary said to him.

"Erm, yes! But I'm doing a late tomorrow." William took the book out of the safe, changed his shift then put it back in the safe. Everything returned to normal and eventually the day came to an end and Gary got ready to go home. He considered calling at Billy's house on the way home and actually drove there and parked outside his house but after a few minutes decided that it would be better to leave everything until tomorrow. Billy was on earlies again and Gary would tackle him then to try and find out what was going on.

Gary had left the office a little bit earlier than normal in order to call at Billy's house and as he decided not to pursue his visit he got home a bit earlier. It was only just four thirty and Gary had expected Angela to have been at home with the girls. He put the car away as usual and locked up the garage and although it was still quite light he kept an eye out for any strangers. He walked up to the front door and pushed down on the handle expecting the door just to open but it was locked. Gary unlocked the security lock and then the normal lock before opening the door and entering. It looked like the house was empty, apart from Sammy of course who was very pleased to see Gary arrive home.

"Angela." Gary called out. "Hello is there anyone home?" He called out again. There was no response. A little surprised but not worried, Gary thought he would take the opportunity by taking Sammy out for a bit of a longer walk than usual and left a hand written note on the kitchen table to that effect. As he reached for the dogs lead Sammy automatically started jumping up and down at Gary's feet. Within seconds they were on their way through the front door this time to a side alley that led round to the lane behind the house. Gary never used the back garden entrance during the day for some reason. It was as if he didn't want to give away his little secret door although anyone looking along the hedge would see it. It was just Gary's way. Sammy stayed on the lead because it was light but Gary was quite pleased to be able to be seen taking the dog for a walk without any fear of being accused of being out after curfew. His intentions all along were to have a couple of attempts at getting nearer to the school so as to look and see what was going on there.

The first route was to carry on along the leafy lane that led to the front entrance to the school. This lane also led to a couple of shops that were sometimes open so he would also have other reasons for walking in that direction. Half way down, the path would be split into two with the upper path going on to the school and the lower path down to the shops. Here, Gary would have to decide which path to take. It was quite possible that Gary would be able to see if there were any soldiers on guard at the front entrance to the school from this position on the path but only if they were standing or patrolling. As he got nearer to the split, he could see a neighbour was approaching from down the path and Gary stood with Sammy waiting for her to reach him and go passed.
"Hello Mr. Newson," the neighbour said as she reached him.
"Hello. Have you been shopping?" Gary replied. It seemed a bit of a stupid question as she had no bags with her but it was the best thing Gary could think of to say. He couldn't actually remember his neighbours name as she lived a few roads away but a lot of the village knew who Gary was.
"Not much to buy but the shop is still open."
"Is the Grocers shop open?"
"Yes but he hasn't got anything to sell."
"Oh. And the other store?"
"Yes, Jacks is open," the neighbour told Gary. She bent down to stroke Sammy. "How do the girls like the fact that they don't have to go to school?" She continued.
"Well they're pretty bored really and fed up." Gary responded not really wishing to talk on the subject.
"They seem to be working on something at the school. Soldiers all over the place," the neighbour said.
"Oh are they. Can you see them from the shops?" Gary asked trying to sound as if it was all news to him.
"Yes, there are loads of them." The neighbour had a quick look around as if she was going to tell Gary a secret and she moved a bit

nearer to him. "Must be going then, goodbye!" She said as she continued on her way down the path. Gary was a bit confused thinking that he was sure that she was going to say something else but then changed her mind and he too looked around only to see another neighbour making her way up the path.
"Hello Mrs. Welham." Gary said as he took Sammy on the path down to the shops.
"Oh hello Mr. Newson," the woman replied as she gave a quick wave.

    Gary reached the shops. There were only four or five units all of which were either closed up or pretty run down. One unit was completely closed and empty. Gary tried to recall what had been there before but he couldn't. Gary walked first to the Grocers shop. It had two customers looking at what food was available but as his first neighbour had quite correctly noted, there wasn't very much for sale. What looked like a few turnips, some very small carrots with more top than carrot and an old cabbage that seemed to have been kicked around the shop. The shop had a number of empty trays that suggested that there had been other vegetables for sale and that there would be again, but not today. There were three more shops which were a Bakers shop, a Newsagents type shop and then a General Store. The Bakers shop would only open if it actually had bread for sale which was probably only about three half days during the week. The newsagents was strange as it tried to sell sweets but very rarely had many available and then tried to sell papers and magazines which very few people could afford. Gary walked along to the next shop which was a junk shop really. There was nobody in there and looking through the window there was nothing on show to suggest that anyone would want to go in there. Some old clothes, a few kids' books, some bits of old furniture and an endless array of china pottery figures. Absolute junk Gary thought to himself. As he looked in the mirror he realised he could see the front entrance to the school and he turned so as to be able to get a better look. There were at least two soldiers on guard at the main entrance and a few more working further down the entrance path towards the main door to the school. Gary looked hard and watched as a couple of soldiers unloaded a box from a lorry. It was obviously quite heavy and they were having difficulty in getting the box down but they managed. Whilst all this was going on Gary could see other soldiers inside the main hall setting up spotlights. He wondered what that could be for. He then cast his eyes back to the main gate and realised that one of the soldiers on guard duty had stood up and was paying him some attention. It was time for him to make his way back home, especially as the light was beginning to go.

Gary headed back up the path to the leafy lane towards the back lane that led to Gary's house but he decided that he wasn't going to just give up trying to see what was going on as easy as that. At the back lane, he turned right, away from the direction of his house and continued along the lane for about another fifty yards. Gary had remembered that there was a part of the graveyard at the back of the church that you could get into from the lane without going through the church. The other side of the graveyard sided on to the school playing field and it was quite possible to get a view of the school from there and so Gary took Sammy into the graveyard. He got no more than twenty or thirty yards in when the Vicar appeared from the far end of the graveyard that connected to the church.
"Hello Gary," he said.
"Oh hello Vicar!" Gary replied in a slightly guilty tone.
"Can I help you at all?" The Vicar continued.
"No not really, I was just looking around."
"For the dogs' ball perhaps?" The Vicar finished Gary's sentence in a fairly positive manner.
"Well er yes, sort of." Gary was trying to think what to say in response when a couple of uniformed soldiers, one fully armed also walked through from the church part of the graveyard.
"Good evening Sir," the first soldier said as he looked over at Gary. "Have you found what you were looking for?" He continued.
"No but I didn't really expect to find it anyway." Gary quickly ad libbed. He had started to regain his composure and tried to talk his way out of his little predicament. "We lost Sammy's ball a week or so ago and I thought it was over here somewhere."
"You're from the village?" The soldier asked. "I've seen you before, walking your dog."
"Yes I live on the lane here." Gary replied pointing to the lane behind him.
"And your name is?" The soldier said in a very dominant fashion.
"Oh yes, Gary Newson". Gary was annoyed that he had to give his name but supposed it was inevitable.
"Well thank you Mr. Newson, no doubt you'll want to be making your way home now," the soldier added. Whilst all this was going on the

second soldier, the one that was armed, had kept his eye on Gary.
"Yes. Thank you Vicar." Gary said as he turned and made his way back to the lane.

Gary went straight home feeling that he had just got out of some possible trouble but had put himself in a very embarrassing situation. He wouldn't be telling Angela, that was sure. When he got back home, his dinner was ready as usual even though he had arrived home early from work. Angela shouted to him as he came through the back door.
"Hello darling, you've been a long time again. Where have you been?" She asked.
"Oh I bumped into one or two people and got chatting, you know how it is," he answered her. As he did he crept up behind her and gave her a big hug and a kiss.
"Don't try and get round me like that Gary Newson." Angela shrugged him away. "Have you been down to that bloody school again?"
"No. We had this argument the other day."
"I'm just making sure."
"Anyway, what if I have been passed the school. There's no law against it." Gary was a bit miffed at being rejected. Angela turned and gave him a dirty look.
"Go and sit down. I'll be serving up in a minute." Angela told him in her masterful voice. "Joan, Katy. Dinners ready," she continued.

Gary went into the dining room and looked around for the paper he had brought home from work on Friday. He flicked through it quickly and came across a report on the shooting incident at the roadblock. He folded the paper back but dinner was served before he got a chance to start reading it. Angela walked in with her hands full of bits and pieces for the dinner table and stopped to stare at Gary sat in the chair. "Oh you just sit there, I'll do all the dinner things."
"Sorry, you should have said something." Gary jumped up.
"I shouldn't need to say anything." Angela slammed the things down on the table and went back to the kitchen. Gary followed her. He tried again to give her a hug from behind.
"I'm sorry darling. I just didn't think. I'll set the table."
"No it's alright." Angela answered as she turned round and gave Gary a little hug. "I'm just a bit upset. Forget I said anything."

Tuesday morning was not really any different to any other day. The alarm had woken Gary first as usual and he had got himself almost ready for work before Angela's alarm went off. Gary was in a bit of a rush to get into work this morning as he had lots of problems tossing around in his head. The biggest was how he was going to deal with Billy. He gave Angela a quick kiss but not much was said by either of them. Joan and Katy were now waking up and both shouted goodbye to their Dad as he left for work. The drive in was fairly normal and Gary had arrived at the Sorting Office a bit earlier than his usual time.
"Is Billy with us today?" Gary asked as soon as he saw the team.
"No. Not a word from him either." William gave him the bad news.
"Do you know what's wrong with Billy?" William asked.
"No. I tried to see him yesterday but couldn't."
"It's unusual for him not to call us." William added.
"Yes I think so too. I'll try and get to see him today." Gary said rather solemnly. He hoped that this was going to be a quick and easy problem.

By 08.45hrs, most of the sorting had been done. Gary sorted through the ongoing files that he had and quickly decided that the task of finding out where Billy was, was far more important. The day staff were starting to arrive and Gary waited ten minutes just in case Billy had forgotten what shift he was on but as he still hadn't turned up so he got his coat and got ready to drive back round to Billy's house.
"If the AP calls down, tell him I'm out and will be back lunchtime." Gary shouted across the Sorting Office floor.
"Will do!" A reply was shouted back.

Gary went straight round to 12, Lansing Road and knocked on the door as before. This time the old man answering the door recognised who Gary was.
"Oh you again. What do you want this time?" The old man said as he indicated that Gary could come in.
"Is Billy in?" Gary asked.
"Nope. And I don't know where he is." The old man spoke in a resigned manner as if his son had moved out.
"Did he come back last night?"

"He didn't even come home from work. He's probably gone drinking with some Postal people," the old man said. He gave Gary a long strange look. "Who are you again?"

"I'm Billy's boss from the Post Office and he wasn't at work at all yesterday." Gary replied.

"So why did you ask if he was at work yesterday then?"

"Well I didn't think I did." Gary replied getting confused. "I asked you if he'd gone out to work but you didn't know. When did you last see Billy?" Gary by now was speaking to both Billy's Mum and Dad. The two of them looked at each other as if communicating in telepathy.

"Must have been Sunday lunch. Billy was here for his Sunday lunch," his Mum answered.

"And you haven't seen him since?"

"No," the old man confirmed.

"Did Billy go out on Sunday after lunch?" Gary carried on with his interrogation. Whilst they were happy to answer he would carry on asking.

"He went out about seven. He usually goes for a drink down 'The Anchor' on a Sunday. I assume he went there." The old man told Gary. "He'll be back, we don't worry," the old woman added. They seemed as if this was a normal occurrence. Gary was quite sure that it wasn't and that they were trying to convince each other.

"Has he gone missing like this before then?" Gary felt he ought to ask.

"When he was sixteen he went off for a week. Turned out he went on holiday to Spain." The old man told him. Gary felt around his inside pocket and produced a business card which he handed to Billy's Father.

"Look, if he returns, can you ring me on this number and leave me a message please." The old man looked at the card and then looked at Gary.

"We haven't got a phone," he said.

"Would you come to the Sorting Office and tell me instead?" Gary suggested.

"I spose so!"

Gary shook his hand and left the house wondering if the idea of telling him about Billy's return had actually got through to him or not. There wasn't much else he could do. The Anchor was the next step.

Gary had made his mind up. Most of the workers would agree with his decision. Gary felt he better go and see the Assistant Postmaster and put him in the picture so without any further delay, up he went to his office.

"Sir, can I have a quick chat?" Gary said to the AP.

"Come in. Sit down. What's the problem?" The AP said in a creepy tone.

"No real problem, just keeping you up to date. Young Billy Simpson hasn't turned up for work for a couple of days." Gary started to explain.

"Well that shouldn't be a problem," the AP interrupted as if he had better things to do.

"True it isn't a problem but as he didn't ring in I thought I'd call round to his house and see what the problem was."

"It's not because of that fight last week is it?" The AP sat upright as if the conversation had all of a sudden grabbed his attention.

"No I don't think so. The point is he's been missing from home since Sunday evening."

"I don't see that is our problem at the moment, Gary," the AP said thoughtfully. "But keep on top of the situation so we know what is happening." He concluded.

"Well I'm actually looking for him myself when I gat a spare half an hour." Gary explained.

"That's not a good idea. Let the Police do that side of things," the AP said sternly as he looked Gary in the eye.

"The Police haven't been informed."

"Why not?" The AP said as his voice went a bit higher.

"The parents don't seem to be that worried and I'm not able to report the facts not being a relative." Gary shrugged his shoulders.

"I still say you should keep out of it. You don't know what these sort of things might lead to." The AP had given his advice and his interest in the conversation seemed to have waned again. "At least you've told me, should you hit any more problems," the AP added.

"Thanks. I'll keep you updated." Gary said as he backed out of the AP's office.

Gary went back to his office and collected a couple of files that he could work on and then drove back into town. By twelve o'clock, Gary had got one or two bits of information to add to his files and he felt he deserved a well earned beer. Funnily enough, Gary decided to collect his reward of a beer in The Anchor on South Quay. It had been years since Gary had been in this pub. Historically the pub was originally used by the fishermen of the town and not many people from outside of that fraternity would visit the pub. As the fishing trade declined, South Quay turned its uses to being a regular cargo quay and the pubs clientele changed to include mainly dockers and visiting crew. It was around this time when a back bar was added to the pub and this was normally where the towns prostitutes used to ply their trade. The landlord at the time, one Albert Green, kept a fairly tight pub in those days. He was an old fisherman and well capable of looking after himself but he had a soft spot for the ladies of the night and looked after them as well. Within two or three years, the docks were shut down and the dockers redundant. The pub went through some hard times with no customers, costing more to stay open than was being spent across the bar so eventually Albert had to admit defeat. He sold the pub to a younger man for next to nothing with the feeling that the pub had seen better days. He was wrong. The new landlord had some money to do the pub up and he spent wisely, smartening up the front bar and changing the back bar into a sort of entertainment room. Most weekends, music of some sort was played at the pub and the youngsters flocked to it like bees to a honey pot. Lunchtimes were quiet but most evenings there was a buzz about the place. Gary quickly eyed the pub up from the outside before stepping in through the side door. There were only two other customers in the pub plus who he assumed was the landlord, behind the bar.

"Can I help you Sir?" The landlord said.

"A pint of your best bitter please." Gary said eyeing the pumps along the bar.

"Radfords?"

"Yes why not." Gary said almost excitedly. The tradition in this part of the country was to serve real ale with about a half inch of head and the landlord here did that perfectly. He produced the completed pint like a work of art.

"Anything else?" The landlord indicated towards the food menu.

"I'll just have a bag of crisps for now thanks." Gary started to feel hungry. He knew he shouldn't eat too much at lunchtime as it would only spoil his appetite for whatever Angela would be cooking for dinner.

"That'll be 2.45 please," the landlord said as he rang the till.

Gary took a quick sip from his pint and then picked up a food menu to give it a look. He thought it would be a good way of engaging the landlord into a conversation. The menu was very basic and built around a basic diet of potatoes or bread. There was a choice of soup of the day with bread, chips, baked potato or sandwiches. The fillings were not listed on the typed menus but written on the blackboard in the center of the bar. Today's soup was pea and ham which Gary thought was quite a good choice to have as ham was almost impossible to come by. For the other fillings, cheese was listed and it looked as if this was the one permanent filling, but there was also 'bacon and onion' and 'pork'.

"You do a good menu for a little pub." Gary spoke to the landlord.
"Does something take your fancy?"
"If I was to be honest, it all does." Gary replied as his mouth watered at the thought of eating.
"Let me know if you want anything," the landlord said as he moved further down the bar in order to dry some washed glasses. Gary had let him give him the slip. He knew he would have to get him talking a bit more than this if he was ever going to find out anything from him.

Gary took a few sips from his beer whilst considering his options. "Excuse me Landlord, I'll have a soup please." Gary finally decided.
"A very good choice Sir if I say so myself," the landlord said as he wrote down his order.
"Where do you get your meat from?" Gary said quizzically.
"If I told you that my menus wouldn't be that special would they?" The Landlord replied.
"Huh no I suppose not. Do you always have a similar type menu available then?"
"No not every week! I try my best to have some sort of meat available but sometimes I'm let down by my suppliers. Sometimes we even get steaks available, in fact I'm expecting some in this week. Don't know how many but it'll be first come first served as always," the landlord was going through the usual motions of his selling technique.
"A mate of mine comes in here and he's never told me about the food before. Billy Simpson. Do you know him?" Gary posed the question. There was a small silence as the Landlord stared at Gary whilst he continued to pour a drink. Gary sensed that he might have gone a step too far and perhaps a bit too quickly. He looked closer at the man

behind the bar. He seemed to have a tough air about him like he was crunching on a mouthful of broken glass. It wasn't an out and out aggressive stance. Gary thought he was also able to wash the broken glass down with a jug of beer if he wanted to. Gary guessed that The Landlord would just ignore his question when all of a sudden he answered.

"Yes Billy's a regular at weekends but then I don't do food at weekends." The Landlord replied.

"Oh I thought he came in here during the week as well." Gary wasn't quite sure how to ask the next question. "He was in here on Sunday though wasn't he?"

"I think so. I don't clock people in and out," the landlord gave Gary a suspicious look.

"No I suppose when he's with all his young mates you can't remember who's here and who isn't." Gary continued.

The conversation took another break as the Landlord walked back to the other end of the bar and started wiping up washed glasses. He then picked up a bowl of soup from the serving hatch and returned with it in his hand, stopped and gave Gary a long hard stare.

"Look mate, people around here don't take too kindly to people asking questions. Unless you're from the Police when people around here just don't take too kindly to people! Do you know what I mean?" The landlord handed Gary his soup. "I think this will be enough to see you ready to be on your way."

"No I'm sorry I've gone about this the wrong way." Gary tried desperately to rectify the situation he had got into. "Do you know what Billy does for a living?" Gary asked the landlord.

"I might do."

"Well look." Gary got out his Post Office identity card and showed it to the landlord.

"What does that mean then?" The landlord asked unimpressed.

"You know that Billy works for the Post Office?"

"He has mentioned it."

"Well I'm his boss and he has gone missing." Gary explained.

"And what's that got to do with me?"

"He was last seen leaving his house for this pub on Sunday evening. Was there any trouble on Sunday?"

"What sort of pub do you think I run here? There was no trouble. There's never any trouble," the landlord replied.

"And did Billy drink in here on Sunday?"
"As I said I think so but can't be sure. It might have been Saturday I saw him," the landlord was being miserly with his information.
"And does he meet a regular crowd in here?" Gary continued.
"Look mate, that card allows you to deliver letters. Why don't you get on with doing that." The landlord left Gary at the bar and he soon became very conscious of the fact that the other two customers were staring at him. Gary finished his soup, paid his bill and left. Gary made his way back to the Sorting Office where he got on with more files. All afternoon, the conversation with the pub landlord went round Gary's mind. His conclusion was that he was going to have to leave things to the Police. He would have to try and persuade Billy's parents to report him as missing.

     As the time got towards five, Gary packed away his things and said his usual goodbyes to the late staff. Gary drove back to Lansing Road and knocked on the door at number 12. Billy's Mother answered the door this time. "Hello, can I help you?" She said in a cheery voice.
"I'm Gary Newson, Billy's boss from the Post Office." The old lady seemed confused. "I called round this morning and yesterday. I'm looking for Billy." Gary said.
"Oh he should be home soon. Come back in a little while," the old lady said as she started to close the door. Gary stopped her from doing so and continued.
"Can I come in? I take it Billy hasn't returned yet." Gary almost pushed his way in. The old lady started to shake in fear. "You've nothing to worry about." Gary noticed that she was worried and tried to calm her.
"What do you want again?" Came a question from Billy's Father who was in the kitchen. "I told you I'd get in touch if he returned," he added.
"I'm here to take you to the Police Station." Gary said.
"What the hell for?" The old man coughed as he spoke.
"You must report Billy as missing." Gary told him.
"No that's the last thing we must do," the old man replied. He seemed to know what he was saying and he stood in a defiant pose as if to say to Gary 'and what are you going to do about it'. Gary tried the sympathetic approach. "What if Billy's hurt? You must tell the Police."

"You might be a boss at the Post Office and handle things differently there but this is the real world here and we know what we're doing thank you. Now I think it's time you left." The old man ordered Gary as he turned him towards the door. Gary left without any further fuss and got back into his car.

He pondered over what the old man had said and thought that he was probably right. If Billy was like many of the youths of today he was probably up to no good and the last thing he would want is the Police being involved. Gary felt he had made his appeal and that it was now up to Billy's parents to make the next move. He then thought about what he would do back at work. He would have to report it to the AP but felt he could give Billy another couple of days. Gary felt happy with that. He was about to start the engine when he noticed that there was a piece of paper stuck under the windscreen wiper. He got out and retrieved the paper, opened it up and read it. 'Friend, we are pleased to see that you are concerned about the welfare of Billy Simpson but must ask that you refrain from your efforts in trying to locate him. I can only advise you that this sort of action will only lead to you getting hurt. Billy is as well as can be expected and will be back at work in a couple of weeks. I hope this will satisfy your curiosity and that this will put an end to your investigation.'
There was no name at the end. This was a bit of a surprise. Gary felt it had 'revolutionary' written all over it and he was a bit surprised that the old man had obviously told someone about his enquiries. Gary had never considered this possibility and he rebuked himself for being naïve enough to not consider it and possibly put himself in more danger than he had realised. Gary read through the note again. Was anyone watching him at this very moment he thought to himself. He checked out of the windscreen and checked his mirrors but there was nobody obvious. He screwed the note up and put it in his coat pocket. There was a lot more to this than Gary had first thought. He drove home.

Dinner was usually ready for six o'clock but it was already 6.15 when Gary got home.
"Where the bloody hell have you been? Why don't you ring and tell me you're going to be late?" Angela shouted at him as he entered through the front door. Gary hung up his coat as Joan, Katy and the dog were all getting excited in the hall at his arrival.

"I had to go and see Billy Simpson's parents." Gary started to explain.
"Why?" Angela snapped back a reply.
"Because he hasn't turned up for work again today!"
"So just sort out cover for him. You don't have to go and see what's wrong with him?" Angela was getting angrier.
"He's gone missing from home." Gary said.
"So they report it to the police." Angela told him straight. "You don't have to get involved. You haven't got involved have you?" She said even more angrily.
"No." Gary tried to sound convincing.
"They report it to the Police and then they find out what's happened to him," Angela continued. Gary was thinking of ways to change the subject when his daughter interrupted.
"What's Sammy got Mum?" Joan said.
"Not now darling, Daddy and I are talking. There's no need for you to get involved is there?"
"But Mum, Sammy is chewing up some paper." Joan added.
"They won't report him missing to the Police," Gary managed to get his reply out.
"Well don't you get involved." Angela told him. "Joan, take the paper away from Sammy darling, don't let him chew it." Joan retrieved the piece of paper from Sammy's mouth and handed it to Angela. Gary took a double take as he realised that the paper was the note that had been left on his car window. It must have fallen out of his coat pocket as he hung it up. Angela took the paper and started to read it. Gary wasn't sure what would happen next. Angela's face turned red as she read the note through. She folded it up and handed it to Gary. "I guess this is yours?" Angela was fuming. She was so mad in fact that she didn't know what to say. Gary turned to head up the stairs. "Don't you think you should explain?" Angela said in a voice that made Gary freeze.
"Explain what?"
"Don't become sarcastic. What bloody investigation?" Angela half cried as she said it.
"Someone obviously didn't like me making enquiries."
"You told me you weren't making enquiries."
"I went to his house. Perhaps the note was from his parents, I don't know."
"You're going to get into trouble. I've been telling you for ages but you just don't listen." Angela started to cry as she said the word

'listen'. Gary tried to put a hand on to Angela's shoulder. "Bloody leave me alone." Angela shouted as Joan gave her a hug. They both looked at Gary. He knew he was probably not going to hear the last of this one and he guessed that there would be no peace this evening. He wasn't wrong as Angela brought up the subject on three separate occasions that evening. Gary had no excuses, he was in the wrong.

Gary and Angela would have argued a lot more that evening but they had a surprise visitor that evening. It was around nine o'clock when there was a little tap on the front door. Sammy growled to confirm what both Gary and Angela thought they had heard and they both looked at each other in bemusement.
"Who would be calling at this time of night?" Angela said to Gary in a slightly angry voice. "It is bound to be someone for you," she continued. Gary got up off his chair and went to the front door. He peered through the glass to confirm that there was someone waiting there before he opened the door. Standing outside, half shivering was a woman in her thirties holding a box file under her arm. She was of medium height and although she seemed on the athletic side she was not as slim as she might once have been. She had shortish dark hair which was mainly straight and a very attractive face. She didn't have model looks but her skin was pale and soft which made her very pretty indeed. Gary thought he recognised her or at least thought that she seemed familiar but wasn't sure.
"Hello Gary, is Angela in?" The woman asked.
"Erm yes! Come in." Gary was still taking in the sight of such a beautiful woman as he invited her in without a second thought. As she passed him, Gary caught the scent of her perfume. Not one he recognised but one he liked. The woman stopped halfway down the hall waiting for Gary to invite her in further. He pointed to the lounge door and the woman carried on in.
"Julie. This is a surprise!" Angela said as the woman entered the lounge.
"Yes I'm sorry to call round at this time but I needed to do it when nobody else was about." Julie replied.
"Gary, do you know Julie Clark?" Angela introduced her just in case.
"Of course!" Gary lied. He knew he'd seen her somewhere before but hadn't placed her as the infamous schoolteacher.
"Would you like a drink?" Gary asked.
"I'd love one." Julie replied.

"Coffee or tea okay?"

"Coffee would be brilliant, thank you." Julie smiled as she replied. It seemed as if she was staring at Gary but he guessed it was just in his imagination. Gary then had a worry that there was no coffee left. If there was, it wouldn't be very good quality. Julie turned to Angela. "Look I need someone to look after some school work for me." Julie started to explain.

"There seems to be loads of it," Angela said half laughing.

"Yes it is a mixture of project ideas and instructions on what the class should be taught. The trouble is, they are in the process of changing my replacement again I gather as Miss Worthington has been recalled back to her original school."

At this point Gary came in with three coffees. He placed them all on the little table together with the sugar bowl.

"Help yourself to sugar." Gary said just to make sure. Julie paused from the conversation and smiled politely at Gary.

"So what do you want me to do with this lot?" Angela asked.

"Well not a lot really. Just look after it for a while. When the new teacher has been sorted out, just let them know that you have all these papers and then leave it up to them as to whether or not they want it." Julie finished explaining.

"Seems simple enough." Angela concluded.

"So why can't you keep it?" Gary asked.

"Gary!" Angela exclaimed in a disapproving way although they both knew it was a question that needed asking and one that Angela would have asked if it had been a friend of Gary's in this position.

"No it's a point I should have explained." Julie said, briefly touching Gary's knee in approval. "I've got to go to London and meet an Education Board who are making enquiries into my conduct." Julie said as she made a funny face in embarrassment.

"Are they still looking into all that?" Angela said with a sigh.

"Yes I'm afraid so and I don't know how long it will take so I'm going to stay in London with my Mother for a while until it's all over." Julie completed her explanation.

"I hope everything turns out alright for you." Gary said sounding quite sincere.

"Thank you Gary." Julie replied. "I suppose I better go. It is late and I'll have to dodge any patrols you know." Julie said as she stood up. "Thanks for doing that for me Angela, it's another worry off my mind."

"Not a problem." Angela replied as she saw Julie to the door.

The next morning, Gary decided that he ought to go and visit his sister Sarah. She had been round to see him a number of times recently but as yet Gary had not been round to hers. Well not her new place anyway. Sarah had managed to buy herself a nice little house on the other side of Waydon. It wasn't actually new but was an old cottage conversion with a new part built on to the side. The finished effect was a rather nice sized house with a sort of old fashioned atmosphere. Gary never enquired about how Sarah was financially as he knew she had come by quite a large sum of money after George had died. He knew that she had not actually inherited it as there was no will as such but George's family had given Sarah a substantial amount of money from George's estate. Sarah was quite a sensible girl and Gary knew too well that she would have invested wisely and that she would probably never have to worry about money again so it was no surprise to find that she had purchased this house in Waydon.

Gary walked through the village and was quite surprised to see two or three new houses had sprung up. One of them was Sarah's house of course. It was very unusual to see any building work nowadays let alone houses Gary thought to himself but obviously if you had the right connections or the money you could get something done. Gary reached Sarah's house. 'The Buckles' it was called. What a strange name Gary always thought whenever he heard it mentioned but Sarah explained that it reminded her of her childhood because she once had a doll's house that she named 'The Buckles' because their Father had used some buckles from an old pair of Sarah's shoes to keep the front of the doll's house together. Gary knocked on the front door.
"Hello who is it?" Sarah shouted from the garden.
"Sarah it's only me." Gary replied.
"Are you lost stranger. Do you realise you are in the rough part of Waydon?" Sarah joked.
"I can always go home again." Gary turned.
"You dare go home now and you'll never be welcome here again." Sarah said sternly as she left her gardening and walked over to Gary at the front door. They hugged and kissed in the continental style and Sarah rubbed her hands on her pinny that she was wearing before opening the front door and pushing Gary in.

"Are you well?" Gary asked.
"Yes quite well." Sarah said in a very confident manner.
"I only popped round to find out what you wanted to tell me the other day." Gary said.
"When was that then?" Sarah said confused. "Would you like some tea?"
"No thanks." Gary replied. "You called round the other day and saw Angela and she said that you had something to tell me."
"I don't remember." Sarah sounded vague. "What day was that?"
"Wednesday I think." Gary replied. Sarah got up and walked around as if it would help her remember.
"I'm going to have some lemonade, would you like a glass?" Sarah said as she walked into the kitchen.
"No thanks." Gary replied.
"I think I know what it was. I thought I had a job interview on Thursday at the Post Office." She said clicking the fingers on her right hand. "I thought it would be really strange working in the same building as you." Sarah continued.
"What job was on offer?" Gary asked surprised to hear of an interview being done at his office. He wasn't even aware that the Post Office were taking on any more staff which he thought he would have heard about.
"I think it was just as a counter clerk." Sarah replied.
"That would have been at The Post Office itself then not at the Sorting Office."
"Post Office, Sorting Office, it's all the same isn't it?" Sarah said.
"No they're completely different." Gary started to explain but he knew that Sarah would not be listening.
"Anyway I never got the interview in the end. I probably didn't offer enough money for it." Sarah said looking coy. "How's Angela?" Sarah changed the subject.
"Alright!" Gary gave a quick answer.
"You two having a difficult time?" Sarah looked at him. "You know I can tell." Sarah started to get into preaching mode.
"I'm sorry but I have to be getting back, we're going shopping." Gary made his excuses before Sarah could get into full flow.
"Alright I'll let you go this time but I'll expect you to come and visit again now you've actually found the place," Sarah said as she kissed him goodbye. Gary made his way back home.

The rest of the day seemed to pass by very quickly. Gary was sat in his chair in the living room. He looked at his watch and seeing that it was still only ten minutes past six declared on his way to the front door, "I'm just going to quickly take Sammy for a walk."
Sammy was already in the hall waiting for his master to take him out and when Gary reached for Sammy's lead he went mad jumping up and down wagging his little tail.
"Don't be too long." Angela shouted from the kitchen.
"Okay." Gary replied in a drone like manner. Gary and Sammy were out in the back garden and through the door in the back hedge before you could say 'Jack Robinson'. It was already getting dark and Gary knew he wouldn't be able to stay out too long this evening. They walked down towards the church but didn't go as far as the church wall before Gary turned round to walk back home. Almost immediately Gary caught site of a shadow ahead of him that looked a bit like someone else walking towards them. Gary had to quickly pick up Sammy and look for a gap in the hedge. There wasn't one to be seen. Gary wasn't sure what to do and by now he had turned and was walking back towards the church. Gary thought if he could get into the graveyard it would provide him with some cover but the trouble was the front gates of the church were lit and this would make him visible for some distance. Time was running short as he could now hear the footsteps of someone walking behind him so Gary climbed over the wall and ducked down the other side.

The person must have seen or heard something of what Gary did as they also crossed over towards the church wall. The footsteps slowed and it was obvious that this other dog walker was looking for Gary.
"Gary is that you?" A loud whisper came from the road. Gary kept quiet. "Gary, are you there?" the voice whispered again. Gary could feel his heart beating faster but soon the footsteps started up again and the unknown dog walker seemed to go off into the distance. Gary made his way back out of the graveyard via the lit gate and then rushed back down the lane and home. When he got in, he could see that all of his clothes were dirty and he had ripped his trousers just around his left knee area. Unfortunately he wasn't the only one to notice his current state as Angela stood at the end of the hallway.
"What the hell has happened to you?" Angela asked sternly.
"What do you mean?" Gary answered in a pathetic voice.

"Well you might think it quite normal for a man to come home from walking the dog with mud all over his clothes and a rip in his trousers but I find it a bit strange. I know you haven't been playing football so no doubt you've been up to no good climbing through hedges again or have you actually decided to take the Army on in hand to hand combat." Angela let rip. She ran out of breath and thought about giving Gary another mouthful but retreated back into the kitchen instead. Gary said nothing and just went upstairs to tidy up a bit.

"By the way you got yet another one of those strange phone calls that you say you know nothing about." Angela shouted up the stairs.

"Honest I don't know who it is that calls. What did they say tonight?" Gary replied.

"Not much. Asked if you were there and then said that it was most urgent that they got to speak to you. I asked if I could take a message but they put the phone down again." Angela told him. "You're not seeing another man are you?" Angela shouted up. Gary huffed and refused to reply.

After about fifteen minutes Gary had managed to change his clothes and washed to make himself look a bit more presentable. He came downstairs to try and sort things out with Angela, or at least try to smooth things over a bit but she was on her way up the stairs as he came down.

"Can we see anything the same Angela?" Gary asked.

"There's nothing wrong with the way I see things. You're the one putting us all in danger." Angela replied.

"How do you mean putting us all in danger?" Gary replied.

"Well what happens to us when they come and arrest you?"

"I'm not going to be arrested. Don't be silly." Gary said.

"You're always out after curfew. You go places shouldn't go. You make enquiries about revolutionary runaways. You play cat and mouse games with the Army. No you're right you won't get arrested." Angela sighed.

"I don't mean to get into any trouble but a lot of these things are things I just feel I have to do. I can't just sit down and let people run my life for me. I need to know why they all of a sudden shut down the school. Why one of my staff all of a sudden runs away." Gary said in his pleading voice.

"No you bloody don't. And you know full well you don't have to. Anyway I need to get the girls baths ready, leave me alone." Angela shrugged off Gary's arm and made her way upstairs. Gary went into the living room and looked at Joan and Katy. Gary sat down in his favourite chair again. The girls came and kissed him goodnight ready to go off to bed.

"Are you and Mummy arguing again?" Katy said in a sad little voice.
"No dear, we're trying to discuss a subject that we don't agree on." Gary tried to comfort her.
"But you both looked very angry Daddy." Joan added.
"Well you know when you have a joint party and one of the guests that you have invited has to sit at the top of the table." Gary looked at both the girls who were paying full attention. "Well if you, Katy decide who sits at the top of the table it might not be who Joan wants to sit at the top of the table." Both girls had no idea what Gary was trying to tell them but nodded knowingly.
"Well Mummy and I have different ideas on things and we talk about them." Gary finished his parody.
"But you shout at Mummy and she shouts back at you." Katy continued.
"Yes, but it doesn't mean that we don't love each other. And we both love you two. Now off to bed and let's not think about it anymore." Gary sent the girls upstairs to Angela and thought back to the argument. It was causing a bit of a problem but he was not going to back down. He looked for the paper so as to take his mind off of it. It lay down by the side of his chair and at last he was able to read the report on the killing he had witnessed. Authorities were unable to give any further details of the deceased the paper said. Of course they know who it is, they're just not saying. There was also a great photograph of soldiers bending over the dead body at the roadblock. It said the lot.

Chapter 4   -   THE UNIT ARE TESTED

As Gary was sat working in his office, the morning's reports relating to undeliverable post were brought up by one of the staff and just dumped in Gary's in-tray. Gary half acknowledged their arrival as he was deep into reading another report at the time but he knew they had arrived. After about half an hour Gary was able to glance over the new reports, each one in its plastic sleeve with the ticked check sheet in it. He turned each one over, dismissing them as he did but as he was about to turn over the third of the four, something caught his attention that made him turn it back. The name of the addressee was a Mr. LONGHURST and although this name seemed familiar to Gary he just couldn't put his finger on exactly why. He looked a bit further and noticed that the actual address was in Waydon, 14, Back Lane to be exact which was basically around the corner to where Gary lived. It grabbed his notice so he read through the brief report from the postman who had tried to deliver the letter which was written on the check sheet.

Not an address that gets a lot of post but was fairly sure that LONGHURST was not the name of the occupants. Held on to the letter for a day and sure enough post arrived the following day for a Mr. & Mrs. HOBBS which was the name I recognised. Knocked at the house to deliver this second letter and Mrs. HOBBS came to the door, asked if there was anyone else staying with her and she confirmed no. The name is not familiar to me as being at any other house in this road which only consists of 22 houses.

Gary was pleased again with the way his delivery staff had dealt with this one. Showed initiative but not with an over enquiring nature. That was his job and this was going to be one he would start work on straightaway. He didn't log it on to the case system as he wanted a couple of days to work on it without anyone else knowing. Longhurst was a name that he had come across recently he was sure. He couldn't remember where or why though. Gary put the papers into a folder but it remained un-numbered or titled. He went to his big cupboard where a lot of the old files were stored away but there was also an old card index box that Gary used to keep that had all surnames of suspects recorded in alphabetical order. He took out the box and looked under 'L' but although there were a number of surnames beginning with 'Long' there were no records for a 'Longhurst'. Gary was sure that it wouldn't be a computer record as the system had only been in use for about eighteen months and Gary felt that the name referred back longer than that but he checked it anyway but with no luck. He decided that the best course of action was to strike whilst the iron was hot. Go and have a look at the place. But first he would have to do a couple of other checks.

The first one was quite easy as he checked the latest residents listing for 14, Back Lane on the disk that the Sorting Office gets from the Information Centre. It was possible that the information could have changed during the week but the Sorting Office got a new disk every Monday which would be correct up to that point. Gary put the address into the system and pushed the relevant button waiting for an answer. After about thirty seconds a reply came up on screen. It said that there were just two occupants who were HOBBS Raymond K, born 1977 and HOBBS Susan J, born 1978. Gary wrote the two Christian names and the years of birth down and worked his way out of the computer system so that his computer was back to normal.

Gary got in his car and decided that he would make his way out to Waydon for himself. Almost as an after thought, he realized that he had forgotten the other basic check that he should have done and decided that it might make sense to call in at the Information Centre. This was the building run by the Ministry of Information. It was where all citizens had to go to register and from where practically all passes and permits were issued. It was a very busy building and had about ten floors. Gary went up to the usual office he called at on the sixth floor. The office door had no title but was clearly marked 'Room 39'. It was the office where any Government official could go and ask for information providing they had clearance of course. Gary often called in to this office and got little bits of information.
"Gloria, hello again." Gary said as he went through the door.
"Oh look out everyone, it's Sherlock Holmes!" Gloria told the rest of the team behind the screen as she saw Gary enter. Sherlock Holmes was the nickname that they had given Gary after he was always there making enquiries. "Who are you after today?" Gloria asked.
"Just a quick check on the HOBBS at 14, Back Lane, Waydon please? Anything added to their record in the last few months?" Gary asked. Gloria looked up at him and smiled.

"For you darling, anything!" She entered some data into her computer. "Did you say number 12?"

"Yes." Gloria completed her enquiry. "Nothing changed for ages. He has to renew his badge every six months." Gloria started to read out to Gary.

"What badge?" Gary intervened with a question.

"His disabled badge. Had it nearly two years now! Says here that he is almost wheelchair bound completely! Shall I go on?" Gloria waited.

"Is there much else I need to know?" Gary asked her.

"No it's all crap really. Ere y'are, have a look yaselves." Gloria allowed her cockney accent to slip out a bit. Gary gave the screen a quick glance and then turned it back to Gloria.

"Oh can you tell me how many Longhursts there are living in the Kentley area?" Gary asked a further question. Gloria typed away and gave Gary a very prompt reply.

"All sexes?"

"No just men."

"In Kentley there are just five. Three in Buttercup Way and two in Bounds Lane!" Gloria answered Gary's query. Gary wrote the two road names down.

"None in Waydon?"

"No none!" Gloria repeated. After Gary had gone, Gloria did what she had been told to do and went back to the page about the Hobbs. Here she entered, enquiry from Mr. Newson, Post Office and also put the date. Gary never realised that Gloria did this every time he did a check.

Gary finished his journey out to Waydon and he parked his car in Back Lane just about opposite number 8. He got out and walked up Back Lane looking at number 14 as he went passed. He could see into the front room of the house quite easily as there were no net curtains hung up. There was nobody to be seen. There was a drive down the side of the house which obviously also had a gate to the back garden. The front garden was well looked after and the front door had a porch to which the front door was also open. In the porch was a pair of Wellington boots. They seemed reasonably new and more like men's size than ladies but then it was difficult to tell. Gary carried on walking passed until he had turned the corner. He was about fifty yards away from his own back garden. He stopped and thought. He hadn't really gained much from this walk passed. He would probably have to spend a bit of time sitting in the car doing observations.

Whilst Gary was thinking over what to do next a bright idea came to him all of a sudden. I'm here checking out illegal post, I have the authority to go passed places I am suspicious of, I'm actually here in Waydon, I'll go and have a look at the school. Gary felt confident that he would be able to deal with any interventions he might encounter from Army personnel and anyway, once he had shown his badge, what else could they do. Gary drove round to the village centre, where the few shops were and parked his car in the only vacant space. He got out and had a quick look around and straightaway he could see a soldier on guard at the front gate to the school. Oh, the realization of just how difficult a situation this was dawned on him. Gary had second thoughts and decided not to approach the front gate but instead he walked round to the shops. All the time he was walking he looked over in the direction of the school but as always there was nothing going on and nothing to be seen. The Army's activities certainly seemed to have come to a halt unless they were only working at night. As Gary got to the shops, there was a hive of activity going on both inside and outside of these shops and it seemed like the meeting place for half of the village.
"Hello Mr. Newson," a call came from one of Gary's neighbours. It was Mrs. Green from number 11.
"Oh hello. How are you?" Gary replied.
"Quite well. What brings you down here at this time of the day?" Mrs. Green asked knowing that Gary would normally be at work.
"I am at work but as I was just passing I've called in to see if they have any bread." Gary lied.
"They've nearly sold out so you need to be quick." Mrs. Green told him. Gary rushed into the bakers and purchased the first piece of bread he could find. He didn't know why bread had come into his mind but it was the first thing he could think of saying when questioned. He returned to his car and started his drive back into Kentley. This attempt to check out the school hadn't gone too well but Gary wasn't going to leave it at that. If only he had a letter that he could show, then no doubt he would be able to get to look around. Gary had another idea.

That evening on the way home, Gary thought of different ways in which he could check out the Hobbs house. There was no view from the back and the only way to watch from the front was to actually walk passed the house or hide behind the bushes in the field opposite. It would be slightly possible to watch from a parked car although you would look quite conspicuous if seen. He then thought to himself, when was the last time he had looked up and down his road and seen someone sat in a car. Nobody was ever about. You were usually only arriving home from work and so Gary decided that he would park his car near enough to number 14, Back Lane and then walk the rest of the way home. The plan seemed to go okay to start with. He had a good view of number 14 and although it wasn't completely dark outside, the front room light was already on. The porch door was shut and the curtains were pulled but you could make out the shape of an adult moving about in the front room without too much trouble. Gary sat in his car for about fifteen minutes when he noticed in his rear view mirror an Army jeep that had stopped at the bottom of Back Lane. It looked like two soldiers were getting out. They were possibly going to patrol up the lane so Gary made for home. As he got out the car he glanced down the lane to see the two soldiers making their way up but they didn't see him. He also glanced at the front room window of the Hobbs and to his astonishment saw what looked like two people stood up. One was holding what looked like a tray whilst the other was taking things from it. Gary wanted to watch some more but he couldn't afford to hang around so he made his way home.

    As he went indoors, there was very little sign of any sort of greeting coming from Angela. Sammy was there to see him but that was about it. Gary walked into the living room and spoke. "Hello." Angela just looked at her watch and said nothing. Gary went into the kitchen and made himself a cup of tea. He didn't have time to argue or even try and explain what he was doing. He let thirty minutes pass and then he got up to talk to Sammy.
"Do you want to go out for a wee?" Gary said to the dog. Gary went out into the back garden with Sammy but made sure he was safe in the garden as Gary left to make his way back to the car. Gary walked back passed number 14 but there was no sign of any movement so he got into his parked car. Watching every now and then he thought he saw a movement at the house. It was just a shadow but it seemed like a movement. It could have been someone going down the side of the house but he had missed it. What should he do? He got out of his car

but then had second thoughts about walking up to the house in case there was someone there. He had completely forgotten about the two soldiers.

"Excuse me Sir, is this your car?" A voice asked from behind him. Gary turned to see two fully armed and uniformed soldiers. 'Shit', he thought to himself.

"Yes it is my car?" Gary replied. "Sorry I was just thinking of something and seemed to have gone into a daydream." Gary replied as he locked his car.

"You know it is an offence to be out after curfew, even if you are only just outside your house," one of the soldiers said.

"If this is his house Seb," the other soldier added.

"Do you have your residents' card?" The first soldier asked.

"I do but I'm actually here on sort of business." Gary said. He pulled his Post Office badge from his inside pocket and opened it for the soldier. "I'm looking at an address where some undeliverable mail was destined for." Gary said.

"Which house would that be then?" The second soldier asked.

"I don't think I'm at liberty to tell you that." Gary was getting pissed off with the second soldier.

"Do you have a residents' card?" The first soldier insisted. Gary produced that.

"It would seem that you only live round the corner. Now I don't know what sort of work you do but I do know that if it was official it would have to be notified to us in advance. There is nothing down on our lists for this road. I'm not saying you're not working officially but I suggest you finish for tonight and make sure it is registered properly for the next time you work on this road." The first soldier had given him the benefit of the doubt and was prepared to let him go.

"Well you know as well as I do we don't tell you what we're doing unless we really have to so the registration probably got overlooked. I'll sort it out tomorrow." Gary knew when he was beaten. He quickly made his way back home.

-

The next day at work, Gary rang Gloria at the Information Centre.

"Gloria, can you do us a favour?" Gary asked.

"Depends darling. Is that Sherlock?" She replied.

"Yes. Do you remember that you said that Mr. Hobbs had a disabled badge?"

"Course I do daarling." Gloria answered in her cockney accent.

"Can you tell me exactly how disabled he is? There was a short pause whilst Gloria looked at her computer.

"It says ere, wheelchair in constant use and that he is more or less house or bed bound. That was from an independent doctor seven months ago. Is that okay?" Gloria replied.

"Does he have an emergency marking?"

"Well he does but it also states he is a fee paying patient so that isn't really that good an indication darling." Gloria knew what Gary was trying to get at as usually any ambulances called to pick up patients would not deal with any calls very quickly unless the patient had been given a proper 'emergency' marking that was authorised through the proper channels. Someone who was completely disabled would be likely to get one of these markings. The check was inconclusive of course because if you had the money to pay for an ambulance you got priority treatment regardless of the injury so even if Mr. Hobbs only had an in-growing toe-nail, he would still get an ambulance.

"Oh damn. Has he always been a payer?"

"As far as I can tell deary."

"Gloria you're a diamond." Gary told her.

-

The next morning Gary got on with his work checking a number of reports he had let slip behind schedule so he worked very hard in order to try and catch up. It was Friday and the weekend was nearly here. Gary's phone rang.

"Hello, Newson." Gary answered.

"Mr. Newson. You've been making too many enquiries about Billy Simpson," said the voice on the end of the phone.

"Who is this?" Gary asked.

"I'll meet you in the car park in five minutes." The voice said and the phone went dead. Gary felt a shiver move up his spine. He had been involved with the old revolutionary movement before and knew that many of them formed the current organisation. Most were well meaning but a few were relentless in their beliefs and goals and wouldn't think twice about killing someone who was interfering. Gary walked around his office for a couple of minutes thinking over his options only to conclude that he had got himself in this mess and he

had to see it through. Eventually he took his coat and briefcase and made his way down to his car. There was nobody about so he got into his car. As he did, a man jumped down from the wall behind and got into Gary's car on the passenger side.
"Drive off and turn left," the man told him. Gary started the car and did as he was told.

The man was about mid-twenties wearing an old grey shirt and a short black coat. He had scruffy jeans on and black shoes. "Okay at the end of the road turn left and keep following the road."
Gary turned into Northgate and followed the road round into Wall Street.
"Just up here you will turn right into Reed Street, follow the road to the end and as you turn left, pull into the left and stop." The man gave his orders like he was conducting a driving lesson. Gary followed the given instructions and he was invited to get out of the car. As they did, a front door opened and Gary was pushed into a small living room where two other men were already sitting.
"Come in Mr. Newson, please sit down." One of them said. As Gary made himself comfortable, tea was poured for him without asking if he wanted any. The voice continued. "You know why you are here? Do you have anything to say about the matter?"
"I am worried about Billy as he is only a young lad and I am his boss at the Post Office."
"Surely his parents should be making these enquiries?" The voice continued.
"Well I've been to see them and they don't seem to be too with it." Gary replied. "I just want to make sure he is okay."
"You can be happy that he is okay," the voice said. "He is well and comfortable but I cannot tell you as yet when he will be able to return to work." Gary thought this over.
"I suppose that'll have to do then." Gary said.
"And no more enquiries!" This statement completed the interview. The man who had come with Gary in the car stood up to indicate to Gary that his time here had finished.
"Wait a while." Said the other man in the room as he indicated to the man in the car to sit back down again. "You have been with us before Mr. Newson isn't that so?" The other man spoke in a very croaky voice.
"A long time ago." Gary replied.

"And why were you with us then?"

"My sister was very much involved with your movement in the old days. Sarah Newson." Gary said her name in the hope that it would mean something to the old man. "She was due to marry George Watson." As Gary added this extra bit of information the atmosphere changed somewhat. The first man to speak to Gary reminded everyone in the room,

"George Watson was condemned as a traitor to our cause. The records show that he tried to betray the movement." The atmosphere was feeling rather oppressive and Gary wondered whether or not he had just signed his own death warrant. He'd forgotten about the way that George had been branded at his death. The old man with the croaky voice spoke again.

"No, not your sister but I think your brother was once part of our movement."

"Oh yes you mean David." Gary replied slightly relieved that the other man had changed the subject.

"David Newson was your brother?" The man who had arrived in the car with Gary said in a disbelieving voice.

"Yes he was." Gary confirmed in a sad voice. The atmosphere had changed back almost instantly and Gary was feeling as if he was being treated as one of the movement himself. The first man spoke again.

"Billy is being pursued by the Police after they broke into an office where we print our information leaflets. He was under arrest but managed to escape and he is on the run at the moment. He does in fact send his apologies to you for not being at work."

"Thank you. I feel better now I know." Gary answered. Gary and the man who had directed him to the house got up and left the house.

"Do you want me to take you back?"

"No I know where I am." Gary replied as he made his way back to town and then to the Sorting Office. He felt himself sweating a little as he walked back and once again thought he might have just got himself out of a tricky problem. All he had to do now was work out what he would tell the AP.

-

Private Rachel Dobbs knocked on the Sergeants office door and waited for her command.

"Come in." Sergeant Foulkes shouted. The door opened and in walked Private Dobbs. She stood to attention and saluted and Ed saluted back.

"At ease Private!" He looked her up and down and noticed that she was holding a file under her arm. He put down his pencil and took in a great breath. "What is it Dobbs?" He asked.

"I've had time to remember a little bit more about the other two cars that were missed on the roadblock Sir." Rachel wasn't quite sure whether or not to admit that she had remembered things she couldn't earlier or not but thought that it would be wrong to hold back anything.

"Let me have a look." Ed held his hand out. "Take a seat." Ed opened the file and looked at the very brief additional report that Dobbs had made. She had already told him the number of occupants in each vehicle and their surnames but she had now added Christian names and car types they were in, although there were no registration numbers.

"Very good Dobbs, or may I call you Rachel?" Ed spoke to her in his ordinary voice.

"Of course you can Sir." Rachel replied.

"Your first report went straight to an Intelligence Field Officer and the comments have come back stating what a good job you did," the Sergeant told her.

"Rachel, you've been impressing them upstairs," he continued. "Have you ever considered a career in Intelligence?" His question was very serious.

"No not really."

"I think you should give it some serious thought as if you ever wanted to, you'd probably never get a better chance of switching than you have now. Let me know if you want any information or advice." Sergeant Foulkes was quite serious and knew that Rachel could easily fit in but it was up to her. Private Dobbs stood back to attention.

"Thank you Sir, I will." She saluted.

"Dismissed!" Ed replied as he saluted back. He would add his little bit to the report and let Major Wooters have it tomorrow.

There was another brief meeting between Major Tannier and the Agent but this time it took place in a public place so that nobody from the military could see. Major Tannier having previously been in the field himself was quite used to meeting like this. Today's meeting was taking place on platform one of the railway station. He would know the time and the place and would always turn up thirty minutes earlier than he needed to. He would sit where he would expect to sit and cast an eye around to see who was about and what they were doing. He would then leave the area and return twenty minutes later. If there was anyone still there from before, he would give them special attention before meeting with his contact. Today's message was quite easy to pass on and Major Tannier sat next to the agent pretending to read his paper. Fairly happy that nobody was listening he would turn to the agent, point out something absolutely irrelevant in the paper and speak the message.

"Those bloody Millers from Greenfields you know, they've been found absolutely negative. Cleared of all guilt! Can you understand that?" The Agent would reply.

"Yes, I guessed that would be the outcome." Without getting up the Agent would then continue, "Well I must be going unless you have any other interesting events to tell me about?" If there was no reply the Agent would then get up and leave but would always leave something behind. Today it was a cigarette packet. It gave details of the date, time and place of their next meeting.

It was quickly approaching 22.00hrs and the members of Unit Charlie 12 were making their way to the briefing office ready to start the night's duty. Unit Charlie 12 would be the only Unit on in Kentley until 08.00hrs but usually patrols were quiet and the night passed without too much activity. There would always be the odd report of strange movements between the hours of 22.00 and 01.00 and then of course people were allowed on the streets from about 05.30hrs not that many had valid reasons to be out. There was also the visiting Army delivery lorry that came in six days a week with the post. It would travel down from Chale, drop off the post at the post office, collect any to go back and would then always call in at Army HQ to see if there was anything to go back to Chale camp. They would normally be calling in about at 06.15hrs and stay for a quick cuppa before moving back.

Nearly all the Unit lived on camp housing at Kentley as they would probably prove to be prime targets if they lived anywhere outside. There were still one or two who preferred to live outside but they were normally members of big local families who would have relations who were part of the revolutionary set up. There would be a professional admiration for each other and very rarely did the revolutionaries attack any of these soldiers when they were off duty. It wasn't considered as the done thing.

      Sergeant Ed Foulkes was already in the briefing room going through notes he had taken during his handover with the outgoing Unit. The two Corporals had their notebooks out ready to write any clear instructions.
"Radio contact will be made and recorded every fifteen minutes." Ed Foulkes looked up and made sure that all of the Unit were paying attention.
"The eight left behind will be split into two groups of four. The first four will be armed and ready to move if there is a need for any sort of back-up whilst the other four will be doing other duties but will make a fourth vehicle to provide secondary back-up. Corporals, you will swap your teams about as you wish at nineties." Ed Foulkes finished the first part of the briefing. He looked up at the room.
"Any questions so far?" Nobody said anything whilst one or two shook their heads. "There are no particular areas that need covering tonight so we'll do a North South followed by an East West patrol." Sergeant Foulkes paused. He thought for a few seconds and then continued. "We'll have a small drill practice at 05.00hrs, everyone on Parade at 04.59hrs". Ed knew that the Unit wouldn't like the idea of drill but then he couldn't let them have it too easy. "Corporals, over to you!" Ed Foulkes saluted the two Corporals who saluted him back as he left the room.

      Everything was sorted by 3 minutes passed ten and the first two patrols were getting into their jeeps and making their way to the Gatehouse. The two Corporals always tried to take the lead at the start of a shift to show the rest of their teams that they were prepared to do whatever they asked their team to do. Delegation was a necessity not a kop out. There was of course a curfew in operation at the moment which although didn't actually specify any exact time was generally taken as sunset. By this time of the evening there shouldn't be any unofficial vehicles driving around nor any private citizens on the streets. It wasn't quite as bad as all that in Kentley as the curfew was mainly only checked out in the town centre area and not in the residential parts. You would still get neighbours moving about a bit late at night and this was accepted by The Army. Everything was quiet. The Unit kept alert and tried to keep their minds on what they were doing. Private Dobbs was usually one of the best for doing this but this night her mind was wandering.

Rachel Madeleine Dobbs was 25 and only had one real friend in the Army, Trisha. They both got assigned to Unit Charlie 12 about a year ago and instantly got on well with each other although it could be said that Rachel would often try to Mother her slightly younger friend. Not many of the Unit knew much about Rachel and she hadn't told Trisha everything. Born the third child of four to a poverty stricken Manchester family, her early days were made up of scrounging, stealing and making do. Oh yes, and fighting! It had been a hard childhood really although she looked back on those days as good days. Perhaps it was her ignorance in those days not knowing exactly what the world was like and how it could be. She had two elder brothers who although would stick up for her were in battle with her to get food. Her father would try his hardest to find enough food for all the family but they soon learnt that if they were going to eat well then they would have to find the food for themselves. They went through a rather bad year when they would fight over crumbs they were that hungry but fortunately things turned around before her younger sister was born. Rachel certainly learnt to look after herself. She was considered by most as a bit of a tomboy but if she put her mind to it she could bring out her better features to become a stunningly attractive looking woman. Rachel was engaged to a lad back home and all seemed well when she got posted overseas. It was only for two years and the plan was that she would leave the Army and get married. Something went wrong. This is where Trisha had not been able to delve too deeply without upsetting her dear friend but it would seem that there was an incident involving a Greek chap that Rachel had trouble recounting. It was obvious that he had either raped her or tried to but after that things get a bit confusing. Perhaps one day, Trisha might learn the real truth.

Rachel had been patrolling a mountain path with another English Private when they had lost touch with the rest of their Unit. They knew that there were armed rebels nearby so they were making their way slowly back to the checkpoint. Then it happened. Her colleague was shot dead and Rachel had been shot quite badly in the leg. Taking cover she hadn't seen the two rebels until they were right on top of her, she managed to shoot one at close range only to find that she had run out of bullets. The remaining rebel fought with Rachel but because of her injury he quickly overpowered her and managed to tie her hands together and she thought she was going to be taken back to a rebel base as a prisoner but the rebel had other ideas. The Greek had noticed that his prisoner was not seemingly naturally dark skinned and he nonchalantly ripped away part of her uniform tunic to reveal the white flesh of her stomach which he thought, or more correctly hoped might be there. With a swift upward movement of his knife, the Greek cut open the remaining part of her tunic and then finally cut open her bra between the cups. This left her front completely uncovered from the waist up.

     Rachel had originally thought that the Greek, who she had been trying to kill would just shoot her there and then but he had other things on his mind. Working her belt free and undoing the buttons he pulled her trousers down so as to get a much better look at the white girl at his mercy whilst also preparing himself to engage in the act of sex. Rachel felt she would probably only get one real chance to escape and so didn't fight against him that much as he removed her trousers completely and then tore off her underwear. She concentrated on conserving her energy. The Greek smiled and purred as he explored his new prize with his fingers, first stroking and then feeling her inside. It only lasted a couple of minutes but for Rachel it seemed like an eternity. She could smell his breath as he moved his mouth and tongue nearer to hers. It was ghastly. An odour which had origins of garlic but contained so much more! The Greeks' body odour was even worse. Rachel closed her eyes and was able to shut her mind to what was going on and for a few seconds. She somehow managed to recall the mountain scenery where she was currently laying and imagined herself being on holiday, relaxing in the hot sun. She had blocked out her current predicament well and she was almost into a state of complete tranquility when the Greek hurt her as he fumbled deeper into her. The pain caused her to jerk rather abruptly whilst also bringing her mind back to her current situation. The Greek reacted as well, removing his fingers from inside of her but then slowly smelling and licking them in front of Rachel, showing her that he was enjoying every second of it. It was no good. He could wait no longer as he now set about undoing his own trousers. In many ways Rachel was sure that her attacker had thought that she had given in but if he did, he couldn't have been more wrong. She tried desperately to free her hands without making it obvious but the knot was strong and not giving way.

Rachel looked around and noticed that the rebel had stuck his knife into the ground nearby but he was between Rachel and the knife so she wasn't able to reach it at all. Then came the moment she had been waiting for. The opportunity she needed. He repositioned her legs so that she was able to receive the full length of his manhood and it meant that Rachel's one good leg was free. She waited a few seconds for him to drop his trousers and pants so as to leave himself completely vulnerable. With all of the training she had received in martial arts, one kick was enough to knock him back on to the floor. The force had not only thrown him a good ten yards or more but the shock of it all made his response quite slow. Eventually he got back to his feet and pulled his trousers up a little. Rachel half pulled her trousers up from behind whilst running to the knife. She was able to cut her hands free on the knife as it stuck in the ground and then she took the knife into her hand just as the rebel landed a kick into her side. The force of the kick had knocked her back to the ground and she had dropped the knife as she did so. Winded and still nursing the wound to her leg Rachel was also slow to recover. She looked up to see the rebel about to land the knife into her chest but somehow she automatically grabbed at a small rock and aimed a throw at his forehead. The knife cut through her skin as her uniform top was still open and it cut into her chest causing a wound about two inches deep but the rebel came off worse. The small rock had hit him right on the forehead above his left eye and stunned him. He fell to his knees in pain. Adrenalin had kicked in and Rachel jumped up so as to land another blow to the rebels head. There was no need as by now he already lay unconscious. It took another five blows to the skull before Rachel was certain. That sight of crushed bone and blood will never leave her. Managing to bring herself to her senses she knew she had killed the bastard but it was a feeling of complete satisfaction that went through her. Rachel hadn't quite finished as she dressed herself and looked back at her attacker. She aimed one large kick to his groin in some mistaken sense that it would cause him pain. The rebel was dead. He would feel nothing. Not even his own knife as Rachel stuck it into his offending private area and twisted it left and right. Rachel felt good. Rachel felt sick. Rachel was sick.

Leaving the bodies of the two rebels behind, Rachel carried her dead colleague on her shoulder as she stumbled her way back to base where she was given a hero's welcome. Although her unit learnt about the attack by the two rebels, they never got to hear the full story. She kept all the details to herself but it was a day that she would never forget. It was a day that would change the rest of her life.

When she left the Army and returned to Manchester she was a different person. Not on the surface as such but in a much more personal way. Rachel wouldn't let anyone show her any love or affection and froze whenever her fiancé tried to touch her. She had even started to get undressed in private not allowing anyone to see her naked. Her fiancé had worked out that there was a problem and he tried to understand the new Rachel but within six months he had finally had enough, gave up and left her. Rachel also started to have moral deliberations about how she had crushed the life out of another human. She worked as a nursing assistant hoping to try and make up for her guilt by saving the lives of others but it wasn't working. She couldn't settle at all. The answer was to go back into the Army which she did. Maybe one day someone will be able to explain it all to her or help her back into a normal life. She didn't socialise very much, would never go out on dates and she certainly wouldn't wear make-up or sexy feminine clothes or do anything that she would consider made her look more attractive. At times she even went through periods of trying to make herself look ugly and unclean so as to put off any sort of interest from the opposite sex. She wouldn't let men anywhere near her nowadays which gave her a bit of a reputation as being a lesbian but she wasn't. For now it helped her get through life. She hoped that one day she'd be able to love again but in the meantime, she would do her duty in the Euro Army.

By 01.45hrs, the first four soldiers out on patrol were back in the mess preparing sandwiches and drinks. As usual the chefs left out a number of things for the night duty staff to choose from. As well as there being plenty of bread and butter there were various choices of fillings. There would usually be a tray of cold chicken and then another tray of either cold pork or beef and quite often a ham joint that could be carved. There would always be a few different cheeses and then a dish of some sort of sandwich filling for the vegetarian pallet. It was also usual for there to be a tray of chicken drumsticks around somewhere. The best thing though about being in the Army was that there were always endless amounts of pickles and sauces laying around. Even mustard if you wanted it. The night duty soldiers would always help themselves to extras if they could get back to the kitchens and some would even take doggy bags home after their shifts as it was common knowledge that although this food was always left out for the night shifts, the first thing done by kitchen staff in the morning was to clear the fridges. Everything was ready for the outgoing soldiers to start their food and drink. Only one Private refrained from eating and kept Sergeant Foulkes company. As the Private was also staying on base during the next shift, around 02.25hrs he would go down and start to have his fill whilst one of the incoming Privates would join Sergeant Foulkes.

The time was 03.08hrs and all was quiet in Kentley. One of the Privates was in Vehicle One and had just radioed in that he was in at the Bus Station in the Market Place where he was awaiting Vehicle Two. After a couple of minutes, the Corporal radioed to confirm that he had met up with Vehicle One. There was silence for the next ten minutes. Sergeant Foulkes was getting bored. This was nothing new really but tonight it was getting him down. Time passed very slowly and the whole office almost jumped out of their seats when the phone rang. One of the Radio Room Corporals answered it.
"Yes Sir. What sort of noises? And have you actually seen anyone out there? Where would that be exactly?" The Corporal continued with his telephone conversation. The rest of the Radio Room flipped into attentiveness and waited for details.
"Are you prepared to give your name?" The Corporal continued and wrote down hurriedly on a scrap pad nearby. "Which room Sir?" He wrote something down again. "Thank you very much," the Corporal finished the call. He turned into the room and looked surprised at the size of the audience he would now be addressing.
"Sounds of some sort of disturbance on Wall Street down from The Angel Hotel. Mentioned movement of people and sounds of voices as well as breaking glass." The Corporal said. Without any hesitation he moved over to the radio and took hold of the microphone.
"Any patrol, any patrol, reports of a disturbance and noise of people from Wall Street, west of The Angel Hotel but from the same side. Can anyone attend?" The Corporal recorded his message as being

around 03.47hrs. By 03.51hrs, Vehicle One had responded to say that they were on their way. At 03.51hrs Vehicle One reported in.
"Vehicle One in Wall Street. Proceeding Eastwards." The Private made his report quickly and clearly.
The Radio Room confirmed receiving his message and waited.
"Vehicle One now level with The Angel. No sign of anything that could be causing the disturbance although have to say that there are a few parked cars about that I don't remember being here earlier." Again the Private gave as much detail as he could over the radio. Whilst one soldier drove the jeep the other kept his eyes moving up front, with a third soldier and Rachel Dobbs looking out behind. All of a sudden there was a noise that came from behind them but sounding like it came from Wall Street. The soldiers tried to spot what might have caused the noise which sounded a bit like a box of metal things falling open on the floor.
"Turn the jeep round." The senior Private ordered the driver. As the jeep was being turned he reported the new noise.
"Another noise heard in Wall Street. Now proceeding west to investigate." This message was timed at 03.54hrs and at the moment that message stopped, the next started.
"Vehicle Two currently at Templegate and will proceed to Wall Street." The Corporal reported. Vehicle One proceeded slowly along Wall Street shining it's searchlight about looking for any sort of movement. As they reached the halfway point the senior soldier held his arm up to indicate that the jeep should come to a halt.
"Private Dobbs with me," he ordered as he got out of the jeep. Dobbs got out of the back of the jeep and joined him at the front of the vehicle whilst Private Bridge moved to the front of the vehicle so as to operate the searchlight. Almost immediately a car turned into West Street from Aldersgate Street. The four soldiers saw it straightaway and froze. The civilian car reacted well and swerved to its right so that it could continue back down to Kings Bridge. It had no lights on but the street lights meant it could be easily seen from quite a distance. The senior soldier ran back to the jeep and jumped straight into the jeep whilst Dobbs got ready to jump into the back. One of the other Privates had already started moving but had to wait until Rachel was safely back in before speeding off. The senior Private picked up the handset.
"Civilian vehicle moving south from Aldersgate Street towards Kings Bridge. Vehicle One in pursuit." The message was timed at 03.55hrs.

He continued. "Initial report says it is a red Ford Fiesta with at least three on board." As this information was being broadcast over the radio, not only could the Radio Room hear it but also Vehicle Two could hear what was being said.

The Corporal was next on to the radio. "Vehicle Two is now turning into Kings Bridge Road and civilian vehicle has been sighted turning into High Street. Do you want me to continue the pursuit?" This is where the Army worked at its best. He knew that the soldier in charge on the jeep was in the better position to make the next decision and left it to him.
"No we'll continue pursuit but will drop Dobbs at the corner of High Street for you." The senior Private replied. The Radio Room just listened on but left it up to the two Vehicles on the ground to get things sorted. Rachel knew that it would be her job to identify to Vehicle Two exactly where the noise they had heard had been coming from so that they could investigate that further and she was ready to jump out of the jeep as it turned into The High Street.
"Good luck Boys," she shouted as Vehicle One shot off in continued pursuit of the civilian vehicle which had by this time driven across the Market Place and into the High Road.
"Immediate Response Vehicle awaiting instructions," the call came from the Corporal. The senior soldier wasn't sure if it was his call or not but he made the reply.
"Join Vehicle Two in Wall Street, IR Team." He told them. The time was now 03.56hrs. Sergeant Foulkes all of a sudden saw an opportunity that he couldn't resist. Now that the IR Team had been mobilized one of his Unit had made his way to the Radio Room so that Back-up could be called for. Sergeant Foulkes told him what he was going to do. He was going to take one soldier and go and give Vehicle One some back-up in their pursuit of the civilian vehicle. The tactics being used out there looked like they were trying to split the Army's strength so another vehicle would be useful.

At 04.00hrs, Vehicle Two and the IR Team radioed in to confirm that they had met on Wall Street and that they were dispensing foot troops to further investigate the earlier noises. "Dobbs I need you to show me where you have already looked." The Corporal asked. He would have to quickly get a plan together to search the back streets and empty buildings to see what all the fuss was about. By now everything on Wall Street was quiet again but Dobbs knew where to centre their search from before. The Corporal took three men with him passing on instructions to the other Corporal to provide cover with the remainder. Dobbs quietly indicated where they had thought they had heard the noise coming from and the five moved towards Reed Street which was a narrow road off Wall Street. Although there was housing in these streets, the frontage that was on Wall Street was mainly made up of derelict and empty shops and storage rooms. They were ideal places for revolutionary factions to hold meetings, store weapons do almost anything in fact. Without actually saying anything the Corporal indicated to Dobbs and another soldier to move to opposite corners of Reed Street. The Corporal and the other two moved forward swiftly to take up positions before, after and opposite to the entrance to a back passage that obviously led to the rear of the shops. Another member of the Unit had been watching what the team had been doing and decided it might help if he shone the searchlight down Reed Street in the direction of the back alley entrance. Almost as soon as he did a shot was fired in the direction of the light which appeared to have come from a high elevation and from one of the shops. Two soldiers immediately fired back at the direction of the shot. There had been a couple of other shots fired at the covering four and in particular in the direction of the searchlight. Perhaps it hadn't been the best idea to turn it on. The Corporal had some difficult decisions to make now.

      Vehicle One had managed to keep in touch with the civilian vehicle as it turned right out of The High Road and into Northgate. There was a temporary loss of sight for a few seconds but the soldier was a good driver and as he crossed over Ferry Bridge the vehicle was in sight again.
"Vehicle One please report your position?" This message came across the radio from Sergeant Foulkes.
"Proceeding south down Ferrybridge Street."
"I'm going to give you back up so please keep your position reported." Sergeant Foulkes answered.
"Still on Ferrybridge Street. The civilian vehicle seems to be signaling ahead."
"Can you see any other vehicles?" The Sergeant said anxiously.

"Not sure but think a vehicle may have turned into the Refuse Centre." The Private continued. "Yes our target vehicle has also turned into the Refuse Centre and we will proceed in there."

"No, do not go any further than the gates." The Sergeant replied but it was too late as Vehicle One had already gone passed the normally locked gates and into the further reaches of the Refuse Centre. At the end of the entrance road was the choice to now go left or right. The normal choice would be left around the one way system but Vehicle Two was ordered to come to a halt. By this time, Sergeant Foulkes and one of the Privates had also turned into the road leading to the Refuse Centre but as he approached the gates the driver brought his jeep to a halt. He awaited further instructions from Sergeant Foulkes but meanwhile one of the Unit had seen what looked like a fire round to the left of the Refuse Centre.

"Fire spotted here at the Refuse Centre on the left hand road as you come into the site. Sergeant Foulkes do you copy?" The radio message came through.

"I told you not to proceed. Are you actually in the Refuse Centre?" Replied Sergeant Foulkes.

"Yes Sir. Once round the bend take the left hand route and we're about three hundred yards ahead of you." The two vehicles sat side by side as everyone just looked at the blazing refuse lorry in front of them.

"Permission to attend the fire Sir?" The soldier shouted to Sergeant Foulkes.

"Do you have any equipment?"

"No but there is firefighting equipment over there, Sir!" He pointed to a hose sitting next to a tank. It was quite conveniently placed to put the fire out as had the fire been a further fifty yards away, they would have struggled to reach it. The fire was out in about three minutes. That was the good news. A familiar noise came from behind them which suggested that something else was also on fire. It suggested that the people in the cars were just kids out to have a bit of a laugh. Sergeant Foulkes saw it differently hence his instructions not to proceed into the Refuse Centre. When he saw what the problem really was he cursed even more. Two vehicles were now alight and blocking their exit from the Refuse Centre. They were stuck. The call went into HQ at about 04.08hrs from Sergeant Foulkes, "Can the Back-up team bring a ramming vehicle to the Refuse Centre as soon as possible."

"They are on their way to Wall Street Sergeant," came the reply.
"What's happening?" He asked in an attempt to keep control of things.
"Wait one. Please switch to channel 7." HQ ordered him. On this channel the duty Radio Room
Sergeant brought Sergeant Foulkes up to date with events back at Wall Street. Sergeant Foulkes switched as requested.
"Can you confirm that we have trained ambulance on stand-by as well please?"
"Do you wish for an ambulance sent now?"
"No just ensure there is a trained driver available. When it is safe we'll arrange a rendezvous."

After the first volley of shots had finished and the searchlight had been turned off, the Corporal shouted across to the two Privates at the other vehicle.
"Is everything okay?" He shouted not thinking about using the radio.
"Yeah I thought the searchlight would help."
"Could you make out where the shots were coming from exactly?"
"No but Hildred got a shot off." The Private let go of the transmit button. "Patrick have you been able to see anything?" He called across to his colleague who was crouched by the rear of the vehicle.
"Patrick do you know where the shots came from?" He said again a bit louder.
"Have you anything to report Vehicle Two?" The Corporal said in an agitated voice on the radio. The soldier had taken a few steps back and come up behind his colleague. As he touched his shoulder he said, "Oy Patrick, are you ignoring me?" Private Hildred's head fell back and then his body collapsed back into his colleague's arms.
"Arggh!!" A shocked cry came followed by "Shit!!" He made his way back to the radio. "Hildreds a gonner Sir!" The Private reported.
"Stay where you are. Are you hit at all?" The Corporal said almost automatically whilst trying to think what he should do next. Both the search team and the cover were in pretty awkward or bad positions and should they show themselves were easy targets for any sniper in a high enough position.
"No I'm alright," he replied.
"Back-up required at Wall Street immediately. Please confirm. Armoured vehicle preferred.

Confirmation and ETA imperative!" Corporal King passed his message back to HQ. He expected Sergeant Foulkes to be the next voice on the radio but there was silence.
"Can you see anyone from the search team?" The Corporal asked.
"Dobbs and one other Sir," the reply came. The next voice on the radio was the duty Radio Room Sergeant.
"HQ to IR Team. Back-up will be dispatched in two minutes. ETA 04.08hrs."
"Thank you HQ." The Corporal replied. He had to try and get in touch with the other Corporal if he could as there had been no indications as to whether or not any of the search team had been shot or not. The other Corporal was almost as much in the dark. He had confirmed that his team were still alright but wasn't sure if there was still any cover. He indicated to both Privates to move up whilst he got another Private to prepare a firelighter. It would be lit and thrown down the back passage where the three on the other side of the road should be able to see if there were any people down there or not. The Private threw the stick and it flared for the normal ten or twelve seconds as it was supposed to. Another Private was in the best position to see down the alley and there must have been at least half a dozen people down there. There was another response with fire coming from the back alleyway and the back windows of the shops. The search team fired back but their position was a lot worse than they had first thought. There were also rebels hiding down the other back alleyway and the firelighter had also given away the positions of both Dobbs and her colleague. Both were shot at from behind and both hit. One in the shoulder and Dobbs rather badly in the leg. She was bleeding quite a lot and the soldier could see the two of them from his position. He managed to attract the Corporals attention with a small whistle and tried to communicate their problem. They had to get out and back to the Vehicle.

    Back at the Refuse Centre, one end of one of the cars was burning quite a bit less than the rest. Sergeant Foulkes took two of his Unit aside and discussed his plan. Hitting the car at a point where there wasn't too much flame, he felt that they could get the vehicle back on to its wheels. If it worked properly they would then be able to push the vehicle on its wheels a little bit out of the way and could then drive passed one side of the burning mess. There was always the risk of causing an explosion but Sergeant Foulkes was happy that the jeeps were strong enough to take anything else. Private Bridge was given the task of trying to get the vehicle on its wheels but on his first attempt he hadn't quite been able to push it over. A second attempt was driven back when flames started to rage around the petrol tank but after he had tried a third time the vehicle easily fell on to its wheels. A soldier in the other vehicle then pushed the vehicle right out of the way and continued on his way out of the Refuse Centre. Vehicle One followed the same track and soon the two vehicles were on their way to Wall Street.

Three back-up soldiers had arrived at Wall Street in an armoured vehicle. They reported their arrival on the radio.
"Back-up reporting our position on Wall Street just opposite The Angel Hotel."
"HQ to back-up vehicle, receiving you loud and clear. Wait for instructions from Corporal King," the radio officer replied. At the time this was going on, a Private appeared, moving out of Reed Street. He was trying to get a message to Corporal King but it wasn't that easy. He crawled under window level along the front of the shops until he was level with Kings vehicle.
"On the count of three I want back-up to fire all along the top of those shops opposite my vehicle." Corporal King instructed. "One, Two Fire!" He gave the instruction. The Corporal and his companion also fired intermittently looking for signs of where return fire might be coming from but none ever came. The Private ran back to the Immediate Response vehicle and gave Corporal King the bad news about Dobbs. In return, he got the bad news about Hildred. Before he sorted out getting the two injured soldiers back a report needed to be made back to Sergeant Foulkes the exact size of the problem here. He turned to Corporal King and asked if the Sergeant had been keeping up with things but all that the Corporal could tell him was that the Serge had been trapped at the Refuse Centre and that nobody knew exactly what was going on there. A couple of shots rang out from the shops and the back-up vehicle returned fire but it lasted only seconds.
"I guess that there are about three with weapons up there and maybe one in the shops passed Reed Street." The Corporal said as the Private took hold of the microphone.
"Sergeant Foulkes from Vehicle Two, do you read?"
"Read you loud and clear. We're about four minutes away. What's going on there?" Sergeant Foulkes asked him. The soldier gave a full

account and it soon became obvious that they were in trouble. The Radio Room Sergeant cut in and advised Sergeant Foulkes that he had already alerted two further Units and that he would have a third ready to support them in about twenty minutes.

Reed Street was one of the roads in the part of town that was probably the most over-populated. Most of the housing in this area had more families living in them than was healthy and it was quite often a case of three generations of a family all living in the same house and sharing bedrooms. Poverty and sickness was rife in this area but the kids were happy enough. Every town had a similar area.

Sergeant Foulkes started to get the situation sorted out and his first job was to get some support to one of his Privates who was completely stranded. He decided to take both of the vehicles with him into Wall Street from the west and hence they could back-up the soldier. Just as he got there, the Corporal appeared at the right corner of Reed Street holding up one of the wounded soldiers. There was blood dripping from his elbow and he was clearly in pain. The two of them kept tight up against the shop front in Wall Street and when the order was given, three of the Unit drove at some speed along Wall Street shooting at the shops whilst cover was also given from the remaining three vehicles. At the same time the armoured vehicle drove nearer to the Corporal so he only had about thirty yards to run to get to cover. As it happened, no fire came from the shops at all. The Corporal bundled the injured soldier into the armoured vehicle but continued running himself to join up with Corporal King.
"Nice to have you back Corporal."
"Yeah I suppose it's good to be back." They looked at each other and laughed. The only thing now was to get Dobbs out. She was in a worse state than the other soldier as she couldn't really walk properly but there was one other member of the Unit with her and he made sure she didn't pass out. They had both appeared on the left corner of Reed Street but Rachel Dobbs wasn't looking too good. She was close to passing out whilst holding her leg so as to stop some of the bleeding. She knew she had been in worse situations but the pain was beginning to take its' toll on her. After a couple of minutes the armoured vehicle had secured a position where they could take her on board. Whilst this was going on, cover fire was given and her colleague kept a guard in case any fire came from the back alleys but the armoured vehicle had

got it's passenger and was off leaving him on his own. On the count of three he ran zigzagged back to Vehicle 2 and relative safety. Sergeant Foulkes had now got two more Units waiting to come on to the scene and what he wanted was Wall Street blocked off at the two ends. To the east just passed The Angel Hotel and to the west right at the junction with Aldersgate Street and Royal Street. Once these blocks had been started it was just for the Unit Charlie 12 vehicles to get behind them and then they could plan properly how to clear the shops.

It wasn't long before the two ends of Wall Street were blocked off and this brought with it a greater fear from those hiding up in the shops. A few shots fired through the air in the general direction of Corporal King but he knew it wouldn't be long before he was out of it. Corporal King got into the driving seat of his vehicle and was ready as the first two vehicles then continued along Wall street to the blockade at the other end of the road. Corporal King joined them and they were let through. The soldier quickly got the vehicle ready to move but first Sergeant Foulkes had to get Hildred's body into the back of the jeep. Another Private was there to help and they both stopped briefly to consider picking up their unfortunate colleague but common sense prevailed. However it was an opportunity that the snipers just couldn't resist. Shots were fired at the two of them and Sergeant Foulkes got hit in the back of the leg.

"We're going to have to leave him boy, get in the jeep." Sergeant Foulkes shouted. The driver realised what was going on and started to move away slowly expecting his colleagues to jump into the back as he was moving but the Sergeant just couldn't jump and the Private was still holding Hildred in his arms. The jeep stopped and The Sergeant scrambled into it with some difficulty. As he looked back he could see the other soldier still carrying Hildred. He jumped out of the jeep again. "Get in the bloody jeep. Drop him." The Sergeant ordered. It was as if he couldn't be heard. Sergeant Foulkes' leg was starting to hurt and he was feeling the pain. The driver tried to get the vehicle nearer but the other soldier was still very exposed and two shots went straight into his chest as he dropped to his knees still with Hildred in his arms. Another shot caught Sergeant Foulkes in the arm but he still grabbed hold of the injured Private and tried to pull him to the jeep. It was no good, he too had breathed his last breath. The Sergeant soon

realised the situation and jumped back towards the jeep whilst holding on.
"Go, go, go!!" The two soldiers were past help. Their bodies would be retrieved by one of the back-up Units. It was time for Unit Charlie 12 to lick its' wounds and get on out. Ed Foulkes wasn't happy with the way things had gone that night. He didn't really want to hang about the area that long either. He knew that many of the people living around Reed Street were ill. Illnesses that had been long forgotten. Brought on by starvation and a general lack of hygiene. Many houses had up to twenty five people living in them. They weren't pretty places to look at.

   By 08.00hrs, residents from the Reed Street estate were out demonstrating about heavy Army tactics and the fact that they were living in a police state. Unofficially there were reports of three deaths of residents stating that they were kids who had been playing in the old shop storerooms. The demonstrators came out into Wall Street but were blocked from going too far by the Army blockades. Cars were turned and set alight. Some shops were smashed. Rocks and bottles thrown at the Army blockades but no more shootings took place till the following evening. The day after, the Army searched the entire line of shops along Wall Street but found nobody. The demonstration was over. It hadn't gone as planned and the planning committee for the revolutionaries were a bit disappointed. Things would be different next time.

-

   Sarah called round to Gary and Angela's again but Gary was the only one in this time.
"Hi anyone at home?" Sarah shouted as she rang the doorbell. Sammy barked.
"Come in, the door's unlocked." Gary replied. Sarah walked into the living room.
"Sorry if I'm disturbing you I didn't realise you worked when you got home." Sarah apologised as she saw Gary working away at the dining table.
"No I don't usually but as I was the only one in thought I'd grab the opportunity." Gary told her. Sarah moved closer to see what Gary was doing and she noticed a piece of post on the table.

"Oh are you delivering mail. Mr. Longhurst, what is that then?" Sarah quizzed. Gary immediately covered up the envelope with the newspaper that was also on the table.
"Sorry I can't let you see what I'm doing as it is secret." Gary panicked.
"Ooh secret eh?" Sarah joked as she got even closer. "Are these spies you're delivering to?" Sarah continued to joke about it.
"No they are pieces of mail that are not addressed to the correct addresses and I have to check them out." Gary explained.
"So where does Mr. Longhurst live then?" Sarah asked.
"Sarah, I can't tell you."
"Oh it's got to be in the village somewhere," she continued to tease him.
"It might be. It might not." Gary started to collect in his papers and put them away.
"Go on, tell me where he lives." Sarah started to beg.
"I don't know where he lives. The address on the envelope is not where he is recorded as living which is why I'm checking the place out." Gary scrambled the papers back into his briefcase.
"So what do you do to check the places out?" Sarah asked.
"I'll just go passed the address and see what there is to be seen there. I'm not saying another word. Please Sarah, leave it alone." Gary pleaded. Gary picked up the paper and turned to the article about the shooting incident. "What about this poor woman who got shot the other day then." Gary said as he pointed to the article and handed the paper to Sarah to read.
"Yes I was told that you were stopped by the roadblock." Sarah said as she read the report.
"Yes, I saw the whole bloody thing more or less. The woman never had a chance." Gary started to recall the incident. Sarah was very much engrossed in the newspaper report. "It was a terrible thing to have to witness Sarah." Gary continued. "Seeing someone shot down in cold blood."
"Yes it can be." Sarah was paying more attention to the newspaper than what Gary was saying.
"I said seeing someone shot down in cold blood…" Sarah interrupted him.
"Yes I heard."
"But you don't seem to be listening." Gary sounded hurt.

"Oh sorry. I have read about the shooting but my newspaper never had a photograph with the report. Anyway you weren't that late home were you?" Sarah finally finished her sentence.
"How do you know?"
"Oh Angela told me. She's not been very happy with you recently, getting home late and things." Sarah told him.
"What sort of things?" Gary asked.
"You know!" Sarah gave him a knowing look. Gary picked the paper up from the table.
"Nothing but bad news nowadays," he said.
"Oh it can't all be bad surely!" Sarah added.
"And another thing, that revolutionary schoolteacher, you know the one who was arrested by the Army and banned from the school." Gary started to tell her.
"Yes I did hear about the incident." Sarah confirmed.
"She has left a load of papers here for us to look after." Gary finished.
"Oh what sort of papers?" Sarah asked curiously.
"Oh some project papers in a cardboard box upstairs in the bedroom."
"Have you looked to see what you're actually looking after?" Sarah asked.
"What do you mean?"
"Well they might be secret papers that the Army are looking for." Sarah said half jokingly.
"Do you really think so?" Gary said with surprise. He hadn't actually thought much about what was in the papers.
"You never know. She was arrested on suspicion of holding some secret papers wasn't she?" Sarah said.
"Was she? I didn't know that." Gary replied.
"Yes it was in the papers." Sarah said. "Anyway, none of this is any reason for you to start drinking." Sarah changed the subject.
"I'm not drinking too much thanks and I can look after myself." Gary replied sternly.
"Angela has told me that you have started to drink and I believe her."
"Well I've got a lot of things on my mind." Gary replied hoping that would be good enough for an excuse.
"What troubles?"
"One of the blokes at work is having problems and I've got to try and sort them out." Gary said.

"You know you'll get through it Gary. You always do. But you always drink when things get on top of you. It's not good for you." Sarah reprimanded him.
"I'll be alright." Gary responded. There was a break in the conversation with both taking in all that had been said.
"Just use your loo please," Sarah asked. "I know where it is," she added. Gary was annoyed with himself for getting caught out having his work all out on the table. The fact that Sarah had seen the envelope was bad but fortunately it was only his sister who had seen it. If it had been someone from work, Gary might have been in worse trouble. He knew he had to be more careful if he was going to bring work home with him again. And then Sarah was starting to get on his case about drinking. He hadn't realised he was drinking more but obviously Angela had mentioned it to Sarah. Where was Sarah? What the hell was she doing in that bathroom? Gary went upstairs to find Sarah in his bedroom looking in one of the big drawers.
"What are you looking for?"
"There's no towel in the bathroom and I know Angela usually keeps them in here somewhere."
"Bottom drawer but one." Gary said.

    Gary and Sarah were both very pleased to be back on speaking terms. To see his sister just feeling at home in his house was good. This was how it should always have been. Gary thought back to that little period when it all went wrong. Their brother David had been shot at a demonstration and both of them had taken it very badly. Their younger brother, the one they both tried to protect. Gary knew that Sarah had taken David's death badly but it was he who was being blamed by their Mother and Father. It was he who was being told that it was his fault that David had died. The family was showing signs of falling apart but nobody seemed to care how Gary felt. Sarah was dealing with her grief in her own way. She was angry, more angry than she had ever been before and of course Sarah started to take up the fight where David had left off. This was not Gary's way. He tried hard to keep his Mother and Father from getting any worse and he had no time to grieve. It was probably at this point in time when Gary and Sarah started to drift apart. They had been so close before as children. Gary needed his sister but she wasn't there for him. Sarah needed her brother but he was too busy looking after their parents. Then when his father died things got even worse. Sarah threw herself into the revolution and left the family behind altogether so it seemed. Those were bad times. Those were the worst of times.

-

The phone went in Major Tannier's office and the Major was surprised to hear the voice of Operation Hunting's agent on the other end. He knew that a lot had been happening on this case just recently but they had their next meeting already agreed and it was unusual for an agent to make contact quite so often.
"What can I do for you?" The Major asked. He then listened with intent concentration as the agent asked if there had been any mention of any local media report on the events that took place at the roadblock last Thursday.
"Well now you mention it there was a small report I saw last week but it didn't say very much," the Major replied. The agent seemed a bit annoyed that he had known but had not said anything.
"I don't see that there is any problem. They have no idea what the road block was about and have obviously taken the line that Tetridge was shot because she tried to do a runner," the Major seemed a bit confused about all the fuss. The agent then explained that there was a photograph that went with a story that was printed in one of the local newspapers. This probably meant that there may have been a team hiding about at the roadblock waiting for a possible incident like this to happen. The Major started to click. They'll have notes and as the agent pointed out, it is unlikely that this was the only photograph taken. The Major knew what was required. He would get the newspaper to get both reporter and photographer into his office and get what he could.

Whilst the agent was on the phone, Major Tannier was able to relay the last little bit of the report from Sergeant Foulkes about the Redbridges and John Cleaveley. As he expected, the reply was that further checks should be done on the two families and details passed to the agent as and when. He agreed to try and have it all done before their next meeting.

Chapter 5   -   THE LONGHURST FILE

Kentley had only existed as a small village before the 1990's but it grew rather suddenly when the population of London became so overcrowded that the people were suffering starvation and disease almost to a plague epidemic. The Government of the time had been warned by the World Health Organisation that London couldn't survive any further overcrowding so a scheme was set up to move thousands out of London and rehouse them on the East coast. Desperate measures were called for in order to clear certain areas where doctors had seen early signs of the plague. It was quite a brave move by the authorities as they declared emergency after emergency in hand picked boroughs of London. The first areas to be evacuated were done under the pretence that the drinking water in the area had been contaminated and that everyone had to move out so that the water board could put things right. As expected, the residents argued and complained as they were shifted into temporary homes like the previously empty Army barracks around the Thetford forest region. The stress of leaving an area you had been born and raised in was tremendous but promises were made that they would be able to return to their homes as soon as the problems were sorted out. Not surprisingly, that was never an item on the agenda as far as the Government were concerned and it never happened.

Kentley was one of a few villages that were earmarked as relocation places and nearly seventy years on Kentley had now got its own real identity. It had been through a couple of years of bad times when all of the east coast of England became a target during the Middle Eastern War and found itself the recipient of hundreds of chemical bombs. The shore was still pretty much out of bounds for various reasons. The main reason most kept away from the beaches was because the water had previously been so contaminated that it almost smoked with acidity. Dead fish and other sea creatures were a regular sight on the beaches and it took a long time for the authorities to clear most of this up. It was also one of the main reasons for having an Army barracks in Kentley. A lot of new barracks sprung up around the same time all situated either on or very close to the beach so that Army personnel could clear the beaches of rotting fish etc. The Kentley barracks was no different but long before the Army had finished their task of clearing the beaches they had been taken over by the European Army and put to other uses. A lot of the east coast beaches were still thought to have a number of unexploded bombs on them. Most sensible people didn't venture down to beaches that had no official clearance and Kentley was full of beach that had not been officially cleared. For a few years the sea was also used to dispose of excess sewerage. There was no sign of the seas actually ever getting any better so local authorities that could not afford to dispose of their areas waste still decided to use the sea. Kentley had piping going directly out to sea where you will now find the 'Refuse Centre'. European Law did eventually put an end to this practice for a while and paid for proper sewerage but then came the Aegean war and things changed again.

    Kentley was very much like many other small towns although having a rather large barracks it did get certain advantages that other small towns didn't easily get. However, the folk of Kentley were soon very much in the same boat as everyone else with mass unemployment, poorly paid jobs when you did get employed, shortfall of food for the population which soon turned into heavily overpriced food when it was available. The consequences were that most ordinary people had no job, no money and very little food. Having said that, morale remained high and everyone helped everyone else out as much as they could. Certain jobs were seen as essential and if you had one of these you were quite honoured and in many ways far better off than most. Working for the Army was even more of a step up the ladder. Army personnel were all very well paid and lived a life in the barracks totally differently to that outside. Government officials were also seen to have certain extras pushed their way whilst civil servants or other government workers had steady jobs with a slightly better income than most.

    As you might imagine, most of the young men and youths in Kentley today have had to grow up through a state of almost complete poverty. Although many would have spent their two or three years conscripted to the Army, this was very much a two edged sword where they might get well fed and their standard of living improved but at any moments notice they might get called out to some war in Europe where the chances of returning home alive was quite often no better than 50 – 50. In addition, they would be treated like the enemy whilst working on the streets by friends and relatives who were demonstrating against the Euro Army. Most conscripts got out as soon as they could. Not to be able to go out and work but to be able to have an element of freedom to show which side of the power fence they were sitting on. Local Kentley lads were pretty much all anti-Army but some were pro. Life in Kentley certainly wasn't easy. The chances are you lived in a house with another family who were related to you in some way. It wasn't that easy to come by new housing in the town so if you weren't prepared to move out into the country you lived where you could. Quite often daughters would be brought up in the house they were born in and then move in their husbands when they got married. The houses themselves were not in that good a state. Nobody could afford builders, painters, carpenters etc. and those businesses mainly went by the wayside. It was usually an Uncle Jack or a Cousin Norman in the family who would be able to mend things in the house. They would normally have been previously skilled labourers who had no jobs anymore or natural handymen either learning the skills from older relations or teaching themselves from text books or magazines. Whatever, as a family member none of these jobs were done for money. It would be mending the plumbing in return for fixing a car or building an extension to a house in return for installing some windows. Most families had some sort of skill that they could bargain with and those that hadn't would give food in return. There wasn't a lot of money around so people weren't actually able to buy very much anyway. As a consequence, most families became very self sufficient with the bigger families doing better than the smaller families.

You would also find that a lot of Kentley is run down and full of boarded up shops. Signs that at some time in the past there had once been a thriving community and some sort of economic market but not nowadays. Crime was also quite rife around the town but then people who lived in Kentley were quite streetwise and usually able to look after themselves. The one thing that had changed was that most people respected their neighbours a lot more than they used to. Most people realised how much hardship and strife you would have to go through to acquire certain things and it was very unusual for a local neighbour to vandalise anything close to home. There was also a lot of mistrust as well though. It may not seem that these two things would fit in well together but they did. If a neighbour was in trouble, you would always help them. If a neighbour was being attacked by a stranger you would always go to their aid but if a neighbour asked you what you thought about the Army, or what your political views were about a certain subject you wouldn't trust them at all and would probably not say a word. It was a funny life.

-

After the battle at Reed Street, three of Unit Charlie 12 had been admitted to the military wing of the hospital at Kentley. As with most hospitals in Europe, Kentley was run fairly much entirely by military staff and was for the use of the Army before anyone else. There were some private nurses who were not paid by the Army but they would usually be confined to an old ward or two at one end of the hospital which catered purely for the general public.

Ed Foulkes, Matthew King and Rachel Dobbs had been looked after in the military end of the hospital which had all the latest technical equipment and top of the range care. This part of the hospital was out of bounds to non-military people and was very strictly guarded. Every little wound and illness was cared for right around the clock for anyone in this section and all efforts were made to ensure that nobody suffered.

Ed Foulkes was probably the most injured out of the three as he had suffered both leg and arm wounds. A bullet had gone right through the back of his lower calf damaging the muscle a little but it was at least a fairly clean wound. He had also been grazed by a bullet on his upper arm. This needed after care but wasn't a real problem. Matthew King had also been grazed by a bullet on his leg whilst he had also torn a ligament in his knee during his efforts in the battle. He would be requiring some physiotherapy but shouldn't be too long before he would be back on duty. Rachel Dobbs meanwhile seemed to have the worst injury out of the three. A bullet was lodged in her thigh and she had muscle damage. She had lost blood and she needed more urgent care for the first day but she too would be back fit and well before too long.

-

Although a lot of the basic checks were being done by usual Army sources through Major Tannier, our agent decided that they could do a little bit more checking themselves on The Hobbs. Looking through the details on the Hobbs, the address 14, Back Lane, Waydon had been checked out meticulously and everything pointed to just two people living there. They were Raymond Keith and Susan Jennifer Hobbs. Dates of birth showed him to be forty eight and her to be forty seven and that they had been married for twenty seven years. There didn't seem to be anything out of the usual about them. It was a bit of a shame really that the Army, and in particular Army Intelligence, always kept themselves to themselves. Just as a number of other government departments did, the Army received weekly lists from the Ministry of Information relating to who was living at what addresses and then they enhanced that information with their own. There was also employment, medical and licensing information available from the MOI and usually the Army would add this to their own records. Any checks required by the Army in relation to road blocks, raids etc, any safety and intelligence checks were always done at their own offices so that nobody knew who the Army were looking at. Although this had obvious advantages and on balance would always have to be the way they did things it was a real shame. Had they gone to the MOI to get the check done, they would have been told that the Post Office was also making enquiries about the very same people at the very same address. The Army didn't always know everything.

The agent checked another sheet of details that had been printed. Their car, a yellow Mazda Celine, registration number CHL 25 BDG had been purchased by them that year. They must have some money the agent thought but then read on. The vehicle was purchased through the national disability group and was not costing the Hobbs as much as one might have thought. It came with the highest issued grade of parking badges so someone must have quite a disability. The badges were graded depending on the ability of the disabled person to get themselves from a car to a nearby office and it seemed from the issues that somebody was almost completely wheelchair bound. This might also explain the other niggling little point that the agent had yet to answer. Husband and wife traveling home from town but it was the wife who was driving. This was not normal but if it was Raymond who had the disability then that might explain it.

There had been a very new lead that suggested that the agents target was possibly living in Waydon but it seemed unlikely that it was at the Hobbs house. This new lead had not been properly checked out yet but Waydon was the main part of the address that went with it. The agent was hopeful that more would come from this latest lead but in the meantime was forced to go without it. The agent closed the file and got ready for the meeting with Major Tannier. As always, things went very smoothly and according to plan.

"Afternoon Major." The agent said.

"Hello again. Come in and sit down." The agent shut the door and sat down.

"Have you much for me?" The agent was hopeful that that was not a stupid question.

"Not a lot but we have some replies to the checks that you wanted done." The Major answered.

Most of these replies were to confirm that all checks on Brown, the Redbridges and Cleaveley had all proven to be negative. The agent wasn't exactly too surprised to hear this.

"I'm sorry to say that I'm not surprised but it had to be done." The agent said.

"Quite agree. Quite agree!" The Major concurred.

"And do we have anything back on the newspaper report or photographs?" The agent asked.

The major gave a huff and a big sigh. "As yet I have had nothing back but it is early days, I say it is early days and we mustn't expect too much." The Major was obviously annoyed at not having anything to give to the agent. There was a little bit more chit chat but not for long. The two of them went off in their usual everyday manners after a few questions and details had been swapped.

-

Gary sat at his desk composing his various reports about work done and checks made on the different bits of undeliverable or wrongly addressed mail. It was a slow, laborious job but at this very moment in time he was working on the Longhurst file which was of course able to make the job a lot more interesting. Firstly he had to log it on to the system and give it a reference number, or at least that's what he should have done but Gary decided to write the report first. He could then attach the report after he had logged the case. His concentration was broken by William knocking on his open office door.

"Hey boss, I'm just about to put the kettle on, can I have your cup," he said as he came in to pick Gary's cup up.

"No leave it Bill. I think I'll be skipping tea this morning."

"Yeah okay." William answered as he went back downstairs. As soon as he was out of sight, Gary pulled out a half bottle of whiskey from his bottom drawer and poured a little into his cup. Gary thought hard about what to put into the report. He could put the bit in about the Wellington boots but it didn't really prove anything. He could put the bit in about the two shadows moving in the front room but then it begged the question, 'what was Gary doing there to be able to see that?' No he would have to put in the bit about the degree of disability of Mr. Hobbs and his checks on all the Longhursts in the area. As a conclusion in his report, Gary wrote that the letter must be regarded as just simply being another piece of undeliverable mail due to it being addressed wrongly. Gary finished the report and then logged the case on to the system. The file was finished and ready to go up to the AP. Gary was pleased to see the end of that report. It was still worrying him that he couldn't place the surname but guessed it would come to him in time.

Gary thought about what he had out on his desk. He put a few files away but left the rest on his desk. He left his office and made his way downstairs to the Sorting Office floor. He then made his way in between the various tables and got to the back door which opened out to the yard which led to the garage to see if there was a vehicle available to use. There wasn't so Gary returned to his office where there were still a few more reports to complete which Gary carried on working on. The next one was a simple case of the occupant having moved away about three weeks before the letter arrived. Usually when people move they either make sure that everyone who is going to write to them knows what date they are moving or they pay to have a re-direction flag put on. Obviously this person, James Thompson, had tried to do everything himself but as often happens, had forgotten to inform someone of his new address. Gary would suggest that the letter goes to the Birmingham office, which was where Mr. Thompson had moved to, and allow them to deal with it.

Gary was starting to write this one off when the AP appeared.

"Gary. I see you have a case on a Mr. Longhurst," he said. Bloody hell that was quick, Gary thought.

"The one at Waydon?" Gary replied.

"Yes that's the one. What have you done with the file?" The AP said rather anxiously.
"It's in the tray ready to go up to you." Gary told him as he found the file and showed it to the AP to show him the name on it. He expected the AP to just say yes and leave.
"Good I'll take it now." The AP grabbed the file from Gary's hand.
"Okay fine." Gary answered, rather surprised at the AP's urgency. The AP opened the file and took out the envelope. He gave it a quick look and then checked to make sure that it had not been opened. He then gave Gary a little look.
"Everything seems to be in order." The AP turned and was gone, file and all. Now what was that all about Gary thought to himself as he took another swig from his cup. It was very unusual for the AP to come down and collect any files for a start. They would have always been delivered the following morning. On top of that, the AP actually knew that there was a case in existence. That was also quite unusual. Gary also realised that in fact it had only been put on the system about twenty minutes ago. It must have been one of those set-up bits of post that try and catch out Postal Service Managers. Gary had been caught once, he wasn't keen to have been caught again. He started to feel quite pleased with himself for not getting caught.

Gary carried on with his reports until about thirty minutes later when he was interrupted again but by the PM this time. It wasn't very often that the PM came down to Gary's office but here he was.
"Gary, how are things going?" The PM said as he came into Gary's office and sat down.
"Things are ticking over quite well Sir." Gary replied.
"And we've heard no more about young Billy Simpson?" The PM asked.
"I've heard nothing else at all." Gary lied. There was a rather noticeable pause as the PM seemed to pluck up courage to ask the next question. It was almost as if he was too embarrassed to ask it, but he did.
"I see you have a case on a Mr. Longhurst on the system."
"Yes." Gary nodded whilst giving the PM a curious look.
"You've finished with the file?" The PM asked.
"My report is all done."
"Just wondered if I could have a look at the file please?" The PM tried to make it sound like this was an everyday request when it was very

much the opposite.

"I would do Sir except that the AP has got it." Gary replied. Once again the PM paused a while as he took in just what Gary had told him.

"Naturally I suppose, you would take it straight up to him. That would be the normal thing to do. Shame!" The PM replied.

"No he came down and got it. I'd have left it till tomorrow morning. The AP wanted the file straightaway." Gary told him but felt he should have known. Sometimes management up there just didn't have a clue what is going on.

"Okay, thanks Gary. Keep up the good work." The PM went back upstairs to his office. Gary was flabbergasted at these couple of incidents. Not only did the AP know about the case and want the file but the PM knew about it and wanted it too. Even if he hadn't before, he was sure it was a set-up now.

The rest of the day went quite smoothly and soon the clock was showing the time as a quarter past five. It was getting late but Gary knew that the AP was still working in his office upstairs and as Gary's official time to leave was not until five thirty, he thought he had better hang on a little bit. It was nearly half past five when the AP came back down to Gary's office. He had obviously had a busy day from the look of the AP, shirt sleeves rolled up, tie and collar undone and generally looking tired.

"Gary I need to see you for a while but I have some work I've got to finish first. It'll take me about another half an hour can you hold on please?" The AP asked. Although phrased as a request it was really meant as an order.

"No problem. Just give me a shout when you want me." Gary answered with the only answer he could really give.

"Thanks Gary." The AP went back upstairs and Gary continued with his work.

It wasn't very often that either the AP or the PM would want to talk to Gary in their office and usually if it happened, it would be because of some sort of reprimand that needed to be handed out to one of the staff. Gary guessed that this too might be the situation but wasn't sure. The time dragged and Gary was seeming to look at the clock about every five minutes. Gary continued working on a few files as much as he could but of course his mind was on other things.

It was ten past six before the AP came back to Gary's office. "Gary if you could shut down everything you're doing, lock up as if you are getting ready to go home but then come up to my office please." The AP said this again in a way that it was an order rather than a request. Gary gathered as many files as he could and then made his way up to the AP's office. The PM's office was in complete darkness so he was obviously not aware of what was going on. Gary knocked on the AP's door.
"Come in Gary, don't wait on ceremony." The AP was treating Gary quite civilly which was a good sign. "I've called you in here about the Longhurst case." The AP started. This didn't come as any great surprise at all to Gary.
"Oh the Longhurst case! I'm surprised!" Gary answered.
"Why are you surprised?"
"Well it seemed like quite a basic case. Wrong address! Undeliverable!" Gary explained.
"You saw it as quite a normal case then. Please just tell me what checks you did on it." The AP wanted a blow by blow account of the enquiry from when the first postman got it.

Gary went through the case bit by bit and completely from memory. The case was so fresh in his mind, he didn't need to refer to the file at all. Gary carried on with the relating of the enquiry for about forty minutes. The AP would ask for clarification on certain aspects but generally let Gary talk. Gary went through nearly everything he had done, although of course he left out certain aspects of it, and then concluded by saying that his report in the file summed up his thoughts. The AP stood up with the file in his hand and started to walk about.
"I'm a bit confused Gary."
"Why so?" Gary gave his most innocent look.
"It's just that you have done certain things with this case that you don't usually do and I'm wondering why." The AP sounded worried.
"Like what Sir?" Gary asked.
"Well you started working on this case three or four days ago but only logged it on to the system when you had finished with it this morning. That is not normal practice and in fact not as per your job guidelines is it?" The AP sat back down.
"No it's not the normal way of doing things but I picked this letter up

when I first saw it as I was on my way out to look at another letter in the Waydon area that I was going to look at." As soon as the words had been said, Gary thought what a stupid thing to say. Shit, he had gone out to look at the bloody school and this wasn't logged officially either. In fact not only was this not officially logged, there was no letter to actually go and investigate. Gary could feel a bead of sweat start to form on his forehead. Nevertheless, he continued. "So I hadn't logged it on to the system before I left and just decided to leave it till I'd finished." Gary looked at the AP who was thinking. "It isn't what I would call unusual as it happens from time to time, I know it is technically wrong but don't consider it as an offence. Sometimes when you are in a hurry you do things for ease, to speed things up rather than worrying about every rule and regulation. Surely you're not going to tell me that you've never broken a rule." Gary finished summing up his defence. The AP listened to what Gary had to say and even took a couple of notes but then continued, completely ignoring the question that had been fired back at him.

"I also have to ask you why you sat outside the Hobbs house watching it on at least two occasions?" The AP asked. Gary was taken by surprise at this question and his first thought was that the soldier must have reported him after all as Gary had left any mention of observations out of his report. He hadn't mentioned it to the AP in his verbal report either so the soldier must have gone against his word but then Gary realised that the soldier hadn't been aware that he had been watching the house on the first occasion. Gary was quite certain about this as he had easily seen the soldiers being dropped off at the bottom of the road from his car and therefore they couldn't have seen him the first time, or at least not as far as Gary had been able to tell. It therefore must have been someone else who had seen him.

He took in a deep breath and replied.
"I just thought I might see someone male arriving at the house who would have to be someone other than Mr. Hobbs. I really only did it on the off chance." Gary replied.
"What's more you haven't mentioned it at all in your report. Nor to me." The AP stared at Gary as he said this last bit.
"Nothing happened. It seemed irrelevant." Gary replied. Gary sat and thought. It looked like he had got himself into trouble here. Fortunately it seemed that the AP was not fully appraised of everything as he didn't pick up on the other apparent unauthorised

visit. The AP never even asked or mentioned about the other visit in Waydon. Sometimes Gary was lucky.

"Thanks Gary for being frank and honest. I don't think I need to ask you anything else." The AP looked at his watch. "In fact it's high time we both went home."

"Yes boss it is pretty late." Gary replied. "My wife will be wondering where I've got to."

"Does she worry a lot then?" The AP asked.

"No not a lot. Just when I'm extra late. Perhaps I should ring her but then if I get my foot down I'll be home in fifteen minutes." Gary concluded.

"No I don't advise you go home at this time of night in your own car." The AP said.

"It'll be alright."

"Not if you're traveling fast so as to get home quicker. No you must ring the Army Control and arrange for an escort or a lift." The AP gave Gary another one of those orders.

"But they can take ages to sort out." Gary replied in a negative manner.

"In fact I'll arrange for Army transport home for you." The AP insisted. Gary obviously wasn't keen from the tone of his answers and although originally he tried very hard to reject the AP's offer he knew in the end he had little choice in the matter. It actually only took about fifteen minutes for the Army jeep to arrive at the Sorting Office. Both Gary and the AP walked to the jeep. The AP spoke to the driver.

"Are you taking both of us?"

"No Sir, there should be another jeep along any second." The driver explained.

"You're rather in a hurry to get home Gary I'll let you take the first one." The AP took a step back after saying this and Gary was allowed to get into the first jeep.

"Thank you Sir. See you tomorrow." Gary shouted at the AP but his voice was drowned out by the sound of a second jeep just pulling round the corner. Gary looked at his driver.

"Where to Sir?" The soldier who was driving asked.

"Waydon please!" Gary replied.

    As the Army jeep stopped outside of Gary's house, the person in his front garden hid behind some bushes so that they could not be seen.

"Do you need picking up in the morning Mr. Newson?" the soldier driving the jeep asked.
"No I can get in myself, thanks."
"Okay, straight in now, the curfew is in full flow don't forget," the soldier warned Gary as he drove off. Gary stood and watched the jeep turn out of his road before turning towards his front door and bracing himself ready to face the inevitable wrath of Angela. Gary checked again whilst slowly walking up the front path making sure he didn't have any keys in his pocket as he came to a halt and just stood at the front door considering his options before deciding what to do next. He could just knock on the door or could try to see if the handle was unlocked. Obviously he knew that because of the alarms almost certainly being set, as soon as he pushed the handle down it would set the alarm off. He paused for a short moment to compose himself before taking his decisive action when he suddenly became aware that there was a sound and some sort of movement in his garden.
"Sammy is that you?" Gary said in his best doggy type voice as he bent down looking to the lower part of the bushes where a dog might be.
"Er no, sorry it's me," came the reply from the bushes as Julie Clark emerged into the light. She quickly brushed herself down a bit just a little embarrassed at how she had to emerge from the bushes and especially in front of someone she didn't really know that well. She felt a little bit like a burglar having been caught climbing out of a window with a bag of swag over her shoulder but this was not what went through Gary's mind. It was almost as if a Broadway star had made her dramatic entrance on to the stage. On the pavement next to Gary's garden was a street lamp which as Julie appeared from the bushes shone straight onto her almost like a spotlight. As Julie walked towards him, Gary could do nothing but watch. His attention was taken like a rabbit in car headlights. His stare was transfixed as this vision of beauty seemed to be performing just for him.

   It took Gary a few moments to snap out of it.
"Oh Miss Clark, I thought you were in London." Gary said.
"I returned this evening," she replied.
"Has everything been sorted out then?" Gary continued to question her.
"No the case against me has been adjourned whilst I prepare my defence." Julie replied.

"Oh right, Miss Clark," Gary said bit by bit not really knowing what else to say. "So have you been round for your papers?"
"No I've come back for my diary which is at home." Julie replied. "Call me Julie by the way," she added. Gary nodded not really understanding what she was talking about. There was another one of those obvious pauses.
"So you've come to have a look at my garden?" Gary said with a strange look on his face.

Both looked at each other and had the look of not really understanding what was going on. It was then almost instantaneous as the two of them burst out laughing.
"It seems a bit funny but I was actually hiding from the Army jeep. I don't want the Army knowing I'm here but I suppose you'll be telling them now." Julie said sadly. Gary thought this a bit of a strange thing to say but then realised that Julie must think that he was part of the Army having been driven home like he was.
"Oh no, I'm nothing to do with the Army. It is just that I was late leaving work tonight and my boss insisted that the Army had to bring me home." Gary tried to explain. Julie wasn't that convinced.
"Soldiers are searching my house at the moment." Julie continued.
"Oh I see!" Gary lied again not fully understanding what Miss Clark was talking about.
"Would it be putting you and Angela out if I asked if I could just sleep at yours tonight?" Julie asked then smiled one of her sexier smiles in an effort to get the reply she wanted.
"Oh I wouldn't think that would be a problem."
"I need to get back to London tomorrow and with any luck the Army would have finished searching by the morning." Julie continued to explain but Gary wasn't really listening. His mind had wandered to the thought of Julie Clark sleeping, and in his house. It was a bit unusual for Gary to have thoughts like this but he had to admit to being turned on by her and not being averse to the possibility of seeing her in her night clothes. Gary quickly snapped out of it again.

He made his way back to the front door which opened as he approached. Angela had obviously heard some noise and had guessed that it was Gary but she had opened the door without looking properly. Without waiting at all, Angela left the door and made her way quickly back towards the living room. Gary beckoned Julie to make her way

in and hid behind her.
"And just where the fucking hell……..." Angela launched into an angry string of abuse which was obviously aimed at Gary from the living room until it was stopped short in its tracks as Angela stormed out from the living room to see Julie Clark in the hallway. "I'm sorry. I don't usually swear. What are you doing here? I thought you were in London?" Angela said as she invited Julie into the living room. Julie went through the routine of explaining to Angela what she was doing asking for somewhere to sleep for the night. Gary just added halfway through that he had already said it would be okay for her to stay and although Angela didn't really have any great problems with it, wasn't too pleased that he had taken the decision without discussing it with her first. Julie tried to make things a bit easier by saying that she would sleep under a blanket on the sofa and also that she would be out of the house by six thirty so that the girls didn't know. Angela
was happier with this arrangement. Julie was true to her word.

    The next morning Gary was up at his usual time of six fifteen. Although this was always the time he got up he had hoped that it would also be early enough to see Julie Clark before she left so that he could apologise for the way Angela and he had seemed to argue about her staying. Julie had already left. Gary went into the bathroom as usual and then returned to the bedroom to get dressed. Angela was already up and out of bed which was unusual. Gary went downstairs and Angela was there waiting for him.
"She's gone." Gary said.
"Yes I can see that." Angela replied looking away from Gary.
"She'd already gone by the time I got up."
"Oh did you come down to make her a cup of tea?" Angela said in her sarcastic voice.
"Just to see if she needed the bathroom."
"Why did you agree to letting her stay in the first place?"
"I didn't." Gary replied in a high pitched astonishment. "I just said there was no problem as far as I was concerned. She's your bloody friend." Gary's voice had risen in volume.
"Well you were obviously quite friendly coming home with her last night." Angela continued her attack as she got angrier.
"I found her hiding in the garden if you must know." Gary replied
"Oh yeah that's very likely, Julie hiding under one of our bushes." Angela's tone was sarcastic but Gary knew she wouldn't ever believe

him.

"Believe what you bloody want." Gary said as he walked down the hallway and passed Angela, knocking against her slightly as he did. Angela over reacted to the physical contact by pretending to almost lose her balance.

"Don't bloody push me out of the way!" Angela shouted at him. "If you want me out of the way just say so." Angela added.

"Don't be such a stupid cow!" Gary replied from the kitchen. Angela ran back upstairs whilst Gary put on his coat and got ready for work. He went to the front door and opened it. Sammy was there jumping up at him and Gary gave him a little pat on the head. "Goodbye girls." Gary shouted.

"Bye Dad," replies came from Joan and Katy.

"Goodbye Angela." Gary shouted. He waited ten or maybe fifteen seconds. There was no reply.

It had been another usual day at work at the Sorting Office. It was a new experience catching the bus in to work but Gary met a few people he hadn't seen for a number of years and chatted to a few people he had never met before. All very different! Work was no different though. The AP had been in for a while during the morning but said nothing about last nights little session and the PM was not in at all again today. Gary had very little option but to just get on with whatever work he could. After all the problems yesterday had brought, added to the fact that Gary was pleased to have got his car back, Gary decided that today he should get away from work a little bit earlier than usual and managed to get home at just about half past four. As he walked in the girls were there to greet him.

"Hello Daddy." Katy was the first to give him a kiss.

"Hello Dad." Joan was only a couple of seconds behind.

"Are you girls okay?" Gary asked them both as they clung to his hands.

"Yes Dad." Both girls answered. Gary looked at each girl in turn and thought to himself how proud he was.

"We did some work on inventions today." Joan told Gary. "We learnt about aeroplanes, rocket engines and motor cars. All about how they work and what fuel they use and the effect it has on the Earth." She added. "It tells us that we shouldn't allow cars to let off dirty smoke into the air and not to help big companies burn horrible fossil fuels." Joan added.

"We did lessons on different religions of the world." Katy added not wanting to be left out.

"Oh that's good." Gary answered both of them. "Have you got your school books here so I can have a look?" Gary asked. Neither daughter was keen to show either parent their school books so it was almost as if that question had never been asked.

"Can we go out and play in the front garden Mum." Joan asked.

"Yes for a little while." Angela shouted the reply from the living room.

"But I thought you were going to show me your work?" Gary said to Joan.

"We haven't got time now Daddy. Maybe later." She replied. The two girls immediately put their coats on and went out to the front garden to play. Gary shrugged his shoulders and stepped into the living room.

"I'm sorry about this morning. Is everything alright?" He asked Angela.

"Yes I guess so. You had another bloody phone call. Same person! Still no message!"

"When did they ring?" Gary asked looking a bit puzzled.

"Oh about half an hour ago." She replied. Gary scratched his head as he thought long and hard trying to work out who it might be on the phone and what they might want.

"I'm getting bloody fed up with all this." Angela started but although she wanted to go on complaining she had the sense that anything she could say would inevitably be a waste of time. She was fuming but she tried to hide it. Gary on the other hand could immediately sense her annoyance. He said nothing.

As Gary was home at a reasonable time this evening, Sammy was taken on his usual walk down the back lane. There were still not too many people about taking their dogs for a walk and Gary was surprised to see another bloke out walking his dog coming towards them. I wonder if this is the stranger who takes his dog out at night as well. As the other dog walker approached, Gary could see that he had a boxer dog. Not a big boxer dog but one that seemed like a young but fully grown male and all black in colour. This was not a dog Gary had seen before. Sammy was minding his own business but the boxer wasn't going to let Sammy pass without a fuss. The dog growled and pulled at his leash trying to get to Sammy. His owner seemingly struggling to keep hold of him.

"He's always like this," the other owner said embarrassingly.

"Will he bite?" Gary asked slightly concerned.

"I'm not absolutely sure," the reply came. This didn't inspire any confidence in Gary who kept Sammy as far away as he could. The boxer finally passed without any incident. Gary knew that this wasn't the stranger he often heard during the hours of darkness. It was strange though how people you could only hear but not see always formed an impression in your mind as to how they probably looked. More often than not this idea was nothing like how they actually looked.

     Gary thought back to those days long ago when he was first involved in the underground movements of Kentley or at least attending meetings and rallies on a regular basis. It all started of course when he went looking for his brother David after his younger brother had started to not return home after meetings. The fact was that Gary was more or less compelled to go to the same meetings as David to ensure that David came home again. It was the only way that Gary could ensure that peace remained in the Newson household. But Gary had started to look forward to going to these meetings for other reasons. Most such meetings would be held in run down or boarded up old shops or in their storerooms where there was no lighting or power. All the meetings seemed to be the same. A few would have brought some form of lighting with them, candles, torches, matches or if you were really lucky a lamp but regardless of what was available it still meant that most of the gatherers were standing in the shadows or darkness most of the time. At one of those very early meetings Gary recalled hearing a young girl asking a question of the speakers and as usual his mind had not been fully tuned in to what was happening but as soon as he heard her voice it was like an angel was singing from Heaven. Gary tried hard to make out who it was who was talking but apart from knowing it was a girl somewhere to his right, and to the front of the crowd, he could see nothing. Gary heard this girl's voice again at a later meeting and he knew that he just had to meet her. He had already formed this idea in his mind of what she might look like and after the latter meeting where he had heard her speak, as the gatherers were leaving he stood just outside the doorway from the closed down shop asking every female if they had the time or a cigarette or a light. Gary watched as each one he asked answered in a completely different voice to the one he had hoped to hear. Everyone except the speakers had left. Gary went back in to the room and for the first time cast his eyes on this beautiful young girl. Time more or less stood still for a while until the girl came over to Gary.

"It was a good meeting again tonight wasn't it?" The girl said to him. Her voice was everything he had imagined it would be. She was everything he had hoped she would be. Gary was in love.

"Er yes. Very interesting!" Gary just about answered her. "Are you coming to the next meeting?" Gary managed to add.

"I would think so," she replied. "And you?"

"Oh yes, I'll definitely be there." Gary replied as the young girl smiled at him and almost lit the whole room. The girl turned around to where the speakers were collecting their books and papers together.

"John, are you ready yet?" The girl said.

"Yes I'm on my way," one of the main speakers said as he walked over to the young girl and put his arm around her shoulder. "Come on let's get home." The two of them turned to leave the run down room and Gary stared at this man's hand clutching the girl's arm. He looked for signs of discomfort from the girl but it was obvious that she was quite happy with the closeness that had all of a sudden appeared. Gary's heart sunk. It was a strange feeling that in such a short time he could see for the first time a girl who he would fall in love with and then allow to break his heart. It had all happened in about three minutes which was quite some going. The couple walked towards the door but stopped just before reaching it. The young girl turned to Gary.

"Look forward to seeing you at the next meeting," the girl said. The couple continued on their way out as Gary stood motionless. He could hear the man asking the girl 'Who was that?' as they walked away. Gary felt devastated as he made his way home. He didn't go to the next three meetings.

It was nearly a month before Gary was coerced into going to another meeting. Apart from the fact that David had not returned home for a couple of days after the last meeting that Gary had decided not to go to, Gary had been spoken to in the streets that very day and questioned as to why he had not been to the last few meetings. He remembered giving some feeble excuse about being ill and then realising that he had no get out from attending tonight's meeting. Having no real excuse and needing to keep an eye on David again,

Gary felt he had little choice but to go to the meeting. All the way there, Gary was very concerned that the young girl with the angel's voice would be there at that meeting but at least he was pleased to find that that night's meeting was being held in a room where full light could be put on. Gary looked around but the young girl was not there. The speaker who she had left with on that night, was not at the top table either. Gary tried to concentrate on what was being said. It was a talk on a typical subject about how the European Army were again sending our boys and girls to war just so that they could be killed. Something a little bit different at this meeting was that somebody had been specially invited to attend the meeting and had actually turned up. He was a journalist from the local paper who had agreed to be at the meeting and was being grilled as to why such information could not get into the papers if it came from an anonymous source. The newspaper man tried to explain but nobody was that pleased about his reasonings. The journalist was explaining how the authorities would demand to see the anonymous note and would tip the offices upside down trying to find the real author of the note and then they would probably shut the paper down for a number of weeks just to be awkward. People at this meeting started to shout abusively at the journalist and the meeting was starting to get a bit out of control. The top table had had enough and called for silence just before declaring the meeting at an end. There was a bit of pushing and shoving and a definite feeling of annoyance but Gary just prepared to make his way home when somebody tapped him on his shoulder.
"Hello again. I've missed you. You didn't get to the last few meetings did you?" It was the young girl. Gary felt a shiver run up his spine as her voice sung out like a songbird. To then realise that she was talking to him made his knees go weak. He turned and saw the same young girl standing there.
"Oh sorry, but I've not been very well and couldn't make them." Gary tried to sound as convincing as possible. He looked at her smiling face and all the previous thoughts of the fact that she had a bloke, just went straight out of his mind. "It's nice to see you again. You light up the place with your charming smile," Gary added. As he said it he thought to himself, what the bloody hell did I just say!!
"Oh how nice of you to say such things." The girl replied. "Which way do you have to go to go home?"
"I'm heading through the Market Place." Gary answered.

"Oh that's good you can walk me most of the way home then, if you don't mind that is?" The girl all of a sudden blushed at the thought of being very forward. "Sorry, I didn't mean to sound presumptuous." The girl said.

"No problem but I don't want any trouble with your boyfriend." Gary felt he ought to say.

"What boyfriend?" The Girl replied giving Gary a strange look.

"The one you were with at the meeting." Gary answered. The girl paused and then laughed out loud. "You mean John, one of the organizers."

"Yes that'll be him," Gary replied.

"You silly fool! He's my brother." The girl put her arm in Gary's and rested her head on his arm. "Now are you going to take me home or what?" The girl said to him.

"I'll gladly take you home," Gary said not believing his luck.

"Good. I'm Angela. What's your name?" Gary couldn't believe that his angel was called Angela. Gary just excused himself for a few seconds whilst he made sure that David was also making his way home. David looked across at the girl waiting and said he wouldn't upset things tonight. It was like all of Gary's dreams were coming true. Neither Gary nor Angela missed any of the next few meetings and spent hours walking home afterwards chatting about nothing and gazing into each others eyes. They were both madly in love with each other.

Gary was all of a sudden aware of the phone ringing. He had been in a bit of a dream and hadn't heard it at first.

"Hello." Angela said as she answered the phone. "Yes he's here." Gary could hear Angela speaking. Her manner on the phone was pleasant and calm which was in total contrast to her next words.

"Gary it's for you!" Angela shouted from the hallway. As Gary came into the hallway, Angela had her hand held over the phone's mouthpiece and she held a finger up to her mouth to instruct Gary to be quiet.

"It's him!" Angela whispered to Gary. Gary took the phone.

"Hello, Gary here." There was a brief silence on the other end but the sound of breathing.

"I can't say much but is that Gary?" The voice on the other end said. Gary recognised the voice but it wasn't the dog walking stranger, nor the other dog walker he had heard this evening.

"Yes who is that?" Gary asked.
"It's Billy. Billy Simpson. Look I need to see you. Are you at home tomorrow evening?" Billy asked. Gary paused and thought for a moment.
"I should be." He replied.
"I've got to go." Billy said hurriedly. There was the sound of screeching brakes and running but nothing else.
"Hello, are you there? Is there anybody there?" Gary asked in vain as the phone went dead. Gary didn't have long enough to confirm to his complete satisfaction but he thought the voice did sound like Billy's.
"Who was it then?" Angela asked as she heard the phone being hung up.
"Well I think it was young Billy Simpson from work. You know the young lad who's gone missing." Gary told her.
"Oh yes another of those revolutionary louts that you're not getting involved with. Phoning here nearly everyday! And you keep telling me that you're not involved with these anarchists. They only lead to trouble you know." Angela had said her bit. Gary knew better than to answer her back. Whatever he said, she would probably be able to twist it round against him.

-

The time was getting on and Major Tannier was ready to go home. He'd had a long day and was looking forward to a nice meal with his wife and a nice relaxing evening in front of the fire. It was 16.50hrs when there was a knock at the door.
"Come in," the Major answered. His office door opened and a scrawny little man with dark short greasy hair poked his head inside.
"Come in man, I haven't got all bloody day," the Major shouted with a little aggression.
"Yes hello I'm Lawrence Dolbert from the Recorder," the man said rather sheepishly.
"You mean that reporter fellow," the Major bellowed at him. He looked at his watch and continued, "Absolutely bloody useless you lot. You're late. You were supposed to be here about an hour and a half ago but let's see if we can sort something out."
The reporter was directed to a chair and the Major walked around and shut the door. He opened his mouth a couple of times as if to start to speak but just made a huffing noise whilst he calmed down. The reporter started speaking first.

"What is it that you want me to report on Major?" He said in a squeaky sort of voice.

"No you get the wrong idea lad". The Major opened up a drawer of his desk and pulled out the newspaper report on the shooting incident last week. The paper was all folded back so that the report was on the front page. He threw the paper on to the desk in front of the reporter. As he did this the reporter jumped.

"Did you get clearance for this report?" He barked at the reporter.

"No. I didn't think I needed clearance." He replied. Although looking like a frightened animal caught in a poacher's snare, the reporter didn't get where he was today without knowing the rules. Even more importantly, knowing which ones he could break. He knew there was no clearance required for this.

"Well actually you're quite right," the Major confirmed for him. He paused a second in order to add atmosphere to his next sentence. "But you do for the photograph!"

The reporter was now in deeper water. There may well be rules about printing such a photograph as it contained scenes that may be considered as 'matters of war' which he knew he would have trouble with. The reporter wasn't completely up to date with the rules and regulations on photographs.

"Did you take the photograph?" The Major asked him.

"Yes," the reporter answered hurriedly.

"I don't believe you!" The Major replied.

"Honest, I just happened to be there on my way home when the shooting happened. I had a camera with me and managed to get a couple of shots off during all the confusion," the reporter said quite unconvincingly.

"Are you trying to tell me that you were in the queue of traffic, realised there was going to be a shooting and crept up to a position to take a photograph without anyone noticing." The Major looked at him as he said this and just shook his head.

"Well I was in the queue of cars but only had to get out of my car to take the photo." Still the reporter didn't sound too convincing.

"I take it you have registered the camera with the authorities?" The Major knew that most of the media would have a camera registered. It was common practice just in case they needed to take a photo but thought it might throw the reporter. It didn't.

"Of course!" The reply was said most confidently and gave the reporter a sense of beginning to get the upper hand.

"And where is your camera now?" The Major held his hand out. The reporter felt in his pockets, banged his coat up and down and then concluded, "I've left it in the office". There was a short pause as the Major came over and stared at the reporter straight in the eyes.

"I don't believe you". "I could probably have you arrested now on suspicion of obtaining camera film illegally or some such ridiculous offence but that's not what this is all about". The Major lowered the volume of his voice and sat down next to the reporter. "Just tell me who the photographer was and we'll get this sorted ever so quickly". The Major knew of course that there was no offence but guessed that his reporter wasn't quite so sure.

"I don't know who took the photograph," the reporter tried vainly to withhold the identity of his photographer friend. The Major took another look at his watch and thought for a second.

"Now I want to be home soon so as this little problem doesn't seem to be getting anywhere I think we'll start again tomorrow." The Major said out loud.

"What time do you want me in here tomorrow then?" The reporter asked.

"No I cannot trust you to be here at anytime tomorrow so you'll stay here overnight." The Major picked up the phone on his desk. "Can you inform the Custody Sergeant that I'll be bringing him an overnight prisoner over," the Major said before slamming the phone down.

"I can get you all of the photographs that were taken if you want." The reporter sighed as he admitted defeat.

"And negatives?"

"Yes I can get the whole lot. There aren't that many anyway," the reporter continued.

"Okay. Wait there a minute and I'll arrange transport" the Major picked up his phone. There were a couple of rings on the other end and the sound of a voice. The Major listened and then ordered for a jeep with a driver to be in his office in ten minutes. The reporter tried to intervene during the call but the Major was having none of it. The phone was put down with the usual bang.

"I can't take you to the place Major," the reporter said rather sheepishly again.

"Your choice son! Either we go and get the films and negatives now or you're locked up pending our enquiries into your crimes. Now what is it to be?" The Major had lost patience by now. He took another look at his watch and could see this evening disappearing out of the window. The reporter said nothing and was obviously turning things over in his mind. The Army wouldn't really lock him up would they? He pondered on that thought and decided in the end that they probably would.

"As long as I go to the door alone we can do it," the reporter finally spoke.

"Yes as long as we don't lose sight of you." The Major replied and a deal was struck.

Almost immediately there was a knock at the door. The Major barked out, "Enter," and in came a private in full uniform.

"Vehicle ready and waiting, Sir." The Private stood to attention and saluted as he finished his words. The Major turned to him and returned the salute and then led the three of them out of his office. Once they had all left he locked the office behind him. They made their way through corridors to the front desk and out to the waiting jeep. The Major indicated to the reporter that he should get into the front seat whilst he got into the back of the jeep.

"Just down to the Guardroom so I can book the vehicle out and tell them about the change of plan regarding overnight prisoners" the Major said as he tapped the reporter hard on the shoulder. The Private started to speak. "But Major I….." The Major interrupted immediately, "Probably so Private but don't argue."

The major spent about five minutes in the Guardroom before coming back out to the jeep. "Finally got it all sorted" the Major said as he got back into the jeep. "Sometimes the boys in the Guardroom just don't know their elbows from their arses," he spoke mainly to the Private. "There is some activity going on with a jeep already been attacked by stone throwing youths this evening so we're being told to be careful," the Major turned from the Private and spoke to the reporter.

"That's one story you won't be working on tonight. Now whereabouts is this house we're going to Mr. Dolbert?" The Major asked.

"I can't tell you where it is." The reporter replied.

"Don't be stupid son. We're going there so we're going to know where it is anyway. For all of our safety, I need to report to the Radio Room where this Army vehicle is going so tell us where." The reporter again thought for a while and decided it made some sense to tell him.

"Yes well we're going to Garden Lane down by the Bateley Road. Do you know it?" The reporter asked.

"Yes I know it," the Major replied. It was quite a run down area and Garden Lane itself ran on to Downley Road where there had been lots of problems before. The Major picked up the radio mic.

"This is Major Tannier out working on Hotel fourteen stroke four. Do you read?" There was a little static interference but the radio room responded quite quickly.

"Hotel fourteen stroke four. Confirm please?" The reply came.

"That is correct. All details are with the Guardroom," the Major continued.

"Yes Sir, we'll update our instructions. Position please?" The voice on the radio asked.

"We're now approaching Ferry Bridge and our destination is Garden Lane, repeat Garden Lane. Do you copy?" The Major made sure that they knew exactly where they were headed.

"Message received and understood. Radio Room out!" The jeep chugged along its way making slow progress but getting down eventually to Garden Lane. The Major leant forward to the reporter. "Now where exactly does he live?"

"Right at the end on the right hand side." The reporter pointed to the end house. Garden Lane was a funny road as it had originally only been built as an access road to the allotments that run by the side of Bateley Road but then had joined up with some other residential roads to the east and someone decided that they ought to build houses on it. There wasn't a lot of building room on Garden Lane hence only thirteen houses in total were on it. The jeep pulled up outside number thirteen and the Major indicated to Lawrence Dolbert that he should get out and visit the house.

"Go on then. Keep in sight." The Major told him.

"What if nobody's in?" The reporter asked as an afterthought.

"There are lights on. Someone is in."

The reporter got out of the jeep and tidied his jacket whilst preparing himself for the awkward situation he was going to have with Micky Dawson. As the reporter entered the front garden of the house, the Major picked up the radio microphone.

"Unit Tango Seven, please report your position," the Major said as he turned and smiled at the Private.

"Round the corner in Downley Road Sir." The reply came.

"Stand-by!" The Major finished as he looked back towards the house. The reporter was at the front door and looking back over his shoulder at the jeep. The front door opened and in he went.

"Unit Tango Seven please deploy to raid 13, Garden Lane," the Major gave the instructions to the waiting Unit. All the paperwork for the raid had been done back in the Guardroom. The Unit got their door opener ready but rang on the door bell first in case they could gain entrance that way. They were surprised to find Micky Dawson open the door.

"Warrant to search!" The warning was shouted at Micky by the Unit Sergeant as his Unit rushed passed and made sure that every room was safe.

"What's this all about?" Micky said.

"Just sit down there." The Sergeant pushed him into a settee in the Hall.

"Only two others here Sir!" Came the word from the Corporal in charge of security.

"Both under arrest?" The Sergeant asked.

"Yes Sir."

The Major now entered the Garden Lane premises. He looked at Micky Dawson sat on the settee. "Mr. Dawson."

"What's this all about? Are you in charge?" Dawson replied.

"Yes I'm in charge."

"So what is this all about?" Micky Dawson repeated.

"You've been taking unofficial photographs!" The Major said to him.

"I'm a photographer. It's my job to take photographs."

"You took some at a roadblock over the road last week?" The Major asked him.

"Yes but none contravene the law surely?" Micky Dawson was at last happy to know exactly why they had raided his home.

"How many did you take?" The Major asked him.

"Just the one film. Everything's out the back in my studio. You want to see them?" He asked the Major.

"Yes please." With that, the Major and Micky Dawson went out to the studio and Dawson went straight to a filing cabinet. Various folders were flicked through until he came to the one he wanted. Inside the folder was an envelope with photographs in and the cut negatives in protective paper. Micky Dawson handed the lot to the Major.

"This is what you want."

"Are all the photographs developed?" The Major asked him.

"Pretty much. There may be one or two I didn't bother to print out."

"And all the prints?"

"All there except one. The paper will have that," Micky Dawson answered.

"Thank you Mr. Dawson. You've been very co-operative," the Major said to him. He then turned to the Sergeant who had followed both of them to the studio. The Major continued, "Check this place over in case you come across anything he shouldn't have. If there is, lock him up overnight and I'll interview him tomorrow." The Sergeant nodded as a gesture of understanding. The Major turned back to Dawson, "Continue to be helpful and everyone will be out of here quicker," the Major told him. He then turned back to the Sergeant, "Dolberts house should also be turned over looking for anything to do with his report on the shooting incident. Don't worry if you make a mess there. He too is to be locked up overnight." The Major concluded.

The Sergeant saluted, "Understood Sir," and the Major returned the salute and left the house.

-

Corporal Matthew King had now been out of hospital a couple of days and he was well into his rehabilitation programme. His ligament would take a little while to heal properly but he hoped to be able to be back on light duties by Monday. Before then was the big Kentley Bash and he didn't want to miss that if he could help it. It was unlikely that Rachel and Ed would be well enough to attend but he would be there. It was a big function being planned at Kentley Barracks. It was a Saturday night which was great and it was the annual bash where a lot of soldiers let their hair down but it was also a celebration of sixty years of Kentley Barracks being in existence. Just think of it, sixty years. There had been a big party along similar lines ten years ago but the Commander in charge of the base was determined to make sure that they had an even bigger and better party this year. Although arrangements were all marked top secret, invitations went out to about a hundred ex-members of the currently serving Units at Kentley but only if they had actually served at Kentley. There were six different Units based at Kentley but also a number of other military and civilian people connected to the base.

Firstly on the military side, Kentley had an Intelligence section based there. There wasn't an Intelligence section at every base and the size of the section varied a lot normally based on the number of agents being run. Although there was of course Major Tannier he had under him a small team of four uniformed officers, one Corporal and three Privates who would keep records up to date. They would also help with the everyday running of checks, planning certain things plus of course major Tannier had his own secretary working on similar things but mainly those concerning major Tannier. The agents who were being run from Kentley were naturally all Army personnel but nobody was allowed to know who they were or what their agent name was. This of course made it difficult to send them invitations but they would never consider coming to a party like this and showing out anyway. There was also the 'Red caps' on base. The Military Police! They again only had a staff of one Sergeant, four Corporals and four Privates. They would all get invites but apart from the Sergeant it was unlikely that any of them would attend. They tended to also keep themselves to themselves.

  Lastly there were serving army personnel from the Catering, Medical and Transport Corps who were based at Kentley. The Catering staff, who also had additional civilian employees would be very busy anyway. Food was one of the main ingredients of a successful party and preparation for the event would have been going on for months. In addition to the military, there would also be civilian staff working on the base, in the shops mainly. These caused the biggest threat to the base but would all get an invitation to the party even if it was only given to them two or three days beforehand. Lastly there were husbands, wives and partners of serving Army personnel that were not Army personnel themselves. If partners lived on base they would have already been given a security clearance but for those who lived off base, requests had to be made to get them on base and all names checked out to a satisfactory degree before being allowed to be invited. As you can guess, for the Commander, it was a security nightmare.

  One of the Units from Chale had been borrowed for the evening and night watches but certain functions like the radio room and the guard-house had to be manned by Kentley soldiers. The main function would be starting at about eight o'clock and wasn't expected to finish much before two in the morning. A system was set up to cover the two functions from seven till three on a sort of volunteer basis. This was not a new concept and usually worked quite well. Each Unit was asked to provide six volunteers who would work a shift of either an hour or an hour and a half with the Chale Unit adding back up support. The Majors were all in agreement at the plan and guaranteed that they would supply enough volunteers, even if they weren't actually volunteers. It gave everyone the chance to get to the big party at some time with most able to let down their hair and relax. There were of course the entertainers to consider as well but they would be escorted all the time they were on base and unlikely to be able to get into any real trouble. It was quite a headache trying to get everything working together but The Commander always knew he could get it arranged. He had lots of faith not only in his own abilities but also that of his Majors and most of the other personnel based at Kentley. And so it was party time.

Unit Charlie 12 had already had their pre-party meeting and it had taken the usual route with most of the Unit excited and the usual immature ones even more so. There was first the subject of what duties the Unit were going to be taking on over the next month but most people were interested in the requests for partners from outside of the base being authorized to attend the annual party. None had been refused at all so everyone was happy.

The Commander had worked out that if everybody turned up who was invited that there would be just under two hundred people dancing the night away at Kentley base. The Catering Team were well prepared and assured The Commander that there would be enough food if double that number turned up. As always they prepared both hot and cold food for the main buffet which included choice of chicken, ham, pork and beef as the main meats but also had pork pie, various flavoured sausages and game pie to go with them. There were chicken drumsticks of course as well as sliced meats and to go with the colder type buffet were coleslaw, salads, vol-au-vents, pickles and so many different sandwiches it was impossible to try everyone. There was also what was called the hot selection which included curries, chilli, hot pies, mushy peas and various other hot dishes and to go with them were various rice dishes, potatoes and lots of Indian type extras. Now it was usual at these type of functions for each main chef, and there were three at Kentley, to make his or her own main dish. This could be hot or cold, traditional or exotic but each would have a special presentation spot around the buffet somewhere where their dish of the function would be advertised and available. Tonight was no exception and the three chefs kept their specials as secret as possible. Tonight there were two hot dishes as specials both very different. The first was a sort of old fashioned English type dish which consisted of bacon and onion rolled up in a suet roll and a second dish which was a sort of vegetable bake but contained a lot of tomatoes. Both tasted absolutely brilliant according to the guests. The third main dish was a cold one and was a bit like a salmon pate but with a lot of raw fish and rice decorating it. In addition to these main dishes, each chef made a special desert dish as well and The Commander was expected to try all three and award a prize to the best. There were lots of other deserts as well.

Not only did the food have to be just right, the entertainment had to be special as well. The doors to the function hall were open at eight o'clock precisely and within ten minutes there were more than fifty people drinking or waiting to be served. The Army were able to do special deals with a lot of national companies and as a result a lot of the drink was free. Beers, wines and spirits were free for most of the evening whilst bottled alcohol was being sold very cheaply. All soft drinks were free anyway in the Army bars. A musical dance troupe provided the early entertainment playing mainly modern dance songs. Quite a few of Unit Charlie 12 were in attendance right from the start but Ed Foulkes and Rachel Dobbs were not there and were being missed.

There was a short gap after the musical troupe had finished and some general background dance music was played for about half an hour before the entertainment was changed again and a comedian was introduced. His name was Charlie Easter and he was a very well known entertainer. He must have cost quite a bit to book but again the Army had probably pulled a few strings to get him. The place wasn't exactly full but it was buzzing and Charlie Easter was only going to do a twenty minute slot before the buffet was opened. He would do another thirty later on. He told a few jokes and got a few laughs and it sort of broke the monotony of the dancing music. When Charlie Easter had finished, the buffet was officially opened. There were a number of places where you could grab a plate and then start working along the buffet table to grab whatever you wanted. Just as the buffet started, Corporal Matthew King arrived at the function hall together with is girlfriend Anna. They bumped into Major Wooters almost immediately.

"Sorry for being late Sir. Took longer to get ready than expected." Matthew said to the Major.

"Don't worry Matthew, under the circumstances it is just great that you are here at all and you look complete with your crutches so it was worth the wait!" The Major replied. The few that were standing near all laughed including Matthew himself.

"Please excuse me, I'm going to make for the bar whilst it's not so crowded." Matthew said as he and Anna made their way to the bar.

Anna held the drinks whilst Matthew slowly made way to join the others from Charlie 12 who had managed to get to the buffet and back already.

"Hello Ramon." Matthew greeted his colleague.

"Good evening." Ramon had a mouthful of food but managed to get his words out. "Great to see you've made it Matthew. Good evening Anna."

"Hello Corporal." Anna was very shy and not keen to make idle chit chat with other members of the Army. She had met most of Charlie 12 at previous functions and knew which ones she was happy to chat with. "I'll go and get us some food Matt." Anna made her excuses and left him talking to Ramon.

She returned with fairly soon with two plates full of food.

"Food is superb eh?" Matthew exclaimed. The others tried to give an answer although most had their mouths full at the time.

By now the place was really filling up. There were of course a few either getting ready for duty or actually on-duty but pretty well everyone else was here.

It was soon time for the live band to start their opening set. They would also be playing two sets and hoped that they could get a few dancing early on. They were a six piece band playing all sorts of music. It only took about ten minutes for the first couple to get up and start dancing and quite soon the floor was full. Kenton and Trisha had a couple of dances but was more concerned about Rachel to really let herself relax. Rachel had been released from the hospital that afternoon and she would need lots of rest and structured exercise in the next few days. Trisha had been looking forward to being at the do with her friend Rachel but so were the fortunes of war. The two of them would normally have flirted withy unsuspecting soldiers and chatted about how they would imagine each one would look naked or perform in bed. Tonight was not going to be nearly as much fun as previous years for Trisha.

    Although the Army was mainly men, there were still quite a few women invited and it was mainly women who were dancing early on. By ten o'clock the party was really starting to swing and the live band had got most of the floor full of people dancing. The party was now in full flow and it was around about ten thirty when everyone had arrived. All in all the celebration party was a success. Everyone had a good time and there was no trouble in the town to distract from it. The Commander was extremely pleased. As the music came to a close just after two o'clock, the usual party animals were still there. As far as Charlie 12 were concerned only a few were left. Nobody had drank too much that they had become abusive as to do so at such an event was almost a hanging offence but most had been drinking quite a lot. Two or three Privates were still picking at the buffet and they all had small doggy bags so that they could take away some of the cold meat that was leftover. As far as the chef's were concerned, they were very happy with the responses they had received about the food but disappointed that more of the deserts didn't get eaten up. As the night drew to a close they encouraged the activity of collecting leftovers to take home with you as whatever remained would have to be thrown away later on today anyway.

Chapter 6   -   INSUFFICIENT INFORMATION.

    It was another normal day at the Sorting Office and Gary was stuck in his office doing his usual reports as they arrived on his desk. He was still waiting for one particular bit of post to arrive but as yet it hadn't materialised at all. There were four staff on the early shift this morning. Andrea was on public counter duties today so she had just got in and was the one putting the kettle on for the second cuppa of the day.
"Kettle's boiling." Andrea shouted out. This was the signal for everyone to stop what they were doing and make their way to the kitchen.
"I'm so thirsty today." Dee said as she entered the kitchen.
"Check to see if we have milk Dee."
"There's plenty of milk."
"Tea. That's what we want." Gary said as he came into the kitchen and sat down. Andrea was sorting out the cups and getting ready to pour.
"How comes Bill isn't on this morning?" Gary asked.
"Oh he's got the day off today." Micky replied.
"There you are boss. One special cup of tea!" Andrea said in her sexiest voice as she brought Gary's tea over to him.
"Whoa girl!" Dee said getting embarrassed.
"She's only trying to get me going." Gary explained.
"Ooh, I'd love to get you going!" Andrea said as she brought in three more cups of tea. The room laughed as Gary went red. "In fact if I thought it would get you going I'd make you a cup of tea every morning." Andrea winked at Gary and blew him a little kiss. The rest of the workers in the room laughed. Gary just went red. Andrea wasn't worried about hiding the fact that she fancied Gary so much so that it was quite common knowledge amongst most of the staff. Gary was also quite open about telling Andrea that he wasn't interested. They both knew the score.

    It was time to get back to work so Gary picked up the files from his downstairs tray and carried them back to his office. He had to leave early today so he was aware that he must keep an eye on the time. Gary sifted through the new reports and felt a sense of excitement as he looked at the 'return' case. It was a big brown envelope addressed to a Mr. Westlake at 31, Church Walk, Waydon and there was a brief report from the Postman who had tried to deliver it yesterday. Gary gave it a quick look but felt disappointment when he got to the section headed 'follow-up action'. This was a box that was rarely filled in by the postman but if it was it would normally state, asked resident about name or confirmed about names of residents next door. This letter was addressed to an address that didn't actually exist and Gary was surprised to see how far the postman had gone to try and deliver it. Gary knew that there were only a few houses in Church Walk, Waydon with on one side the last one numbered being number 29. There were then no further buildings for about five hundred yards when the next building was Waydon School. In the report, the Postman had put, I wondered if the school was the intended place of receipt. Gary swore as he read this. The postman wasn't supposed to make that connection that easily. Gary swore even more when he read that the Postman had actually made enquiries at the school to see if a Mr. Westlake worked there. Gary's plan hadn't quite worked how he had hoped but at least he now had his letter with which he could approach the school. More importantly he could start off an official file on the computer system, just in case the AP ever came back to him about his visits to Waydon.

Gary had got a phone call during the morning from Angela asking if he could pick the girls up from school that afternoon. Angela was not very talkative and in fact a bit annoyed that she had to ask Gary for the favour. However she had no other options. She just said she had to go out but didn't elaborate any further. Gary never asked where she was going but knew that there would be some good reason for her having to go off. It meant that Gary would have to leave work a little bit earlier than usual but that wasn't a problem.

Gary drove back home to Waydon at a nice safe speed. For once, he wasn't late and could enjoy his journey. The girls had both been going to school at the village restaurant. I say restaurant because that was what it used to be but they had been shut for a few years now. The premises in question was Slater's Farm Restaurant and as the name suggests, before it was a restaurant, it had been a farm. Next to the old restaurant was a barn that had been converted into a small function hall and the teaching staff had asked to take over the whole of the premises and temporarily turn it into a school. The owners were happy and with a little bit of moving about, the premises were divided into seven different age areas. All classes of the same age had to be grouped together but then you had two teachers teaching the bigger classes. It was pandemonium to start off with as not only had Miss Clark been banned, but one of the other teachers had felt so strongly about it all that she refused to come to work until Miss Clark was re-instated. As before, the finishing time for the school was three fifteen but parents were allowed to come and collect their children from three o'clock onwards. The headmistress was a Mrs. Stingberry and she would always wait on till the last pupil had been picked up. As headmistress, she would always be around outside of school when ever she could be so as to get to recognise the parents.

Gary turned up near the restaurant and had to park his car a fair way down the road. Obviously the later you turned up the easier it was to park. Gary hadn't thought about the parking but aimed to be at the school for three fifteen. He was soon at the main entrance. Joan had walked over to join Katy and the two girls waved as they saw Daddy approaching. Gary waved back and the class teacher let the girls go.
"Hello Mr. Newson." One of the Mothers said as he got nearer.
"Hello," he replied not having a clue who he was talking to. The two girls ran to Gary.
"Where's Mum?" Katy said in her demanding voice.
"She's had to go out and will be back very soon." Gary answered. It seemed to be enough for Katy. It seemed to be enough for Joan as well. Gary got them back home and whilst they went up and changed out of their school clothes, Gary prepared them some drinks and a small sandwich.
"Thanks Dad. Can we go out and play in the front garden?" Joan asked.
"Yes. But don't go away from the street."
"We won't." The two girls rushed off outside to see if any of their nearby friends were out playing whilst Gary sat down on the settee and read some of an old paper that was laying about.

It wasn't too late when Angela finally returned back home. She was carrying a big shopping bag full of various vegetables and Gary knew that she had been doing some bartering or working some deals to get some better food. Gary didn't ask where she had been, he was just pleased to see her home. Gary wasn't quite sure what sort of mood Angela would be in when she returned. At least he had managed to do as she had asked him and he hoped that she would be in a slightly better mood.

"Everything alright Gary?" Angela asked as soon as she got inside the door. Gary was taken aback at the tone of Angela's voice. It was almost as if there had never been anything wrong. Angela went straight into the kitchen though and didn't come in to actually see Gary. Gary decided that he had better go and see Angela in the kitchen.

"Yes. The girls have been good. I didn't start any dinner as I wasn't sure what you had planned." Gary replied.

"No I didn't really expect you to. I didn't mean to be as long as this but got held up." Angela answered.

"No problem."

"I'll start dinner in a moment." Angela announced.

Looking up at the living room clock it was about the time when Gary took Sammy for his tea-time walk. As always, Sammy was excited as Gary grabbed his lead down from the coat hook and as soon as it was attached, Sammy was off out to the back garden and straight over to the door in the bushes. It was a little bit lighter tonight and Gary felt that he could walk a little bit further than he would do normally. Sammy was going about his usual business and Gary wasn't really thinking anything in particular as they approached the gap in the hedge where Gary and Sammy had often nipped through to avoid being seen by strangers or Army personnel. Gary looked at the gap with some sort of respect as he talked to Sammy.

"That gap has saved us on many a night eh Sammy."

The dog didn't reply but he did look up at Gary as if he wanted to and as if he knew exactly what Gary was saying. Sammy started to pull towards the gap as if he was going to go through it.

"No boy we don't need to go through there today." Gary said to Sammy. With a bit of a tug, Sammy got the message and the two of them continued on their way. Gary had decided to make his way passed the church and down towards the little cottages so that he might get a little view of the school through the bushes in between. He didn't want to be seen walking around the church again as he had already been caught there and had his name taken so he thought the best idea would be to walk down the lane a bit further and try and get a view from there. Gary didn't want to go as far as the little cottages so he slowed up once passing the church as if Sammy was busy sniffing at things and he looked as hard as he could towards the school building. Disappointingly, nothing much seemed to be happening at the school at all. No sign of any movement although there were lights on. Gary stood and looked around for a while and soon realised that it had started to turn dark. It was time to turn round and make way for home again. Gary hadn't really walked that far so he was quite happy that it wouldn't be that dark by the time he got back home.

Sammy was as obedient as ever and soon they found themselves back at the gap in the hedge. In the distance Gary heard the sound of a vehicle. It sounded like quite a large, heavy diesel type vehicle so to be on the safe side the two of them nipped through the gap and waited to see what was driving down the back lane. It was an Army lorry. Gary could see that quite clearly as it moved slowly up the lane. What Gary didn't expect was the lorry to come to a halt about twenty yards from where he was hiding. Gary could hear the sound of two soldiers jumping out of the back of the lorry and then walking along the road. A lorry door obviously opened and another soldier got out. There was the sound of boots clicking.
"I need you patrolling up and down this short stretch," a rather aggressive voice barked out.
"Yes Sir," two voices replied in unison.
One of the soldiers got back into the lorry and it started off on its way. Gary was in a bit of a quandary as to what to do. He was about fifty yards away from his own house and the door to safety but there was no way he could go back on to the road at the moment. He looked around looking for inspiration but to his surprise found an envelope lying under a rock. Retrieving the envelope he was even more surprised to find that it had the name Gary written on it. It was sealed so had obviously remained unopened. Gary thought that there was no way it could be for him but his curiosity got the better of him and he put the envelope into his pocket. He quickly became aware of one of the soldiers moving along the road so he tried to stop moving. The soldier wasn't even looking at the bushes on the far side of the lane. His orders were to be on the look out for any unauthorised movement down the lane which had been reported to them.
"Steve." One of the soldiers cried out.
"What is it?"
"Are we the only ones on this lane?" He asked.

"No they're dropping off every hundred yards. We've only got this little section to cover." Steve answered. Gary guessed he was in a real situation again. He could go on to the road and get arrested or stick it out. He was tossing over his very few options when a noise broke the silence.
"Steve, Mick. We have a movement heading towards the church. Can you intercept please?" said a voice over a radio handset.
As an almost immediate response, the two soldiers ran off in the direction of the church. Gary gave them twenty seconds and then moved back out of the gap. He quickly looked up and down the lane but could see nobody. Picking up Sammy he ran for the door in his hedge. He had made it back. As Gary came in he was gasping for breath as if he had just run the 100 metres final in the Olympic Games.

"Late again Gary!" Was the welcome from Angela as she looked at her watch. "I told you I'd be starting the dinner and yet you purposely come in late." Angela shouted as she opened the oven door, took out Gary's dinner and dumped it down on the kitchen table.
"I had to wait for an Army truck to leave. It was bloody parked in Back Lane would you believe?" Gary tried to reply but Angela had already gone into the Living room. "I take it you don't believe me then?"
"Look I'm just fed up with you being out after curfew when there's no need for it. I'm fed up with you getting home late from work without you telling me in advance. I'm just bloody fed up with you. You show me no consideration at all." Angela was starting to cry as she spoke. Gary moved towards her as if to comfort her.
"I'll try harder." Gary said.
"That's the point. All you do is fucking try. You don't actually ever succeed!" Angela was now getting angry. Gary wasn't sure what to do. Should he try and calm her down, comfort her because she was getting upset or just leave her alone. He decided on the last option.
"And now when you've upset me like this you can't even be bothered to apologise for it. It's just bloody typical of you lately." Angela waltzed passed Gary and up the stairs. Gary was bemused by everything that was going on. A bedroom door slammed shut upstairs but seconds later Angela was back down again. "You're getting mixed up in all this mess. I need to know now that you can promise me that you will not get involved in anything else." Angela gave him the ultimatum. Gary thought for a second.

"But work requires me……"
"Work requires you to do so much. You go further. I knew you couldn't promise." Angela said as she stormed into the living room. Gary stood in the kitchen for a minute or so looking at his dinner. He thought about what he and Angela had just been arguing about trying to see her side of things but he just couldn't. He thought about the fact that something might have upset Angela this afternoon whilst she was out. Then he thought again about the envelope he'd found tonight.

Gary had left the envelope in his coat pocket. After all the aggravation with Angela had died down he thought he would try and open it and see exactly what it was all about. He was intrigued to find out who the hell Gary might be. He took the envelope upstairs and went into the bathroom, locking the door behind him. He opened the envelope and read the short note inside.

Gary,
    I am writing this in the hope that the correct person gets it. I will phone you at work at 14:00 hours on the first Monday after I see that the letter has gone. Please make sure you are there.
                              A friend.

Gary was none the wiser. Very few people could get hold of Gary's office number so it was unlikely to be him but something made him think. He would make sure he was there at two tomorrow.
"Gary what are you doing in there?" Angela shouted from outside the bathroom door.
"I'll be out in a moment," he replied. Gary unlocked the bathroom door and Angela was still standing there.
"What have you been up to?" She asked him sternly.
"Nothing, honest!" He replied guiltily. As he walked passed her, she didn't notice the envelope held tightly in his hand. Gary would have to get rid of it without her noticing. Angela gave him a scowl as he walked back towards the stairs. She then went into the bathroom herself. It was just the opportunity Gary needed. He quickly made his way back downstairs and placed the envelope and its contents into his briefcase. He could remember roughly the content of the letter so it was not necessary for him to get the letter out again. Oh God, he thought to himself, if only things could have been a little bit better. He knew that Angela and he were having a bad time but they had had bad

times before and it had never got as bad as this. He couldn't see Angela's point of view at all although he realized she was genuinely upset about it all. Perhaps she knew more than Gary did about everything that was going on. The bathroom door unlocked. The sound of Angela coming back downstairs sent the hairs on Gary's back on end.

"You're a bloody ignorant pig, do you know that?" Angela said to him.

"What can I say?" Gary replied shrugging his shoulders and holding his arms out.

"You're heading for a disaster and only I seem to realise it."

"I know what I'm doing. You seem to think I'm putting myself in grave danger every night but that isn't the case." Gary replied.

"You need me to show you?" Angela cried. "It always comes down to me to have to do the right thing doesn't it? Well I'll do whatever it takes to get you to open your bloody eyes Gary." Angela was going red with rage as she said these last few words. Angela turned and went back upstairs. Gary wondered exactly what she meant about doing whatever it takes. Sounded a bit like a threat that, he thought. Gary tried to work out exactly what she meant but never even got near. Angela meanwhile was upstairs working out where she could go with the girls if it came down to leaving him. Gary was fed up with trying to work out exactly what he could do to make things better. His mind wandered again and this time back again to those early days when he and Angela were young and in love.

After walking Angela home that first night it was obvious to both of them that they were made for each other. In a cruel and nasty world, two people had found heaven in each others arms. Angela was of course still very involved with the local revolutionary movement and spent a lot of time going to meetings with her brother John. Gary had got himself a job at the Post Office working at the Sorting Office. Gary would work different shifts but was usually able to get away to meet Angela most mornings and evenings. Angela had no job and she spent most of her time with the revolutionaries. They would be planning this and planning that and whenever Gary saw Angela with the revolutionaries, he was impressed with her enthusiasm. She would always be asking to help organise this or help organise that but as older brothers do, John would persuade her to not get too involved. Angela was very keen to actually get up and talk at one of the meetings and she was allowed to at one of the smaller ones. Gary was in absolute awe of this young girl, his girl, who was prepared and able to talk to a gathered mob. He would tell her how much she would amaze him but then she saw something in him that she didn't see in others. At meetings every now and then, the police or the Army would raid the places and when this happened there was usually a mass exodus of the building followed by sheer panic. On a couple of occasions, Angela had started to get hysterical at the thought of being caught but Gary would calm her down and lead her to a safe way of leaving whatever building they were in. Gary usually took in his surroundings quite fully and was always aware of various escape routes. Gary could always keep calm in a crisis and was usually able to think straight. Angela thought of him as her hero when he was like this.

Angela and Gary were becoming well known amongst the revolutionary organisers and although it was often Angela and her boyfriend, Gary found many of the leaders saying hello to him when he turned up at meetings. The current trend or subject to be talked about was the way that the Euro Army had control over the whole of Europe's food production. It was clear that food was beginning to become scarce on the markets and that the price was rising even for the cheapest foods. Local food producers were smuggled into meetings to give their stories about the way that the Euro Army took all or most of their produce yet none of it found its way to places like Chale or Kentley markets. The normal conclusion was that France and Germany had their pick of whatever food was going then the Euro Army bases and by that time there was none left for the rest of the population. A couple of speakers, fresh back from abroad, spoke of food being stockpiled all over Europe. They would build storage near to where the food was being processed and then stock it there until France, Germany or the Army wanted it and then throw away the rest. There was also a speaker who was one of the management from Potters Peas. They were probably the biggest producer of food locally as nearly all the farm land around grew peas for them. This manager spoke of the Army taking away practically all of their stock but nobody had seen a tin of peas for ages. It just wasn't available.

After one such meeting, Angela was asked to wait behind. Gary of course waited for her. The meeting had almost cleared and the only people left were the Potters Peas employee and three other members of the revolutionary group. Two were regular leaders but the third was unknown to Gary.

"Angela, we want to talk to you alone." One of the leaders said looking over at Gary.

"We have no secrets so whatever you tell me now I will tell Gary on the way home. You might as well involve him." Angela spoke bravely. Gary knew that this was quite a stand to make and she was making it for him.

"We have a job for you." The leader told Angela.

"I'll be helping her." Gary said as he stepped forward towards the top table.

"Then come and join us." The leaders made room for Gary to join them round the table and they unrolled a map of Kentley. "We have learnt from our colleague here that the Army have been using a store-room on the old railway sidings." The leader introduced the third man as Neil and indicated that he should take over.

"For about a couple of weeks, the Army has been using this store-room here." Neil started his tale whilst pointing at a remote building on the map. "The access is via the road down beside the railway station and the Army camp fence."

"How do you know that they've been using it?" Angela was the first to query anything.

"I don't think we need to question our man!" One of the leaders interrupted.

"No, on the contrary, I don't see why I shouldn't be questioned," Neil replied. "I was told about them using it by a contact about two weeks ago and the very next day I sat in a room in the Angel Hotel and watched. Practically everyday it was used but only for about an hour each afternoon around four o'clock."

"And what happens?" Angela continued.

"A lorry will turn up with about four soldiers and they unlock the store and then unload the lorry. Once they have finished, they lock the store back up again and drive off." There was a slight pause before one of the leaders spoke.

"Thank you, Neil." The leader then turned to Angela. "All I want you to do is make sure that you know your way to the store so that on Wednesday evening you can break it open."

"Why Wednesday evening?" Angela asked again.

"We are organising another meeting and will be taking that meeting down to the store where I expect everyone to take a box of peas or whatever other food they have stored there." The leader got rather excited as he explained.
"Provided you have a proper plan of times that the others will be there, I'll do it. I don't want to break into the store and then leave it open for an hour or so. I'll do it just before the people are due to arrive." Angela said defiantly.

So on the day, both Angela and Gary work at the little task they have been asked to do. Angela had already booked a room at The Angel Hotel and had spent the previous night watching the store. Everything seemed to be going just as Neil had told it. Gary had also spent the night with Angela. It was an opportunity neither wanted to miss although Angela didn't want anything getting in the way of her task. Once she was happy with what they were going to do the next evening then they both started to relax. It was the first time either of them had ever slept with someone else and both were a little nervous but the bed wasn't wasted. It was nearly five in the morning before the two of them settled down to sleep and it wasn't a great surprise that they both slept in late the following morning. Angela was annoyed that she had done so but Gary pointed out that two lovers booking a room was perfect cover for them. Gary had to go to work during the day but he went with a big smile on his face.

That evening when Gary got back to the Hotel, Angela was very tense and extremely nervous. Gary tried to comfort her as much as he could and although it helped her a bit, she still felt that pain of anticipation in her stomach. They went through the plans again and Angela had everything timed down to the last minute. She had worked out that from the meeting place to the hotel would take about nine minutes to walk and from the hotel to the store was about six minutes. Giving her self five minutes to break the locks Angela calculated what time Gary and her needed to leave the hotel in order to break the store open just as the meeting got to the hotel. That was her plan anyway.
"Who directs the people from the meeting to the actual store-room?" Gary just asked out of curiosity.
"Ah. That's a good point." Angela answered. She thought for a moment and came up with a solution. "You'll have to walk back

towards them after we've opened the storeroom and lead them to it Gary."
"Why would they take my word or follow me?"
"Once you tell them where you're taking them, they'll just follow. They're expecting to go to a storeroom aren't they?" Angela explained.
"Yes. You're probably right." Gary said.
"I'm always right!" Angela told him giving him a big kiss.

Angela had two sets of bolt cutters, some wire cutters, a screwdriver and a large crow bar just in case. Gary brought along a torch and one or two other things just in case but left most of the planning to Angela. They were both in dark clothing so that they didn't stand out in the night. Ready or not, it was time to go. The two of them left the hotel by the side exit and made their way along Wall Street to the railway station. They walked arm in arm looking like a young couple out late but fortunately nobody else was around. Having got passed the station and able to turn into the dirt track down the side of the station, Gary felt that the most vulnerable part of the plan was over. The dirt track was not lit at all and nobody would have been able to see them making their way down it to the bit of wasteland where the storeroom was situated. The storeroom was actually one of about twenty old buildings that obviously once belonged to the railway. Apart from about four of them, there were still old railway tracks around these storerooms which suggested that they were once rail freight storerooms. The one the Army were using was the one nearest to their base but it was separated by the base fence. When they got to the store, Gary pointed out that there was a power supply running from inside of the Army base to the storeroom.
"They have lighting in the storeroom which I assume the Army had to power." Angela said.
"Do you want us to cut the power?" Gary asked.
"No. Let's just check the locks." Angela ordered. The door of the storeroom was a large sliding door and had three different latches with locks on. Two of them seemed quite easy locks to remove whilst the third was a lot bigger and may take some breaking.
"Let's try and cut the big one first." Gary suggested. Angela gave a thumbs-up. She then produced a large set of bolt cutters and went to work on the lock. Gary helped after a few seconds and between them the lock came away relatively easily. It was just about this time when

Gary heard a motor. He turned to see some headlights in the distance from inside of the Army base. It was a perimeter security check. He grabbed Angela by the arm and pulled her round the far side of the storeroom.
"Is that a car?" Angela asked.
"Ssshh!" Gary put a finger to Angela's lips. The two of them crept back towards the corner of the storeroom to see a jeep with two soldiers in it come to a halt inside the Army base. It was obvious that they were also checking the storeroom. Fortunately, with the storeroom being outside of the fence, all they could really do was make sure it looked intact.
"Where are the bolt cutters?" Gary whispered to Angela.
"I thought you had them?" She replied. Gary looked back round the corner and saw the big shiny bolt cutters laying on the floor right in front of the storeroom.
"Shit!" Gary whispered. The soldiers got the jeep searchlight and shone it on the storeroom door. They moved the light up and down a few times but failed to notice that one of the locks was missing and failed to see the bolt cutters on the floor.
"Nothing to report at the outside north storage!" One of the soldiers spoke into his microphone.
"Understood!" The reply was clearly heard. The soldiers started up the jeep again and drove off on their way.
"That was close!" Angela gave a big sigh of relief. Time was getting on and Angela was concerned that the people from the meeting would be there before they had got the storeroom open but she needn't have worried. Gary could make out what looked like a number of people turning into the dirt track down by the side of the station. He was a bit concerned as he knew that there was a gate nearby that he was certain, the soldiers in the jeep had gone off to check. There was no indication of any problems at all.
"They should be here in about two minutes!" Gary said to Angela.
"Okay, just one more lock to go," she replied. As the final lock came off, Gary and Angela pushed the sliding door back to make the storeroom completely open. They could hear the sound of footsteps coming towards them but also the sound of motors in the distance again. Gary looked up and saw the lights of a jeep from inside the base driving towards them and also another vehicle driving up the dirt track. Things had gone wrong.
"We need to get out of here quick." Gary shouted at Angela.

"Not before I get my hands on some peas." She replied. Angela went into the store and called Gary in to see. There were no peas in the storeroom. There was no food at all. It was an arms store. Rifles and hand guns. At that point the people from the meeting turned up. They didn't look like the normal sort of crowd who would go to a meeting and what's more they didn't show much surprise when the storeroom was seen to be full of weapons. It dawned on Gary quite quickly that this was another faction of the revolutionaries who were after nothing else other than arms and ammunition.

"I'm sorry, but there aren't any peas!" Angela said to the first person who arrived.

"Peas! Who wants bloody peas?" The chap grabbed at the first box and smiled with delight.

"Angela!" Gary shouted. He was keeping one eye on the two vehicles that were approaching thinking that any minute now they would be trapped and arrested. He was surprised but pleased to find that the vehicle that had driven down the dirt track was a revolutionaries' vehicle which had come to load up their booty.

In the confusion, Angela had fallen over a box in the storeroom and had hurt her ankle.

"Gary, help me!" Angela cried out.

"Where are you?" Gary asked.

"Down here." Angela was nursing her swollen ankle but Gary managed to get her to her feet.

"Can you walk at all?" He asked. Angela hobbled a bit.

"Not really but I'll try." She replied. At this moment the jeep from inside the Army base had got to the fence and was shining a light on the subject.

"Stop what you are doing. You are breaking the law!" The warning came from one of the soldiers in the jeep. This was followed by a few shots that were aimed at people in the storeroom. Gary knew he had to get the two of them out of the way. Some shots were fired back at the soldiers in the jeep and it immediately retreated. Gary guessed it wouldn't be long before back up was on the way. He managed to get Angela to support herself on his shoulder and the two of them got out of the storeroom. Angela automatically headed for the dirt track but Gary had other ideas. He took them in the direction behind the storeroom heading towards the other stores.

"The Army will be all over this place soon. We need to go this way." Gary made Angela hurry even though she was in great pain from her ankle. They passed the next storeroom but Gary wasn't convinced that they were anything like safe yet. Another jeep had arrived inside the base to help support the first jeep and the sound of gunfire rung out in the night air on a regular basis. Already, one of the revolutionaries had been shot and they were getting ready to take what they had and get out. The lorry started to drive back to the dirt track but it left the people who had come on foot to fend for themselves.

   Gary and Angela were still making their way passed the old railway stores and every step was a real struggle. Gary kept them both moving whilst he kept an eye out for movement. As they passed the fourth of the storerooms, they came to another fence. Gary wasn't sure if there would be a fence or not but he had brought some reasonable wire cutters with him just in case. Moving to the middle of one of the fences, Gary cut away from the bottom until there was a split in the fence about three feet in length. He pulled the fence back and Angela crawled through. Gary managed to follow without too much trouble. Gary then took the bag he had been carrying on his back, off and opened it up. Inside he produced two dark blue balaclavas. He handed one to Angela.
"Put that on." He ordered. He then produced some gloves and handed a pair to Angela. She didn't need to be told. Lastly Gary produced four bits of wire with which he expertly tied the fence back up again. Unless you were right next to the fence, you couldn't tell that it had been opened.
"Where are we going?" Angela asked.
"We're going to have to try and make it over the train lines and back to the hotel that way." Gary replied.
"What went wrong?" Angela said as she looked at him with a frown.
"You didn't do anything wrong. You were used that was all." Gary told her.
"But we weren't expecting the Army to respond so quickly." Angela continued.
"And they wouldn't have done if it had been peas in that store. That Neil fellow knew all along what was in there. If we'd have known we'd have expected the place to have been alarmed." Gary was furious at the way the revolutionaries had risked Angela's life. They

had no morals and couldn't be trusted. Gary took out a tin of shoe polish from his bag.
"Put some of that on your face. Not too much though."

The shooting continued between the two factions either side of the perimeter fence. The lorry had just about got to the end of the dirt track. Gary saw it turn right. The bloody bastards had got away, he thought to himself.
"Come on girl. We need to move." Gary picked Angela up again and they started to jog or hop on their way. Half way through the storerooms, Gary turned sharp left and made for the railway lines. He could see at least four vehicles now driving down the dirt track towards the storeroom. He knew that the Army would be following behind but hoped that they might stop chasing when they got to the fence. It was about this time when the two of them had got to another dangerous bit. They came out of the cover of the storerooms and were now faced with about a five hundred yard stretch of open land. Most of it was full of old railway tracks which made the terrain a bit more difficult to cross. There were also the odd bushes about but not very many. An Army jeep was driving down the dirt track but not heading towards the storeroom. It was driving further down by the side of the railway towards where Gary and Angela were trying to make for. It stopped and turned on its searchlight, giving a couple of sweeps across the open wasteland and the disused tracks. The jeep turned and drove back. Gary turned to Angela.
"Are you ready?" He gave her a big kiss as they stood up and ran across tracks and wasteland. Angela showed signs that she was about to drop so they made for the nearest bush and took a deep breath. Just about two hundred yards left. They started again and this time made it to the old wooden fence that separated the dirt track from old railway wasteland. Another Army jeep was again driving down the dirt track heading towards where Gary and Angela were hiding. Although it drove up a bit further this time it concentrated its searchlight on the old railway tracks and the wasteland. The beam never came anywhere near to them. Although it seemed like ages, the jeep stayed there for less than five minutes before turning round and going back. Gary waited for a couple of minutes and the two of them crossed over the dirt track and then jumped over the wall to find themselves next to the main railway lines out of Kentley station. They crossed the lines and

reached another wall on the other side. Once again they jumped over it and found themselves in overgrown unused land.

"We can rest here for a few minutes but we'd be better off still walking." Gary said to Angela.

"Let me stop a minute," she replied. They both took the opportunity to try and catch their breaths but true to her word, Angela got the two of them moving again about a minute later. Gary led the way as if he knew exactly where he was going and after about fifteen minutes he led them to another brick wall but one that had a natural grass bank growing against it. They walked up the bank and jumped down the other side.

"We're in the hotel car park!" Angela exclaimed with surprise.

"Of course!" Gary replied with a sense of pride. Angela knew that they would be using the back door to get in so finishing up in the car park was really good. Obviously the hotel was not supposed to let anyone in after curfew hours but unofficially gave a back door key to Angela when she said she might be back a bit late. They both made their way in to the hotel and back to their room. They both sat on the bed and gave a big sigh of relief.

Gary remembered all this like it was yesterday. He remembered the night that followed as well as neither of them really wanted to sleep. They were both far too high to think about sleeping. Instead it was a night of ecstasy that not many married couples experience, but the excitement and the adrenalin made a superb combination that no aphrodisiac could match. What a night, he was thinking to himself. He also remembered reading the papers the following day. Eight killed, thirteen arrested. The revolutionaries called it a success because they had stolen so much weaponry. Angela didn't go to many further meetings after that. She confronted her leaders who of course denied all knowledge of what was really stored there. He had put it down to the group have insufficient information about the job. They came out with some story about Neil telling them on the night not to go to the storeroom. Angela never trusted them again. It just so happened that two days later she got called up to do her conscription. She was made to join for two years but she traveled back to see her hero every chance she had. Gary and she were in love and nothing was going to get in their way. Even when Angela had to go away for almost six months, Gary wrote every week, and Angela wrote back when she could. Both couldn't wait for the day that they would be back together again.

Gary realised that his mind had been wandering again as he quickly remembered that things between Angela and himself were not that good. A lot had changed since those days. Angela had children and dropped out of the revolutionary circles that were once so much of her life. Perhaps she had grown up. Perhaps she had different feelings now about the cause. Whatever it was, Angela no longer had anything to do with her old revolutionary friends. That was a closed chapter as far as she was concerned and she wasn't that happy when Gary talked about it. She wasn't pro The Government but there was no way that she would voice her opinions to anyone anymore. She had definitely changed. Gary had changed as well. If anything he had got stronger beliefs about the right of the revolution. He wasn't an activist, in fact not much of a revolutionary at all but if he had been made to make a decision, it would probably be for the revolution. It would never happen, he thought to himself. Angela and he would just go on living their normal lives. He held this thought for a moment. If only, he thought to himself.

-

The way that things were going locally with Operation Hunting, there seemed to be a need for Major Tannier and his agent to meet almost every other day. Normally, if it wasn't a pre-arranged meeting they would meet in one of two places, either at a designated public place or in his office but the regularity had been getting so much that in order to maintain security things had to change. It was a bit drastic perhaps but not completely unusual but the agent had arranged for the renting of an office in Kentley. It was normal to choose a spare office in a government building somewhere but after looking around at two or three the agent never actually found one that was completely satisfactory. In the end there was a third floor office on the High Street that suited the needs best.

Major Tannier called at the office and the door was unlocked and opened by the agent. The sign on the window of the office had read 'St. Michaels' Import & Export' and gave a local telephone number that didn't exist. Inside there was a desk, two or three chairs for visitors and a filing cabinet. The agent sat back down at the desk

where there was a phone, note pad and a pen. The agent had called this meeting to update the Major with progress but the Major would now be able to call meetings himself by leaving a note under the door or in the letter box downstairs. The agent sat up and started talking,
"I've managed to get a bit more background on our Jenny Tetridge."
"What sort of stuff?" The Major asked excitedly.
"Only background stuff you know. Now that she's dead, people are more prepared to talk about her," the agent said.
"Anything on her current job?"
"Not a thing as yet but there is still time." The Major took this in and then continued.
"So what have you managed to get?"
"Well it would appear that our Tetridge woman was born and bred in Waydon," the agent said with a hint of surprise.
"Why haven't we heard of her much before?"
"I don't know as yet. Perhaps she kept her head down in the early days," the agent said with a hint of uncertainty. "What I can tell you though Major is that she has a sister who still lives in the village."
"Do you know her name?" The Major asked.
"No again I hope to get more later but thought you might be able to identify sisters who were born in Waydon around that time," the agent said in a sarcastic tone.

After a brief pause, the Major handed the envelope of photographs to the agent. Almost with a feeling of opening a Christmas present the contents were spilled on to the desk and the agent frisked through them with the occasional 'Yes', 'That's a good one' and 'Oh yeah' as the anticipation of what the agent could get from the photographs became too much to contain. After about twenty five minutes, the agent picked out six photographs and asked for them to be blown up in particular areas. The Major undertook to get this done and kept the six photos away from the rest.

-

It had now been 11 days since the battle on Reed Street and after all the events that Unit Charlie 12 had been through recently it was quite surprising how good the morale of the team was. The funeral of Private Hildred was held back in his home town of Belfast and a detachment from Unit Charlie 12 attended. Ed Foulkes had wanted to try to get to the funeral himself but this had proven impossible. It required a lot of organising just trying to get the bodies back to their loved ones let alone then arranging for some of the Unit to be at the funerals. Major Wooters had taken Charlie 12 off normal duties until further notice to make it easier.

     Sally Foulkes had been given the afternoon off to go and see her husband in the Military Hospital. She wasn't allowed to go and see him when he was first admitted as any soldiers arriving with fresh wounds whilst on active service are taken to a ward that is off limits to non-Military personnel. As soon as things were evaluated, soldiers are moved to other wards where they can receive visitors and Ed had by now got over the worst and was mainly being given rest.
"You alright darling?" Sally sat next to Ed's bed and held his hand.
"Yeah I'm okay." He smiled as he looked at her stroking his bare arm. The two kissed briefly.
"I've let your Mother know and she sends her best."
"Oh you shouldn't have bothered her." Ed was annoyed about what Sally had done but wouldn't let it show if he could help it. "You know she only worries."
"Well yes but she'd have moaned if we hadn't told her."
"That's maybe."
"And I'm the one she would moan at." Sally fussed around with the bedclothes a bit just to make sure her man was as comfortable as he could be. "Not like being at home is it. Any news when you might get released?"

     Ed was due to be out of hospital tomorrow and then back on duty about a week after that so her time would be short. There were two or three others that were sent to hospital from Unit Charlie 12 and Corporal King and Private Dobbs were two of those three. Both had already been released and should be back on duty soon although Rachel was still finding it hard to walk properly. The rest of the Unit tried to carry on as normal and it gave Kenton Bridge and Trisha Logan a chance to talk and work out their differences. They had both gone to both funerals and now things were getting back to normal they were beginning to appreciate each others company again. Kenton had so much he wanted to tell Trish that he felt that if they could get away from HQ for a couple of days so much could be sorted out between them but he didn't have the courage to ask her. He didn't have to worry as Trish came to him and suggested that they have a dinner in Chale at the weekend. They booked into a hotel in Chale but into separate rooms.

Saturday was the night they had dinner and Kenton had spent the morning buying a new shirt for the occasion whilst Trish went and had her hair done and took in a manicure at the same time. She wanted to feel special and make Kenton proud to be with her. They booked at one of the top restaurants in Chale and sat down ready to order. Usually it would only be the rich that would be able to eat at such a restaurant but Kenton and Trish were able to show some Army identification and eat at much lower prices than the restaurant would normally charge. Food was not easy to come by so the restaurant paid extra to get what it wanted and then charged its customers for the privilege of eating there.

Both Kenton and Trish felt a bit like royalty and although they were able to afford the reduced prices still found the food very over priced.
"Are you any good at ordering wine?" Trish asked.
"Do you want wine?" Kenton replied with a hint of surprise.
"Yes, if we're having a nice meal then we should have wine." Trish finished. Kenton couldn't really argue too much as he had drunk wine before and found it did make a meal if the wine was right.
"I know some wines but can't say I'm an expert," he admitted. Kenton continued, "But let's order our food first," he said as a waiter came to the table. Despite being one of the best restaurants around, food was not that easy to get hold of so the menu was a fairly limited one. Both ordered a prawn cocktail to start with but whilst Trish had a fish meal, Kenton stuck to the chicken special.
"I'll order some wine please." Kenton added.
"I'll bring the wine list Sir." The waiter replied. There was a brief silence before Trish spoke.
"Isn't it funny how you think you know someone but you don't!"
"Are you talking about me?" Kenton replied in a guilty tone.
"No, I mean Patrick. Or should I say Michael?" Trish said as she looked at Kenton. She looked into his big brown eyes and started to lose herself. She wondered what he'd seen with those eyes. He smiled and Trisha remembered how lovely he looked when he was happy. She hoped it was her who made him happy.

"What do you mean Michael?" Kenton finally replied.
"Didn't you notice anything in Belfast?" She said sternly.
"I didn't realise there was anything to notice and anyway we were there to say goodbye to a colleague not to start investigating anything." Kenton played with his napkin as he felt that this conversation was going nowhere.

He wanted to get round to telling Trish about his background to see if she would still be interested in him but this was proving more difficult than he had expected.
"Well the first thing you should have noticed was that everyone in the family kept referring to him as Michael. That in itself is not unusual."
"True, as a lot of people are known by their middle names." Kenton added in support.
"Ah but then I heard one of the family saying that how tragic it was that the two should both die under the same circumstances." Trish made her first point.
"I never knew he had a brother, did you?" Kenton's interest had been raised a bit.
"No I didn't so I looked around the graveyard after the funeral to see if I could find him."
"And did you?" Kenton was hooked.
"Well it wasn't that difficult really as although his Mother went straight back to the wake his Father stayed behind and stood at another grave." Trish finished her sentence with an air of achievement.
"And what was his name then?" Kenton had asked the exact question she had hoped he would.
"Well you'll never believe it but his brothers' name was Patrick Henry and he was born on the twenty first of March 2004."
"And what's the problem with that then?" Kenton shrugged his shoulders. Just at that second the waiter turned up with their first course. Kenton watched Trisha as she seemed so excited at being served in a restaurant. It took him back to the first time he fancied her when he caught site of her playing in a netball match. Her enthusiasm and excitement gave her a sort of sparkle which shone out amongst the rest. It was an innocent type of quality that Kenton liked. He had never been turned on by the fact that Trisha was prepared to chase him but she had a lot to offer that he wasn't sure if she realised was there.

As the two tucked into their cocktails Trisha continued with her

tale. "Well that was our Patrick's date of birth according to Army records." Trisha had almost got to the real point.
"So he had a twin brother?" Kenton suggested.
"No. You haven't caught on have you?" Trisha felt a slight disappointment that Kenton hadn't realised what she was about to reveal.
"No I haven't, I'm sorry." Kenton replied.
"Our Patrick Henry was actually Michael Patrick and although everyone thought he was 21, he was actually only 19. And he was actually born in Liverpool. What's more that would explain why Private Lewis was always trying to look out for him. I think he knew." Trisha made her final point. Kenton thought about it for a few seconds and told Trisha that she had a point. He was then a bit worried about what she was going to do with this information.
"Are you going to report it?" Kenton asked with a worried look.
"No. What's the point?" Trisha said. "Let sleeping dogs lie," she added.

  Kenton was a lot happier. The two of them continued their conversation throughout the meal and things were going so well that Kenton was finding it harder and harder to bring up the subject he had wanted to talk about all night. The one point he desperately needed to tell her was that he wasn't actually officially single but he was a widower. It came as a shock to Trisha who had no idea but she wanted to know. His wife Malitia was his schoolboy sweetheart. They had known each other since they were five or six. He pronounced her name Ma-lish-er but spelt out her name so that Trisha would know how to spell it properly. He explained how he had been a bit of a lad in his early days and they had got married when he was fully involved in local crime. Kenton admitted that he was in to all sorts of trouble. Dealing drugs! Extortion! Robbery with violence! He was proud to say though that he had never used a gun before joining the Army. Malitia had tried to get him out of all his bad ways but only two months after they got wed, Kenton was arrested for breaking and entering and got sent down for twelve months. She would visit him everyday and he promised her that he would change his ways when he came out. He did everything to keep that promise. He went on a course to learn computerised engineering and times were hard whilst he was learning. Malitia would go out to work and half of the money was spent on his course but they both thought it would be worth it. He passed his exams with flying colours and got a small job quite soon afterwards. The two of them went out to celebrate with a couple of friends and they got a bit drunk. Malitia was driving back and this stupid kid in a stolen car swerved across the road in front of them. She lost control of the car and they drove into a brick wall. Kenton explained that he got out of the car and dealt with the little punk who had also crashed before he realised just how bad she was. He got an ambulance but Malitia died on the way to hospital.

Kenton thought back to that fateful evening and found it hard again not to be overtaken with guilt because of how he had reacted. At the time, he only had one thought in his mind immediately after the accident and that was to kick ten tons of shit out of the little sod who had been driving the other vehicle. Kenton went straight over to the young lad who was still half stuck behind the steering wheel. He could have only been about fifteen years old but that didn't stop Kenton. He pulled him out from the car probably breaking one of his legs as he did so. He laid into the young boy with a couple of full on punches before pushing him to the ground and laying a full kick into the lad's chest. There was another young lad who had managed to get out of the crashed car from the other side but he legged it as soon as Kenton started to make for the car. Kenton hadn't even considered that Malitia might be badly hurt. All he felt was anger. It was this fact that Kenton found hard to live with. He was more concerned about beating the life out of some young kid whilst leaving his lovely Malitia to die.

Trisha listened to his story and finished up with tears trickling down her face. Kenton went on to say that he never thought that anyone would ever take Malitias' place in his heart and he joined the Army to get away from the area where he had all of his memories. He wanted Trisha to know all this but hadn't been able to tell her before and when it got close to being able to tell her, things would go wrong and they would split up. He told her that he didn't want that to keep happening and hoped that she could still love him. By the time Kenton had got to this stage, they had finished their meal and were walking back to their hotel so as to be in before the curfew. Trisha was holding his arm very tightly and as it was reasonably cold, Kenton put his arm around Trisha. They didn't have far to walk but Kenton was concerned as he knew that he had told her a lot more about himself tonight than he had wanted to. He had never told anyone outside of his family about this side of his life and he had certainly told her a lot more than she could have guessed. Kenton was particularly worried that it could spoil the whole weekend. He needn't of worried. Everything was cool and what was more, they had booked one more room than was really necessary.

Chapter 7   -   THE LISTS

Gary had been excited all day waiting for this moment to arrive. He had pretty much decided that two o'clock would probably come and go without anything actually happening but Gary was in for a shock. He just happened to look up at the clock on his wall as it said 13:59 hours and at that very moment his phone rang. Was this the call? Could this be just a big hoax? Gary answered the phone in his normal manner.
"Hello Newson." Gary spoke with a slight nervousness in his voice.
"Hello Gary thanks for being there," the voice on the other end replied. Gary thought that the voice sounded familiar but it wasn't one that he could instantly recognise or attempt to put a name to. He was however pretty sure it was the same voice that he had heard in the back lane though which he guessed sort of made sense.
"Are you the person who left me the letter?"
"Yes that was me. Sorry for the way I've contacted you but I need to be careful. Would you be prepared to meet me in person?" The voice replied.
"I don't know who you are?" Gary replied with a very cautious tone.
"You do know me. You will recognise me, I promise," the caller said in an effort to put Gary more at ease. "Would you be prepared to meet me please?" The voice spoke in such a desperate manner that Gary felt he had no option but to agree. Gary wasn't quite sure if it was the right thing to do or not but the voice sounded familiar, like a long lost friend that he just couldn't put a face to, nor a name for that matter. Gary decided that even if he did agree to meet, he didn't necessarily have to go through with it.
"Yes okay. When and where?" Gary replied trying not to sound uncertain.
"How about in half an hours time. It's best to get this done now rather than wait. A place of your choosing so you know where you are and may feel a bit better about meeting me," the voice said. Gary thought for a second or two. He was a lot happier that he was able to choose the place but then he hadn't really got any idea what sort of place he ought to meet a stranger. Should it be an empty place or full of members of the public? Gary didn't know. The thought was painful. Suddenly it came to him.
"I'll be in the library, reference section. Is that okay?" Gary asked. There was a slight pause so Gary just added, "Do you know where the

library is?" Gary had always assumed that the stranger was from Waydon or at least from Kentley. There was now a small doubt that the stranger might just know Gary from somewhere else.
"Yes. I'll come and re-introduce myself," the voice replied and almost immediately the phone went dead. Well that was a bit of a turn up for the books. Gary was the person the envelope was intended for. This had revolutionaries written all over it.

Gary guessed it wasn't the local revolutionaries though. He hoped that they would be able to recognize each other. It seemed most likely that the stranger knew him at least. Gary wondered if he was being set up. What could he be being set up for? There seemed to be no plausible answer to that question. For some reason, Gary was quite excited about it all. His heart was starting to beat a little faster and no doubt the adrenalin had been racing a bit. Gary tidied up his desk and put away his files as if he was packing up for the day just as the Assistant Postmaster walked in.
"Gary, are you off out again?" The AP asked.
"Just following up another couple of reports boss!" Gary lied.
"Okay, I won't stop you now but can I see you briefly when you get in tomorrow morning." The AP didn't put this as a question or a request but more of an order.
"Yes will nine o'clock be okay?" Gary asked.
"Yes see you then." The Assistant Postmaster said as he sped off back towards the work floor and then up to his office. He didn't acknowledge any of the actual workers as this was not the management way. Anyhow, he was too busy doing far more important things. Within a couple of seconds he was gone. Gary wondered if it was a follow-up to the questioning about the Longhurst case. He had hoped that that had all finished. Gary told the staff he would be out for the rest of the day and he made his way to his car.

It wasn't far to the library and Gary knew that this afternoon it would be open. He quite enjoyed being able to look through some of the large amount of books that the library had access to. Local history was a particular favourite subject and he would often look through old lists of Kentley's residents and old books that showed the shops full of business. As he browsed he came across a big reference book entitled 'Kentley in the twentieth Century'. How times must have been then back in the old 1900's. Gary found it hard to imagine sometimes, even though he had been alive in the 1900's him self. How things had changed. Gary found another old book which gave a brief history of the railways decline in the Kentley area. There was an old picture of Kentley station as it used to be around 1984. Grand, smart and full of life! There were passengers and taxis, busses and paper sellers in the picture and he could imagine what the atmosphere must have been like back in the 1980's. There was also an area next to the station that Gary had completely forgotten had been there.

"Hello Gary. May I join you?" A voice came from behind. Gary had almost forgotten what he had come to the library for. He looked up at the man and recognised him instantly. It was a little weird to take on board but things were starting to drop into place all of a sudden. Not only did he recognise the stranger as his old Assistant Postmaster, the one who had given him a hard time about opening that letter, but he all of a sudden remembered his name.

"Bloody hell! What are you doing here?" Gary asked still shaking his head with amazement.

"Well I've come to meet you," the man answered a bit confused with Gary's question.

"Oh yes of course. Sit down," Gary pulled out the chair next to him. Gary could hardly believe it was the old Assistant Postmaster. The only one who had really put Gary in his place in the past. Gary didn't work under him for too long but had a sort of respect for him.

"Good to see you remembering the old days," the AP said.

"Yes I love to look through these old books." Gary said a bit embarrassed.

"Well you're probably wondering why I've been trying to make contact with you? You do recognise me don't you?" The man suddenly had doubts.

"Yes of course I do. Mr. Longhurst, I seem to recall. Not a name I could ever forget." Gary tried to sound convincing.

"Long Hurst. That's right!" The man repeated his name in a very deliberate manner.

"Yes. Andrew Longhurst." Gary said with renewed confidence.

"You do remember." Andrew replied.

"You did sort of disappear under rather strange circumstances if you don't mind me saying and nobody at work really ever explained why you went?" Gary said. "All they would say was that you were too ill to come back to work."

"I'll try and explain." Andrew told him.

Andrew looked around to see who else was in the library but apart from an old woman on the other side of the reference section and the two members of staff who were chatting at reception, the place was empty. What a bloody good choice of place to meet he thought to himself. "You might have guessed by now that I am involved with the revolutionary movement known as 'Phoenix'. Have you heard of us?" Andrew asked.

"No I don't think so." Gary replied.

"Well we're a global movement whose aim is to try and restore Europe back to its former greatness where Britain has control of its own destiny and isn't reliant on the handouts from Germany and France. I won't go on too much."

"I know a lot about what is happening." Gary assured him. Andrew was trying to keep his voice as quiet as possible so that nobody else could overhear the conversation.

"I started off working for the local sympathizers and got involved in organizing little rallies. Handing out leaflets here and attending riots there but a couple from the National Party soon caught on to where I worked and felt I could offer them much more if I was to go underground. My position at that time was Postal Service Manager, like yourself but it wasn't long until I got promotion to AP and came into my own."

Gary stopped Andrew from talking by touching his arm.

"Interesting as this is, should you be telling me all this?" Gary asked in a worried tone.

"Normally you'd be right but I need you to help me and didn't think it fair to ask for your help without letting you know why it was needed." Andrew answered.

"I haven't said I'd help." Gary replied.

"I know but I have checked out your current activities and know you come from the same side of the fence as I do. If you know what I mean? We appreciate you're not as deeply committed as many, that's not a problem as long as you're not pro the European Army and we don't think you are." Andrew explained.

"Okay, carry on." Gary sat back.

"I'll even give you some restricted information about me that you could use against me if you wanted to." Andrew told Gary. "I'm an undercover agent going by the code name of Captain Flint. Not even the local revolutionaries know that." Andrew told him. Gary was immediately impressed with the thought that he had been given some restricted information. Then Gary was a bit surprised to think that this man would trust him to tell him such information.

All of a sudden Gary got worried. Surely this was definitely information that Andrew shouldn't be telling him. "But now you've told me that I'm in a position to blow your cover right out of the water." Gary turned and looked at Andrew as he said it.
"Yes if you were to walk into an Army HQ and tell them, and only then, if they in turn were to actually believe you." Andrew replied.
"But you've put me in a very awkward position haven't you. If you were to be arrested in the next couple of days by the Army, I'll have a load of bloody revolutionary sympathizers chasing after me won't I?" Gary said with a worried expression.
"I think I got to know you a little bit when you worked for me and I have been doing some checks more recently and we're fairly convinced that you are not going to hand me in." Andrew replied. "In any case, I'm not going to tell anyone that I've told you my code name."
"Okay well tell me more." Gary hurried him.
"With my new position at the Post Office I was quite soon able to overlook what work people like yourself and others did on the mail. Members of 'Phoenix' would send me details of suspected or identified Euro Army agents and I in turn could then either arrange for their mail to be looked at, intercepted or if one of their names came up in a case file I would look at the file and try and push cases in the right direction." Andrew explained. Gary sat and stared for a few seconds.
"What is it?"
"I'm just trying to remember back to any times when you made me do something with a file that I didn't agree with but I cannot remember you interfering at all."
"I would also use my influence with others. It would only be as a last resort that I would have to come and order you to do something and you're right, I don't think that situation ever arose. Anyway as a consequence of all this work I was doing I had to write up a list of Euro Army undercover agents," Andrew explained. "Also as part of my work, I would look at the mail going to various people who were quite high up in the local revolutionary circles or if there was a visiting agent just to make sure that you didn't check out one of our people too much. Subsequently there was also a list of local revolutionaries."

"Intriguing!" Gary put in a comment to prove that he was still paying attention.

"Lastly I also need to tell you that I was working for a much higher undercover agent than me known to me only as Robert Stevenson. He is a highly trained operative who runs a network of assassins and through them arranges most of the Phoenix approved killings. He has been working for the last couple of years on a big hit list of retired and currently serving high ranking Euro Army officials. The Revolutionary Party leaders have decreed that they are all to be assassinated and Robert Stevenson will organise each one of them. It is in everyone's best interest that the list of targets doesn't stay in the same place for too long so the list gets sent to different trusted undercover agents who hold the list for a short time until it is needed again. So when it was my turn to look after the list, they stayed in my safe at work." Andrew had more or less completed this part of his story and he sat back to take a breather.

"So these lists have been in your old safe at work all this time?" Gary asked.

"That's where I used to keep them but they're not there now." Andrew replied.

"So where are they now?" Gary asked excitedly.

"Well I'll move on to the period around the time of my disappearance, about six or seven months ago when things went wrong." Andrew said.

"Please carry on." Gary hurried him up again.

"One of the top Phoenix people in London was very interested in the work that was going on and he wanted to see the list of Euro Army agents, or at least suspected agents, for himself. I was asked to get the list to him somehow so I took steps to get it out of the safe at work ready for it to be taken to London in the next few days. Then came that fateful morning when I received the phone call from my contact in London telling me that they, The Euro Army I mean, had got information that Andrew Longhurst was working as an agent for the revolution. Some bastard had given them my name." Andrew spat as he said the last sentence.

"How do you know you were ratted on?" Gary asked.

"Oh we have our agents and they have theirs. Some are double agents, ours working for them and theirs working for us. It's all a bit of a game I suppose but anyway someone in our little locality circle was feeding information about me to the Army. I knew that it was likely that both my house and place of work was going to be searched soon so I had to quickly try to retrieve the list and get it to another safe holding. I was still waiting for confirmation of where I could take the list to and perhaps rather fortunately I panicked a bit and moved the list, plus some other papers I was holding and put them somewhere close by that would probably not get searched."

"So where did you put them then?" Gary asked curiously.

"Well it was quite easy really. I put the lists into another envelope, waited for you to leave your office and put the envelope in your safe." Andrew said with pride.

"You put them in the safe. My safe?" Gary said in a slightly high pitched voice. Gary had forgotten where they were and he looked around to see the staff looking at the two of them. Gary raised his hand as a sign of an apology and then lowered his voice again. The staff got on with their work. "That means I've been at risk for the last six months or so of being accused of holding onto revolutionary documents." Gary went red in the face.

"Hold your hat," Andrew replied. "You were perfectly okay. Who goes through the documents in your safe?"

"Nobody but that's not the point."

"You've so much old crap in there you don't even know if an extra envelope has been added or not. The envelope had my writing on it. It was quite safe, nobody would question the contents. Anyway, the idea was to come back and get the lists in the next few days but things went from bad to worse."

Andrew took a deep breath. "What happened?" Gary asked in anticipation.

"Well I got to my house and started to get ready to make my exit but it then dawned on me that I'd better sterilize the place first so that they wouldn't get any evidence of my other papers, but just as I was burning the last few sheets I got another phone call to say that the Army were on their way. Bloody close call because as I went out the back door and was jumping over the garden wall at the back, my front door was knocked down. I literally jumped over into the old man's garden and landed slap bang in the middle of a manure heap that the old man used for his allotments. A soldier called me over as I headed across the garden and he even asked me if I knew Andrew Longhurst. I told him I knew the bloke from the house they were in and that he had left about ten minutes previously. I think the soldier was so pleased to get some information and so keen to get away from the smell of manure he went charging off back into my house whilst I escaped."

"That was a bloody close call then."

"Yes too bloody close. If they'd briefed their soldiers a bit better I'd have been done for there and then." Andrew laughed a bit as he remembered that particular incident. "I didn't clean the house properly unfortunately and the Army soon discovered who I was and some of the other sort of things I'd been up to. I've been on the run ever since and now I'm back to try and clear up my mess but of course whilst having to keep my head down."

"Did you find out who gave the Army your name?" Gary asked.

"Yes but I don't think you would have known him at all. He was a local lad who had appeared quite keen to get involved in the local revolutionary scene and on occasions helped me out a little bit. We eventually found him out by feeding him false information and he has been properly dealt with." Andrew said.

"And the lists?" Gary continued to question.

"Yes the lists." Andrew drew a breath. "I was still waiting for approval that my contact in Waydon would still be able to take the lists so I had to get word to someone that I was unable to get the list to them, then I laid low." Andrew paused.

"You have a contact in Waydon?" Gary sounded surprised.

"We have contacts and agents all over the place. You'll be surprised."

"What sort of people?" Gary asked without really thinking.

"I can't tell you of course but people in all walks of life. People you wouldn't even start to suspect. Unfortunately there aren't many living close to Waydon and I think on reflection it was lucky that I hadn't already passed the lists to them as subsequent events seem to suggest that The Army were obviously well aware of who the contact was." Gary thought about what Andrew had just told him and his next line was just an automatic reaction.

"Is that why the school was raided by The Army?" Gary had started to put two and two together. Andrew looked at Gary in a funny way but very briefly.

"I can't say anything on that subject. The person I was to give them to managed to pass the message on to London somehow and it was decided that it was too dangerous for me to try and retrieve the lists back so we left them till things died down a bit." Andrew finished.

There was a short pause and Gary touched Andrews arm and bent his head down as if he wanted to whisper something.
"I think we ought to change the subject a bit." Gary suggested to Andrew.
"What do you mean?" Andrew had got carried away and he hadn't noticed what Gary had. The two staff had been watching the two of them chatting for the last few minutes and were getting more and more suspicious. It was time to leave. Gary shoved a local history book in front of Andrew as if it was the book they had been discussing. After a few seconds, Gary closed the book and returned it to the shelf. The two of them got up from the table and started to make their way towards the exit. Andrew said thank you to the assistant who was stood at the desk as they passed by. The two men left the library.
"Shall we drive somewhere?" Gary asked.
"I've got to get back to Waydon somehow so if you're offering." Andrew replied. The two men got into Gary's car and set off for Waydon.

Andrew started the conversation as the car drove through the town. "You know that the Germans and French are still controlling European affairs I suppose?"
"Yes that's how I understand it." Gary replied.
"They're controlling fictitious little wars all over the place where they send other European troops off to be murdered so as to keep the population down. There is starvation in most European countries but not France or Germany. We're getting ready to rebel. The old British Army is ready to reinstate themselves when the big revolution starts and we've got American arms to help." Andrew started to go into one of his talks.
"Yes I know, I know." Gary replied.
"Sorry. I should be more controlled." Andrew apologised.
"There is something else you need to know about. Recent things that have happened at the Sorting Office in just the last week." Gary said.
"Like what?" Andrew asked.
"There was a letter for you which became the subject of a case file sent to me. Normally I would have done a few checks and sent it on its way but firstly I recognised the name. I couldn't remember exactly where from to start with but of course I know now. Also the address was in my own village of Waydon so I checked the letter out further than I perhaps should have done. Initial checks didn't show much so I

did some observations on your house."

"You've been doing observations on me?" Andrew queried.

"Yes. Don't get over excited about that it's all part of my job. Anyway it would appear that unfortunately others were also doing observations at the same time."

"How do you know?" Andrew asked.

"They asked me at work what I was doing observations on the place for and I never put that in my report so I must have been seen. Bad thing is if they saw what I saw, you've been sussed." Gary exclaimed.

"What do you mean?"

"It didn't take much to find out that Mr. Hobbs is restricted to a wheel chair but you could see your shadow walking about most nights." Gary told him.

"Oh. I see."

"Anyway, I didn't put that in my report either but the report has gone upstairs like a bullet. I put the details on my computer and the AP was down asking for the file about twenty minutes later."

"Bloody hell that is quick. Either they have my name on a list or they are checking you out as well."

"Well thirty minutes after that the PM was down after the same file." Gary added.

"Shows they are working from different sides, doesn't it?" Andrew shook his head.

"I have been wondering if I have been watched or not. What are you going to do about these lists then?" Gary asked.

"I need you to get them to me," Andrew replied.

"I'm not touching them if they're watching me at work for God's sake. I'm not happy about doing that." Gary told him.

"You haven't got to do much and we'll be most thankful to you." Andrew tried to convince him. "Firstly I need you to check that the envelope is still there. It's a brown envelope with 'Staff rosters 2023' written on it."

"Yes that's still there. I saw it the other day." Gary replied.

"Just see if you can get the lists. My sister will be in touch with you in a couple of days to see if you have any news. You can drop me off here." Andrew said as the car just entered Waydon. Andrew got out and quickly walked off. Gary continued on his way home.

As Gary approached home he was reasonably happy that he had managed to get home at a good time for once and hoped that

Angela might be in a better frame of mind than she had been recently. He put the car away in the garage and walked in to be greeted by Joan and Katy as well as Sammy.
"Hello Daddy." The girls both said.
"Hello. How's your Mum?" Gary tried to get the low down.
"I'm alright thanks." Angela said as she too came out see him. The two hugged but it was one of those 'I'm not too sure hugs' a bit like celebrities give each other when they meet on television. Gary was pleased that at least Angela was seemingly nice.
"Daddy! Are you taking Sammy out tonight?" Joan asked.
"Yes I would think so." Gary replied.
"Can I come with you?"
"As long as Mummy agrees." Gary replied.
"As long as you're back before five thirty." Angela told him.
"Katy. Do you want to come?" Gary shouted through to the living room.
"No thanks!" Came the reply. The two of them put their coats on and got Sammy ready to go out. As usual, Sammy was away as soon as Gary put the lead on him. Gary and Joan chased behind.
"Be careful." Angela shouted.
"We will."

Tonight's walk was quite different. Gary chatted away to Joan about school, homework, make-up and boyfriends. This last subject was a bit awkward as it had never come up before. Although Joan was aged thirteen, she was a very young thirteen and had never shown any interest in boys or men as far as Gary had known. Obviously things were changing. There were no names but it seemed obvious that Joan had a boy in mind when she talked about love. Gary did his best to steer her away from really awkward questions without lying or refusing to answer anything and Joan seemed reasonably happy with the answers she was getting. It certainly helped cut the dog walking short and they were back home just before half past five.
As Gary got in he noticed without too much trouble that the atmosphere had changed.
"Who is Andrew?" Angela asked as soon as he got in the back door. A number of things went through Gary's head. Had he left the letter from Andrew laying about. No he didn't think so. "So who is Andrew?" Angela repeated.
"He is an old boss of mine. Why?"

"A woman just rang to leave you a message. She will leave it a few days until she collects the package you're preparing for Andrew. That was the message. What is that all about?" Angela threw down the tea towel that was in her hand.

"I'm doing a little job at work that he is involved with."

"Rubbish. Why would a woman ring you at home to leave you a message if it was work." Angela held back her tears. Gary knew he was not going to be able to explain this one away very easily.

"Honest. It's some papers that I'm getting from work for him." Gary hadn't even convinced himself as he said it.

"I know when you're lying Gary Newson. It sounds very much to me like your passing over secret papers to a revolutionary agent. That's what it sounds like. Tell me you're not Gary, please tell me you're not." Angela pleaded.

"He isn't an agent," was all that Gary could say.

"I've asked you not to get involved. I've begged you to think about your family. Yet still you do this sort of thing. I'm sorry but this is just the last straw." Angela growled.

"You've got nothing to worry about. I'm not getting too involved with this bloke. He just needs something from work." Gary tried to explain.

"Then why doesn't he just go to work and get it? Why does he need someone to pass a 'package' to a woman? Why has that someone got to be you?" Angela just shook her head.

"It's nothing honest."

"I will not put the girls in danger. I think you need some time whilst you think about where your priorities lay. What comes first? Revolution, work or family? If you can answer that question correctly, let me know." Angela said.

-

      The Intelligence agent for Operation Hunting had not been letting things go slack. A lot of intelligence was normally obtained by getting out into the field and meeting people and talking to them. It wasn't the only way to find out things but it was surprising how much you could find out this way from so little effort. Another meeting was held at the offices of St. Michaels' Import & Export. Major Tannier did most of the listening on this occasion.

"Well I think I've got to the bottom of our Ms Tetridge," the agent started the conversation.

"What have you found out?"
"Turns out that her maiden name was Clark."
"And her sister?" The Major asked.
"Yes, Miss Julie Clark. She's the school teacher in Waydon who we thought might be holding the lists. We've got nothing on her at the moment to confirm this of course." The agent answered. The agent looked at the Major as if expecting another question but one never came so continued. "Both Jenny and Julie were training to become athletes and both decided to start training as teachers but Jenny went to a different college to her sister. There she met a Dutchman who took her back to Holland and married her," the agent completed more of the picture.
"Was this Dutchman in the Army?" The Major asked.
"No he was a sympathizer and obviously had similar ideals to Jenny." The agent continued, "Anyway it would appear that the marriage lasted only a few years and our Jenny returned to the area, everyone thinking that she was Dutch."
"Is there anything you want done?" The Major asked with hope.
"No we know what we want to know. We'll leave it at that."

The two then chatted about the photographs, which were still being waited for and things were being brought to an end when the agent remembered the one thing that needed to be said to the Major.
"Oh yes, the Hobbs."
"What about them?" The Major asked.
"The husband has a number of entries in his record about disablement, hospital visits etc."
"Yes I've looked at the records."
"Have you seen the last time that Mr. Hobbs was actually seen by anyone?" The agent put the question to the Major with a satisfying tone.
"No. Please enlighten me."
"Well it was nearly three months ago."
"That isn't that long is it?" The Major said confused.
"No maybe not but the rumour going around the village is that Mr. Hobbs cannot get out of bed that easily. In fact he is almost house bound." The agent had made the point.
"So what are you trying to say?"
"Not much except that you wouldn't expect the Hobbs to go shopping would you?" The agent put the point to the Major.

"And your point again is?" The Major asked
"Well if you could write to Mr. Hobbs and conjure up some of reason why he might have to come into the office and we'll see how easy it is for him to actually make it". The agent was happy that this more or less concluded their affairs for today but just got reassurance that contact would be made when an appointment had been agreed.

-

    The very next day at work Gary couldn't wait to get into his office and unlock his safe. He arrived at about his usual time and said hello to the early shift.
"Tea will be ready in about ten minutes boss," came the shout from one of the early shift.
"Okay I'll be down again for tea." Gary replied. He dashed straight up to his office and dumped his briefcase on the desk. He hurriedly took off his coat and hung it up and then unlocked the safe. It wasn't unusual for the safe to be unlocked this early it was just that Gary would normally settle in first before doing so. Depending on how Gary felt, settling in could take ten minutes or an hour. Gary took his work trays out of the safe and put them on his desk and then he looked into the safe to look at all the other rubbish he had in there. There was more than he had realized with a number of sealed envelopes all bunched together at the back. Gary took these out and sifted each one in turn. The second one was entitled 'Staff rosters 2023' just as Andrew Longhurst had said. Gary put the whole bunch of envelopes back into the safe and went off for his early morning tea.
"Alright boss?"
"Yeah thanks. How are things going with the sorting this morning?"
"We seem to have got more in today than usual." One of the team informed Gary. "But we're getting through it okay," he added.
"Have any of you met the new lad yet, Barry?" Gary asked.
"Yes I met him the other day," replied Andrea. "He seemed quite nice and keen to learn the job."
"Do you think he'll be okay then?"
"Yes he'll fit in well." Andrea assured him.

    Morning tea lasted for about another ten minutes and then Gary got up to return to his office. His main thought was that he had probably about half an hour before the AP came in if he was going to do anything with the envelope. The AP wanted to see him this morning so he knew he would be in earlier than normal. Gary walked passed his office and upstairs to the management level. He ventured down to the AP's office just in case he was in but of course it was empty. The PM's office was also unoccupied but for some reason the door was open. Gary stepped inside to look around just in case there were any problems but everything seemed okay. Gary was about to turn and leave when he caught sight of the PM's little stationery pile on his desk. Amongst the collection were some empty envelopes of the same type that were used to store the so called staff rosters from 2023. Gary looked around and took two of the envelopes. He returned to his office and put the unused envelopes in his briefcase whilst he then sat down and got on with his normal everyday work.

   The day seemed to be dragging for Gary. He wanted to make sure that most people had left before he took his next course of action. With most of his work finished for the day, Gary made sure that both the managers had gone and only the late shift were working downstairs. It wasn't that unusual for the Postal Service Manager to work late so nobody questioned the fact that Gary was still in his office at six fifteen. Gary had waited long enough and he decided that if he was ever going to do this then it had to be now. He took the dreaded envelope from the safe and placed it on his desk. He then took one of the blank envelopes from his briefcase and started to write the same heading on it, in the same sort of writing as was on the envelope he had taken from the safe. It was a reasonable copy even if Gary did say so himself. Gary then put some folded sheets of blank paper in the envelope and sealed it and put it in the safe in place of the other envelope. He put the original in his briefcase, loaded up his safe and locked it. Within a minute he had his coat on and he was out of the office.
"See you later." Andy Gray shouted out.
"Yeah okay. Have a good night boys." Gary replied. The drive home was a bit fast but Gary got home just before seven.
"You're bloody late again. Where have you been this time?" Angela started on him as soon as he got in the door.
"I had to work late, something came up." Gary replied.
"You never tell me. You didn't phone. I've just about had enough of this Gary, I won't take anymore." Angela stormed off into the living room more or less in tears. Gary daren't ask about any dinner but he

crept into the kitchen to find a saucepan on the cooker which contained a sort of casserole. It had vegetables in and probably some sort of off cut of meat that Angela would have got hold of. Gary warmed it up and served himself a bowl of it which he ate in the kitchen.
"Eating in here eh?" Angela said to him as she stood at the kitchen door.
"I guessed this was for me."
"I think you can cook your own meals from now on Gary. If you can't tell me what you're doing then you look after yourself. I'm going to bed. Don't disturb me when you come up." Angela made it very clear what she thought. Angela was looking for Gary to say something to show that he was still interested in their marriage but there was no hint of a conversation coming from him. Gary just carried on eating the casserole. Gary felt that whatever he had to say, Angela would find fault in it so decided it was better not to say anything. At least then Angela didn't shout at him. As soon as Angela had gone upstairs Gary poured himself a drink and then got his briefcase and went into the living room. He undone it and took out the envelope and placed it on the table. As much as possible, Gary unsealed the envelope without tearing the paper. He knew it would be impossible to reseal it so that nobody could see that it had been opened but he thought that if he could get the same envelope back in the safe so that from the front it looked unopened that would do. It took about twenty minutes to get the flap open. Gary tipped out the contents. There were clearly two lists.

He was quite surprised to find both sets of lists quite small. Both were on notepaper sized sheets as oppose to A4 sized, one on white paper and the other on blue. Gary looked at the names on the lists for ages and although he seemed to recognize some of the names they didn't really mean anything to him. They were mainly military ranked people and mainly foreign sounding surnames. He continued to look at the list just in case it started to mean something or at least until he started to get tired and he felt it was safe to go to bed.

As always, the thoughts of what he had been reading seemed to circle round in his mind. There were details that suggested that the Euro military were targeting areas that were believed to be anti-Europe and that they would cause food shortages in those areas so that the residents suffered. It talked about food deliveries being stopped or at least hindered and the prices being falsely inflated. It showed that the military and in particular France and Germany seemed to be orchestrating things. There were also details about hospitals being forced to let more people die. It all went round in Gary's mind.

The next day, Gary spent most of his day wondering what the hell he should do about the lists. He thought about the fact that the authorities may have already set him up and were waiting to catch him in possession of the lists but there was also the impending visit of the old PM's sister. He wasn't sure what he should do but felt that he would not be able to get out of giving the old PM the lists. He was going to have to remove them for him in some way. Gary worked late again that day, an activity that became almost habit forming. He would be very busy doing suspect reports if anyone were to come in but he was in fact in the process of typing out the lists again for his own use. The original idea was to put the original envelope back into the safe and give the PM the copies but Gary's plans seem to change by the hour. Gary looked again at the list of names. There was also some writing relating to EU orders and something about a 'document of intent'. Gary read through it but it still meant very little.

On that first day, Gary was late home again and Angela was already in bed when he got home. Sammy jumped up and down in vain as he was not taken on his usual walk and Gary slept downstairs on the settee. Things were getting really bad in the Newson house. Gary also had a half bottle of Scotch in his briefcase which became a comfort to him. Angela may have been in bed but she didn't sleep.

Over the next few days, Gary continued to work late in the office and get home after Angela had gone to bed. The two of them were already beginning to live separate lives. At work, Gary was quite surprised that he was left mainly to his own devices. Very few people would call in to speak to him but there was one occasion when the AP stopped by to ask what he was working on.
"Hello Gary you seem to be hard at it." The AP said.
"Yes you know how it is. I've got a bit behind with some of my reports and need to catch up a bit." Gary replied. The AP came in and picked up a case file from Gary's desk.
"But these are old case files. This one's nearly five years old?" The AP pointed out.

"Yes I know." Gary replied.
"So why have you got so many old case files?"
"I always use the old files to see what I've done in the past. The cases may be old but the techniques don't change. You'll be surprised how useful they are." Gary picked up an old case file from his desk.
"You don't always use old files do you?" The AP questioned.
"No but if I'm stuck on where to go next to find out about a particular address I recall a similar case from before and look and see what I did to sort it out. It works every time." Gary assured him.
"Right okay. I look forward to reading your reports." The AP said as he left. That was a bit close, Gary thought. He's getting suspicious I think, thank God I'm nearly at the end. Gary wanted to finish what he was doing and he worked even later that night. It was nearly eight o'clock when he left for home. Technically, Gary should have got in touch with the Army HQ to tell them he was traveling late but he didn't bother. Other nights he hadn't seen a sign of an Army patrol but tonight was going to be different. Gary had only just got on to the Bateley Road and he was flagged down by an Army jeep.
"Excuse me sir but can I ask what you are doing out at this time of night?" The soldier asked him.
"Sorry but I've had to work late." Gary replied.
"Where do you work?"
"I'm the Postal Service Manager at the Sorting Office." Gary told him.
"Have you got identification papers please?" The soldier asked. Gary handed him his own personal ID card, his work pass, his car owners' certificate but he couldn't find his residents pass.
"I seem to have mislaid my residents pass." Gary had to tell the soldier.
"Where do you live exactly?"
"Number 3, Jamesland Road in Waydon!" Gary told him.
"If you could just park your car over there and get out we'll need to do a few checks." The soldier pointed to where Gary was to park and he did so. Gary had a quick look around and although he had noticed three soldiers when he had first been stopped it was obvious that back up had arrived just to make sure that there was no trouble. Gary got out of his car as he was instructed.
"I'm just going to quickly frisk you to make sure that you are not armed." The soldier told him. The Army personnel made various checks to ascertain whether or not Gary was who he said he was and

after about half an hour they had got enough replies from checks to be happy that he was. The only problem they had now was what to do about his residence as Gary could not find his pass.

"Mr. Newson, we are almost ready to let you on your way but we've sent a patrol out to your house to see if someone can vouch for you. Is there anyone at home?"

"My wife should be but she might be in bed." Gary replied with a feeling of impending doom.

"Well let's hope she's not a heavy sleeper." The soldier replied.

After about another ten minutes Gary was told he could be on his way. He was warned that in future he should contact the Army before setting out on a journey during curfew hours but nothing would be done about this occasion. Gary had watched them search his car, search him but fortunately they only looked very briefly into his briefcase. If they had been looking for documents, they weren't doing a very good job. Gary was confident that they had only stopped him because he was out late. A much bigger challenge was yet to come when he got home.

As Gary walked in he was a little surprised to find Angela up waiting for him.

"Just great!" Angela said shaking her head. "Absolutely brilliant!" She continued.

"Sorry, did they wake you up?" Gary asked.

"Did they wake me up? Did they bloody wake me up? The whole street is awake because of the noise they made. You've really done it this time." Angela was going red again with anger.

"I must have left my residents card in my other coat, I'm sorry." Gary tried to apologise but even he could see there was no use.

"Firstly you're sleeping down here tonight on the settee but you can sleep in the bed tomorrow night." Angela told him. Gary looked confused.

"What are you getting at? If you want us to sleep separately I'll sleep on the settee tomorrow night as well." Gary tried to be gracious.

"Sleep on the bloody settee tomorrow night if you want. I won't be here to care either way." Angela gave him such a dirty look that Gary felt as if his heart was literally being scratched at. Angela went up to bed leaving Gary to ponder on his new situation.

Gary tried to get himself comfortable on the settee that night but it just wasn't working. Various thoughts went through his head about what he could try and do tomorrow to stop Angela and the girls from going but he just couldn't agree on the best course of action. Gary tossed and turned but just couldn't seem to get to sleep. He would look up at the living room clock which had apparently moved on about ten minutes since he last looked at it. Gary got up and walked around a bit to see if he could clear his mind of his troubles but as soon as he got back on to the settee, they kept flooding back to him. He even did some press-ups to try and tire himself out. Nothing worked. Gary thought back to Angela's words, 'I won't be here to care either way' she said to him. The words repeated themselves a couple of times as Gary studied Angela's face as she was saying the words. He never thought he would ever hear her say anything like it. His mind wandered back to the times just after Angela had got out of the Army. Those two years had been very tough on both of them especially the last year. They actually went a period of over six months without seeing each other. Gary would write to Angela at the Kentley base but he would have no idea where she was until he received a letter back telling him what she had been doing for the last few weeks. He then remembered that great day when the letter arrived at his Kentley home. The family was living in Concord Avenue in those days in an overcrowded two bedroomed house. A letter was in amongst the mornings' post which Gary immediately recognised as an Army letter and he just knew it had to be from Angela. There was a partly written letter and then another memo attached to an invitation on a card. The memo read;

Dearest Gary,

I have been very busy lately dashing here and dashing there and as you can see I have even been back to Kentley base a couple of times. I would have rung but on my two visits have so far spent just the night and then five hours on base before being rushed off on another assignment. I have enclosed a half written letter that I started during a ceasefire in my last encounter in Spain and have now had to go off somewhere else.

As you will see, there is a party at the base next Saturday if you can make it. I should be getting back about mid-

afternoon on the same day. Hopefully I'll get a chance to get home and get changed. I'll ring as soon as I get home.

Love you always

A

xxxxxxxxxx

Gary could remember that letter to this day and practically word for word. Angela did get back that afternoon and she did ring him and they did go to the party. Gary had hoped that Angela would ring him as soon as she got back to the base but it was nearly six o'clock when she rang. Angela also lived in Kentley in those days, with her parents and her brother John. Gary remembered being a little put out when he learnt everything that had happened that day but then he was so pleased to see Angela that he put it all behind him quite quickly. It didn't come to light until later on that evening when Angela suggested that they leave the party early and the two of them began to discuss things in a bit more detail.
"I thought you were going to get back a bit earlier than you did?" Gary said to Angela.
"I got back late morning."
"Why didn't you ring me?" Gary said with a sorrowful whine.
"I had things to do." Angela replied.
"Things! What things?" Gary asked.
"Just things. Things so you'd be happy." Angela answered. Gary wasn't quite sure what Angela meant but guessed it was time to stop the inquisition.
"There's another party on tonight as well." Gary said.
"I know!" Angela replied as she looked at Gary and pulled a funny face. By now the two of them had left the Army base and were walking along the High Road towards the Market Place. "Perhaps we should go to this other party, what do you say?" Angela said. The party was being held by the unofficial revolutionary party and Gary had been invited through an old friend.
"Yes. It should be quite a good party." Gary answered. "But hang on a minute they won't let you in if you're a member of the Army will they." Gary pondered on this latest problem. "Not only that but I've left my bloody invitation behind." He continued.

"Who says I'm in the Army?" Angela said.
"They'll know you're in the Army." Gary replied.
"Well I'll just have to show them my discharge papers then, won't I!" Angela said letting the penny drop.
"Discharge papers!" Gary turned as he said it. "Discharge papers. You're kidding." He said.
"No. I have here my official discharge from the European Combined Forces." Angela said as she took out a many folded piece of paper. Sure enough it was her official discharge papers. Gary picked her up and squeezed her so tight she almost burst. They kissed quickly, looked at each other and then kissed some more before Gary put her back down again.
"I can't believe it." Gary said.
"I've been moving my things back home all afternoon." Angela explained. "And I wanted it to be a surprise for you."
"It was certainly a surprise." He replied.
"Hey do you feel like partying?" Angela said as the two of them made their way to the revolutionary party, party.
"You bet," he replied.
"Well it's also quite lucky that I have brought an invitation along with me." Angela said.
Gary was often amazed by some of the things that Angela did. Tonight was no different.

Gary remembered this party as being the start of some slightly better times in his life. Angela was back home and they were still very much in love. It was almost like having one of your arms sewn back on again after so many months. Gary and Angela went everywhere together. Gary was actually earning a wage so he was able to buy things for her and Angela had managed to save a lot of money from her Army pay so she too always seemed to have money. They went back to a few revolutionary meetings and at the first couple of meetings, Angela was treated as a bit of a celebrity having just come out of the Army. She would get up and tell the gathered crowd about certain things that had happened but she would normally tell Gary afterwards that he wasn't to believe every word she said as she was asked to make things sound a lot worse than they really were. It was probably a couple of months later that the two stopped going to meetings. They would still go out of an evening but quite often spend their evening drinking, or even just in a hotel room. They were so much in love that it wasn't long before Gary asked Angela to marry him. Angela accepted immediately but had to tell Gary that there were possible complications. She had just found out that she was pregnant and they both agreed that they didn't want their first child to be born outside of wedlock. The very next weekend, they drove away and spent the week in London arriving back the following weekend Mr. & Mrs. Newson. Yes, Gary remembered these happy times but then realised that he had been day dreaming. Or at least casting his mind back to how things used to be. With a bit of a bump he came back to how Angela had been with him that evening. Where had it all gone wrong he thought?

Gary kept on thinking about where it had all gone wrong and found himself driving, well at least sitting in his car saying those words, "Where had it all gone wrong?" There was no easy answer to it and the best thing would be to get out of the car and have a little walk around to try and clear his head. Gary got out and noticed that there were a number of other cars also stopped. The whole picture was a bit fuzzy as if he was trying to sober up from one of his all night drinking sessions and he was totally unable to focus properly on anything. He could make out cars and people in them but nothing was that clear that he could actually see what type of cars they were or who the people were inside. He became slightly aware of some movement just up ahead of him and Gary made his way towards the movement. It was a strange sensation as it was as if everything else around was practically at a stand still apart from this little incident ahead of him. Gary was also moving of course. He looked up whilst he was still moving and could see a couple of uniformed soldiers running about with automatic machine guns ready to be fired. It was a very unconscious thing but Gary seemed to increase the speed he was travelling at, almost like he was being carried on air so that in seconds he had reached the point of the incident. It was the shooting at the roadblock of course. Gary knew it was but was somehow hoping that it might be something different. Gary was aware that there was a figure in civilian clothes running away to his right and the uniformed soldiers were chasing that figure but he automatically looked down to where he had seen the dead blond woman only to find that there was a body covered with a groundsheet just exactly where he had seen one before. Once again, everything seemed to be running in slow motion like it had all been captured on film and that a cinema audience was watching a playback. As before there was not much sound although it wasn't completely silent. Gary stared at the groundsheet with a feeling of impending doom as if he knew exactly what was going to happen next. In fact he did know what was going to happen next. It was almost as if he was writing his own nightmare and was completely powerless to stop himself. He stared at the partial bit of blond hair that was not covered by the groundsheet. He wanted to look away but without any control of his actions he started to look closer at the blond hair. He was unable to look anywhere else.

    Although he knew what would happen next, he was still shocked to see the shape underneath the tarpaulin sheet apparently starting to move. The woman's arm grabbed hold of the edge of the sheet and threw it back in one fast clean movement exposing the full extent of the murdered victim laying underneath. Gary looked at her blond hair which was covered in blood. He then looked at her jumper which again was completely blood soaked. Most of her body had splashes of blood on it including her face. The woman started to cough and her head moved. Her eyes opened and immediately caught the staring eyes of Gary. He was still unable to turn away from her. She smiled at him and then started to get to her feet. As before, although there were soldiers all over the place they seemed completely oblivious to what was going on right in front of them. It was quite weird as if Gary was living in one world whilst the soldiers were living in another. They were all more concerned about the other incident that was going on behind Gary. The incident where the woman with the blond hair was trying to escape the roadblock. Gary continued to watch as the blond woman got to her feet. Originally her face had been blurred somehow although he was able to make out particular aspects of her face at different times. Never before had he been able to make out the whole of her face but now he could.
"Yes hello Gary." The woman said. "Yes you now know who I am." She continued. Gary of course had absolutely no idea who she was but it was definitely the woman he had seen lying dead at the roadblock. The woman continued to get to her feet and started getting into the motions of running whilst she kept her stare fixed on Gary.
"I need to tell you," she said. The words 'Tell you' repeated over and over as Gary was lifted by powers unknown into the allotments behind the fence where the woman was running to. Gary was powerless to do anything to help, he could only stand and watch as it seemed as if the

woman was only running to the allotments in order to continue to speak to Gary. That seemed to be her goal in life, nothing else mattered. She had jumped over the first fence but the second fence required a bit more technique to get over and she had got to the fence and was ready to climb it. All the time her eyes never stopped looking at Gary's.

"Watch her! Watch her! Look out for her!" The woman kept repeating those words as she seemed unable to just climb over the fence.

Watch out for her!" She repeated. Once again the endless repeating of the words was interrupted by a loud crack of gunfire as she was shot from behind. Her body jerked as the bullets hit her and she started to fall to her knees but she held on to the fence to keep herself standing for as long as she could. As before, the bullets exploded out of the front of the woman's stomach through her thick jumper, splashing blood everywhere. They literally tore through everything even though her jumper was already covered in blood, it had not previously been ripped apart like it was now. Another loud crack rang out as another load of bullets ripped into her body. All the time she kept her eyes transfixed on Gary.

"Watch out for her!" The woman said again as she started to fall to the ground in slow motion. Her voice was loud as if she was talking straight into Gary's ear. The soldier responsible for the shooting was directly in line behind her. As she fell, Gary became more and more aware of the soldier standing right behind her with the automatic weapon. The blond woman fell to her knees as more of the soldier was visible. Gary was staring at the woman as she fell and only had a blurred image of the soldier behind but it was obvious that the soldier was holding an automatic and that smoke was coming out of the barrel. The woman dropped to the ground completely and although she did not move her lips Gary could hear her saying to him,

"Watch out for her! Watch out for her!"

Gary slowly looked at the soldiers' boots and then gradually lifted his gaze up the soldiers body. The usual camouflage trousers and the gun could be seen. He worked his way up to the soldiers face but it was all blurred. It was obvious that the face was blackened with camouflage type paint so they could not be seen that easily but none of the other soldiers seemed to be wearing any. Gary's attention was then taken by some movement of the soldier's hands as they started to lift the gun more in the direction of Gary. He was sure that he was about to get shot and watched as the soldier pulled the trigger. There was no movement of the gun just a small sound of the trigger being pulled.

Gary woke with a start. He was sweating profusely. He wiped his forehead and looked around in an attempt to work out exactly where he was. After all that time Gary had obviously got to sleep and he had dreamt the same dream again but this time he had been woken up by the sound of the front door slamming shut. Sammy was sat on the floor looking up at Gary with his tail wagging.
"What is it boy?" Gary said to him as he stroked his head. All of a sudden it dawned on him what the noise had been. He jumped up and quickly put his trousers and jumper on and rushed up the stairs. Angela was not in bed. The wardrobe door was open and half the things were missing. He turned and went into Joan's bedroom. It was empty. He went into Katy's bedroom. The same! They had gone after all and left him sleeping on the settee. Gary could hardly believe it. He went back downstairs to look at the clock which said ten thirty. No wonder he had missed them.

Gary felt he ought to tell Sarah what had happened just in case she bumped into Angela around the village so off he went round to Sarah's house. He rang the door bell.
"Come in, it's not locked." Sarah shouted.
"Don't you think you ought to find out who it is before telling someone they can come in?" Gary questioned his sister's relaxed approach.
"Wouldn't be such a surprise if I did that," she replied.
"Sorry I haven't come round to argue, in fact I'm not stopping but felt you ought to know that Angela and I had another big argument again last night and she has finally decided to leave me." Gary explained.
"It was on the cards stupid." Sarah showed no sympathy.
"I know you told me." Gary slumped into a chair.
"So what are you going to do now?" Sarah asked him.
"Have another drink I suppose." Gary replied with a wry grin on his face. "I know I know!! That's the last thing I need to do."
"Do you want her back?" Sarah asked.
"Of course I want her back. I love her." Gary replied immediately.
"Good, then that's a start. I can't promise anything but I'll try and get in touch with her and find out how she feels but you've got to stop drinking." Sarah told him.

"I'll try." Gary replied.
"You'll have to try harder than that," she barked at him. "Now what will you be doing?"
"I will stop drinking." Gary said a little more positively.
"That's better."

-

  Gary had loads of things on his mind. Angela and the girls moving out was just about the last thing he needed although he should have seen what was happening. Perhaps because of all the other things that were going on was why he failed to see where his marriage was heading. All he could feel at the moment was anger. He loved Angela. He loved the girls. He worked hard to try and keep the family fed and clothed and although he knew he didn't earn a massive amount of money, it was a fairly good wage compared to a number of other families he knew. What had gone wrong? He then had the problem of the lists. Having been contacted by this old friend could he be walking into a trap. All of a sudden a strange scenario came into Gary's head. The authorities were suspicious of Gary so they plant the envelope in his safe and get one of their old employees, who for all Gary knew might still be an employee, to get Gary to hand them over. He could be working against Gary trying to get him to show revolutionary tendencies. The idea stayed with Gary for a while but then he was sure it was the same bloke he had heard in the lane and the way he was contacted in the first place meant he had to be for real. Could he trust the old AP? Gary couldn't be sure but then what did he have to lose.

  That evening there was a knock at the front door and Gary was at first surprised to find a middle aged woman standing at his front door.
"Oh you must be Mrs. Hobbs." Gary said.
"That's right," the woman answered.
"Do you want to come in?" Gary held the door open and the woman stepped into the hallway. Gary looked at the woman and was quite surprised to find that she was not quite how he had imagined her to be. Although obviously from a well educated background, Gary could tell by the way she spoke, it looked as if she had also come from a well brought up background. For instance the woman was wearing a Barbour coat and they were not very easy to get hold of. In fact Gary

would have said that practically only the old Royal family and perhaps some very high ranking Army officials would be able to buy them nowadays but then this coat had obviously seen better days. It had been looked after but was old. She had a Pringle jumper on and brown corduroy trousers which were then tucked into her posh olive-green 'Hunter' boots. She suggested that she was rich whichever way you looked at her.

"I have a message from my brother. He would like you to meet him next Tuesday at the Social Centre about three o'clock. He needs to know if you will have a package for him?" The woman spoke as if she had been practicing the lines from a written script, which she quite possibly had. "Do you have something for him?" She repeated.

"Tell your brother that I hope to have something for him by then." Gary replied. The woman having finished her mission turned to leave without saying another word. Gary shut the door and then went upstairs to watch the woman from his bedroom window. By the time he had got up there, she was no longer able to be seen. What a funny set up, Gary thought to himself. Perhaps I ought to check them out a bit more.

-

Operation Hunting is going very well again the agent thought. When you think back to last year and all the problems and failures it was good to see how well things had turned round and just how much intelligence was being collated. The file was becoming quite thick and a little awkward to follow in places but generally the information flowed through it quite sensibly. Again in the last couple of days, a lot more had been added to the file and another couple of leads needed following up. The agent had written out some orders for an assigned Unit to observe the Hobbs house and follow any men who left the house. They were also asked to follow any movements of Mrs. Hobbs by car. All this was passed through Major Tannier who would pass it on to one of the Kentley Units to work on. Just a forty eight hour job.

Quite soon the conversation came round to the photographs that the Agent had asked Major Tannier to get blown up.
"I've got the photos you wanted."
"Oh good let's have a look," said the agent excitedly.
"You listed six that you wanted blown up and here they are," said the Major. He spread the photos around the desk. "I took the liberty of

getting one of those blown up a bit more," he continued as he showed the agent.
"Very good work!"
"And from these we can establish that the first letter is a 'B'." The Major said proudly.
"And that definitely looks to me like an 'ER' at the end", the agent added.
"And then from this final one we have a 'P' and what looks like an 'O' following on from the 'B'."
"So when we put all of this together what do we have?" The agent asked.
"Well I'm going with BPO then the year and something ER," the Major answered.
"I'd say about four or five years old wouldn't you?"
"Yes seems about right to me", the Major answered in full agreement. The agent wrote a few notes and then thought for a few seconds. "I don't think we're looking at switched plates here so if we go with the model, make and colour, and let's say three years either way I think we'll have it."
"Have we got any good photos of the man in the car?" The agent enquired.
"No not really. One or two shots bur he is keeping his head down."
"Just show one or two of the photos to the troops involved in case they ring any bells."
"Leave it with me", the major replied. "I should have that done by tomorrow afternoon. How urgent do you want the results?"
"As soon as you can pop them round do so. I can then pick up any post as often as I can and I'll get them soon enough", the agent replied.

    Once again the two of them had engaged in some small talk about changes to certain military procedures when all of a sudden the Major remembered again something he'd forgotten about.
"Oh by the way, one of the top brass in Strasbourg wants to see you".
"What the devil for?"
"To discuss Operation Hunting of course," the Major said. He was a bit surprised that the agent hadn't guessed the reason for themselves.
"So who's coming then?" The agent asked.
"Nobody! You're going there." The Major continued, "We'll transport you to Lakenheath and from …."
"Hold on. What are you suggesting?" The agent interrupted.

"We'll sort out all the arrangements," the Major told the agent.
"No you won't," said the agent. "I'll book my ticket myself." On saying that, the agent got things ready to go and then started to lock up the office. "It would make a lot of sense for me to travel by domestic airline so as to keep under cover but you could do me a little favour."
"Yes what do you want?"
"I want you to continue with making arrangements to send out 'an agent' to Strasbourg as and when we get details and send one of your other staff instead. I'll let you have further instructions later", the agent concluded the conversation. The two left the office together but shook hands and went separate ways.

-

      Sarah quickly popped in to see Gary at home. Gary was in the living room sat at the table just thinking about life. There was an almost empty glass of whiskey on the table. Gary heard the door open, followed by the friendly knock on it to signify a friend. Gary quickly finished the drink in the glass and looked around for somewhere to put the empty. He hurriedly hid it in the old rubbish drawer but looked a bit embarrassed as he did so.
"Hello, put all your secret work away?" Sarah joked as she came in.
"Hell I don't know what to do when you come round now." Gary replied.
"What do you mean?"
"It's a choice of either getting all my work out of the way or the empty bottles!" Gary joked as he replied this time.
"You're in a good frame of mind." Sarah said.
"Not too bad I suppose. Bearing up."
"I've good news and bad news for you. How do you want it?"
"As it comes."
"Well I've managed to see Angela and she is quite happy to talk over your problems with me." Sarah told Gary.
"Is that the good news or the bad news?" Gary asked.
"That's the good news. I wasn't sure she'd want to chat about you at all."
"And the bad news?" Gary asked.
"She couldn't care less if you were dead at the moment."
"Oh I guess that's not as bad as it could be then!" Gary responded.

"She's hurt Gary. It'll take time. But at least I can communicate between the two of you. Look on that as the good side." Sarah shook her head. "I must get going. Now don't forget, no drinking."
"I know, no drinking." Gary repeated.

-

    Gary started to have a deep discussion with himself about whether or not he really had a drink problem or not. This afternoon was another one of those times when he felt that a debate was required on the subject. Gary didn't go to the pub that often like a lot of people so surely that was a plus showing that he wasn't an alcoholic. But then he thought that he had been drinking at home a lot more and remembered emptying the bin the other day full of empty bottles of whiskey and vodka. Another good point he thought as if he was really an alcoholic he would drink anything he could get his hands on and probably much cheaper drink than whiskey and vodka. Then he remembered that he'd been drinking wine quite a bit lately as well and he had a bottle of gin at work that had come from somewhere but he was convinced that as he kept his drinking to just mainly two different types, it proved that he was not an alcoholic. Anyway, and this was the real test, Gary didn't feel that he had to drink everyday. Alcoholics had to have a drink and Gary wasn't like that. Gary could stop for a while if he wanted to. For instance, he said to himself, I didn't have a drink yesterday did I? He thought for a moment and answered himself, well alright I had a couple of glasses of whiskey when I got home but that was all. I didn't drink the day before. Ah yes I finished off that bottle of Gin in the office. The day before I got completely drunk on vodka and I had a couple of bottles of wine with dinner the day before that. By now he had gone back over a week and still he couldn't think of when he last went a day without drinking. Then it dawned on him. He hadn't drunk anything so far today.

    Gary had bought a new bottle of vodka for the office which was conveniently laying in his bottom drawer. He looked at it then looked back at the clock. He looked at the bottle again and with a determined thought of mind he shut his drawer and packed up ready to go. Gary had a little job of his own to do before he actually went home. A little shopping. He left a bit earlier than usual. Gary was after a particular sort of something and he knew it wouldn't be easy to get one in Kentley. Certainly not a new one and possibly not an old one either but he knew that if he was going to find one he would have to go to an old bookshop he knew on Aldersgate. Gary had visited the place a few times and knew the proprietor quite well. Ben Thatchwell owned the shop and he knew Gary. Gary set out to walk over to Aldersgate, leaving his car in the car park rather than driving there. He fancied the walk. It didn't take long and within twenty minutes Gary had arrived. The whole area was in a pretty terrible state with many old shops boarded up and many houses apparently uninhabitable. As Gary made his way towards the shop a young boy of about seven or eight had stopped playing whatever game he had been involved in to watch Gary. The child had that look of empty pockets and stale bread and eyes that had seen pain. He was also accompanied by the desolate stench of poverty. These could never be regarded as indications of an auspicious existence. As Gary reached the shop he stopped and turned to look at the young boy who had been watching him. The boy ran away immediately.

    The shop was well run down and badly in need of a coat of paint but Ben still had a reasonable trade going even if he couldn't afford to keep the shop in proper order. Gary opened the front door and walked in. A bell rang as he did so. Ben was in the back room but didn't bother to come through immediately as this often put new customers off. Gary browsed the novels section. Alistair MacLean, Wilbur Smith and George Orwell all had big sections full of their novels. Some paperback, some hardback and varying conditions as well. Gary was always keen to look at the novels in the shop and spent many an hour just looking through a few pages of many famous novels.
"Hello Gary. How the devil are you?" Ben said as he made his way through from the back room.
"Quite well thanks Ben." Gary answered.
"Are you here to see Joe?"
"No I'm actually just looking around." Gary replied.
"Something particular?" Ben continued his interrogation.
"Maybe," Gary said. "I may need your help in a little while but for the moment I'm just having a great time looking at what you've got."
"You're into detective novels aren't you?" Ben said hopefully.
"I like them but I wouldn't say I was really into them as such." Gary answered.

"Just got a collection of Arthur Conan Doyles in. Good condition. Give you a good price on them." Ben was always quick to try and sell.
"Er no thanks."
"Or we have a decent copy of 'Mel's Book of Thoughts' if you're looking for something for someone special. You know; the lady in your life."
"Huh I don't think so." Ben would have carried on if Gary hadn't said anything. "I might give them a look in a bit but I just want to look at some of your non-fiction first." Gary knew that Ben was trying to sell and he didn't want to upset the old man but he certainly wasn't interested in buying any collections and certainly not poetry.
"If you need me, just ring the bell." Ben retired back into the back room and left Gary free to browse to his hearts content. Joe was of course Ben's son and an old schoolfriend of Gary's. They had been in the same class practically all the way up to leaving school but Joe had taken an extended time off due to some form of whooping cough that he had contracted in one of the later years and was kept in school an extra year so as to catch up with the work he had missed. Despite this, Gary and Joe had kept in touch after leaving school and still considered each other as good friends. Gary made his way round to the non-fiction section which was full of reference books and illustrated picture books. Gary again looked for the local history section and picked up the book he sort of dreamed of owning one day. It was titled, 'Brown's Kentley History' and told the story of how the small village was first formed and then grew into the town of today.

Gary read little bits from various books, flicking through pages when the bell on the front door rang again. It was automatic to look up and see who was entering the shop.
"Well bless my soul if it ain't Gary Newson." Joe Thatchwell said as he entered.
"Hello Joe." Gary answered as the two shook hands and gave each other a small hug.
"What brings you down here then?" Joe asked.
"Just looking around." Gary answered.
"And we haven't got what you want?" Joe shrugged his shoulders as he spoke.
"I don't know. I haven't finished looking yet." Gary replied. Ben then came through from the back.
"Hello boy. Has it been a good day?" Ben asked Joe.

"Yes Dad. Not a bad day at all. Have you seen who's here Dad?" Joe pulled his father through to look at Gary.
"I know son, I know. We've already said hello." Ben told him. Joe turned to Gary and asked,
"Are you going to stop for a cup of tea?"
"Yeah I don't mind but mustn't be late away of course." Gary replied. Joe and Ben both went through to the back and left Gary in the shop to continue perusing the books. He looked at a few books on cars and ships and then some sport books, all very colourful and full of big photographs. He then found the atlases and maps sections and Gary looked out for any old street guides to Kentley but naturally there were none at all. Ben had some English towns and cities but not very many. The selection then went on to foreign cities and Gary sifted through a box of foreign city maps.
"Cup of tea is ready. Do you take sugar Gary?" Ben asked as he came through with a mug of hot tea.
"As it comes please." Gary replied. The three of them sat down and started to chat about old times.

    The three of them sat back down and talked about old school friends that Ben could remember. There were quite a few as a lot of them would call into the shop to see Joe. In fact Gary remembered that the book shop was often used a meeting place for a lot of his mates. The discussions went on a bit and soon all three had found an old bottle of cheap whiskey to have a little drink from. They drank a couple of glasses of whiskey before they realised that the bottle was getting to the end.
"I'll have to go and get another one." Joe said as he lifted the bottle and looked at the small quantity left.
"Not on my account." Gary said. He stood up. "I've got to get home yet," he said as he looked at his watch. Gary did up his coat getting ready to leave. He would appreciate the walk back to the Post Office to get some air.
"Did you find anything you wanted Gary?" Ben asked, indicating the book shop.
"Just one thing. Totally forgot about it, sorry." Gary walked back into the reference bit and came back with an old street map in his hand. It was quite worn and folded but only about five years old. He showed it to Ben. "How much do you want for this old map?"

"You can have it on the house Gary. What the bloody hell do you want a street map of Strasbourg for?" Ben said.
"Just like to look and see how other cities in Europe used to be." Gary answered. "And if you're prepared to let me have it for nothing then I will return it to you when I have finished with it. I probably only need it for a couple of weeks." Gary replied. Gary said goodbye to Joe and Ben and gradually made his way back to the car. So much for not drinking today he thought to himself. Ah well, perhaps tomorrow.

Chapter 8   -   THE FOOD CENTRE

Another meeting was arranged between Major Tannier and the agent as there was some new intelligence, or at least new information to be passed over. The Major had used the usual system of arranging the meeting between them where he sent a typed letter to the agreed drop. The letter would contain mostly a script to do with ordering goods or something similar. It was all rubbish. Somewhere in the letter though there would contain a name of a place, a time and a date. This would be the meeting place. The Major had chosen that this meeting would take place in an old churchyard in one of the villages north of Kentley. It would mean driving to the venue but this wasn't a problem. Both arrived around the same time but separately and from different directions, the two of them looking as if they had come to pay some further respects to a dearly departed family member. The Agent had arrived first and was looking over a fairly newly dug grave. The Major gradually made his way over.
"Hope you're not too concerned with our meeting place today." Major Tannier said.
"Not at all! There's nobody about at all. It'll do fine," the agent replied.
"I have some news." The Major kept his words short. At last the results of the checks on the car registration numbers had come through and the Major was able to pass over a typed list of the numbers, car details and owners details. The Major took an envelope out from his inside coat pocket and he handed it to the agent. The Agent in turn removed the typed list from the envelope and unfolded the paper, perusing all the details very closely. For once the checks hadn't taken too long to be done and the agent had got the result that was required. Although there were four Ford Mondeos and two of them blue only one checked out to be in the region and seemed to fit in with everything else. The full number had checked out to be 'BRO 19 GER' and the registered owner of the vehicle was shown to be a Michael David Swindley who lived at 11, School Lane, Waydon.
"Yes this seems to fit the bill." The agent said looking at the list again.
"You will note from the report further on that we have also done some other checks on Swindley." The Major added. The agent turned the sheets over and read the relevant part. On receiving the results of the checks, a few extra checks were done on the local address. Everything

confirmed that the address was correct and up to date. Swindley had owned the car for the last eighteen months and he lived in the house all on his own.

"I would like the cottage checked tomorrow. Do you think you can arrange that?" The agent asked. It was really more of an order than a request but as the agent was outranked it had to be put politely.

"If that's what you want, I shall try and get it done."

"A couple of other things though." The agent paused.

"Am I going to like the sound of this?" The Major said in anticipation.

"Probably not but it is important to me. In fact I feel it is very important to the whole case. I want Unit Charlie 12 to be the Unit that does the call. They must be the main unit that enters and searches the house." The agent made this point very clearly.

"I follow your thinking." The Major concurred nodding his head. He didn't say so but he was already thinking along the same lines as the agent.

"There is more though. I also particularly want Private Rachel Dobbs to play a main part in the search of the house. She's very much impressed me with her reports and she seems to have got a particular feeling for this case. Assure me that will be done Major, please." The agent pleaded.

"I'll do everything in my power to make it so," Tannier replied.

"Even if it means talking nicely to Major Wooters?" The agent added a little sarcastically.

"Yes even if it means I have to tell him how bloody good he is." The two kept their heads bowed throughout most of this conversation as if they were praying but both sniggered at The Majors reply. "Are we any nearer to getting these lists then?" Major Tannier thought he would just try his luck.

"You know I can't tell you anything precise like that." The agent wanted to update him but wasn't allowed to.

"Yes I know, sorry." The Major forgot himself briefly but knew he shouldn't have asked. He'd heard little snippets about these so called lists but wasn't absolutely sure what their full content was or indeed what relevance they played. He knew that there was a great importance being put on their finding them. He had also guessed that they were lists of names. He knew no more than that. The agent knew only a little more. Business had been completed. Without saying anything else the agent left the grave they were stood in front of and departed. Major Tannier left no more than two minutes later. There was nobody else to be seen in the graveyard at all.

Major Tannier wasted no time in speaking to Major Wooters to try and get arrangements made for a raid of the cottage to be made the next morning. The two spoke on the phone and although relatively awkward, Major Tannier felt he had got Major Wooters on a good day. "You want the raid to be done by Unit Charlie 12?" Wooters queried the request.
"Yes this is part of an on-going operation and we would like the same people involved if that is possible." Major Tannier explained.
"But they are on-duty now and not due off till ten." Wooters told him.
"Surely they can be replaced this once, allowed some time off and then they could be ready for tomorrow morning." Tannier suggested.
"I suppose it could be done." Wooters agreed. As far as Major Tannier was concerned this was Wooters on a good day. He didn't really argue the point and without too much hassle agreed he would do what Intelligence wanted. Major Tannier then went on to ask if it could be arranged for Rachel Dobbs to be the main person involved in the search operation. Wooters did come back with a few lines on how cheeky it was for Intelligence to tell him how to run his own operations but once again after making his point, Wooters seemed happy to comply with everything that Major Tannier wanted. Major Tannier was quite relieved that things had gone so well with Wooters today.

Major Wooters played his part and the message got down to Unit Charlie 12 almost immediately. They were very quickly relieved that afternoon and allowed to go off duty for the rest of the afternoon and evening. The Unit would be aware that there was some special mission that they were going to be part of and most of them talked amongst themselves trying to guess what they might be doing. Only Major Tannier knew at this stage but he would brief his Sergeant soon. Everything went to plan and the Unit were briefed at 04.00hrs the next morning. By 05.00 hrs, Unit Charlie 12 were in Waydon and in position. Nobody knew what the usual movements of Michael Swindley were but a check on his work status had shown that Swindley was recorded as working as a factory worker for Potters Peas in Lavenham. This had been put in the briefing and suggested that this might mean an early start to work. The cover would be just right as this would leave Swindley free to do things in the afternoon or morning without having to take too much time off work. He would have enough time to operate as a revolutionary agent and still travel back home with the workers at five o'clock in the afternoon after having worked a full early shift or alternatively could operate in the morning and then get back home to start work in the afternoon. No approach was made to Potters Peas themselves to find out what shift Swindley may have been working that day just in case indications of their interest were let slip. The plan was to hope that he would still be in the cottage at the time they planned the raid even if he was working an early shift. The agent wasn't entirely convinced that Swindley was this great revolutionary agent everyone had all been looking for so the only course of action was a raid of his house.

It was a bitterly cold and slightly frosty morning as Unit Charlie 12 got out of the back of the Army lorry at the bottom end of School Lane. There was a crisp dew on the grass and soldiers left big boot marks everywhere they stood. Try as they did, it was also impossible for a group of soldiers not to make visible puffs of hot air as they breathed in the cold night. Sergeant Foulkes was glad to be back out on duty again even if he was still in some pain. He dispatched one of his Corporals down to the end of School Lane with instructions not to let anything in or out until told.
"Private. Two men over to the other side of the road", the Corporal ordered.
"Yes Sir!" The reply came.
"Anyone looking like they were thinking of turning into this road, stopped and detained. Take details of their identities and report but do it with the minimum of fuss and as little noise as possible."
"Understood, Sir!" The Private answered as he ran off with the two soldiers he had been allotted and they took up a position so that oncoming motorists wouldn't be able to see them till it was too late.

Sergeant Foulkes made sure that the rest of this team kept their eyes open for any movement from the nearby houses. The rest of the unit got back into the Army lorry and it continued driving up the lane. Sergeant Foulkes relayed a few more instructions and then he marched up the lane after it. The lorry came to a halt just about thirty yards passed the target house and the rest of Unit Charlie 12 got out again. Corporal King started to get a team of three to stand guard and stop any traffic coming down School Lane whilst the rest of the team

prepared for the raid. Sergeant Foulkes could see his breath quite clearly in the morning frost as he marched up the lane. He wasn't unfit but still recovering from recent wounds and so the march required a lot more effort than normal. All of the Unit were cold but disciplined enough not to stamp their feet to try and keep warm. Sergeant Foulkes approached the rest of his team.
"Are we ready Corporal?"
"Yes Sir."
"Where is Private Dobbs?"
"She is around somewhere Sir."
"Here Sir", came a response from Ed's left.
"You understand what you are doing?"
"Yes Sir. I've been fully briefed and I know what I have to do, Sir," she replied. The plan was to put in a telephone call to Swindley whilst Dobbs was at the front door looking and listening for signs of movement. As soon as signs indicated that Swindley was up or moving, the call would cut off. Then a second call would be made about two minutes later and when Dobbs was happy that Swindley was up again she would knock on the front door. She was only partly in uniform so that she could appear to be like a civilian through the front window. With everyone ready, Sergeant Foulkes made the first phone call. Private Dobbs heard the phone going and indicated with a thumbs up but then heard the sound of not one but at least two dogs barking and howling at the sound of the telephone ringing. It wasn't absolutely clear exactly where the dogs were but the sounds moved enough to suggest that they had some sort of freedom around the house. All of the Unit in position outside of the house could hear the dogs and a general feeling of disappointment went through them on hearing them. It wasn't anything that they couldn't handle but just another problem to overcome. Sergeant Foulkes kept his eye trained on the house and in the direction of Private Dobbs but he was the first to see a bedroom light going on upstairs. It was obvious that Swindley was getting out of bed and making his way downstairs. Private Dobbs could see through the letter box that Swindley was on his way down so she gave her signal for the phone to be hung up. The phone discontinued. Unfortunately the dogs didn't. They both continued to howl and bark so loudly that it seemed that the whole village would be woken. It caused some amusement to some of the Unit. A couple of minutes soon passed and eventually the dogs were quiet again but the Sergeant put in his second call and the whole lot started again. Private

Dobbs knocked at the front door and the dogs barked.

Everything went according to plan as Swindley answered the door to Rachel Dobbs as he tried to answer the phone to Ed Foulkes. Rachel pushed her way in quite quickly and took Michael Swindley by surprise as she pushed him to the floor with her weapon. It all happened so quickly and efficiently but then seemed mysteriously to come to a halt almost just as suddenly. Within ten seconds the back up squad had made it up the path and were also on their way into the house. They were greeted by a bit of a strange sight as they got there. Two large dogs were stood growling and snarling at Private Dobbs who had halted part of the way down the hallway whilst Michael Swindley was down on his back shouting. It appeared that Swindley only had to give the word, or a little signal and the dogs would attack. Private Dobbs meanwhile had trained her gun on the dogs as they seemed to be the area of most danger to her.
"What the fuck!! Who are you? What the bloody hell?" Swindley stuttered as he looked up at the uniformed woman who was by now leaning over him with her knee firmly and painfully planted on his chest. Swindley was also able to ascertain that there were a lot more uniformed people entering his house and he raised his arm quickly to signal the dogs to heel.
"Tell the dogs to back off." Private Dobbs seemed to be finding it hard to get through to him.
"Look, who are you? What do you want?" He just continued. As the next couple of soldiers burst in, the soldiers who had all come to a halt were pushed forward and ultimately Private Dobbs was also pushed. She resisted being pushed completely off of Swindley but the motion still lurched her slightly nearer to the dogs. In the excitement of it all one of the dogs got agitated and snapped at Private Dobbs.
"Get the dogs off or I'll shoot them, I fucking promise." Private Dobbs shouted in a loud voice. As she said this she looked down at her left hand which despite being gloved was now bleeding from the wound the dog had inflicted upon her. The two dogs were still well trained and despite this small misdemeanor had retreated back to their positions. Rachel meanwhile had a handgun pointed in the dogs' direction. She was certain she could take them both out if necessary.
"Sabre, down boy," Michael Swindley ordered and almost immediately the two dogs seemed to relax.
"Can you put them in the kitchen?" One of the soldiers asked as

Sergeant Foulkes entered the house.

"Is everything under control Private?" He asked.

"We're just getting there Sir," she replied. At this point, Private Dobbs started to get back to her feet to allow Swindley to get up off of the floor. He did this quite gingerly and then took a few seconds to dust him self down and regain his balance before continuing.

"Kitchen boys," Swindley ordered as the two dogs followed him into the kitchen. He closed the door and turned to face the Sergeant. By now he had recovered some of his composure but was still only just beginning to fully realise what had happened. "What the bloody hell is this all about?"

"You are under arrest on suspicion of inciting and organising revolutionary actions," the Sergeant continued. "Anything you want to say in your defence, say now." As he spoke the words he had already retrieved his trusted black book and was trying to read the caution verbatim. "Do you understand the charge?" He continued.

"Well sort of."

"Do you have anything to say?"

"Is this all a big joke?"

It wasn't a big joke and eventually Unit Charlie 12 had taken over his house. The dogs were taken away by a special army unit and Swindley was arrested and taken away back to Army HQ awaiting questioning. As the raid had been well planned it only took half an hour to get things ready for a search. Charlie 12 were left with the chore of turning his house upside down looking for any papers that might relate to revolutionary matters, any secret hideaways, names and addresses, lists or anything that they could talk to him about. They were also looking for papers relating to the car and keys to drive the car back to Army HQ as well. Private Dobbs had been instructed to accompany the man back to HQ and she sat with him in the back of the jeep that had come to collect him.

"What am I supposed to have done?" He asked her.

"I can't tell you anything at the moment, you know that."

"But is it something to do with work? Have I been reported as stealing something? Can someone tell me what I've done?"

"Please Sir, I cannot say anything to you at the moment. Wait till we get to the proper interview and then you'll know." As she spoke to the man her initial instincts were that this was not the man in the car at the roadblock. Michael Swindley was a nervous little man and Rachel was certain that she would have homed in on his nervousness straightaway at the roadblock. It is quite possible that he lent the car to someone else of course. It took another five hours before Charlie 12 were finished with Swindley. They had interviewed him but he maintained that he was not in the roadblock and that he had never lent the car to anyone else. He used the car everyday he went to work and once a week to go shopping in Chale. He never went to Kentley. He confirmed that he worked for Potter Peas in Lavenham as his records showed and all of his papers were in order. He was even able to say that at the time of the roadblock he would still have been at work and that he was sure that his boss would be able to confirm this. There was no option really but to let him go. Private Dobbs asked Sergeant Foulkes to hold on to his car which he did officially and then they released him.

"Why do we want the car, Private Dobbs?" The Sergeant asked as he rubbed his tired eyes.

"Sir I don't think that this was the car from the roadblock Sir," she replied.

"Why not?"

"Just looking at it, it is far too battered to have been the car that I saw, Sir." Dobbs continued, "And I've heard rumours Sir, that there are photographs of the car at the roadblock," she said with confidence.

"And what if there are photographs, Private?"

"I think we should compare Sir."

"Very well Private. Well done," Ed Foulkes said. He was pleased again with Rachel's input. The car would be locked up and the report would suggest that the agent comes and compares the car with the photographs just in case. Under normal rules, the car would have been returned to the owner immediately unless it was involved in some sort of crime or offence as the owner would have the right to put in a claim against the Army for non-availability. This was seen as tardiness in the Army if an innocent victim made a claim and therefore Sergeant Foulkes was reluctant to hold on to the car for any longer than was really necessary. He wouldn't normally go against his own intuitions but Rachel was on a roll at the moment in this case and he didn't feel that he should argue with her over this request. The report wouldn't make too much interesting reading anyway and he needed something else to go in it. The car may well be something to have got from the raid.

-

Whilst all this was going on, Martin Saunders tucked into his light breakfast as he contemplated the things he had to do today. He sat at the breakfast table eating toast and sipping his orange juice. The table had a slight wobble as it was an old farmhouse table but Martin replaced the wedge of paper under the short leg to keep it level. Not many people were able to get hold of orange juice nowadays. Only two or three years ago it was a part of everybody's diet as the media pushed down our throats about how good and healthy it was for you. Then it got difficult to import. Martin had a regular supply of orange juice. There was also a bowl of cereal on the table which most people had for breakfast. Not many could always afford to have milk, or at least not fresh milk with it but again Martin never seemed to go without. He thought again about what he had to do. His car had been backfiring a bit so he decided that for most of the morning he would generally check the car over to make sure it was okay. As he finished his breakfast, Martin Saunders started to prepare for the days work. He opened the bonnet of his blue Mondeo inside the garage.

-

It was Sunday morning and Gary had slept in. As usual he had downed a few drinks the night before whilst watching the television and he awoke that morning with a bit of a hangover. Rubbing his head only seemed to make it feel worse so he stopped doing it. His throat and tongue were dry and feeling like a piece of old leather had got inside his mouth. He thought about the fact that if Angela been there she would have probably made him feel a lot better and have made him some breakfast by now but then she wouldn't have let him lay in late in the first place. She would probably have got him some aspirin by now as well but it was the thought of breakfast that made him feel hungry but he knew very well that there was no food in the house and certainly nothing that he could eat for breakfast. He could almost smell bacon being cooked and could practically taste a fried egg. He sat up and wondered what he would do today. There wasn't too much he needed to do so in the end he decided he would clean the car. He got washed and dressed and then went down and drove the car out of the garage and into the road. With a bucket and sponge he tackled the task of cleaning his car from top to bottom. It took a while but after he had used the leather on it, the car started to look nice and shiny and Gary felt he had achieved something for his troubles. There was a rumbling in his stomach which reminded him that he still hadn't eaten anything today.

As he was getting to the end of the cleaning, Mrs. Hobbs appeared out of nowhere next to the car.
"Oh you gave me a fright!" Gary exclaimed.
"Did I? I'm sorry about that," the woman replied.
"Yes you did. What are you doing here anyway?"
"I have another message for you. Can we talk inside please?" The woman asked politely whilst pointing and leading the way into the house. Gary followed her to the door and they both went into the living room. The woman sat down on a chair at the table. She crossed her legs and brushed down her thick pleated skirt as Gary studied her brown brogue shoes. He looked at her thinnish legs in her flesh coloured tights and then studied how she was dressed generally. Very elegant but so out of date. It reminded Gary again of pictures he had seen of the old Royal family back in the mid 1900's. Nobody dressed that way anymore.
"So what is the message?" Gary asked.
"Due to certain circumstances of which I am not aware, the meeting place needs to be changed. You must now meet my brother at the Food Centre an hour later than planned. That will now be at four o'clock. Be waiting for him in the middle of the civilian area. You must have the lists with you," the woman said again in a robotic type fashion. It was almost as if she had been practicing her lines all week and this was her one performance. She did however have the crucial information written down on a piece of paper. She handed the paper to Gary who automatically took it.
"Look I'm not happy about this. Why is the meeting place being changed?" Gary asked.
"I don't know I just deliver the messages." Gary wasn't very happy about the change but quite quickly realised that he was going to be unable to argue the point under these circumstances. He would just have to go along with it. He pondered on Mrs. Hobbs part in all this.
"Are you a member of the revolution then?" Gary asked her a direct question. It was a strange question to ask and it came from out of the blue. The woman jumped back as if she had been hit and her voice tone changed to a more natural one. This was just not the sort of question one asked anyone nowadays.
"I certainly am not." She replied indignantly.

"Then why are you delivering these messages?" Gary continued to question her.
"I'm doing this for my brother you know." She replied.
"You're doing the work of a revolutionary sympathiser and you could be arrested." Gary said this to try and frighten her or at least get some different sort of reaction.
"I have nothing to do with all this revolution. I'm not happy that my brother is so involved but then he is my brother. I only used my husband's identity card to get my brother home to Waydon. I knew nothing about the woman who got shot. I just want my brother to sort things out and get out." The woman said all this as if it had been on her chest for ages. It was a bit like a confession of war crimes. She was obviously under a lot of pressure and not capable of dealing with it. Gary was surprised as to just how much information the old woman told him in such a little time. He felt he was beginning to understand the woman a bit more and was convinced that she was just mixed up in all this out of some misplaced family loyalty. He knew exactly what she must have been going through from his own experiences with David. Usually, brothers and sisters would not expect to involve other brothers and sisters in their business but let each one get on with their own lives but it was obvious that Andrew Longhurst was desperate. Gary also thought how at risk Andrew would be should the old woman ever be arrested. They wouldn't need to torture her. I wonder if he realises.
"Okay, tell him I'll be there." Gary sighed out loud as he gave the woman the answer she wanted. He was beginning to start to feel sorry for her. She was looking so vulnerable. Perhaps that was why Andrew Longhurst was using her. Because she was so easy to use.
"Will you be there on Tuesday?" Gary quickly added a last question.
"Where?"
"At the Food Centre," Gary added.
"I'll probably be taking him there so no doubt yes." The woman answered in a resigned voice. Gary got up and led the woman to the front door. There were no further words spoken, no formal words of goodbye and the woman briskly left the house and was quickly on her way. Gary shut the front door and walked into the kitchen looking for a bottle to drink from. The written note was still in his hand. He looked at it again and then screwed it up and threw it on to the kitchen table. There were the remains of some whiskey in a bottle on the table which Gary picked up and downed in one swift movement. 'That's

better' he thought.

-

John Silver was working hard again today having finished tuning his car yesterday. He sat at the heavy oak desk in the lounge of his little home. He had now been given the go ahead to go ahead and work on the next target who had probably been picked out almost a month ago but he had to wait for the confirmation before actually doing anything on him. John Silver was really looking forward to getting back out there and preparing a dossier ready for the hit. He knew what he had to do and he would take as much time as he needed to make sure that he checked every possible twist or turn so he could deliver what was expected of him. Mariano Zwolle was another retired politician. He used to be a member of the Dutch Parliament and a very influential one. Mariano was in his late fifties and had got himself a nice little pension fund that he and his family could live on for the rest of their lives. John Silver had only basic details of Mariano Zwolle. The file already contained his new address and a description of what he looked like. By the time John Silver had finished it would contain a lot more than that.

Mariano Zwolle had worked hard and fair as far as he was concerned. In his time he had been involved with a number of very nasty people but he had a conscience and no fear that anyone wanted to cause him any pain. The news of Dario Vidmar had just reached him and he had felt a small regret at the way that he had died. Mariano had worked with Dario a few times and although he wasn't as horrible as many of the others, he had helped to enforce many regulations that Mariano had not been happy about. Mariano had also heard the other year about the suspicious death of an old Italian General. The name given wasn't familiar but he thought that he looked a lot like a General Cassino that he had also met a number of years ago. Nobody would be mourning his departure, he thought to himself.

John Silver had managed to find out that Zwolle had recently purchased a sort of retirement house in a little town called Boxmeer in the east of Holland and he had already been over there to find the exact place where he lived. It was a reasonable sized house in its own grounds near the Maas canal. John knew he would have to spend a bit more time over there and he had got himself a little holiday cottage nearby which he had already stayed in once. Some of the local people wondered who he was at first but having a female with him from the second day, he had been less suspicious and he hoped that if he were to stay there again, he would go fairly well unnoticed.

-

Sarah called round to see Gary again but even after three rings of the bell, there was still no answer at the front door. Sarah looked through a hole in the side fence into the back garden where she could also catch a glimpse of the living room window but nobody was to be seen so she returned to the front door and gave it one final knock. Hopefully he isn't still in bed, she thought to herself.
"Alright, alright who is it?" Gary shouted as he answered the front door. "Oh it's you!" He continued as he saw Sarah. She gave him a quick look up and down and realised that he hasn't had the best of nights. He hadn't shaved and his hair was a complete mess. Bits sticking up here and there.
"You're pissed out of your skull aren't you?" Sarah said fuming.
"I've had one or two but I'm only a little bit drunk." Gary replied as he led them both into the living room. He slumped down on to the settee and indicated that Sarah should sit wherever she could. Sammy is keeping quiet in his basket. The living room is a mess. Sarah daren't think about venturing into the kitchen.
"I've come to talk about Angela," Sarah tried to talk to Gary but he was already half asleep. She slaps him round the face. "Oy wake up." Sarah shouted at Gary.
"I'm up early tomorrow. I need to sleep." Gary slurred.
"Why are you up early tomorrow?"
"I'm going into work early so I can finish early. Got something to do." Gary only just about finished the sentence.
"Is there something I can do? Where have you got to go?" Sarah asked but it was no good. Gary had fallen back to sleep. Sarah decided that she should just cover him with a blanket and let him sleep it off. It's no good trying to talk to him in this state. As Gary slept, Sarah noticed a tumbler on the floor which she picks up and smells. She places it on the table and then decides to take it through to the kitchen. The sink is half full of washing up and there is a pile of unwashed clothing on the chair. She places the tumbler in the sink and

notices an empty bottle of whisky stood on the corner of the kitchen table. Sarah took a general look at all the mess. Bits of rubbish all over the place. She started to tidy the place up a bit but after a few minutes decided that Gary would probably see it as interfering. Out of some sort of concern for her brother as well as a very idle curiosity, Sarah looked through the kitchen cupboards looking for food. A mouldy couple of slices of bread and half a bag of sugar seemed to be the full listing of anything that could be remotely mistaken for food. She was beginning to realize what sort of task she had taken on but then she knew she would see it through.

Gary had set the alarm on his wrist watch and an alarm clock in the living room as well so that he would be up early today. It was just five o'clock and with a bit of luck Gary would arrive at the Sorting Office at the same time as the early shift. If he could get there just a little bit before six he would also be performing one of his annual management duties, checking that the early shift came in on time so despite the headache and the horrible dry feeling in his throat, Gary whisked through the early morning washing process whilst Sammy was let out in the back garden. He was on his way to work by five thirty five and by putting his foot down at places where Gary knew he could, he arrived at work at five to six.

He was impressed to find that he was the third person to arrive that morning as two of the team had already arrived and were getting the sorting boxes in order ready for the mornings work.
"Good morning!" Gary gave out with an apparent happy shout.
"Morning Boss. Are you checking up on us or is there a job on?"
"Just doing one of the early shifts that I have to do every now and then." Gary explained.
Gary made his way to his office and got on with his reports and actually got one or two finished and ready to pass on up the line. It was quite a busy morning and Gary found the mid-morning coffee a bit bland so he added a few drops of Whiskey to it to help it on its way. He felt better for that and much more able to face the workload.

By two o'clock, Gary was ready to go. He checked again that he had the lists in the envelope as he took his coat down from the stand. There were two hours before he was due to meet so he would probably have a walk around the town to clear his head. He left his car

in the car park and took a quick swig from the half bottle of vodka kept safely in his coat pocket. It was a bit of protection. An oasis in times of need. That would be it for this afternoon though as he needed to be on top of what was happening. Just as he was leaving the car park, Andrea appeared from the Sorting Office.
"Gary, are you heading off home?"
"No. I'm going to do some shopping in town," Gary shouted.
"I wondered if you could give me a lift."
"Sorry but I'm leaving my car here and walking into town."
"No I don't want to go into town, I'm hoping to visit my friend Georgina in Waydon." Andrea looked on hopefully knowing that Georgina was actually on holiday. If she could get Gary to give her a lift in his car, perhaps when she found no answer at her friends he might invite her round.
"I'm not going home yet."
"That's alright, I'll wait. How long will you be?"
Gary was annoyed about the personal intrusion but knew he had to put her off. "I've also agreed to call in and see an old friend this afternoon and he's not very well so don't feel I can cancel." Gary turned and set out for the town not waiting for Andrea to reply. Andrea cursed a little but resigned herself to admitting defeat on this occasion. 'I'll get him one day' she thought to herself.

    Gary had walked into town and then along the riverside for a while to kill the last minutes of his agonising wait. At half past three Gary decided that he would make his way to the Food Centre. He originally thought that four o'clock was a bit of a strange time to meet here as the place shut at five but he was surprised to find the place very busy when he arrived. The Food Centre was really a sort of market place, or more an enclosed outdoor market. There was of course the main entrance but there were a couple of side entrances and there were also the exits behind all the stalls where the tradesmen loaded and unloaded. Gary looked around and realised that this would be an easy place to disappear from in a hurry if you wanted to. The design of the Food Centre was quite basic but it seemed to work. There was probably a Food Centre in every major town and city. Once you had entered through the main entrance, you found yourself in a big open plain. The shape of the Food Centre could be square or circular or a combination of both but Kentley's was square. Around three of the sides were permanent stalls which were available for hire and usually traders would take out quarterly or annual leases for a stall. The traders would then arrive at the back of their stalls and place their wares on the stalls. Food was not always that readily available and it could often arrive at strange times of the day hence people would sometimes visit the Food Centre but leave without buying anything only to return later when better food had been made available. Today was an extra busy day and there were a few traders who had brought their own stalls and set them up in place to make a second three sided square inside the first. Right in the middle was mainly open although Kentley had three benches that were sometimes used but otherwise the floor space was being crossed by the buying public if they weren't just walking round inspecting the quality. This was something you had to do as well.

Gary walked around a bit and checked out a couple of stalls he knew quite well. Lamb's the fish merchant was his first stop. Gary checked what he had for sale. Some fish heads that looked quite fresh, some roe that was described as cod roe but Gary thought this most unlikely, some herring, some smoked haddock and then some home made fish cakes.
"Any white fish at all?" Gary asked.
"I'm expecting some Whiting but not sure if it'll be here today or tomorrow. We have some prawns and crabs also coming later this week. Are you interested?" The fish merchant was always keen to sell his fish before it arrived.
"No not this week but will you be getting any crabs again?" Gary replied.
"Who knows?" The fish merchant shrugged as he continued to rearrange what fish he had for sale. "I'll always get it if I can."
"See you next week then." Gary walked on. The next couple of stalls were vegetable stalls and Gary didn't even bother to check out what they had. He was able to grow most of what he wanted and there was rarely anything out of the ordinary selling at these stalls. Most of the vegetables looked as if they had been there at least a week. A lot were covered in earth to hide a whole manner of things. The next stall was a meat stall and this was much more interesting.
"Can I help you Sir?" The cry came from the meat trader.
"Do you ever get any chops?" Gary asked.
"Chops are so dear that even if I got any I wouldn't be able to sell them. Or at least not at a price I paid for them," was the reply.

"I have some Food vouchers to get rid of." Gary added.
"Yeah but Food vouchers alone aren't much good to me." The trader wasn't keen.
"So you'd take vouchers and money?"
"Only in advance." The trader was sounding more interested in doing a deal.
"How much then for proper steak?" Gary was getting serious.
"The price of steak, good sized cuts and nice and thick rump is about nine E's a steak." The trader told him. That sounded to Gary like a reasonable price. The trader continued, "I'd want full price in both vouchers and money." The trader looked at Gary. "And I cannot guarantee I can get them next week." Gary decided that that was a bit too much.
"What about Lamb chops?" Gary asked again.
"Again nice good size, I have to sell for six E's a chop. If you're buying with vouchers I'd need another two E's per chop in money. How does that sound?" The trader felt he might have got a deal. Gary looked to see what money he had in his pocket.
"I want four chops. I'll give you full payment in vouchers plus six E's in cash." Gary offered.
"You drive a hard bargain Sir but okay you have a deal."
"I'll give you the vouchers up front and the cash on delivery." Gary continued.
"No way! Cash now and vouchers on delivery if you must but I'd prefer all up front."
"Can I trust you?" Gary said with a grin. "Oh alright then!" Gary handed over the vouchers and the six E's to the meat trader who in turn gave him a receipt and sales voucher for the four lamb chops.
"When will you have them?" Gary asked.
"Next Tuesday or possibly Saturday if you can call?" Gary was pleased with his purchase and went on his way.

The next stall was another vegetable stall and Gary noticed that nearly all there was for sale was carrots. Most had some sort of mould on them but people were still sorting through and buying the less affected carrots. There were sweets, drinks, bread, cakes, fruit, some eggs and some cheese and then various other stalls selling spices and other cooking ingredients. The stalls on the inside that weren't always at the Food Centre seemed to be selling mainly tinned food. There were loads of people about still. Some rushing around, some walking slowly and then some just standing about. There were of course the usual two armed soldiers on guard. They kept out of the way but were watching all the activity around the Centre in case there was any trouble. It wasn't unknown for a fight to erupt due to someone being overcharged or tricked into buying something they didn't want. There was also a number of people that would hang around waiting for traders to either bring their prices down or even dump old food. It was quite disturbing seeing people fight over rotten food but it happened. They would grab carrots, potatoes and various vegetables even if they were wet with mould. With some careful cutting you could still make a nice vegetable soup from a couple of pounds of rotten vegetables. Fruit was often the same as well. Unfortunately traders knowing how desperate people were for food even if they were ready to dump it they would rather sell it for almost nothing or take it away again. It was at these times when trouble was most likely to break out. Desperate punters trying to get rotten food off of greedy market traders. Sometimes things got well out of hand and the soldiers would have their hands full with a mob of hungry citizens on one side and angry tradesmen on the other. It wasn't pretty to see. Gary looked at his watch. It was ten minutes to four.

Gary continued to walk around the Centre slowly and he noticed more people just standing around. One was Frank Braidwood. As Gary approached him, Frank recognized him and gave him a friendly nod.
"How's it going then Frank?" Gary asked.
"Things are going to happen today." He replied in a slow deliberate style.
"What do you mean?" Gary asked again.
"Lots of strange faces hanging around today. You're another. The signs are bad. I don't like the vibes. I sense trouble." Frank muttered in a low voice. As soon as he had finished he walked off towards the main entrance and left the Food Centre. He didn't rush. He just sauntered towards the exit as if making his dramatic departure in a film. Gary stood there a bit bemused trying to take in all that Frank had said. He concluded that Frank thought that something was about to go off. If only he knew what Gary was there to do. Obviously Frank was one of those who could sense tension. Gary took a hold of him self and continued on his walk around the Centre.

As it turns out, Frank wasn't the only one who thinks that something is about to go off as earlier during the day, Unit Charlie 12 have been told that they were to report back for duty at 14.00hrs this afternoon. More often than not at present, if there was an important job about to take place that required Army personnel to attend it seemed that Unit Charlie 12 were always the Unit that were involved. Today though there had been no briefing about what was expected to happen and that was quite unusual but the whole of the Unit were understandably on edge. In fact the whole of the Unit were there fully equipped as if a battle was about to start.

    Gary made his way to the middle of the Food Centre where he was supposed to meet the old Postmaster. Gary tried very hard to be as normal as he walked around. His collar was up and his hat slightly down as decided to make his way straight to the centre piece. He chose not to sit down but he stood uneasily, hopping from one foot to the other waiting and looking. He had hoped to have seen at least one face he recognised but everywhere was full of strangers. Some seemed to be just hanging around like he was but most were doing their shopping or selling their products like they did every other day of the week. Gary spotted a couple of kids playing with a ball near to one of the side gates. They were lining up some old bottles and then kicking the small rubber ball towards the bottles hoping to knock over as many as they could. Rather unsuccessfully as well unfortunately. Another brief look round and suddenly a movement caught Gary's eye. A tall chap had just entered the Food Centre through the main entrance but he was dodging in and out behind other people in the Centre and it was difficult to catch a good glimpse of his face but Gary's initial instinct was that it was the old Postmaster. After a few seconds, Gary's thoughts were confirmed.

    Gary felt the tension in his body as he stood still just watching the old Postmaster walk towards him. Andrew Longhurst was dressed in a sort of business suit with a long black raincoat and he seemed to be looking everywhere except for where Gary was standing. All of a sudden, he stopped and looked to his left. Gary wondered what the problem was. Had he seen somebody or something that spooked him. A couple of seconds later, the old Postmaster dashed to his left and up to a stall where he brought some apples. Having done this, Andrew

Longhurst continued on his way over to where Gary was standing in the middle of the Food Centre.

"Gary how are you?" Andrew started.

"Fine thanks. I have the lists." Gary answered.

"No hurry." Andrew replied scratching his ear. "Let's just look around for a minute. See anyone you recognise?" Andrew casually perused the Food Centre.

"Funnily enough I don't see anyone I know and I was expecting to. Didn't your sister come with you?" Gary asked.

"Yes she's there waiting for me just outside the main entrance." The old Postmaster answered. Gary looked at the main gate and saw a woman stood against the wall opposite. She looked very much like the woman who had come round to organise this event but in fact from this distance it could have been anybody.

"Oh yes I can see her now." Gary replied lying.

"Just calm down a bit and make it look as if you and I are having an idle gossip. Soon we'll mingle into the background." Andrew said as he continued to keep his eye on as much of the crowd as he could.

"How much longer do we have to keep this up?" Gary said starting to get a little impatient. He was already nervous and this delay wasn't helping him very much but the old Postmaster was playing it very cool.

"Just pretend we are having a nice little chat like we haven't met for ages. You keep on talking and when I say you can give me the lists." Andrew told him.

"What do you want me to talk about?" Gary asked.

"Anything, just talk." All the time, Andrew Longhurst was looking around whilst Gary told him about the first time he saw a game of Teamball on the television. When the old Postmaster was absolutely happy he interrupted. "Okay I'll have the lists now!" He ordered Gary. Gary removed the envelope from his inside coat pocket and flicked the envelope open so that the old Postmaster could see inside. He didn't let go of the envelope though. Gary watched as the old Postmaster looked inside the envelope and then looked back at Gary.

"Are you happy?" Gary asked him still holding on to the envelope but feeling the old Postmaster pulling at it.

"I will be when you give me the lists. Let me have them please." He said forcefully. Gary let go of the envelope slightly surprised that Andrew Longhurst didn't ask anything else or look at the lists any closer. Just as Gary let go of the envelope, the sound of a shot whizzed passed them. Gary could hear it very clearly. The old Postmaster ducked and looked in the direction of where the shot came from. Then another shot hit one of the metal posts near to where the two of them were standing whilst it became obvious that the Army guards on duty at the Food Centre have also heard the shots and are grabbing their guns properly, ready for anything. Both Gary and Andrew look at each other realising straightaway that they were probably the targets of those first two shots. From almost nowhere, two further uniformed soldiers enter the Food Centre and fire a couple of shots up in the air. Civilians either drop to the floor or run for cover. There are also two plain clothed soldiers who produce handguns and start to close in towards the middle of the Food Centre. "Thank you Gary. You have done well getting these to me." The old Assistant Postmaster said as he shook the envelope in his hand. "You've guessed we've been sussed so bloody well get out if you can as quickly as possible." Andrew said these last couple of words whilst turning away.

    The old Postmaster only had time to worry about his own safety and he moved towards the main entrance. People were running in all directions and many had already fallen to the floor but Andrew felt this was probably helpful as he doubled back to make his way to one of the rear exits. He had seen uniformed soldiers over by the main gate and he knew that they would be headed his way. As Andrew made his way out of the central seating area he realized he had a small open area to try and negotiate before he could get to one of the rear exits. Andrew was less than twenty yards from relative safety when one of the Army soldiers who had been with the agent appeared from behind a post right in front of him. 'Shit!' He thought. He felt for his gun but the soldier was ready to fire. Andrew knew it was all over. Why was the soldier waiting? 'Shoot you bastard' Andrew thought to himself, as a shot was fired. Andrew waited for that feeling of cold pain but nothing seemed to happen when he realised that the soldier had been shot dead. Andrew looked to his right to see a man in a black leather jacket having just fired his gun at the soldier. Andrew knew the chap as 'Saunders' but knew very little else about him. He was pleased to have seen him this afternoon. Andrew continued to run for the rear exits and yet another soldier appeared and shots exchanged between him and 'Saunders'. Neither seemed to get hit but an old lady carrying her bag of shopping fell to the ground.

It was absolute pandemonium around the Food Centre. Although in fact there were not that many shots being fired it seemed like the place had become a free for all with shots being fired by everyone and at everyone. Gary had started to freeze. Everything had happened so quickly that he did not know how to react. Looking around he could see soldiers lying wounded and civilians lying wounded and himself right in the middle of it all. Then all of a sudden emerging from the crowd came a face he recognized and a voice he knew.
"Mr. Newson, bloody run!" The voice shouted.
It was young Billy Simpson who was running towards Gary. He was waving his arm around trying to tell Gary to get out of the place. Gary was pleased to see Billy. He had always guessed that the revolutionaries had told him the truth but to be able to see it with your own eyes was the ultimate. Gary still stood still.
"Bloody well get out of here before you get shot," Billy shouted at Gary as he got closer. He was only about twenty feet away by now. Shots were still ringing around the Food Centre, and Gary saw Billy stumble. He watched as Billy hit the ground in a heap. He waited for him to get up but Billy just raised his head before it slumped back to the ground. Billy was dead.

All of this seemed to happen in only a few seconds. Gary was still very much still in the middle of the Food Centre and certainly not sure what to do for the best. Shots were being fired and people were getting killed. Gary turned back to where the old Postmaster was expecting him to still be there but he had already made a run for the rear of the Centre. Gary looked over in the direction of the main entrance and to a little place a bit further outside where he was expecting to see Andrew's sister. Even she wasn't there. Everyone had reacted far quicker than Gary and it was time for him to start to make a move.

Although not wanting to be seen, the agent for Operation Hunting is standing in the shadows watching everything that is going on at the Food Centre. Having been advised by the normal Army that there was a rumour of a riot being started this afternoon at the Food Centre the agent took the unusual step of getting two uniformed officers from out of the area to work as a screen. The agent was of course armed and ready to use a gun if necessary but if possible needed to make sure that they remained anonymous to as many people as possible. The main reason for being here is that at last the two people the Intelligence were after were due to show themselves in the public. The dreaded list was going to be handed over. The list that for years had been keeping many Intelligence agents in work but had never been seen. It was surmised by many who would be on the list but nobody really knew. There was also the mention of a possible second list. This was just too much to hope for.

The agent and the two soldiers kept well back and out of sight not wanting to frighten anyone off. All around the Food Centre, although it appeared to be very low key you could sense an air of caution. Both sides knew that this was a piece of history waiting to happen. The agent wasn't going to let a chance like this pass by without actually being there to see that the list is captured. All that was definitely known was the meeting place and expected time. A local revolutionary would be handing over the lists to a previous local revolution leader who was now calling a lot of shots. There had been one of the ex-local authority members arrested only the other week who had been turned in by one of his relations. He was reported as stating anti-military thoughts or inciting revolutionary action or some such thing. There was a rumour that he was also part of the same group of revolutionaries that they were now looking for. The Agent took a mental note of everyone's thoughts but kept an open mind generally.

Keeping an eye out for two people possibly meeting, the agent saw a man start to walk across the middle of the Food Centre from a distance. This person had an air of confidence about them almost as if they were acting a part in a play and the agent had to make sure that this was not just an innocent person out for an afternoon stroll but the person they were really looking for. Gary Newson strolled around the Food Centre just as calmly as you like. He took in the surrounding area like a painter trying to capture a vision. The Agents first thought was that this was someone who was probably waiting to meet his wife after the end of a very boring shopping spree.
"What the bloody hell does he think he's doing?" The agent said quietly.

"This could be our man," one of the soldiers said to the agent. The agent looked left and right for signs of another person but none were obvious. "We don't have a meter," the agent said, head shaking from side to side.
"Don't you want me to set a sight on him anyway, just in case?" The soldier enquired.
"No not yet." He replied.
"But we have him cold?" The soldier continued. Gary Newson came to a halt near the middle of the Food Centre as if he was waiting to meet someone.
"He's got to be our target, why can't we shoot?" The soldier asked anxiously.
"No wait until I tell you. He could be here to meet his bloody girlfriend for God's sake." The agent said with a small tone of disapproval. It was about this time when the next man came into view, obviously heading for Gary.
"No surely not." The agent said, as if the agent couldn't believe what was going on. It was quite brazen for them to use such a public place for such a meeting. The two of them met in the middle of the Food Centre. Right in the bloody middle. In front of loads of people. It just didn't seem right.
"I have him, do I shoot?" The soldier asked.
"No wait one."
The two men shook hands and made a little bit of small talk.
"I've got both in sights, just need your order." Again the soldier almost pleaded with the agent.
As the agent watched, Gary's hand reached inside his coat pocket and he appeared to be trying to get something out. Seconds turned into minutes and everything turned into slow motion.
"I need your order to shoot," the soldier said.
"Wait." The agent told him.
Gary and the old Postmaster stood looking at each other with an eerie silence. Gary showed him the envelope with the list in but kept hold of it. He opened the envelope and showed him what was inside. It is now obvious to everyone that this is the handover.
"Permission to shoot?" The soldier asked. "Trained and ready," the other soldier added.
The agent still waited wanting to be absolutely sure.

"No I want to see that the list is handed over first," the agent replied. The list was now in the hands of both Gary and the old Postmaster. The agent could wait no longer.
"Shoot to wound," the agent ordered. "You can kill the tall one but I need the other one alive."

So all the different factions were doing their bit in the Food centre that afternoon. The agent. The Army. The Spy. The go-between. The revolutionaries and unfortunately, also the everyday public. Even Martin Saunders was there to add his experience to the proceedings. Andrew Longhurst didn't actually know Saunders that well but had been introduced to him a couple of year ago and recognised him straightaway as one of the revolutionary hit squad. They all had a similar air about them he thought. Andrew didn't actually know the hit man was going to be there but he was very pleased when he did show up. Saunders meanwhile, knew that his job was only to play a supporting role and he thought to himself that if he stayed much longer he would be in far greater danger than he really needed to be. His new mission would now take precedence over any local organised events so this was likely to be the last time he would get involved in anything similar. Nevertheless, he felt quite smug again at the way the Army had failed once again to arrest a wanted man who was there right under their noses. Despite thinking so smugly to himself at his ability to remain free, Martin Saunders wasn't stupid enough to not realize that things could change so dramatically, and very quickly so he should take the opportunity to escape from the scene whilst he was able to. After all he still had a pretty busy day ahead of him.

Still there was quite a state of panic around the Food Centre. People were running here there and everywhere. One or two lay dead or wounded on the floor whilst some had just tripped over. Other quick thinking individuals were already picking up dropped food from the dead. Others were quite blatantly taking food from the stalls. The Army were in a muddle about what to do first. Chase after suspected gunmen. Stop the looters. Their instructions had not been made that clear. Gary realized that he has still to get out of the Food Centre. In the confusion he had made his way to the main entrance via the back passages behind some of the traders' premises. Two armed soldiers were standing about five yards inside the Centre but there was enough room for Gary to get out behind them. He did so and made a run for it. "There he goes!" A shout came from the Food Centre. A shot whizzed over Gary's head and another couple of shots were also fired in his direction. Gary turned his ankle but he continued to run until he could make the relative safety of a small passage way that ran down to the bus station. Gary couldn't afford to stop moving despite the excruciating pain that was coming from his ankle as he was sure that at least one soldier would be giving chase. For a few yards he found it a lot easier to hop rather than run but this slowed Gary down so it was back to running. It seemed like hours but in just under ten minutes Gary had jounced his way to the car park of the Sorting Office. He was able to unlock the gates to the car park and leave them unlocked whilst he started his car as quietly as possible. Driving at this time was risky but assuming that there would be soldiers searching around the Food Centre area there was no way Gary was going to drive that way out of Kentley. For the first mile he drove in short bursts, turning into roads and parking in case any soldiers were about but none were to be seen. For the last stretch out of the town it was drive fast with lights on low but with the condition of Gary's ankle this was not very easy however soon he was on his way towards Waydon. He kept up his speed relatively but turned the lights out so he couldn't be seen from a distance. Eventually he entered the village.

    As Gary approached his house he slowed his driving down so that the engine wouldn't make too much noise. It was okay to be speeding through the village but as he approached his own house he didn't want neighbours to know that he had got back late in case they were the type who might inform or at least give him away if they were later questioned. As always he put the car in the garage and walked up to the front door but with his ankle damaged it was very difficult to walk. He sort of dragged his right foot rather than lift it up and then down again. The pain was getting worse. As Gary got his key out he noticed that the light was on in the kitchen and there seemed to be someone moving about in the house. Perhaps Angela had decided to return. Perhaps she had just come back for some things. Gary opened the door.
"Angela is that you?" Gary shouted as he stumbled into the hall and fell to the ground.
"Hello." The reply came but the voice was not Angela's.

"Who's there?" Gary said in his bravest voice as he felt of his twisted ankle again. He was in great pain and in no position to defend him self should the stranger be of a mind to attack him. He looked up towards the kitchen door. Straightaway he recognised the woman who emerged from the kitchen. For a few seconds it took away the thought of the pain coming from his ankle, but this soon returned.

"Hello Gary." Julie Clark spoke in a soft voice as she popped her head around the kitchen door.

"Oh it's you!" It was all that Gary could think of answering. As he said it he thought to himself 'What a bloody stupid thing to say'.

"Are you hurt?" Julie said noticing that Gary seemed unable to move properly. She held out an arm to help Gary back to his feet. It was obvious that he was having trouble putting any weight on his right foot so she positioned herself under his right arm to support him as he hobbled into the living room and sat himself on a chair.

"Thank you." Gary said. "I have to ask, what are you doing in my house?"

"I came to see Angela and the front door was open. I came in but there was nobody to be found. I was looking for a piece of paper to leave her a note." Julie explained. There was a small embarrassing silence.

"There's a note pad over here in the writing desk if ever you want some." Gary spoke to Julie. "If you ever get caught short there's usually only one or two bits of paper hanging around here or there. Just help yourself in future." It seemed like a very surreal conversation as he talked about Julie using scrap paper in his house but he wasn't really thinking straight at all. "So you're back from London again are you?" Gary continued in a suspicious tone. "Angela has moved out for a while." Gary told her.

"Oh I didn't realise. I'm sorry to hear that. Yes I'm back from London and for good I believe." Julie said as she smiled at him. "What have you done to your ankle?"

"Nothing I've just sprained it a bit." Gary said feeling the pain. "So what did you get up to in London?" Gary asked Julie.

He was still a little uncertain of exactly what to make of Miss Clark but he felt an instant sexual attraction as he checked her up and down. Although she had a coat on, it was undone so it revealed that she had a tight fitting black dress on. In all the excitement, her breathing had become more pronounced and Gary could see the bulge of her breasts, under her dress, moving backwards and forwards in a seemingly inviting manner as she breathed. The gap at the top of her dress also allowed him a view of her bare skin from her chest to the top of her breasts and he was also able to make out a part of the intricate patterned lace of her black bra that she was wearing. Gary's mind worked overtime as he tried to imagine how the whole bra might have appeared. His eyes followed the curved outline of her breasts. He wanted to touch them, caress them, see exactly what they looked like. He could imagine but it wasn't like he was able to see them for real. Gary had realised that there was a pause to the conversation as they were both looking at each other.

"I was there to answer that charge of not being fit to be a teacher. I thought I'd mentioned it to you." Julie replied after a few seconds.
"Perhaps you did yeah." Gary sort of remembered it being mentioned but wasn't really that sure. "I thought you were taking something to someone. Don't know what gave me that idea." Gary tried to sound calm as he said it but he was already finding his arousal uncomfortable. He hoped that Julie had not really noticed but the bulge in his trousers was impossible to hide.
"No I didn't see anyone to give anything to." Julie replied. She had been studying the manly figure in front of her. He was tallish and looked strong enough, ready to protect her from any danger but it was his distinguished chin that she found so attractive. She imagined Gary grabbing her and lifting her to his lips and then she started to imagine the rippling muscles in his arms and thighs as he did so. Julie cast her gaze towards his legs to see if they were how she had hoped they would be. She didn't fail to notice that he was showing signs of arousal. All of a sudden something grabbed her attention. "Oh look!" Julie said as she pointed down to Gary's foot. "There's blood coming from somewhere," Julie said as she lifted Gary's foot and placed it on a stool to keep it up. She started to unlace his shoe. Her heart started to beat faster. She was actually touching him.
"What are you doing?" Gary asked.
"It needs looking at. I've had some first aid training," Julie replied.
"Look could you get me a drink?" Gary was starting to feel the pain in his ankle even more. Julie got up and looked around the room. "Oh sorry! There's a bottle of Whisky in the kitchen cupboard and a couple of glasses if you'll join me." Gary said.

Julie went back into the kitchen and soon returned with the bottle and glasses. She poured a couple of drinks out but Gary downed his in one. Julie poured him another before returning to tending to his ankle. She removed his shoe and sock and looked at the wound. It was difficult to tell immediately what it was but Julie realised it was a bullet graze. She washed the wound and then bandaged it. Gary was starting to lose consciousness but Julie kept him talking whilst she saw to his ankle.

"Don't put any weight on that ankle until tomorrow." Julie would tell him. Gary muttered a few words back but nothing that was really comprehensible. Julie finished dressing the wound. She took his other shoe off and laid a blanket over him. She then realised that she hadn't left her message. A quickly written note would have to do to tell Gary that she had been given her old teaching job back at Waydon school. She left the note under his glass and finished drinking her Whisky. She bent over and kissed his forehead before turning out the lights and leaving the house.

Gary had fallen into a strange state somewhere between sleeping and unconsciousness. Although Julie had left, he was still imagining her being there with him in the house. She was still tending to his injured ankle. He watched her hands skillfully bandaging the wound.

"Now keep still Mr. Newson." Julie said sternly.

"But it bloody hurts," he replied.

"Well of course it hurts silly. But if you don't do as you're told it won't get any better." Gary looked at her and saw that she was now wearing one of those starched white hats that nurses wear and what looked like a white apron. He wasn't quite sure what was going on but he seemed helpless and unable to do anything about it.

"Now that should be better," Julie said as she finished bandaging his ankle. Gary looked at his ankle and then saw that he was actually wearing pyjamas. Thick blue and white striped ones to be exact. In fact he was in a bed. There were other parts of him bandaged up although none of them hurt like his ankle did. On closer examination it seemed that he was in a hospital ward where there were loads of other men with wounds and battle scars.

"Nurse!" He cried out but nobody was listening. "Nurse, where am I?"

"Mr. Newson. Stop making a fuss." It was Julie who had returned to his bedside to comfort him and keep him quiet. "Look we'll try and get you out of here if you can keep quiet."

It seemed like a good idea to shut up and keep quiet so that's what Gary did. He looked around at all the others who were also in beds. All seemed to have been shot in one part of their bodies and all had bloodied bandages on them. It was more like a war field hospital scene.

"Gary, I've been told that I can take you home as long as there is someone there waiting to look after you." Julie had appeared as if from nowhere and had her coat on.

"Angela will look after me," Gary replied.

"Are you sure she's at home?"

"Yes she's at home."

"I don't think she is." Julie was shaking her head as she told him. "I can't leave you on your own!"

"She'll be back."

Almost as if by magic Gary was now in the driving seat of his car with Julie in the passenger seat. They had left the hospital and were making their way out of Kentley towards Waydon. Gary was in pain but was still driving. Julie was just sat in the passenger seat. Up ahead there was a queue of traffic and the car came to a halt. Gary got out and started walking along the line of queued cars towards the front where there was a military roadblock. Nobody else seemed to be getting out of their cars. They were just sitting there like crash test dummies. The pain had gone from his ankle and it was almost as if he was flying, or at least hovering along the road. As he got nearer to the roadblock a familiar scene started to roll over again. The cars started to become fuzzy and he only became interested in some movement of people up ahead of him. Again everything around him was almost like painted scenery or extras in a film who had been told to just blend into the background whilst Gary continued to move swiftly towards the commotion ahead. Once again he found himself watching uniformed soldiers with automatic machine guns running in all directions but generally chasing after the civilian clothed blond woman who was running in the direction of the allotments in the field next to the road. There were voices shouting but very quietly and it was obvious that there was pandemonium and confusion. He had managed to touch his feet down to the ground and he looked away from the woman who was running and gazed down to the ground only to see the groundsheet which covered a body. He knew what to look for and yet again it was there, that little bit of blond hair that was protruding from under the groundsheet. Every effort was made to turn his head away but he just couldn't. It was as if two people were holding his head forcing him to look at the groundsheet. He knew he didn't want to. The sweat was dripping from his forehead and he tried with every muscle but he couldn't move.

Again he knew what was going to happen next but it still frightened him when the body under the groundsheet started to move. An arm appeared from one side of the sheet and grabbed hold of the groundsheet throwing it back with a swift single movement. Although her arm was obviously moving, the rest of her body lay completely still. The arm returned to its proper position and the body was to all intents absolutely stone cold dead. Her jumper and t-shirt were soaked in blood and part of her torn torso was visible where the bullets had ripped her apart. Gary was concentrating on the murder victim on the ground but behind him the chase was still going on in slow motion. Once again, only the blond woman being chased and the soldiers chasing her were properly visible whilst everyone else was blurred. Gary looked back at the body on the ground as she started to cough and move her head in the way Gary had seen before. She opened her eyes and immediately caught Gary's attention in such a way that he couldn't stop looking at her. Another couple of soldiers ran in slow motion past the two of them as if they were not there. Everyone was blind to Gary and the dead woman who by now was getting up on to her feet. She was the woman Gary had seen at the roadblock but there was something else quite familiar about her. He couldn't quite put his finger on it but it was there in the back of his mind.
"Hello Gary." The blond woman spoke to him again like they were old friends. Was she someone he had worked with or perhaps someone he had gone to school with.
"I need to warn you don't I." The blond woman was by now on her feet and becoming more aware of what was going on around her. Gary considered that she might have been someone who he had met at one of the revolutionary meetings but then he was sure he would have been able to remember such a woman had he met her then. There weren't many women that Gary instantly took a sexual liking to. There was Angela of course and he had to agree that Julie was another but this

blond woman was in the same group. He began to think hard about where he might have met her before when she all of a sudden started to run towards the allotments. As she ran off, Gary followed her with his eyes so as to keep her in view. Away in the distance he could also see the blond woman starting to climb the fence to try and get into the allotments.

    Gary suddenly found himself standing in the field that the blond woman was trying to get to. The soldiers were behind her and were barking out orders but they were very quiet and muffled even though they were shouting them out. Gary was again trapped in the field and could do nothing to stop what was happening. The blond woman was staring at Gary all the time.
"Watch her! Watch her! Look out for her!" The woman just kept repeating these words as she seemed to be trying in vain to climb over the fence. Once again all the words were interrupted by the loud crack of gunfire as she was shot. Her body jerked forward again this time as her stomach exploded outwards. Blood went everywhere and the woman started to fall. Another shot fired out loud as more blood spurted out. The woman never even blinked but kept looking at Gary as she fell to her ultimate end.
"Watch out for her." These words kept repeating around in Gary's head. The blond woman fell slowly to her knees as once again Gary saw the uniformed soldier appear behind her holding the smoking gun. As the blonds words started to fade there was a strange laughter that took its place. It was difficult to say if it was the blond woman laughing or one of the soldiers as it was not possible to say if it was a woman's laugh or a mans laugh. It was just a horrible laughter. As the blond woman fell finally to the ground, the soldier could be seen in full. Still the face was not distinct. Gary could clearly make out that the face was camouflaged but he could get a clear view of it. Who was the soldier. Was it the soldier who was laughing? Gary couldn't be sure of that. He again watched as the soldier lifted the automatic machine gun that was beginning to point directly at him. He watched as the trigger was being pulled but there was no loud bang, no bullet, nothing at all, just the clicking sound of a trigger being pulled. Gary lost his balance as his natural reaction was to turn away from the gun. He started to fall to the ground as the laughter subsided.

Gary woke suddenly and took a few seconds to remember where he was. He was still sat in the chair with his feet up on a small stool. The note that was left under his empty glass immediately caught his eye. It stirred him into picking the thing up and he read it. Realising it was from Julie he studied every part of it not really taking in the content. The style of the writing. The curve of particular letters. That certain feminine neatness that was impossible not to notice. He smiled as he looked at the note in his hand. It made him feel good.

-

John Silver rushed a bit but managed to catch a night flight into Strasbourg where he picked up a hire car before driving up to his new holiday cottage on the outskirts of Boxmeer. He got a few hours sleep before getting up and making the most of the fresh air and bright sunshine. It was about nine in the morning and there were a number of people walking about the town on their way to work or just out on their way for a day of job hunting or looking for a good deal on food at the local market. Holland was no different to England as far as everyday lives were concerned and as many people were suffering in Boxmeer as there were in other similar sized towns. John started to unload his bags that he had in his car but took his time until one of the neighbours saw him. The Dutch woman recognised him as the Englishman who had visited before and she gave a slight wave. With the excuse of coming out to sweep the path she carried her broom out and spoke to him.
"Hello, nice to sees you again." Her English was reasonably good but as she was fairly certain that Martin could not speak a word of Dutch she always spoke in his language. It was quite normal for English to be the main language of communication in Europe.
"Oh Hello Christine." John Silver replied as if he had only just noticed her.
"Are you being here for another week?"
"Well I am here for two weeks but then I am hoping that Jane will be joining me and we may spend sometime elsewhere in Holland."
"The weather is good at the moment. Is there anything you be needing Mr. Saunders?" Christine had quenched her curiosity.
"If you have a little milk it would mean I could have a cup of tea before going to the shops. I will give you some back this afternoon."
"I go and fetch some."

John Silver had achieved what he had wanted to by making sure that one of the locals had seen him and actually spoken to them. There was of course nobody by the name of Jane but he would try and arrange for the same female agent to join him in the next couple of weeks and get them to stay for a couple of nights so that she would be seen. It was something that was done quite regularly. It all helped him to fit into the community. The milk arrived and he put it in the fridge with the three pints he already had there. He made a quick call on his mobile phone to try and make some arrangements for the female agent to join him before sitting down at the table and prepare for his mission. Time had come for him to work out where he would set up in order to keep a watch on Mariano Zwolle. The times and days were most important. He worked on it for a few hours before concluding with a plan he was reasonable happy with. Martin decided he would relax for the rest of the afternoon, perhaps by going into the village to do some shopping. It would be an early night to catch up on the sleep lost last night. The time by now was just after two o'clock.

Chapter 9   -   RECOVERY

Gary started to wake up. It wasn't an instant thing and in fact took about fifteen minutes before there was anything remotely sensible going round in his head. Even then it was only basic questions like, where am I, what day is it. Gary couldn't properly answer either at the moment but he could see that he was sat in a chair with his feet up on a stool and a blanket half over his legs. He was beginning to recognise that he was at home. 'It's time I got up' Gary thought to himself. Gary was aching all over his body and the awkward angle that he found himself in didn't actually help him very much at all. In fact it was probably a contributory factor to him aching in the first place. He was still sat in the chair with Julies note held tightly in his hand but he had one arm slightly trapped under his body and his better leg at such an angle that Gary wasn't quite sure how he could have laid like that. He looked at the note and waved it around. He tried to focus on it properly in an effort to actually read what was written on the paper but gave up after a few tries. He looked at the little table to his right and in particular to the empty glass. Gary changed his attention and started focusing on the strange printed pattern on the glass and then realised that it was of course an empty glass he was staring at. If anything was going to get him up, it would be his need for a drink. His mouth was dry but there was a lingering taste of whisky at the back of his throat.

Gary had made up his mind that it was time to get out of the chair. He started to move different parts of his body quite deliberately but he could feel the pain in his ankle and he knew that getting up wasn't going to be an easy task. It was a necessary one. Slowly he put his weight on his hands and pushed himself up out of the chair. It wasn't very easy. The whole procedure was in fact most awkward and very strange looking had there been anyone there to watch. To start with all of his weight was put on his left leg but because he had been asleep he wasn't able to keep it all on one leg and he had to place his right foot down on to the floor. As he did so, the pain that shot through his ankle was immense and it sent a shock right through his body forcing him to start to fall forwards. Gary's head missed the table by millimetres but he managed to stop his fall by keeping himself up on all fours, hands and knees to the floor. This seemed like a fairly comfortable position and one he stayed in for a couple of minutes whilst he thought and planned his next move. Gary manouevered himself towards the little table and took the empty glass in his hand and then set out for the kitchen.

"Don't be stupid," Gary actually said out loud as he realised that this was the wrong approach and he placed the glass on the living room table and then continued on his way out to the kitchen. Having got to the kitchen the next step meant he had to get back on to his feet. This wasn't quite as difficult as he thought it might be as he climbed up the kitchen furniture and put most of the pressure on his left foot until he was able to stand reasonably properly. Gary regained some of his breath before attempting the next part of the task. Gary reached up and pulled open the door to the top cupboard. Quite close to the front Gary found another full bottle of whisky. He reached around to do a sort of search.

"Down to the last two," he said out loud as he shook his head and tutted. It was as if he was telling someone off for not having purchased anymore bottles but of course he was the only one he could tell off. Gary unscrewed the bottle top and took a small swig before putting it back on and making his way back to the living room with it. It was hard work and by the time he had got back to the living room, Gary was tired out. He collapsed back on to the small settee.

The whisky was not one of the proper whiskies that you could buy but in fact a very cheap brand. It cost just two and a half E's a bottle and was usually available in great quantities at various shops and stores everywhere around. It was one of the few things that the current government made sure was available in full supply to the people. Well, that and also the cheap Vodka and cheap Gin. All the bottles carried the distinctive red and black labeling that the military government used for most of their products. Not that they actually made the products but of course they were in charge of certain manufacturers who would have to work for a pittance and give most of the profit to the government. They would normally have two standards of product available to buy. One would be the most basic quality which would be identified by a black label with a red diamond on it whilst the top quality would be identified by a red label with a black diamond on it. Although there was such a great fuss made about the two different standards, neither were particularly good and if you wanted something that was decent or actually tasted good you would have to buy one of the private manufacturer brands if it was available. Usually these were only available from specialised spirit retailers but sometimes other general shops would stock them. There was no license needed nowadays to sell spirits or beers that were destined for home use, or at least consumption off of the premises. The government would not stand in the way of private industry as they received a lot of their taxes from successful businesses. Unfortunately, as the government controlled the market place, although it might be possible to produce the stuff, it wasn't always easy to sell your wares. For instance, the production and sale of the cheap whisky probably made the government somewhere in the region of around ten million E's a year in profit. There were always plenty of desperate people about that were in need of cheap drink even if they might have preferred the better quality but this was often priced a bit out of the reach of many. If a private brand lowered its prices to compete with the government product or somehow became more popular so as to threaten the government products sales, the military would either just confiscate the private brand from a number of outlets on some hiked up charge or would stop the company from delivering the product to the shops by finding their vehicles all faulty. Whatever it took, the private brand would be forced to cut down on its production and hence the government brands would retain their sales. The outcome of these sort of tactics meant that private businesses concentrated on supplying the smaller upper portion of the market creating proper quality goods. Funnily enough, it was mainly government bosses and the military who were their main customers.

    Maybe a few years or so ago, everyone would be drinking good quality products whether it be whiskey, vodka or gin. As the price of better quality rose and the availability of poor quality drink increased, people got used to inferior tasting spirits and nobody complains anymore. Rumours of how the cheap spirits were made had long been passed around but no actual proof was ever published. It was said that on occasions, the government would confiscate a whole load of proper decent spirit, let's say whiskey for instance, and would then mix it with a raw alcohol like ethanol to produce the government product. It was most unlikely that this was the case as any 'free' quality product would normally be diverted to military use but the rumours still went around. The government had set up a number of production plants around the country and was probably one of the biggest employers. The pay was never that good and turnover was high with many in and out of work at the same factory at regular intervals. If you went into most homes in the country you would find that most had a bottle of quality brand whisky, vodka or gin in their homes which were only used on special occasions whilst everyday drinking would comprise of cheap government bottles. Quite often, families would keep the good quality drink for years before opening it. Gary had drunk all of the quality brand spirits he had a long time ago.

    A pain started to return. It was of course his ankle that was giving him this pain so Gary took a closer look at it. He had forgotten about the events leading up to his injury and was beginning to recap on exactly how he got into this state.
"I have been shot!" Gary again said out loud. "I've been bloody shot!" Saying it helped Gary accept the fact that he had got himself into a very dangerous situation yesterday. He was in fact very lucky that his only injury had been a bullet graze. He shook his head as he thought about the bullets whizzing passed him as he stood with the old Postmaster in the Market Place. 'They were shooting at me. Actually trying to kill me' he thought to himself. Next came the long process of trying to establish what had actually gone wrong with the meeting, when it had gone wrong and then trying to come to some conclusion as to whose fault it was. Gary mulled it over in his mind. Had he actually been set up by Andrew Longhurst? There was definitely a long delay after they first met before he wanted Gary to hand over the envelope with the lists in. Gary had expected to just meet him, say hello, hand over the envelope and go but the PM wasn't in any hurry at all. Was he waiting for people to be in place? What would he gain from doing that? Gary thought through various different scenarios but each time couldn't get to a suitable solution where the old Postmaster would have done what he did for his own advantage. There was certainly something that Andrew Longhurst wasn't happy about. Gary recalled being asked if there were any faces in the Market Place that he knew. At the time Gary thought this was just idle chit chat but on reflection it was obvious that Andrew had been spooked by something. Then there was the fact that Gary had bumped into Frank Braidwood who was also spooked by certain things. Gary tried to recall what it was he said. 'Too many strange faces around today, something's gonna happen, I don't like the vibes' was what he remembered. If only Gary had listened to him. Gary thought Frank a bit strange himself and had passed off his comments as being those of a drunkard or madman. He wasn't as stupid as Gary thought he was. It was no

good. The only conclusion that Gary could come up with was that both he and Andrew Longhurst had been set up by someone else. He was fairly happy that Andrew wouldn't put himself in that much danger so he doubted that he had double crossed him. Someone knew what was going on though! There were a number of people around who seemed slightly familiar to Gary but none he could actually put names to.

Gary then sat back and poured himself another whisky. He picked up the glass and looked at the dirty marks around its rim. There were lip marks all the way round. Not left from lipstick but just his own lips having imprinted their pattern on the glass as he'd drunk from it. There were also dirty finger marks around the glass. Gary thought that perhaps he ought to wash the glass so he knocked back the whisky and prepared to get out of the chair. It wasn't easy. He looked at the bottle and decided that he would wash the glass the next time he was visiting the kitchen. He poured another drink. Gary thought about the general state of things. Him self! His house! The whole situation he was in. How had he got involved in such a situation in the first place? Almost like a bolt of lightning Gary suddenly remembered about young Billy Simpson. He had also been at the Food Centre. Gary knew that Billy had been working for the revolutionaries so guessed that they were probably fully aware of what was going down that day. Then there was also the other bloke who shot the soldiers. He was very calm Gary thought to himself and appeared to be very professional but he was clearly a member of the revolutionaries. Perhaps there had been a leak and they had guessed that things might not go according to plan. That was probably why Andrew had changed the meeting place and time at such a late stage. It would also explain why he was apparently on edge during the meeting. Gary felt they had tried to play it carefully so as to avoid showing out. It hadn't worked. Gary was aware how important these lists were to the revolutionaries. He had been told that it might be the last ingredient to start off the big one. The revolution that everyone had been waiting for all these years. Gary didn't think that any sort of revolution would really change very much. That was if there ever was a revolution. He knew that the party also thought he had these sort of feelings and wondered if they perhaps didn't trust him. Perhaps they were the ones shooting and in fact shooting at him.

The feeling growing inside him as he went over these events was starting to evolve into one of absolute anger. It wasn't something that Gary liked to feel but he couldn't help getting annoyed. Why couldn't Gary just have a normal job, lead a normal life, do normal things. Gary was thinking back to his wife and family. He missed Joan and Katy, and he missed Angela. They would probably still be here with him if he had been a little less concerned about the Government. Gary tried to look at himself and in particular he started to question his reasons why he felt so strongly about what he was doing sometimes but in general didn't really believe any of it. Gary realized that Angela too had her political beliefs. She must have done because of her involvement all those years ago. She must have her own view on things now even if that view had changed. She was just able to keep them separate from her everyday family life he supposed. Gary was starting to feel sorry for him self. He finished off his drink. He needed something to take his mind off of things, all the trouble he had got into. He tried to remember back to when he was a bit younger and could spend time just watching the fields. There was something most soothing about watching the green fields around where he lived. The crops would all wave in the wind as they swayed in one gigantic movement as the wind blew. Gary could watch the fields for hours. He needed to watch something that would relax him now.

Gary decided to put the television on. It took a few minutes to warm up but eventually a picture and some sound started to come through. The television was tuned into channel 1. It was no real great surprise to find that there was a programme about how well the British were doing in the wars to protect the folks back at home. There would always be a little bit about some new leading figure in a country overseas somewhere who had made a declaration that they would attack Britain. This would lead next to more troops being sent off to some neutral country where we would be fighting a newly identified enemy. In reality, we would be sending troops off to quell some rebel faction or sort out civil unrest. Gary was certain that there was no real threat from the regularly identified terrorist leaders but always had a niggling doubt in the back of his mind. He couldn't work out how they could get so many people to be filmed making verbal threats against Britain. Perhaps some of them were real. Gary switched to channel 2. This wasn't much better. It was a programme advertising vacancies in government backed industrial jobs. There was a very posh woman who read out the particulars of the job and then a couple of smartly suited chaps who would then interview other workers at the place where this new job was. As you can probably guess, all the workers interviewed were happy, well nourished, clean living and full of praise for their employers. They couldn't stop themselves from giving all the details of all the good things about working in the particular job and at some time through the interview the question would always be asked 'And are there any down sides to working here?' but nobody could ever think of any! Gary watched and listened for a short while until the inane content of the whole subject came too much for him to take.

Gary retuned the television to channel 3. This channel wasn't actually broadcasting at the moment but had a few fixed pages which took it in turns to be shown on the screen whilst mindless music was being played. The main screen showed a map of Britain with the words 'Unity and Trust written over it. The next page then advertised the next programme to be shown on that channel. It wasn't due to start for a couple of hours and was a choral recital which was very boring. According to the next page, after that there would be a programme talking about wild flowers. Even more boring Gary thought. The Britain map then reappeared. Gary decided to turn the television off. He made his way over to the radio to see if there were any stations broadcasting at the moment. There were no fixed radio stations anymore but a varied amount of local broadcasters who would play music or interview local celebrities if they could get a license. There were also the odd couple of stations who would be giving out local news. Gary found one known as the Chale Hail.

Gary listened to the station which gave local information about events going on in Chale. There was nothing really of interest until…..

"Last night in Kentley there was a small incident in the Food Centre when four revolutionary activists tried to incite local shoppers to riot. The authorities are not releasing any names at the moment but are looking for two of the men who managed to avoid arrest. A large scuffle was witnessed before shots were fired by the activists into the innocent public and three people were badly wounded. Again full details of the victims have not been released at this stage. We are pleased to say that Military forces were quick to arrive on the scene

and were able to arrest two of the activists whilst restoring calm and order without firing a single shot. There is also a further report stating that the two activists may have committed suicide soon after being arrested but this has not been confirmed."

Gary listened hard at the news which as usual was full of lies about who had fired at whom and how the Army had done everything by the book. He knew that it was the military who had fired first and not the revolutionaries. Anyway there weren't four activists there, only two. Billy and the man in black. Where had they got the figure of four from, he wondered. It soon dawned on him that they were referring to him and Andrew. The local news had by this time gone on to some other subject. Gary took a couple of large swigs of whiskey. No names had been mentioned but he knew that he was probably one of the wanted men.

      It was about a quarter past twelve when there was a ring at the door. 'Who on earth could this be' Gary thought to himself. His immediate feeling was one of being inconvenienced. It wasn't going to be an easy job answering the door and Gary considered it a bit of an unwanted task that he had to perform. Was it The Army coming to arrest him? Gary immediately dismissed that thought as if they had been the ones calling there wouldn't have been just a ring at the door. They would have broken it down by now. Gary sighed as he took in a deep breath. He got up slowly, hobbled to the front door and opened it. Julie Clark was there, standing outside. Gary was surprised and lost for words. The fact that he was also a bit out of breath didn't help matters.

"Oh hello. Sorry to bother you." Julie said as soon as the door opened.

"Hello." Gary's annoyance had disappeared immediately and he changed the tone of his voice to be as warm as he could make it under the circumstances.

"Are you okay?" Julie continued.

"Yes thanks and how are you?" Gary asked back politely. There was that strange feeling of uncertain embarrassment in the moment. Neither was really sure why they felt embarrassed but both did.

"I'm fine." Julie could see that Gary was having difficulty standing on his right foot and she looked at it to such an obvious degree that even Gary knew she was looking at it. "Are you sure you're alright?"

"No not really I'm in a lot of pain. My ankle hurts." Gary replied as he sighed again being reminded of the pain. There was an awkward silence for a few seconds but Gary soon snapped out of it. "Would you like to come in for a minute?" Gary took a short step back and indicated with his arm that Julie should come in.
"Yes if that's okay." Julie entered and went straight into the living room. Not being rude at all, she hang around the table rather awkwardly as Gary followed in behind. Gary pulled a chair from the table in an effort to try and make his guest feel more comfortable but the pain in his ankle was getting the better of him and he had to quickly sit back down in the armchair to take the weight off of his foot.

    Julie looked around at the mess in the living room and then looked back at Gary. She wasn't quite sure what to say and as it happens didn't say anything.
"Now I have to ask you. Were you here in my house helping me last night or was I dreaming?" Gary put the question to Julie.
"No you weren't dreaming." Julie laughed as she replied at the comment Gary had made. "I was here. I was actually trying to leave a note for Angela." Julie replied as she looked around the room and indicated the note on the floor under the table. "There it is," she said as she picked it up and handed it to Gary rather embarrassed. This was mainly due to the thought that she had just waltzed into someone's house and sorted things out without being invited. It wasn't the sort of thing she would normally do but she felt she knew Angela well enough to come into her home but then of course, Angela hadn't actually been there. The current situation she found herself in was also a little embarrassing as she stood there with her note in her hand. "I put it under the glass. It must have fallen on to the floor."
"No I did read it earlier. My ankle started to hurt and I must have dropped it. I don't know how to thank you." Gary said somewhat embarrassed himself. He was more worried that Julie might have thought that he had thrown the note away.
"Don't mention it. I just called round to make sure you were okay." Julie continued.

    Gary found it difficult but he got back up on to his feet, grabbed Julie by both arms and gave her a kiss on her forehead. It was a strange thing for him to do but one he enjoyed. When he had gone to kiss her it was an automatic reaction of his in an effort to show how thankful he was that he had someone who was there to help him. Afterwards, the kiss seemed to take on a completely different meaning and it was a moment he wished he had taken more time over. She looked up at him and he stared down at her. He stood tall and strong and despite his injuries Julie looked at him as a sort of hero back from battle. For a few seconds neither said anything but both realised how they felt. Their minds were racing and a thousand thoughts must have run through them in seconds. Julie's heart was beating a little faster and Gary fixed his gaze on her breast as it swelled in time to her breathing. He could see a patterned lacey top, which Gary imagined was her bra. He concentrated on her flesh whilst deciding whether he should make the next move or not. Julie looked at his forehead. The effort in getting back on to his feet had caused him to sweat a little and Julie watched as his face seemed to glisten. He was unshaven but the contours of Gary's jaw were heightened by the dark course bristles. She looked at his eyes and almost fell into him there and then but she quickly regained her composure. She felt a shiver move through her. Gary noticed the horripilation on her exposed arms. Each single hair on her arms seemed as if it was erect as they stood protruding from the goose bumps now so prominent. There was another one of those still moments. Gary slowly moved his mouth nearer to Julie's. Although they both clearly wanted to let things take their course, there was something not quite right about the moment. Julie knew it was wrong so spoke to break the moment. As she did so she moved in a way so as to regain some more of her personal space again. Unfortunately there was a gripping inclination inside of her telling her to move forward once more but she fought against it.

"Oh I also took the liberty of stopping off and picking up a walking stick for you." Julie produced an old walking stick that she had been holding in her hand. It was an opportunity to try and change the subject. She would have been happy for Gary to have kissed her just then but things needed to be just right. "I don't know if the size is okay but at least it might help you take the weight off of your injured foot if you're going to be walking around."

Gary moved back and took the walking stick from her and tried it out. He walked up and down the hallway. He had to bend down in order to use it and it appeared to be rather uncomfortable for him.

"It's just great. You are lovely, thinking of me like that." Gary tried to sound pleased about the walking stick but in truth it wasn't a lot of help.
"Don't mention it. I'd do it for anyone." Julie knew that wasn't true but felt it was the sort of thing she ought to say.
"No honest. You've been my Saviour, looking after me. I owe you." Gary moved towards her considering giving her another kiss. It might have been fairer to say he was hoping to give her another kiss or at least see a little bit more in the way of encouragement.
"Well I'm sort of in my lunch break and I've got a lot to do so I think I ought to be going" Julie said, raising her hand slightly stopping Gary from moving any closer. It wasn't a harsh push saying 'no' but more a gentle touch saying 'not quite yet'.
"Please come and see if I'm alright again. Anytime!" Gary said.
"I will," Julie said as she smiled at him and went on her way.

    She wasn't at all sure if what had happened back then was the same for both of them. She hoped that Gary wasn't offended by her calling round. It was an awkward moment but it had given her a nice feeling inside. Gary stood and watched Julie leave and didn't close the door until she was out of sight. He watched every little way in which she walked. He also felt good. He slowly made his way back into the living room and sat himself down on the settee. Gary then picked up the note from Julie and he read it through again. This time he tried to take in what the note was actually about. It didn't say much except to say that the school was being returned and Julie would be going back there. Gary studied the writing carefully again looking at the pretty way that Julie had written her Y's and G's. He kept looking at the note for about ten minutes before it dawned on him that this would put an end to his interest in the school. Because of all that had been going on, he had not had the chance to go and visit the school on the pretence of making enquiries into an undeliverable letter. That letter was still sitting in his briefcase along with the file. Gary was caught between choices as to what he should do next. On the one hand he should start putting the details of the case on the computer system just in case the Postman asked about it or even worse asked the AP about it. This meant that there had to be an outcome. Gary would have to write the file off somehow. Gary could always just burn everything and hope that nothing was said. No this was the wrong way to do it. After a few minutes of thought he came up with the idea of stating that he had left the envelope with a soldier who had told him that there was a Colonel with roughly the same name working at the school. He would have to find out the name of a soldier who was working at the school and hope that nobody actually asked him about taking the letter. In the meantime he would burn the bloody thing. It wasn't the perfect solution. Not ideal but the only way that Gary could see of getting out of it.

-

Back at Army HQ in Kentley, Unit Charlie 12 were finally stood down from duty. Everyone was tired as they had all been working quite a lot of hours recently with very little time off. The whole Unit was together in one of the day rooms. It was the office where all orders would be given out and of course whenever a Unit returned from a mission, they would have to meet up again for further orders. Sergeant Foulkes was undoing his belt and adjusting the implements attached to it as he stood up at the front of the room. The Unit stopped what they were doing, ready to listen to his orders. "Okay, listen up. We've all been working hard and you all worked well today. Your duty has finished for today. Dismissed!" He stood to attention and gave a little salute as he gave these orders and the Unit responded in the proper fashion by returning the salute. "And if anyone is interested, I'm on my way to the bar and I'm buying." Sergeant Ed Foulkes added. A big cheer and some applause went up from the bulk of the Unit
Ed Foulkes was pleased to see his Unit through another tough assignment without any injuries. There was just one casualty as far as the Army was concerned but it turned out to be a Sergeant from the Battersea base in London. Nobody knew who he was or what he was doing here but he was definitely shot whilst on duty at the Food Centre this evening.

Most of the Unit were talking about the so called 'job well done' but with differing opinions. They agreed that they had managed to get one of the two targets they were told to arrest but then only after losing him and then having to shoot him. They lost the other meeter altogether. Some of the talk was that someone from the Army actually prevented the second man from being captured. There was a lot of confusion out there when it first went down but there were definitely some working against rather than in unison.

"Serge, is it true that we got the right man?" asked one of the Privates.
"Yes, I'm told we got the number one target."
"And what about the person he met?" Private Bridge continued firing questions.
"Unfortunate but he got away."
"Do we know exactly how he got away?" This came from yet another Private as nearly all the Unit were now taking turns in questioning their Sergeant.
"No I don't but I know it wasn't our fault." Ed finished his pint.
"Who's for another?" He continued as he made his way back to the bar. The Unit started talking amongst themselves again. There were still lots of questions left unanswered. There was one of the Delta 5 team who was knocked unconscious somehow. And then there was the gunman nobody had noticed until it was too late when he had shot the soldier from Battersea. Private Rachel Dobbs thought she recognised him but couldn't think where from.

    Major Wooters made his way back to his office where he rang Major Tannier. Not surprisingly, Tannier was not best pleased at the result and in fact told Wooters what he thought of his band of reprobates who probably couldn't control a piss up in a brewery. He confirmed that the dead man was the revolutionary runaway that they had been looking for and had been expecting but he was no good to them dead. He complained that there were not enough troops employed, that they didn't seem to know what they were supposed to be doing and just took part in a free for all shoot out. Major Wooters took it all with a pinch of salt. He knew that his teams had done well and that the Intelligence had underestimated the situation in the first place. It was normal for them to blame another Unit. Tannier also queried the mention of another plain clothed gunman. Nobody knew who he was, where he went or anything. That wasn't quite the case.
"One of the Units actually saw this man earlier on during the evening", Major Wooters said.
"Did anyone get a description then?" Tannier replied indignantly.
"Yes quite a good description". A full detail was then given to Tannier who could not argue that at least one of his soldiers was not sleeping on the job and might have just helped save the day. It was all Wooters could do to stop himself laughing at Tanniers response but the Intelligence Major hadn't finished yet. He then went on to explain that although the list they were hoping to retrieve had in fact turned

out to be two lists they were not pleased that things were not controlled properly after the point that the lists were handed over. The lists may well have been passed on to anyone in the two or three minutes between the swap and Unit Charlie 12 luckily shooting our target. Major Wooters decided the time had come to stand up for his teams.

"Now look here Tannier, you may think that things went wrong out there this evening well if they did I say it was mainly your fault." Wooters barked down the phone.

"Don't talk such crap man." Tannier replied.

"You told me there would only be the two of them at the Food Centre."

"I never said that there would only be two of them, dear chap. I believe I said we were expecting two suspects."

"No you clearly stated just two."

"You might have got that impression but it is an assumption that you jumped to. I would never tell you that there would only be two. You have to allow for occurrences." Tannier said.

"Occurrences huh! Occurrences!" Wooters nearly fell off his chair in rage.

"Admit it. You were ill prepared for this mission and it is you that put your own men in danger." Tannier added some salt and rubbed hard.

"A very low key affair please, that's what you said," Wooters shouted back to him. "There were at least two others with guns who were working the Centre that night, it was more like a city railway station." Major Wooters huffed.

"Can't your boys work a railway station then?"

"Not when we're told we're in a graveyard, No!!" Major Wooters sat down and tried to calm himself. His blood pressure was rising and he needed to take one of his pills. He produced a small little tin from the inside of his jacket and opened it. He took out a small pill and swallowed it down with no trouble. The brief pause gave him a chance to think and calm himself. "Have the report with me tomorrow."

"You'll get it when I'm ready to give it to you." Major Wooters slammed the phone down in a fit of anger. Wooters wasn't quite sure if he was more annoyed with Tannier or himself for reacting as he did. It wasn't very often that the two of them argued and this one was long overdue. Wooters knew he was in the right this time so he felt a bit better. He knew very well that by tomorrow Tannier would probably ring him on the pretence of some trivial subject but really to see if he was okay and then nothing else would ever be said about it.

Tannier for his part knew that he was in the wrong. He decided that he would let a bit of time go and then ring Wooters tomorrow just to make sure that everything had been forgotten. The agent for Operation Hunting had phoned in and wanted to see him so he quickly composed himself and made for the Hospital where they had arranged to meet. Again there was a similar discussion about the lists, the death of the revolutionary runaway and the other gunman.
"I take it he got away?" The agent said.
"Yes I'm afraid so,"
"Did anyone get a good look or description of the man?"
"Yes," said Major Wooters. We have a good description to go on and I am hoping to get a name and an address. One of the Units was clever enough to have got a description. I'll let you have it straightaway.
"That's great. Can you also try and make sure that Private Dobbs gets to see it. I value her opinion very much and I'd like to know what she says," the agent finished.
"I'll make sure she does." The Major concluded. The two departed from the hospital in the same way that they had arrived. The agent leaving first and The Major afterwards. He spent a few moments looking around the remembrance garden. It listed numbers of people who had died in the hospital over the years mostly Army personnel. The Major looked around to try and find a particular name he started his career with. So many names! What was it all for, he thought to himself?

-

Sarah had made her mind up that she wouldn't give up on trying to get Gary and Angela back together again. She knew how good Angela was for her brother and of course she wanted the best for him. It wasn't going to be that easy but at least she had got to know Angela a lot better in the last few months. They were able to speak to each other more than they had done before. She wouldn't tell Angela everything. She opened up to Gary quite a lot and she wouldn't tell him everything. In fact there wasn't anybody she had ever been able to tell everything to. Not even George. The relationship between her brother and her had been through some rough times but they both had a general understanding and trust. For a long time now she felt she

had a responsibility for looking after Gary but she knew damn well that he would look out for her in return. She persevered with her task and called round to see Gary again. With any luck he wouldn't be in as bad a state as he was in when she last time she called round. Sarah was pleased to find him sober even if he was still walking funny.
"What's up with you?" Sarah asked as she walked into the house.
"It's my ankle. I've had a bit of a problem with it. Gary replied.
"What sort of problem?"
"Nothing I can't sort out." Sarah insisted on checking Gary's ankle and she was surprised to find it very well bandaged up.
"Who did this for you then? It's been done rather well." Sarah asked looking at the bandage sensing that it had a woman's touch. Had Angela been round perhaps.
"Oh a friend of mine called round and sorted the ankle out a bit. Is it okay?" Gary replied with his own question.
"Well whoever did this has really made a good job of it but if you've swollen your ankle it needs a bit more space," Sarah talked as she unbound the bandage. As more came off she could see what looked like blood. "Did you cut it on something?" Sarah continued to open the bandage. Gary didn't reply. One because he thought it a stupid question to ask and two because he was in a lot of pain. Sarah finally took all the bandage off and removed the dressing. "Shit! You've been shot!" Sarah exclaimed. "When did this happen?" She asked.
"Yesterday at The Food Centre." Gary told her wondering how she was able to tell that it was a bullet wound.
"What the bloody hell did you think you were doing there?" Sarah said in an angry voice.
"Oh you know, minding my own business." Gary lied.
"Don't give me such crap. The only people who were there last night were revolutionaries or Army. What were you doing there?" Sarah continued to sound very angry. She continued to look at Gary's foot whilst she questioned him about his affairs.
"No it wasn't. You've been listening to rubbish on the radio again. It was people shopping, just trying to buy an honest crust and then the Army took it upon themselves to cause a massive disruption." Gary got a little carried away with his reply.
"And you've been listening to revolutionary propaganda haven't you. Probably mixing with the wrong sort." She tutted and shook her head as she told him off. "So what were you buying then?"
"Well nothing as it happened. I just happened to be there waiting to

meet someone." Gary said.

"Oh yeah. Who was that then? It wasn't Angela, that I'm sure." Sarah gave him a sly look.

"Just a friend that's all."

"But who then?" Sarah wouldn't drop the subject.

"It's none of your damn business but it wasn't another woman if that's what you think." Gary guessed Sarah was concerned.

"But there was a load of shooting wasn't there?" Sarah wasn't going to be happy till she'd got to the bottom of this.

"Well I think I heard the odd shot. I left as soon as it all started and didn't hang around." Gary said quite convincingly.

"Well you obviously didn't leave quickly enough as you still got shot didn't you!" Sarah twisted his foot a little just to emphasise her point.

"Ow yeah, I suppose I did get shot, I don't really remember." Gary replied.

"You know that a couple of people were killed at the Food Centre last night." Sarah continued.

"Yes I've heard on the news".

"One was that bloke Longhurst you were checking out the other day." Sarah said. There was a moments silence as Gary felt a cold chill run up his spine. Sarah continued to attend to his ankle but she noticed his reaction. She twisted the ankle again. It made him sit up rather abruptly and he stared at Sarah.

"Andrew Longhurst got killed?" Gary said in a questioning way as his mouth dropped.

"That's what they said on the radio. I recognised the name immediately." Sarah told him. "Was that who you were meeting by any chance?"

"I told you, I was just meeting an old friend. Why would it be him who I was meeting?" Gary said still in shock about the news of his death.

"Sorry I thought he might have been someone you knew."

"No his name was in one of many files I work on. Just a coincidence."

"They say he was a revolutionary agent. You know, one of those activists. Kill or be killed is their motto. What were you doing meeting him?" Sarah kept asking. She slowly started to inspect the wound on Gary's ankle.

"I said it wasn't him I was meeting." Gary replied.

"But you do know him don't you?"

"Yes I know him and in fact I bumped into him the other day."

"What just like that. How do you know him?" Sarah asked again.
"He was my old boss at The Sorting Office" Gary told her. "I didn't know he was a spy or anything but I knew he'd sort of been in trouble before. It was why he left work quite quickly," Gary explained.
"Is that why you were checking him out the other day?" Sarah saw some pieces falling into place.
"Sort of." Gary realised that he was telling Sarah far too much.
"You didn't know he was a revolutionary then?" Sarah asked again all the time checking out the blooded wound.
"No of course not. You don't think I'd get mixed up with that lot again do you?" Gary felt quite emotional as he answered. He all of a sudden realised that the news of Andrew Longhurst's death had affected him. "You wouldn't get involved with the revolutionaries again would you?" Gary turned the tables on to Sarah.
"No bloody way." Sarah answered with feeling. "After what happened to David and then George how could you think such a thing." Sarah was in full flow. "I hate them all. I want nothing to do with any of them".
Gary and Sarah sat and stared at each other both quite exhausted from letting off steam.
"Those revolutionaries are bad." Sarah added. "Don't get mixed up with them again. Promise me." Sarah held Gary's hand as she asked this last bit. "We've got enough problems getting you and Angela back together without you getting involved with anything else."
Sarah concentrated on cleaning Gary's injured ankle again. She bathed away a lot of the old blood and wiped it with some cleansing spirit before putting on a new dressing. "Bloody good job you've got some medical stuff here."
"Yes quite lucky."

Sarah left Gary with his new dressing on and made her way back home. Gary was content to just sit down in the chair in the living room and watch the telly. It was 'Teamball' day and Gary was quite pleased that he was able to sit down and watch it. There was only about ten minutes before the programme came on so Gary didn't have long to wait. As always that very recognizable theme music started and everyone knew it was time for 'Teamball'. Once again the voice began; *"I hope you are all sitting in your seats now as you won't be for long. It's time for another challenge of Teamball with your host Johnny Johnson."* The voice delivered this message in the most exitable tones you could think of and the camera switched to the compere of the show, Johnny Johnson. The top man was dressed in his usual style again tonight with a large lapelled, shoulder-padded bright red sparkly suit jacket on. Every time he turned, it would catch some light from somewhere and sparkle. He had a normal white shirt on and a tie that was mainly black but had three little lights on, one pink, one green and one blue that lit up in sequence every now and then. Johnny Johnsons hair was as spiky as it had always been but today it was jet black. To go with all this he had his regular heavy framed black rimmed glasses on. For once the weather had not been very kind to them and it was pouring with rain very heavily. To combat this, Johnny Johnson had a large umbrella which carried the programmes logo on it. The sections of the umbrella were coloured alternately yellow and red and every now and then Johnny would spin the umbrella around.

"Hiya folks! Are you ready to be entertained?" Johnny Johnson started off with his usual opening lines. *"It's the country's most popular event and it's nearly time to start."* He delivered the lines in his usual excited manner as he jumped around kicking his almost abnormally thin legs in the air as he did so. He always wore very tight fitting black trousers so that the thinness of his legs could be fully appreciated and he had very large thick soled shoes, again mainly black. The compere would normally throw his arms around but with an oversized microphone in one hand and an umbrella in the other, he was finding this almost impossible to do this week. Holding out the hand with the microphone in it, he continued.

"As you can see we should have brought our macs with us today or perhaps our swimming costumes as it is absolutely throwing it down here but never fear, we will be having the times of our lives and we'll soon forget the rain." Johnny allowed the camera to show just how wet it was before he introduced the teams. He looked back at the camera. *"And can you remember who our reigning family are? Yes that's right they are the posh lot from Swindon, the Howley-Smythes, I said that posh lot the Howley-Smythes."* Johnny continued to talk in various high pitched tones and silly voices whilst pulling silly faces at the camera. He was still nodding his head up and down most pronouncedly but despite all of this movement his glasses never seemed to move an inch. If you had been watching this for the first time you might have thought that his glasses were actually stuck to his face somehow but he would always prove that this wasn't the case by

just moving his glasses in short sharp movements to the left or right in a funny manner to get another laugh. As he introduced the winning family from the last show, the camera zoomed out so as to get Johnny Johnson and all of the Howley-Smythes in view. All six of the team were wearing brand new sports shirts, different from last week but each shirt had the family members name on their back. As well as this they all wore the same very obvious top of the range track-suit bottoms and training shoes. The whole lot of gear must have cost quite a lot of money unless they were sponsored or knew someone in the sportswear business. The whole team jumped up and down excitedly waving both hands in the air. The crowd were very vocal, cheering loudly whilst Johnny Johnson ran around the Howley-Smythes doing silly jumps.

"Hopefully you'll remember our champions who successfully beat the Philpotts a couple of weeks ago. I have here the leading member of the family, Mother Howley-Smythe. Marilyn, you did very well last time were you pleased with your tactics?"

"Yes we tried to do a little planning and most things worked a treat."

"And how do you think you'll get on today, being the pushers this time?" Johnny Johnson pulled a funny face and mimicked a big laugh as he put this last question to her. He also acted out a pushing motion by moving his arms forwards and backwards in front of him.

"We have some new moves this week. We'll see how it goes." Mrs. Howley-Smythe sounded very confident. The camera followed her as she returned to her team but then it flicked back to Johnny Johnson.

"And fellas, do I have a bit of a treat for you as I also have right next to me our new darling of the game, Geraldine!"

The camera turned to the young slim girl who still looked every bit a model but also looked somewhat embarrassed by all of this new attention. Johnny Johnson put his arm around her waist and gave her a little squeeze whilst looking at the camera and making a pleased expression. Johnny Johnson continued interviewing.

"Hi Geraldine are you looking forward to today's game?"

"Oh yes. Very excited," she said in the appropriate manner.

"Have you been told that we have received lots of letters and enquiries asking to find out about you?"

"Well I have seen one or two."

"I think all the men are glued to the telly tonight just watching you Geraldine. What do you think about that?"

"I'm just getting on with the game Johnny." The young Howley-Smythe family member came across superbly. Sexy but serious.

"So how old are you Geraldine?"
"I'm going to be twenty in a couple of months time."
"And have you got a boyfriend?"
"No not at the moment." Geraldine gave a coy smile to the camera as she answered.
"Wow!" Johnny Johnson jumped up and kicked out his legs. *"That's good news hey guys."* He looked at the camera again as he said it. *"Well today it was the Howley-Smythes choice of venue and they have chosen to come to their home town of Swindon for our event today and particularly to this playing field. We have plotted out the usual course and 'oh dear' we've found a rather stony bumpy section but there is still lots of flat grass around. Let's just meet the champions again."*
As usual at this point the live camera switched to a pre-recorded film where the members of the Howley-Smythes were introduced. A voice gave out their names, their relationship to the family, age, height, weight and hobbies. When it came to Geraldine they also gave her vital statistics. As the camera swept to James it closed in to show the wound over his eye. Apart from that, all the Howley-Smythes seemed to have got off without too much in the way of injuries. Whilst television viewers were seeing this, back in Swindon, Johnny Johnson had an opportunity to complain about a couple of the supporters in the crowd who had been making rude gestures behind him whilst he was doing his introduction. He turned to one of the military personnel who was involved in crowd control.
"Oy, I don't know if you're new but if one of those fucking wankers sticks his fingers up at the camera again I want you to stick your fingers up his fucking arse!"
There was a quick warning and the camera went back to Johnny Johnson who immediately turned back to camera and was as composed as ever. *"And so it's time to meet the challengers. Let me give a big welcome to the Breakspears who have travelled all the way down from Manchester to be with us. Let's hope it wasn't a wasted journey for them."*
We once again got a pre-recorded film of the Breakspears being introduced. They looked more like the normal sort of family that the programme attracts. They were all dressed in different types of sports wear although each one had a red top on and a red hat of sorts even if they were all different designs. One of the family members looked like he could easily have been a doorman or security guard and not somebody you would want to have an argument with but the rest of

them all looked quite regular. Johnny Johnson came back into view and he had a quick chat with the leader of the Breakspear family in his normal fashion ensuring that they had a rough idea of the rules and admitted on air that they fully understood them. The whole Breakspear family then did their little jump of excitement although one had to say it was a bit subdued. There was a distinct lack of confidence amongst them.

As always, although most people had a fair idea of the rules of Teamball, there was always the odd occasion that would turn up where everyone looked at each other and said 'Well is there a rule about that or not'. If there was, Johnny Johnson would be on the spot with the referee who would stop play and enforce the rule whilst Johnny Johnson would be on hand telling the watching public what was going on and what he thought about it. It was probably the case that the referee, or should I say referees, made the rules up as they first went along. There were only three official referees, two men and a woman, and they took it in turns usually to referee the games. These referees were employed by the makers of Teamball and they were pretty much in charge of how the game was played. Today's referee was Tony Hastings, the eldest of the three at 45. He was slightly overweight and losing his hair but he was very popular. And pretty rich. The object of the game was well known. It was the champion's task to push the large giant leather ball along the 50 yard course and the challengers' job to stop them. The organisers would also put certain obstacles on the course so that it wasn't a simple job of pushing the ball the length of the course and the easier the course, the more obstacles were put on it. This was considered to be a top category course or one of the easiest and hence there were 5 obstacles. Todays included a large tree trunk which was almost three quarters of the width of the course. This would be an obvious spot for the challengers to try and hold off the champions. There was also a large brick construction containing a couple of iron girders. There was a small ditch that had been dug, a fairly sizeable old metal tank and lastly a burnt out van that had been rolled on to its roof. The Howley-Smythes took a good look at the course and planned their approach that morning. They had till twelve o'clock to order their five implements but in fact had only asked for four. This meant that they could ask for a fifth during the game but it may take some time to arrive. This would be a good time to ask for a 'time-out'. Tactics were really required.

The referee gave the five minute countdown warning and both teams made their way to their respective ends of the course. The Howley-Smythes were slapping palms with each other and looking really up for the game. From the last game, they were believed to be quite acrobatic in their game and the audience, already more excited than usual was looking forward to some spectacular feats. The rain had started to ease off a little but it had made the ground fairly slippery. This wasn't what the champions really wanted but they would just get on with their task. All stood behind the ball, the Howley-Smythes gave a howl of anticipated victory as the referee sounded the one minute warning. The crowd joined in with the digital clock.

"*Forty, thirty-nine, thirty-eight........*" As this was going on the Howley-Smythes took up position behind the big ball. Father Harry and his brother James looked for the best place to put their hands on the ball, bearing in mind they needed to avoid razor blades, glass, knives and any strange liquids that might be coming out of the ball. They weren't allowed to actually touch the ball until the rocket went off but by then they would know exactly where they were going to put their hands.

"*Twenty-seven, twenty-six, twenty-five.....*" The rest of the family would be placing their hands and pressure on to the backs of the two men touching the ball.

"*Sixteen, fifteen, fourteen....*" The challengers, the Breakspears were all behind their line waiting to run up the course to attack the ball pushers. It was normal for the challengers to just make one big rush up the field and get to the pushers as quickly as possible so as to stop the initial momentum of the first push but they would be up against some sort of defensive wall in front of the ball or some of the family members trying to prevent the challengers from grabbing at the pushers near to the ball. When the Howley-Smythes challenged in the last game they of course ran up to the defensive wall in front of the ball but then somersaulted themselves over it so as to get to the ball pushers unopposed.

"*Ten, nine, eight...*" The crowd was really being worked up into a frenzy by Johnny Johnson as the countdown reached its climax.

"*Five, four, three, two, one.*" There was a big shout and scream as the rocket fired to signify the start of the game. All six of the Howley-Smythes pushed at the leather ball and it started to roll along the course. Harry and James managed to keep at least a couple of hands on the ball at all times and soon the ball was moving. The Breakspears started their run up the course, avoiding the obstacles on the way of course. Two of the men in the team and one of the young girls were running faster than the other family members and were obviously going to get to the Howley-Smythes before the others but then the Howley-Smythes put their first plan into operation. As the ball kept being pushed by Harry and James, the other four members of the family ran around to the front of the ball. This seemed like a normal defensive pattern, employed by many team but it wasn't. Instead of waiting for the Breakspears to get to them, the Howley-Smythes ran and attacked them. They reached the advanced three and managed to fell them all. The Breakspears hadn't split up at this stage so all three were pushed on top of each other. This enabled just two members of the Howley-Smythe family to keep all three of them down whilst the other two waited for the rest of the Breakspears to catch up and join them. Only two of the remaining three reached the melee next and the remaining two Howley-Smythes kept them occupied for some precious seconds. It wasn't until the last Breakspear joined the ruck that the Howley-Smythes found it hard going to keep them all at bay and had to rely on tripping up one of the Breakspears who had broken through the defensive line to keep them back before a call went up to retreat. Whilst all this had been going on, the two men from the champions had managed to push the leather ball nearly fifteen yards down the course. This was very good going indeed but the initial push came to a halt as the Breakspear family finally managed to pull the men away from the leather ball. It really was a very good plan from the Howley-Smythes and possibly one that could have worked completely successfully five times were they of a mind to ask for a time-out at the end of each push and then repeat what they had done. They didn't.

There was a lot of pushing and pulling and a little of illegal punching going on with all twelve of the contestants spending time getting up off the floor. There was one really big battle going on between one of the Breakspear men and James from the Howley-Smythes. The Breakspear man kept a fairly good hold of him but every now and then James would break free and try to push the leather ball. All the others were also well involved with their counterparts from the opposition but the Howley-Smythes had quickly learnt to try and throw one Breakspear member on to another so as to get a man free to push the ball. Still less than ten minutes into the game and the Howley-Smythes had managed to get their second push at the ball. They moved it three or four yards but then had to change direction to make for the only gap passed the large tree trunk. They had obviously decided to go round it rather than over and it meant pushing the ball an extra few yards but it seemed to be the right idea. The Howley-Smythes kept on going whilst they pushed the leather ball diagonally heading to the gap. It was hard work and slow going but they moved it regularly. Then there was a bit of a breakthrough. One of the younger Breakspear girls had taken a blow to her side and she was fairly winded and out of the equation for a while. This allowed a Howley-Smythe, Mark to be exact, to help James and Harry continue to push the ball to the gap. They got it in line with the gap and immediately called for a 'time-out'. This gave everyone, including the winded Breakspear some time to capture their breath but the rules were also that at the restart, the two teams had to start behind their respective lines again. When the game restarted, the Howley-Smythes took advantage of this and got the ball moving through the gap and passed the tree. All six of the team helped with the pushing this time and the ball moved another ten yards before the momentum came to a finish. They had now moved the ball over half way and had used only twenty minutes.

The game continued in a similar fashion and with still fifteen minutes to go the ball was less than ten yards from the finishing line with only the ditch to really avoid. It was inevitable by this time that as the Breakspears had no new ways of stopping the Howley-Smythes it was a case of when they won rather than if. They did so with seven minutes left on the clock. It was the Howley-Smythes second victory and the crowd was in sheer ecstasy. Johnny Johnson jumped for joy as the ball went over the line and Tony Hastings signaled for the fireworks to be let off to signify another win for the champions. They only needed to win their next challenge and they had won a holiday. Johnny Johnson completely ignored the losers as usual and celebrated with the winners.

"Harry you've won your second Teamball, how do you feel?"
"Well Johnny." He gasped for breath as he spoke. "*I haven't quite taken it in yet but I think it'll feel great.*"
"And if you win your next game, it's the holiday!!" Again, Johnny Johnson kept speaking in funny high pitched levels to add to the

excitement. He then turned to the camera, "*Hey fellas, you know what this means. We'll see the sexy Geraldine again.*" Johnny Johnson grabbed hold of her and pulled her into camera shot as soon as he had said it. "*Blow them all a big kiss Geraldine.*" She obliged most willingly. The Howley-Smythes were allowed to get on with their celebrations as Johnny Johnson moved away from them still looking and talking to the camera. "*So the Howley-Smythes, yes that posh lot from Swindon, have won their second Teamball. Can they win a third and get that holiday of a lifetime. Tune in for the next game of Teamball, till then, byesee bye.*" Johnny Johnson finished with this same sort of silly voiced message every week and as the music started, the cameras pulled away and upwards as Johnny Johnson and the referee, Tony Hastings waved, the Howley-Smythes all waved and the Breakspears could be seen lying flat out on the ground. As usual, Johnny Johnson would continue to jump up and down as he waved so as to stand out from the rest. He didn't really need to jump to stand out, but he still did. As the camera panned out more it was possible to see more of the supporters in the stand. Most were just jumping around celebrating but there had been a couple who seemed determined to try and create havoc. You would probably only have noticed it if you were particularly looking for it but the camera caught a view behind the stand which captured one of the military officers hitting one of the trouble-makers over the head with his truncheon. The civilian went down quickly and took another couple of kicks before the director managed to get the cameraman to pan left and the incident was out of shot. No viewer really noticed anything.

    Gary enjoyed the show very much and he had sat right through the programme without drinking a drop. He picked up his glass and downed the remains. He thought about the possibility of his family taking part in Teamball one of these days. It wasn't very likely though, only a dream he thought as there wasn't really anybody fit enough in his family to make up a team. Perhaps one day a local family might enter and he could go and watch them. If they happened to win then perhaps they might choose Waydon as the venue. Gary continued to think about this possibility and imagined that the television camera teams were setting up down at the Waydon playing field. This would be the perfect place for a game of Teamball. Waydon playing field was a little bit out of Waydon but not that far. It was fairly big and well enclosed and had dressing room facilities. It would be just perfect. Gary had lived in Waydon for a while now and had actually grown very fond of it. Although many years ago it had only been a very very small village, it had become, a few years back quite a proper little town. Gary started to imagine himself taking visitors to the village around Waydon showing them all the landmarks that he knew of. He went through his imaginary talk until he realised it would all be about farming and peas. Quite boring really!

-

John Silver sat in his car as it was parked in the street near to the entrance to the picnic area on the other side of Boxmeer. He had his newspaper which he pretended to read and the small set of binoculars which were required every now and then. Less than a hundred yards away was the entrance to the drive which led to the house where Mariano Zwolle lived. John's eyes peered in its direction regularly. He was waiting for some movement and he didn't have to wait long. An estate car emerged from the drive and turned in his direction. There was a man driving it. He was wearing a velvet coat and brown trilby type hat. He had a grey moustache but John was happy it was the man he had been waiting to see.

He waited for the car to pass him and then he started his own car and turned round to follow the estate car from a distance. Nobody drove that fast so it was quite easy to keep up with his target. The car stopped at some lights and John slowed down so as not to be right behind the car for too long. The estate car turned right and John did the same. Another car had managed to get in between them and John felt a lot happier being able to use it as slight cover. He followed the car into the center of Boxmeer and watched as the car parked in one of the side streets. He did the same but a bit further down the road. The man got out of the car and John Silver was able to follow him. He didn't go far. The man went into the local bank. John went in as well and was lucky to be able to find a little seat where he could sit down and take a closer look at the man he had been following. He was happy that the description he had, matched the man he was looking at. To help though, the man from the estate car was obviously asking the cashier for a cheque to be cashed. John Silver queued up near to the man and overheard the cashier calling him Mr. Zwolle. It couldn't have been any easier.

John went back to his car and waited for Zwolle to return. It was nearly half an hour before the target returned and he was carrying a small paper bag with a distinctive yellow and green marking on it. It was some sort of product symbol but John Silver couldn't really make out what it was. As Zwolle returned to his home, John Silver made sure that his target turned into the drive and then he drove passed. He would return that evening to get a better look of the area surrounding the house.

Chapter 10   -   THINGS GET WORSE

Gary had had an unsettled night. Although he had slept a bit he had been constantly waking up through the night and consequently felt very tired when he woke. The actual feat of getting up the stairs to the bedroom had been a real achievement and one he was quite proud of but he now had to get up on his bad ankle again and this was not going to be easy. At first he fell on to his knees as he got out of bed and he considered crawling to the bathroom but after getting as far as the bedroom door changed his mind and pulled himself back to his feet. He completed his ablutions and toileting in some agony and then slipped on a rough pair of trousers before making his way down the stairs. He had to be careful but he made it to the hall and in particular to the phone. He telephoned the early shift at the sorting office and told them he would not be in to work today.

As Gary put the phone down he tried to walk without the aid of the walking stick but he just couldn't put any weight whatsoever on to his right foot. He nearly fell a couple of times but managed to stop himself but just standing on his left foot. With the use of the walking stick, Gary made his way back into the lounge and he dumped himself into the chair. Gary contemplated what he might do for the rest of the day. His ankle was beginning to hurt a lot more and he guessed that the dressing might need changing again. He considered phoning his sister but thought twice about bothering her. The pain was difficult to cope with so he decided that he had to at least get up and go into the kitchen to get another bottle of whisky. This he did and started to drink mouthful after mouthful until the pain subsided a bit. It wasn't the most sensible thing to do but an easy option. Whilst all this was going on, Sammy had gone to the back door and was barking to say that he wanted to be let out.
"Alright boy! I'm coming." Gary made his way to the back door and let the dog out. Sammy went straight to the shed, sniffed around a bit and then went about his business as little dogs do. Gary looked over at his vegetable plot and thought he would give it a little look to see how things were coming along. A lot of the vegetables he was growing seemed to have taken quite well. He had some parsnips, potatoes and beetroot planted. All of these would be good for swapping if he didn't want to eat them. To the right of the vegetable plot, Gary had constructed a sort of glass cloche where he had some tomatoes

growing. These were slow to come along but at last there seemed to be signs of little green tomatoes forming. Gary was aware of Sammy moving around the garden and could see that he had made his way to the back gate. Not a problem usually but today for some reason the back gate was partly open and Sammy had made his way out to the back lane. Gary hobbled after him.

"Sammy, come in here. Sammy. Sammy." Gary shouted out his orders but there was no response. It was strange for the dog to go out of the back door on his own Gary thought, but if there had been a cat or another dog around, that would explain it. It was also unusual for the back gate to be open. It wasn't possible to unlock the gate from the lane and Gary was adamant that he had left it bolted when he last came in that way. Sarah wouldn't have unbolted it either he thought but he was more concerned about trying to catch the dog than worry about how the gate came open. He hobbled nearer to the gate.

"Sammy. Sammy you bloody monster, get back in here." Gary shouted out again as he got to the gate expecting to see Sammy outside wagging his tail. As he looked out he couldn't see the dog from the garden. He would have to actually go out through the gate and look up and down the road it would seem. Gary wasn't very happy as the pain was starting to return to his ankle as he hobbled further towards the gate. Gary went through and saw Sammy on the opposite side of the road being stroked by a man who was crouching down in front of the dog. Gary was totally unaware of the person on his left as he felt the sharp pain at the back of his head as he was hit with a dull thud. Gary collapsed to the ground, unconscious.

Gary felt the pain in his head as he started to regain consciousness again. He rubbed the back of his head at the top of his neck and he could feel the bump and the cut where he had obviously been hit. He was still very groggy and a bit confused as well as cold and he opened his eyes but could see very little except darkness. There was a single narrow beam of light above him which looked like the sun from outside trying to break through to the room he was definitely in. He was cold. Icy cold. As he moved his eyes a little he began to appreciate the desolate bleak situation he appeared to be in. All of a sudden Gary realised that he was in fact laying on the floor, on his side with his arms constrained. He tried to move them but he had had his hands tied together and they were seemingly tied to a piece of wood. He then started to feel the terrific pain in his right ankle. His ankles had also been tied together and the rope had been tied over the wound and it was beginning to cut into the wound and hurt a hell of a lot. Gary tried to move but it was impossible.

He shouted out. "Is there anybody there?" Gary wasn't sure what he thought he might achieve by doing this or who might be there to hear him but he shouted again anyway. "Help me. Can anybody help me?" There was a horrible silence as if he was the only person left alive. He looked around about him but it was too dark to see too much. He could tell that he was laying on a stone floor but on some sort of mat or carpet. It was only thin and not really much protection from the freezing effects of the floor. It had probably been put there for him to lay on but he had managed to crawl off of it partly and his head was actually on the stone. He couldn't make out where the walls were. Everything was dim and shadowy. He couldn't tell if there were any walls or even if there was a door. He might be down a cellar he thought. Wherever he was, he was isolated. The one beam of light only showed another bit of stone floor. Gary decided that moving around was a waste of time so he laid still only to become aware of a very quiet sound. It was a rhythmic sound but in very small quick bursts. Like little footsteps.
"Oh shit!" Gary said this as realisation struck him that it was probably the sound of a rat or a mouse or some similar creature. He never found out but he did catch sight of the end of a large looking tail as it passed under the single beam of light. That bloody thing better not come anywhere near me, he thought to himself. He needn't have worried as the rat was in fact more frightened of his new room mate than Gary was of the rat. Gary worried about the rat for another half hour or so until he started to think about other things. Who is it that has me locked up here, what do they want of me. Gary ran the incidents of the last few weeks around in his head, the meeting with the old postmaster, the shooting at the Food Centre, the whole mystery surrounding the arrangements, the actual lists themselves and the postmasters' explanation of what they were for. He guessed that he was probably a guest at one of the European Armies secret interrogation camps. The sort of place that people said you never returned from.

Gary stopped as he heard in the background some footsteps, heavy and forceful and the clinking of metal, likely to be some keys he thought. The footsteps stopped and Gary could hear what sounded like a key being inserted into a lock and then being turned. A squeak of an unoiled hinge was the next sound and then the footsteps started again. This time Gary was able to make out two separate lots of footsteps. They got louder and stopped very close to him. There was the sound of a bolt or two being pulled back and then a lock being unopened. Lastly there was another key inserted into a lock which was obviously a door to the cell he was in. As the sound of a door being pushed and more unoiled hinges being used, Gary saw a silhouette of light appear around three sides of what was a square door. He tried to look passed the door but the light was too strong for him to spend long enough looking at it to focus. He could make out a shape of a man and he seemed to be in some sort of combat uniform. Gary felt himself being lifted from either side and then a cloth bag was put over his head. Gary felt comfort at this to start with as it sheltered his eyes from the light but as it was tied around his neck it soon became yet another pain for him to have to endure.

He was dragged from his cell and his right ankle started to give him lots of pain as it knocked against the soldier's feet and other hard bits of concrete. They had a little bit of trouble trying to get him through the cell door but after that he was just dragged along what Gary guessed were a number of passages. The sound made it seem that he was in a corridor and from time to time he could hear the sound of some electrical buzzing coming from above him. He was uncertain whether these were lights or fans or possibly some sort of electrical defence to stop him from moving down the corridor should he manage to escape from his cell. This was of course very unlikely at the moment. Gary was finally taken through another small doorway and sat down on his wooden stool that was still tied to his body but this time his hands were cut free and so were his legs. The relief he felt from having his right ankle freed was almost like being on a high from drugs but he soon started to feel the down of pain from the bullet wound which had still not been tended to. The cloth bag remained on his head and there was a silence of sorts as nothing else happened for a while. Gary could hear breathing and could smell tobacco so he was sure that there was at least one person in the room with him. The ties around the bag were now being undone and the bag was removed. Gary was confident that he was sat in the middle of a room just on his stool but within seconds a lamp was turned on and a bright light shone in Gary's eyes so that he could not look at anything else. He moved his head to the right in an effort to turn away from the brightness of the lamp but this was greeted with a fist to his right ear. His ear whistled with the aftermath of the punch he had received. He still tried to turn away from the light but another punch hit him on the top of the cheek. This too started to hurt. He soon learnt not to turn his head. A foreign voice (sounded a bit like a Mexican voice) started.

"What were you doing last week at The Food Centre?" The voice sounded clear and precise.

"I was buying food of course." Gary knew what they wanted him to tell them but he still came out with this smart arse answer. Not surprisingly it was greeted with a whack from a cane over his right knee. The pain shot through him like lightning.

"I'll ask you again Mr. Newson, what were you doing in the Food Centre last week?"

"I was meeting an old friend."

"And who was this old friend?"

"He used to be my boss a few years ago." Gary felt he shouldn't give up all he knew, or at least not that quickly but he tried to make up a believable story that would account for what he did.

"And his name?" The voice was very direct. Gary felt the pressure.

"Mr. Longman." Gary lied of course.

"What is his first name?"

"I don't actually know his first name I only ever called him Mr. Longman."

"Are you sure that is his name?"

"Yes that's how he was introduced to me when I worked for him." Gary replied wondering how long they would allow him to keep giving them all this crap. He guessed that they already knew the old postmasters name but he continued for a while.

"Where does he live?" The voice was still very calm.

"I don't know that either." There was a brief pause to the proceedings as some papers were turned over. Gary couldn't be sure where the papers were but he knew they had a few pages to them.

"How do you know his name is Longman?" The voice gave its first indications of being annoyed.

"I don't know that is his real name but I assumed it was. I never really spoke to him that much at work except when things went wrong. I was surprised to see him again." Gary was trying to think ahead about how he could explain having an envelope he wanted to hand over. He had a few ideas but was really having to think on the move.

"And why did you meet him at the Food Centre?"

"We arranged to meet there."

"Why?"

"He wanted an address of an old colleague." Gary hoped that this answer was good enough for them.

"Which colleague?" The voice was quick to come back with this and Gary hadn't considered such a question might get asked.

"One of the old sorting office girls. I guess he wanted to look her up again." There was a small silence again and then a whack from the cane as it came down on to his already hurting right knee. There was then another whack on his right arm just above his elbow. Gary winced as the pain from this last blow remained a lot longer than expected.

"You must think I am stupid Mr. Newson. What was in the envelope you gave to the man you met at the Food Centre?" The voice had returned to its usual calmness.

"I don't actually know what was in it." Gary was crying as he answered this last question still feeling the pain in his elbow.

"You expect me to believe that you don't know what was in the envelope?" The voice replied and gave a little laugh at the end.

"Honestly I do not know."

"Then where did the envelope come from, my friend?" The voice said the last bit very slowly. Gary had come out with this answer without really thinking about it. He wasn't quite sure what to answer now.

"It was in my safe at work." Gary gave a slurred answer as he felt more pain coming from his ankle.

"So what was inside the envelope?"

"I never opened it. I don't know." Gary blubbed as he answered. There was no follow up question but a brief stop in the proceedings as somebody got up and left the room. Gary guessed it was his interrogator but he couldn't be sure. The door was left partly open and Gary could hear murmurings from a distance. All of a sudden the cloth bag was put back over his head and he was dragged back to his cell. As he was dumped back into his cell and the bag was removed but his hands and legs were not tied again. He was laying back on the mat which he could now make out as an old thin mat, full of stains. There obviously had been some sort of pattern to the mat but over time it had worn away and now all you could make out were the number of different stains it contained. Gary took a quick look around his cell before the door was shut and the light disappeared. That single beam of light which came through a small hole somewhere in the ceiling continued to remind him that it was in fact still day time out there somewhere. He had forgotten about the creature sharing his cell but went over what he had said at the questioning that had just taken place. He had tried to be as honest as he possibly could be without telling the Army anything they needed to know. The last thing he wanted on his own conscious was that he might spill the beans and cause someone else to be arrested and put through hell. But then he thought back to all those other revolutionaries who had not spared a thought for him and his family when they had involved him in their activities but then he decided that he had probably volunteered more than being press-ganged into anything.

The silence was deafening. Gary listened to himself breathing. He imagined himself back in his little garden and then the worry of what might have happened to Sammy hit him. Strange that with all that he was going through he felt more concerned about his poor little dog. He was probably walking around Waydon trying to look for food. There would be little animals out there for Sammy to try and catch but then there would be bigger and more experienced dogs also out there. Poor little Sammy, Gary thought. As this was going over in his mind he fell asleep.

Gary stirred after a few hours and straightaway noticed that the beam of light that had shone powerfully through the hole in the ceiling had gone very dim. He guessed that this meant that it was night time outside or at least evening. He thought about the fact that there would be a moon that would probably show some sort of light but then he considered that it might well be the middle of the day but raining outside. No that couldn't be the case as he would surely get some rain coming through the hole. But he then thought that if it was just cloudy but not raining that that might be the cause. In the end he came to the conclusion that he hadn't got a clue what the time was, whether it was day, evening or night. He couldn't really say how long he had been locked up either come to that. He began to get depressed. There was another sound of metal chinking in the distance. It grew louder and Gary could hear the footsteps. The sound of the iron gate were heard again as it was unlocked and pushed open. The footsteps came to his cell and he heard the bolts being slid back and the door being unlocked. As the door opened, he could make out two uniformed men, both looking a bit Eastern European and they went through the same routine with the cloth bag and then dragged him to what Gary believed to be the same room he had been taken to before. It seemed about the same distance away as before. The very same thing happened. The bag was removed. The spotlight went on. Gary turned his head away automatically and he was immediately punched on the side of the head. This time he only moved his head away the once. His ear began to hurt.

"What was the name of the man you met in the Food Centre?" The voice was the same. It was a bit more aggressive than before and straight to the point this time. Gary all of a sudden realized that he had forgotten what he had given as the old postmasters name last time.

"The old postmaster." Gary answered after a pause. Almost immediately he was hit on his left knee with something.

"I asked you what was his name? What was his name?" The voice almost shouted out the last sentence. Gary could remember giving 'Long' as part of the surname but he just couldn't remember what he had said.

"Mr. Long." Gary stopped at this point and thought. He looked right into the light but he couldn't remember. Another blow hit his left knee as he stopped answering. "Longmore." Gary ended his answer in the hope he wouldn't get hit a third time. It was hard to actually try and remember what the old postmaster's real name was at this point and Gary tried to remember what name it was that he shouldn't say. Then he remembered he had said Longman. "I mean Longman."

"And what is his first name?"

"I don't know his first name." Gary was a lot more comfortable having got Longman back in his mind.

"Where does Mr. Longman live?"

"I don't know." Gary felt his shirt being ripped open to reveal his back.

"Now Mr. Newson I don't want to use the whip so give me the truth." The voice was back to its calm controlled state. It was strange but Gary's first thought was who is Mr. Newson. Newson he kept murmuring.

"What was the question?" Gary's mind was all over the place. He was hungry. Tired. He was also in so much pain he couldn't feel anything, just a sense of pain everywhere. It was almost as if he had cut off the bits of his body that were hurting but he still knew that he was in pain.

"Where does Mr. Longman live?"

"He lives in London somewhere. He never told me where."

"And where was he living locally?"

"With his sister in Waydon somewhere!" As Gary said the words he felt the guilt come over him about what possible comeback there might be on the poor sister who had taken him in. He imagined that there were troops standing by just waiting for his word to go in and kill her.

"And what was in the letter you gave him?"

"Just names of people." Again Gary realised as he gave this answer that it wasn't what he had said during the last interrogation. He tried to think what he had said last time and seemed to recall he had said that he hadn't even opened the letter.

"So you opened the envelope?" The voice was swift to reply with this follow up question.

"I looked at it quickly to see what was in it."

"And you read it?"

"Well I looked at the list of names and then sealed it up again."

"And what sort of names were on there?" By now Gary had regained a little bit of his senses and was able to keep to some sort of plausible story.

"Just names and addresses. I thought they were going to be people I would know." Gary was probably saying more than he should but at least he felt he had some sort of control over what he was saying.

"So you read all the names and addresses?"

"I looked at them. I'm sorry."

"What names can you remember?" The voice sounded as if it was a lot nearer than usual.

"I cannot remember any of them." Gary felt the whip being placed at his back as if someone was lining up an aim. He quickly continued with his answer. "Honestly I cannot remember any." It was no good. The whip lashed across his back sending a jerk right through his body.

"You wouldn't lie to me would you?" The voice sounded as if he was enjoying the whole incident.

"Honest I cannot remember anything." Gary found it hard to speak. The whip lashed against his back again. Another jerk went through Gary's body but this time it forced him to try and be sick. His body was going through the motions of being sick but very little was actually being regurgitated. Some bile and a bit of blood but Gary was still being sick nevertheless and his body tried extremely hard to force up something that just wasn't there.

There was a brief break in the proceedings as the guards forced Gary back into the chair he was sitting on. His hands were again tied behind his back and hands were placed forcefully on each shoulder to stop him from lurching forward. He had stopped trying to be sick by this time and he turned his head slightly to the right to see the hand that was placed on his shoulder. Another punch hit him full on in the ear. It hit him so hard that he nearly fell off his chair.
"Just tell me one name and all this can stop." The voice was gentle and soothing. Friendly and comforting.
"I don't remember any. There were some addresses in Kentley but not all of them. Some were foreign. I didn't really read them properly." Gary spurted out his answer in bits. He was still crying from the pain he was suffering.
"Take him away." The voice sounded annoyed. Gary was dragged back to his cell. He was left in silence again, the bag having been put back on and removed but his hands left tied together.

Gary tried to move but he only went through the motions of being sick again and it was better to just lay still where he was. His knee, ear and back were hurting as was his ankle from the bullet wound. Gary guessed that if he didn't get some water soon he might not live to see another day. It was useless to call out as he knew that nobody could hear him and if they could they wouldn't come and help. He started to think over the latest session with the voice but his mind couldn't concentrate on anything. He thought about his cell door opening and guards dragging him to the room. He must have been dreaming. He could see the light but he couldn't hear the voice anymore. It was a muffled sound. He could imagine himself being dragged back to his cell and being thrown into a room full of rats. The rats spoke to him.
"Welcome back Mr. Newson. Can you hear us? Are you alright? Hello." The rats were standing up on their hind legs as they talked to him. They chatted away to each other in between talking to him.
"Mr. Newson can you hear me? Hello, are you there?" The rats dispersed as the cell door opened again and Gary was dragged back to the room. Again he could only see the light. He couldn't hear any voice and couldn't feel any pain. Was this death? Gary wasn't sure. He thought back to his childhood with his brother and sister playing in

the garden. His Father was also in the garden sitting in the deckchair. Gary tried to focus on his Father and as the European voice spoke as his Father's lips moved as if he was speaking.
"Tell me what I want to know." His Father looked at him in the way that His Father had done many times before when he was angry with Gary. "Tell me Mr. Newson, tell me." Gary's sister Sarah joined in.
"Tell them Gary, tell them." Sarah could be heard to say.
"Yes go on. Tell them everything." It was David's voice this time. Gary couldn't see David but he recognised his voice and could hear him. Everyone was telling him to 'Tell them'. They started to walk around him and then finished up spinning around his head. Gary watched them as they span off into the air and into nothing.

"Mr. Newson, are you okay?" It was a different voice. One Gary had never heard before. He tried to open his eyes but he was weak and this simple task was very difficult. He managed to get them open a bit and he could make out a shape of a man next to him. Gary realised that he was now laying down in some sort of bed. He was almost naked apart from something wrapped loosely around his waist.
"Try and swallow some water." It was a woman's voice. Gary felt the edge of a plastic cup against his lips and the wetness of the water contained inside. He sipped a little and then tried to sip some more. Gary tried to move his arms up to help and although he quickly realised that his hands and arms were free from their ties they were both too weak to be lifted to help.
"That's better. Don't try and drink too much in one go Mr. Newson." The woman took away the cup but then brought it back to let him drink again. Gary was beginning to be able to open his eyes a bit further but his vision wasn't that brilliant. He had a shadow blocking the view to his right but he was able to make out the man who had first spoken to him. He was a bearded man wearing a simple buttoned up shirt, although not fully done up, a black tie and very basic dark blue denim trousers. He was a comforting sight to see as he looked very normal. Gary tried to turn his head but the pain was horrific as he did.
"Don't move at the moment." The woman spoke from his left.
"You have many wounds and injuries my friend. We will tend them and get you back home as soon as we can." The man added. Gary tried to speak but found it hard to move his mouth.
"Who are you?"
"My name is Peter. This is Marie. We are from the Kentley

Revolutionary Movement. I will tell you more when you are stronger but for now it is important that you rest." The man spoke to him in a very sympathetic manner. Gary immediately wondered how the Army had managed to capture him and even more, how the local revolutionary party had effected his escape. Perhaps they had managed to arrange for his release. Gary had loads of questions he wanted to ask and lots of thoughts going through his mind but agreed that he was in no fit state to do very much at the moment.

Over the next couple of days, Marie tended to Gary's wounds and fetched and carried for him providing him with everything he needed. She fed him little by little and after a day he was strong enough to sit up and move every part of his body even if they still hurt a bit. His jaw bone had been fractured and a doctor had come in and operated on him whilst Marie had looked after his bullet wound. Gary's eye wasn't quite as bad as they had first thought. It was feared that he might have lost his sight or that the retina had become damaged but in fact it was just a mass of blood from some internal wound that had got around the eyeball. He was badly bruised around his eye as well as other parts of his body and his back was covered with welts but they were treated and would soon heal. They assured him that there were no bones broken elsewhere.

After the second day, Gary was up out of bed. He found it very hard to stand up let alone walk so a crutch was ordered and it arrived within a couple of hours.

"You are being given very special treatment my friend." Peter said as he came in to see how Gary was recovering.

"Where did the crutch come from?" Gary was mildly curious.

"Well we thought you could do with one so we arranged for one to be picked up."

"You mean you stole it."

"No not stolen. It will have been removed from one of the local hospitals." Peter said calmly. "In time it will find its way back there I have no doubt. Nobody will suffer from its loss."

"I have to thank you for everything." Gary knew he had a lot to thank them for. "How did you get me out?"

"Get you out?" Peter found the question rather a strange one.

"Out of The Army prison!" Gary was a bit confused that Peter didn't grasp what he meant at once.

"As I have said I have a lot to tell you." The man sat down on a chair next to the bed. He rubbed his brow as if he was finding it hard to think of what to say. Peter eventually spoke again, "You weren't in an Army prison."
"Yes I was. I was kidnapped outside my house and put in a cell." As Gary said this, Peter shook his head. Then he nodded. Gary was very confused. "I was then interrogated by some European Army General or something and beaten. You can see my bruises and other wounds." Gary was annoyed that Peter didn't seem to believe him.
"You weren't taken by The Army."
"Well who the bloody hell else took me then." Gary was even more surprised at this comment.
"I'm sorry to say that it was we who took you." Peter bowed his head in shame as he said it. Gary's mouth dropped open as he took in just what Peter had told him. A few seconds passed.
"You took me?"
"Well sort of yes. You have to understand what has happened." Peter hoped to carry on with his explanation but Gary wasn't going to let him.
"Do you mean you have been interrogating me? You lot have tortured me. Nearly to my death. And now you nurse me back to health again. What….." Gary couldn't finish his sentence, absolutely lost for words to describe how he felt at that moment. He felt betrayed.

"Do you know exactly what went on at the Food Centre the other night?" Peter approached his difficult task from another angle.
"Yes I know what went on. I met up with one of your exposed agents and handed him some bloody lists that he had inadvertently left behind, in my safe. In my bloody office I tell you. Yes I know what went on." Gary tried to keep calm but his blood was at boiling point. Marie, who was also in the room tried to intervene as she could see that Gary's blood pressure was probably getting dangerously high.
"I think we should leave this for a while to give Mr. Newson a chance to calm down." Marie aimed her instruction at Peter but it was Gary who replied.
"Calm down! I'll give you bloody calm down. I want to know everything and I want to know it now." Gary pushed the nurse away from him as he said this. Peter had to bite the bullet and give Gary as much detail as quickly as possible for his own good.
"Yes you passed over some lists to one of our agents. And yes you're

right he had been exposed. But he had not been arrested by The Army as they obviously knew he needed to get the lists. It wasn't known for certain but suspected that they knew he was back in the area and may well have had some idea where the lists were but we couldn't be sure. That's why you were approached. We had made efforts to try and retrieve the lists without your help but had been unsuccessful and time was running out." Peter sat back in the chair ready to tell his long story.

"I got the lists and gave them to your man as instructed." Gary said in an abrupt manner.

"Yes but we never got the lists." Peter said quietly.

"How comes. I gave them to A....." Gary was about to come out with the old postmasters name when all of a sudden it struck him that he might not actually be talking to one of the revolutionary party at all. It might be a way of getting the facts out of him. He decided to just let Peter do the talking.

"Yes you gave them to our man. We do not know his real name. I am only one of the local party and didn't really know him, I just knew he was an agent with full clearance from London. The Army also knew of the lists and they were just as anxious to get their hands on them. I also know that he was well aware that there was a possibility that he would be arrested as soon as he got the lists from you. It was always possible that The Army knew where and when the lists were going to be handed over so plans were made to switch the real lists for a set of false ones. One of our local boys was doing the swap. I think you knew him. Billy Simpson."

"What do you mean knew him?" Gary could guess what the answer was going to be but he still had to ask.

"I'm afraid he was shot during the incident."

"Shot!" Gary was still saddened to actually hear what he suspected would be said.

"Yes he got shot." Peter moved forward in the chair. "We never expected The Army to kill them but they did. He managed to get away from the Food Centre before he finally died and the Nationals have been questioning him as much as they could. He never really managed to say very much before he died so I'm told but what is clear is that he had neither of the lists on him. Not the original one that you gave him nor the false one that he was going to change it for. I am also told that Billy was taken by The Army even though he was definitely dead. They would have found nothing on him but a list. When we recovered

Billy's body and belongings neither of the lists were there either of course. We have to assume that The Army got both the real lists and the false ones."

"So you suspect me of setting up an ambush? I got shot at as well." Gary was incensed.

"No we don't suspect you at all."

"So why did you put me through what you have done in the last few days." Gary found it hard to understand what exactly Peter was trying to tell him.

"We didn't actually know you'd been taken. The London boys came down and took you, it wasn't us. I don't know if they had someone watching or someone reported back to them but it was very unusual to use you in the first instance as you aren't even a fully established party member. You were only allowed to be used on the agent's instructions. His instructions were of course questioned at first as we didn't really know who he was but he was adamant that you were okay."

"Well I'm glad that someone trusted me." Gary began to take a grasp on what had been going on.

"Gary, we trust you. It's just that the agent obviously didn't get the word back to London. Due to the fact that he must have known that The Army was closing in he worked under his own arrangements. None of the meeting was cleared by London. They came down and it was they who grabbed you and have been treating you as an Army agent. We were contacted a couple of days ago to be told that they had an Army agent who they needed to get rid of and that they were holding him in the Kentley area. When we got there we found you." Peter tried to apologise. "I'm sorry but they just did it without telling us."

"So where are they now?" Gary wasn't sure if they were still waiting to question him.

"They've taken our word that you were not to blame and have returned to London but they wanted to know what else you knew of. I have to report back in a few days."

"So what will your report say?" Gary asked innocently.

"I still have to ask you what you know." Peter replied. "Do you remember any details from the lists?"

"No because I didn't really look at them properly. I gave them a quick glance to see if I recognised any of the names but didn't actually take that much notice of who they were." Gary tried to sound convincing even though he was lying through his teeth. Gary was becoming an expert at it nowadays.

"You might remember later." Peter sounded happy with Gary's reply.

"Tell me what else has happened then and I'll tell you everything I can remember." Gary knew he wouldn't tell Peter anything he hadn't already revealed to the London Revolutionaries but he would have to tell him something. Peter continued to explain more of the situation surrounding the Food Centre incident.

"You now know of course that we had Billy Simpson working for us. He was put into the sorting office to try and get the lists back but then got arrested and his cover was blown. We do have another agent working within the Postal Services but I am not aware of their name. I just know that we get information from them every now and then. Unfortunately it seems that we also have an Army agent working very close. It is assumed that they were put in to flush out our London agent but we are no nearer to identifying who it might be. Just be warned that when you do return to work, they might know that you have been working for us."

"But your own agent will be trying to find out who the Army agent is so will they make contact with me?" Gary racked his brains to come up with a name of who the likely agent might be.

"No that's very unlikely. Our undercover agents don't like to tell anyone apart from their agreed contact. I remember once we had an agent working deep and they were giving good intelligence to us but their contact got killed in a car accident. It took us nearly six months before we could set up a new contact as we didn't know who the agent was and they didn't contact us for ages." Peter seemed quite happy to chat with Gary about these sorts of things. Things that Gary didn't think he should have been told.

Peter carried on for a while more chatting about various problems connected with undercover agents. All was going quite smoothly but then his tone changed to a far more serious one.

"So tell me Gary, what can you remember about the lists?" Peter was straight to the point.

"Very little, honest."

"But you opened the letter and looked at the list?"

"I've told you that, yes."

"Just trying to clarify." Peter paused to think about his next question. "Did you copy the lists at all?"

"No. I looked at them but didn't recognise any of the names. There was an address in Westbank. I'm certain of that because I remember thinking it was just down the road but I cannot remember the number, 23 or 27 I think." Gary put on his confused look.
"And the name?" Peter was getting a bit fed up with the lack of information coming from Gary.
"No idea. No idea at all." Gary shrugged.
"That is all you can remember?" Peter started to resign himself to having to admit that they had lost the details for good.
"I'm sorry but I just didn't bother to try and remember." Gary sighed.
"What exactly were the lists then?"
"I don't think I can really tell you that." Peter replied.
"Well I seem to have worked out that they are names of agents but are they Army agents or.." Gary swallowed as if in pain but was actually trying to stop himself from saying the wrong thing. "Or were they ours?"
"To be honest, I think the lists contained names from both sides. I don't really know but what I do know is that there was one list that was very important. It contains some foreign names. People who attended a meeting." Peter had already said too much.
"I did see a load of foreign type names and addresses." Gary felt it was okay to mention this.
"And what were the names?" Peter gave one last try.
"No I just didn't take the details in at all. It all seemed rubbish to me."

Peter chatted with Gary for about another two or three hours whilst Marie tended to Gary's wounds. Obviously the cheek was quite a bad injury but so was Gary's ankle but he received constant attention for the next couple of days. Peter popped in to see Gary whilst he remained with them at the base and he told Gary about the current threat to The European Army from America.
"We get on very well with the US you know." Peter said cheerily.
"What the revolutionaries you mean?"
"Yes. The Americans would like to topple the European power if they could but they are biding their time before moving." Peter spoke with an air suggesting he was well informed.
"Are they going to try and take us over then?" Gary sounded surprised.
"They are not too keen on the current French German power at present and consider Europe as a relatively major threat to them. They would

like to have some sort of entente cordial with Europe but if not they want Europe toppled." Peter went on.
"Sounds quite frightening really."
"Not really. They would be pleased to see the old British Army and Government re-installed and we are trying to negotiate a deal where that happens." Peter slammed his fist down on to the table he was sat next to as he said British. "It's all a long way off I suppose if I was to be perfectly honest, but I live in hope of seeing the day."
"I'm surprised they would want to bother with us, we're so far away."
"I know they have troops in Asia already and the attack when it comes may not come from the West." Peter smiled as he said this. It was a knowing smile.

    Gary's ankle was said to be on the mend. Marie gave him one last dressing and packed some fresh bandages for him to take home with him. He was reminded that he should use the crutch as much as possible and keep the weight off of his ankle whenever he could. Gary knew he was going to be allowed to go home and couldn't wait to be able to see the sun again. His eye was also getting better but he still had some blood swimming around in it that would eventually go. Peter came in one last time to say goodbye to him.
"So you are leaving us Gary."
"Yes. Thanks for what you have done." Gary shook his hand.
"Sorry that you got injured. It all stems from that bloody Food Centre incident of course. If we ever find out who the bitch is that set it all up, well we'll……" Peter couldn't think of how to finish the sentence.
"Bitch! You said bitch! You know it was a woman who set it up?" Gary asked.
"Oh damn, yes. Well we think so. I shouldn't really tell you. We only got the intelligence in yesterday but we are reasonably happy that The Army agent who was after Flint is a woman."
"So she knew we were meeting?" Gary was very curious.
"Look I'm not supposed to tell you any of this but we were told from one of our agents that the troops were in place around the Food Centre that night and it was a woman that ordered it. It's likely she is someone very close who heard what was going on. She must be very clever."
"Someone very close to what?" Gary wanted to know more.
"Who knows? Close to us in some way. It wouldn't be the first time we had an informer amongst us. Close to Flint possibly. Maybe close

to you? We just don't know." Peter started to turn to leave. Gary pondered on his words. 'Maybe close to you', he said a couple of times over in his head.
"I'm afraid we have to blindfold you again to get you out of here. You are one of us I know but you do not have clearance to know the identity of this place. We'll get you home and one of the local revo group will make contact. Good luck." Peter walked out of the door as two other men walked in with a blindfold, balaclava and a cloth bag.
"Blimey! You're not taking any chances are you?"

Gary was walked quite a long way but soon he was out in the fresh air again and able to hear the noise of the town. He thought he might be able to make out where he was but the truth was he had no idea. He was bundled only slightly roughly into the back of a car and driven around for nearly an hour and a half before he was dropped off right outside the back of his house. During the journey, Gary was thinking about what Peter had said just before he left. Had Gary let slip a vital clue about his meeting with Andrew Longhurst. Surely there wasn't anyone that Gary knew who was a spy for The Army. He wasn't sure about the old AP's sister. At first he had felt sympathy about how involved she had apparently been made to get. Perhaps after all she wasn't such an easy pushover or perhaps Andrew had pushed her too far and she had turned. Gary wasn't convinced either way.

-

Since Angela had moved out she had found it very hard to start living her life normally. Gary hadn't known that Angela had been to the doctors on a couple of occasions and he had diagnosed that she was stressed out about something in her life and needed a break. She didn't think that this was the sort of break that the doctor had intended but it served it's purpose. The three of them had moved into an empty cottage on the other side of Waydon, funnily enough only about sixty yards from Sarah's place. Angela had known that it was standing empty and she had asked favours and used what influence she could to persuade the owners to allow her to live in it until they returned. She had managed to get them to agree. Using her influence with people she knew, she was also able to get the cottage at a very cheap rate. She couldn't really afford to rent anything much on her money and she didn't want to go to the Housing center and ask them to put her into a

new house for various reasons. Firstly it would be most unlikely that she would get housed in Waydon which she particularly wanted and what's more she preferred it if the authorities didn't know her business. Her biggest worry was how the girls would cope with the change but she needn't have worried. After a few days, Joan and Katy had easily settled in to a new routine and the weekend was soon upon them which meant that they needed to go shopping. The girls didn't mind going shopping as it often meant that they would be treated to some little surprise. As Angela had left the car with Gary, they caught the bus into Chale.
"Are we going shopping all day?" Joan asked.
"Not all day but for as long as it takes." Angela gave a typical parent answer.
"I don't want to go shopping." Katy added her two penneth.
"Well I'm sorry about that but we've got to go." Angela was a bit shocked at Katys' statement but guessed she was a bit down.
"And when will Dad be back?" Joan asked.
"Yes. When can we see Dad again?" Katy cried.
"I don't know at the moment. Soon hopefully!" Angela was near enough ready to cry again.

-

Once again a meeting was arranged at the offices of St. Michaels Import & Export between Major Tannier and the agent.
"I've used this office a bit more often than I had originally intended so we will not meet here anymore" the agent started the conversation.
"Yes I quite understand".
"I took out a bloody three month lease as well and I've hardly had it a month" the agent went on.
"Well I can ask if it is of any use to one of the other agents" the Major asked tentatively.
"Yes, as long as they don't use it for meetings".
"Of course not! Observations, storage, it's not a lost cause".
The agent fiddled about in one of the drawers and then sat back comfortably. "I think we're a bit behind in updates of reports", the agent said.
"Yes there are one or two reports to keep you up to date with. Where do you want me to start?"
"Start with the oldest".
"Okay".

The oldest report was with reference to the photographs that had been taken from the newspaper reporter's friend and developed. The Major had his small briefcase with him that contained a number of different files and he bent down to open it and searched inside for the relevant file.

"The photographs", the Major started.

"The ones from the roadblock?" answered the agent.

"Yes. We've shown the photos of the man in the car to a few soldiers who have been involved with things a bit more recently but nobody seems to be able to recognise him at all. I've had the best shot sent to Strasbourg but again nothing. You have to admit that the pictures of him are pretty poor," the Major concluded.

"Yes true but it's worth the effort," the agent replied. "Did Corporal Dobbs get to see the photographs?"

"Well it's funny you should ask that as she particularly asked to look at them".

"She knew that we had some?" the agent added suspiciously.

"You know how it is. Rumour goes round the base. You cannot keep everything secret".

"So did she recognise the man?" the agent asked without really thinking. "Hold on she has already seen the man, she knows what he looks like, what was she doing looking at the photographs?" the agent continued.

"Well it would seem that she wanted to look at the photographs of the car," the Major explained. He went on to explain that Dobbs had specifically asked for a comparison to be made to the car seized from Swindley's house to the car on the photographs of the roadblock. She thinks that we are talking about two different cars. He continued to say how certain parts of the photos had been enlarged to find five distinct differences that prove that we have been dealing with two vehicles, same make, same model, same colour, same registration number but two different cars.

"You're bloody right, that Dobbs is good".

"It was her doing then?" The agent asked.

"Oh yes. She said that she didn't think that Swindley was the same bloke as the chap at the roadblock but also the car seemed a bit different".

"I told you didn't I," the agent said again with a feeling of satisfaction.

"So this means we have two vehicles driving around on the same papers." The agent continued.

"Yes, well at least we did but again Dobbs insisted that the Swindley vehicle was impounded so only our man is now driving around in one." The Major nodded as he corrected himself.

"Well I suppose that's a bit of a help but I now know that he is not Michael Swindley I'm back to square one again", the agent said and slammed a fist on the desk.

"I also have the report on the house search from Sergeant Foulkes and his subsequent follow up at Potters Peas", the Major handed the agent a new report.

"Don't see any point in reading that now, he is not our man", the agent waved the file away.

"Well yes you are right but you should have a little look at page seven", the Major insisted. The file was taken by the agent and page seven quickly found. As the agent read through the report, the Major whistled a bit. He knew that he could point out the relevant part straightaway but that wouldn't be how the agent would want it.

"Just a brief mention of one of Swindley's colleagues thinking he lived in Greenfields," the agent looked up at the Major. "Is that the only point?"

"Well I thought it quite possible that this may be where our man is actually living," the Major added.

"I don't see that it is that strong enough to go on."

"Well I do have more," the Major added with a feeling of having been caught out.

"Have you done some checks in Greenfields?" The agent asked surprisingly.

"No I haven't. It is in the report from Unit Charlie 12 that came through today. The report of the Food Centre incident. I nearly missed it but have followed it up." The Major passed yet another file to the agent. The agent had a quick flick through the report but it was at least twelve pages long so turned to the Major to get straight to the point.

"Well what did you nearly miss?" The agent asked him.

"Almost right at the end, Sergeant Foulkes does a quick recap and wonders if his Unit could or should have been better prepared for the chaos that was to follow and he concludes that despite the fact that there seemed to be more people about than usual and the report of the strange car parked nearby, he didn't think he was to blame for underestimating the situation." The Major read from the file in a knowing tone.

"And the car was?" The agent had realised what the relevance of this passage was.

"Yes, I got back to Sergeant Foulkes who was unable to tell me," the Major responded jokingly. The agent grimaced at the thought that they had been so near. The Major continued. "No, I had to make a few enquiries and finally got to the soldier who spoke to the man in the car".

"He actually spoke to him?" The agent said excitedly.

"She spoke to him, and no it wasn't Private Dobbs this time. We do have some other females in the Army you know," the Major answered. "A Private Westley was doing the rounds and patrolling the Food Centre as normal leading up to our operation".

"She knew we had an operation running?" The agent queried.

"Come on, we don't tell everybody but we do tell the soldiers in the vicinity to keep their eyes open". The Major took a deep breath. "She spotted this car parked on Northgate with a man in and he just seemed to be parked there sizing up the area. She at first thought that he might be one of us but then thought she ought to challenge just in case. As she took a few steps towards the car, it started up and drove away," the Major did a good job in drawing the picture.

"So what did she get?" The agent was almost begging.

"Nothing. Well not then anyway", the Major was having fun teasing this story out. "She was due to go off and decided to have one more look around the area before heading back to HQ and would you believe it the same car, with the same bloke in was parked up in Westbank. So she called for back up and actually questioned the man".

"Did she get a name?" The agent was almost bursting.

"Yes. A name, address and confirmation of the registration number of the car but you're going to be surprised," the Major finished his little story. He searched around in his pocket and pulled out a piece of paper on which the name and address were written. Michael David SWINDLEY of 11, School Lane, Waydon.

"So he has false papers," the agent said angrily.

"It would appear so but the soldier did have a quick look around the back seat of the car. I think looking for any weapons or the like. She only saw a big envelope addressed to a Mr. M. D. S.... something but at an address in Greenfields not Waydon."

"Did she query it?" The agent asked hopefully.

"No. It wasn't until I spoke to her that it came back to her mind".
"The envelope was addressed to Swindley though?"
"Well here's the biscuit. She doesn't think it was. She couldn't read the surname properly as she quickly saw it but the more she thinks about it, the more she thinks it ended in something like 'ers'," the Major added.
"Anything else you think she can give us?"
"No I think she has told us everything she can remember at the moment."
"I'll need to get address details for everyone registered in Greenfields first thing tomorrow", the agent continued. "Where would you normally get that from Major?"
"The Information Centre or if you want to keep it quiet, from the Postal Office."
"No get it from the Information Centre please. I'll call in at your office at ten thirty for it," the agent concluded.
"Aren't you off to Strasbourg tomorrow?" The Major queried.
"Yes, but I'm going to be a bit late aren't I."
"Ten thirty it is then," the Major said assuredly.
"Couple of other things please?"
"Go ahead," the Major indicated the agent had a free rein.
"I'd like details of when Unit Charlie 12 are on duty over the next three or four days and can I have the use of your assistant Carol for a few hours tomorrow." The agent thought for a second. "That's if you can spare her, I get on well with her you see," the agent added.
"Consider it done," the Major was glad to assist. He left the agent behind using his energies in planning what he should do next. The agent picked up a few personal things from the office before locking the door for the very last time.

    The following morning our agent was up sharp and early getting ready for the long day ahead. A small overnight bag was packed ready and the briefcase with Operation Hunting files in was almost complete as it sat on the kitchen table. A list of what was needed had been neatly written out and our agent was going through the items systematically. File; yes that was in the briefcase. Intelligence Identity; yes that had been packed and unpacked and was now sitting on the kitchen table waiting for a decision as to exactly where it should be put. Identification of this sort would be required in Strasbourg but would be a problem if shown in the UK. Letter of introduction; again that was packed in the briefcase. Passport; out on the table. Tickets; again out on the table. The one thing the agent had still not managed to get hold of was an up to date map of Strasbourg but that would be sorted out on arrival. So our agent was ready. As was previously mentioned, the agent did not want anyone to know too much officially about the way this journey to Strasbourg was being made. Eventually though the journey was underway but not before calling in to Major Tanniers office to collect the required lists and details and to drop off the office key for his secretary Carol.

There were also a few last minute plans to organize.

"Has everything been arranged for my travel from the base Major?" The agent asked.

"Yes, you leave here at seventeen hundred hours this afternoon where you'll be travelling under Operation Rat Race as Agent Jones," the Major informed the agent.

"And they'll be checking into which hotel?"

"The Hotel Cavalier on Henningen Strasse", the Major confirmed.

"And then?"

"They will leave the hotel at nineteen hundred hours and will not be seen again until nine the following morning when arriving for breakfast", the Major smiled as he completed the plan.

"Yes I like it," the agent confirmed.

"If you have any problems you can contact within those two hours. What name are you using this time?" The Major asked.

"I have travel bookings made under the name of Pat Jenkins," the agent confirmed. "Obviously when I book into my hotel I'll become Agent Jones".

"Do you know where you are staying yet?" The Major asked.

"No. I'll look for a hotel when I get there."

"Well safe journey and I hope all goes well at your meeting," the Major saluted. The agent returned the salute and Pat Jenkins walked from the Army HQ to the station.

The main thing to check during the trip was the list of residents registered in the village of Greenfields. There were three thousand, two hundred and seventy nine to be exact and they were listed in order of street and house number. What a bummer the agent thought. I'm going to have to go through every single one. With note-book and pen, every surname beginning with an 'S' was looked at to see if the forenames could possibly start with an 'M'. There were the obvious ones like Michael, Martin and Mitchell but there were also other ones to consider like anyone who had the name Edwin was often known as Michael or if their name was Emmanuel they might be known as Manny. There were surprisingly few. Only five in Greenfields which was quite a nice number to work on. Three of them had middle names but only two had a middle name beginning with the letter 'D' and one of those was aged seven and last seen at the local clinic about three weeks ago according to an entry relating to a new card being issued. This basically left just two suspects. Martin Saunders and Malcolm David Salter. The agent was pleased as the train was just about pulling into London and two names had emerged. On reaching London, the agent rang through to Carol in the office.

"Hello is that you Carol?" The agent was in a bit of a hurry trying to get to the airport in time to check-in and realised straightaway it could only be Carol on the other end.

"Yes Hello. Have you got anything you want me to do?" Carol answered in her most efficient manner.

"I have a couple of people I want you to check out for me. As much history of them as you can get from birth to the present day," the agent replied. With little effort, the details of the two suspects were taken by Carol and she assured the agent that she would ring back at a certain time to give an update. The agent was happy and continued to the airport.

Carol was known for her efficiency and she was back on the phone before take-off time with a fair bit of information. Taking each suspect in turn, Martin Saunders was born in Kentley on the 15th. October 1995 and had a Catholic upbringing attending church and school of that religion. He remained in full time education at the local college until he was twenty when he moved with his family, back to Ireland. According to records, he had lived in Kentley all the time whilst he was here as a child and then the housing records stopped. This coincided with the families move but then Martin Saunders had moved back just about six months ago looking for work. He stayed in lodgings in Kentley until he got the current job he has, working as a shop assistant in the general store in Greenfields since he has managed to purchase a cottage at 37, Lavender Lane. The second was Malcolm David Salter although there is a small problem in as much as he is currently registered as Malcolm David Slater. He was born in Chale on the 4th. September 2004 and went to school and college at Chale before joining the Euro Army. He had a distinguished career earning two medals for services abroad and was expected to continue but refused a promotion and left the Army last year to take over the running of a small pub, The Green Dragon, in Greenfields where he lives, just under a year ago. This is where the problem lies as all the papers relating to the pub are in the name of Slater and not Salter but I think we have to assume it is the same man.

The agent pondered over the couple of new bits of information a while and then asked Carol if she could try and do another couple of favours. Drive to Lavender Lane and see if there were any vehicles parked nearby and call in to The Green Dragon and speak to Mr. Slater and see what she thinks of him. Carol said she would oblige.

Carol Whitehead was very good at her job as secretary to Major Tannier and as a civilian employee saw and knew a lot more about the Army than most. She knew that technically she was as much part of the Army as any of the soldiers were but she felt she had a better job than most. She was often given little assignments to do by the agents run by Tannier and she would often fly overseas to collect documents that needed to have that personal touch and the number of different cities she had visited was almost listless. Born on the Isle of Wight, Carol was the daughter of a hotel owner and she had expected to probably grow up into that business when she got older but being very fit and sporting she also played tennis at a professional level for a few years before an ankle injury ruined her chances of making it big. Her parents still ran the hotel she grew up in and she had an official job which meant there was no requirement for her to join up and do her time in the Army but luck or fate had its own intentions for Carol.

Carol had to deal with her injury and spent many months having extensive physiotherapy. As the truth about how bad the injury sank in to Carol she found herself at a health centre in Chale, a long way from home. She contemplated returning to the Isle of Wight and discussed the fact with the only person she had really befriended in Chale, a French Sergeant who had shown some time to listen to her story. She soon fell for the charming Jacques Tannier, now Major Jacques Tannier of course and when he took up his new post in the Intelligence Office, he knew just the woman he needed to help him run things properly. They made a great team.

Carol thrived on little tasks like the one she had just been set by the agent whom she knew as Pat Jenkins. Under the current operational plans though, the agent was only being referred to as Agent Jones. Without a word to Jacques, Carol drove out to Greenfields and stopped at The Green Dragon. She gave the place the once over from the car. Quite a nice little pub she thought to herself and she was not disappointed when she entered and went inside. She took a quick look around as she moved up to the bar. There was a fairly good looking lad stood behind the bar, wiping glasses with a dish towel. He was probably in his thirties, Carol thought.

"Can I help you Madam?" The young man from behind the bar said.

"Oh thank you yes, I'll have a half a lager please," Carol replied in a friendly tone as she eyed the young man.

"Haven't seen you in here before, are you visiting our lovely village?" The barman said in a gentle manner which was not too intrusive but searching enough to possibly have some people a bit on edge. Carol sat herself on one of the stools stood next to the bar and then ran her fingers through her hair to make herself presentable.

"Well funny you should mention it but I'm looking for a pub that has a meeting room. Do you have one?" Carol acted as cool as ever. She watched the barman pour her drink and couldn't help notice him give her a sly look as he was doing so. He had a handsome face and a warm smile.

"Well we have a back bar. How many is it for?"

"Oh only about a dozen, fifteen at the most I would guess", Carol went on. "I was told to come and see you, Mr. Slater as they thought you'd have a room. It is Mr. Slater isn't it?"

"Actually the name is Salter but you can call me Malcolm," the barman said forcefully. "When would you be needing this room?" He continued.

"One afternoon next week. Probably Thursday or Friday. Would that be a problem?"

"No it doesn't get used that often at the moment."

"And would you charge me?" Carol said in her most seductive tone. She also made a point of making sure that she made full eye contact with the barman and she held his gaze before giving him a little wink.

"I don't think so," the barman said with a smile that almost broke out into a laugh. "No there would be no charge," he confirmed. Whilst all this was going on, Carol had been served her lager and she had paid

for it and been given change. She continued to look around at the place. Only three customers but then she guessed it would get busier later and would be the sort of pub that would risk flouncing the curfew laws. She was happy that this barman knew how to run a pub.
"I'll have a little look at one or two other pubs but will probably be in touch tomorrow," Carol lied as she got up and left. Her next mission was to drive passed Lavender Lane which she found with no trouble. No sign of life there and no vehicle parked outside but there was a garage to the side of the house that she could not see into. Carol phoned through her findings to the agent.

Everything had gone smoothly on the journey over to Strasbourg and the agent was now safely booked into the Kaleida Hotel in Station Square and getting things ready for the meeting that evening. The agent never checked into a hotel that had been previously arranged as it was far too dangerous. Having not been able to get hold of anything but an old map of Strasbourg before arriving, a tourist guide was one of the first things on the list of things to get. The instructions were clear that Agent Jones was to report to the Euro Army HQ at twenty hundred hours with required papers and ask for General Poullon on arrival. A quick look at the map showed that it was too far to walk to the Army HQ so it was a taxi job. The agent arrived at the given time and followed the instructions to the letter. The Army Headquarters was some impressive building. It was about twenty five stories high and the frontage of the building was made almost entirely of glass. The steps leading up to the entrance helped the first timer to see the full glory of the entrance hall bit by bit as they made their way up the steps. Big black marble walls, carved into modern art type shapes formed the centerpiece of the entrance hall with the Information desk situated in the middle. Off to the right were further black marbled walls full of gold inlays that led to the lifts.
"General Poullon is not here but I have been instructed to take you to see the Commander-in-Chief", said the front guard. "Please follow me", he ordered.
"Did you say the Commander-in-Chief?" the agent asked the guard.
"Yes. Is that a problem?"
"No I wasn't expecting to meet anyone that important", the agent started to sweat a little at the thought. The two entered a lift and the guard pressed a button. Everything was silver and highly polished both inside the lift and in the corridor. There were no clear indicators

to say what floor the lift was on but all of a sudden it came to a halt. The guard grabbed a small bunch of keys that were connected to his belt and he picked a small one out and put the key into a keyhole in the lift and turned it. He then pressed another button and the lift moved up again. As the lift came to a halt, the doors slid silently open and the guard beckoned the agent to leave the lift. Assuming that the lift would open into a corridor, the agent was surprised to be in a large office.

"Hello. Come in Jones," the voice came from the far end of the room. The agent walked towards the voice. "Hello Sir." The agent looked ahead but there seemed to be nobody there to be talking to. "You wanted to see my report on Operation Hunting Sir," the agent continued. At that point a uniformed man appeared from behind a screen that had been giving the impression that it was part of the complete wall at the back of the room.

"All in good time agent. Have a drink," the Commander asked showing that he already had a drink in his hand.

"Thank you Sir I'd like a gin if you have one", the agent asked nervously. A drink was poured and accepted.

"How rude of me, I'm Commander Martin Busch. Please call me Martin, but only whilst we are in this room".

"Oh yes thank you, you can call me………..," the agent still quite taken aback was interrupted.

"I'll only ever know you as Agent Jones and that's good enough for me. Please sit." Eventually the agent started to regain some composure and the two of them sat down and discussed all the various elements of Operation Hunting. Martin Busch was very impressive with his huge and exact knowledge of many aspects of the file. It was almost as if he had written the file himself but then there were things that the agent started to tell him that left him agog. Martin Busch went on about the list and although the agent had a fair idea what he was talking about, having never seen it was at a loss as to exactly what the list contained. The agent knew it had names on it and that it was some sort of hit list but having not actually seen the list itself had no idea how many or what names it contained. Martin Busch was asking questions as if he had actually written the list himself and wanted to know how much the agent knew about the list. Perhaps that was it. He had lost the list and agents had been working to recover it. One hour and twenty five minutes later the meeting came to an end and the agent was on the way back to the Hotel.

As our agent departed from the hotel, the mobile phone rang. "Hello. Yes. Can you confirm the date for me please?" The agent received a call that might prove to be most interesting. It was from the Ministry of Information in Belfast and was in answer to a call that had been made by Major Tannier the previous night. He had been tasked to check something out and get back to the agent but instead of doing that he got the MOI to ring direct.

"So that was St. Jude's?" The agent confirmed. "Thanks very much." The call came to an end. At the airport a few changes had to be made and instead of flying directly back to London, the agent was going to go via Belfast. It wasn't difficult to sort out and the agent would only be spending about two hours in Belfast. Whilst there the agent spoke on the phone to both Major Tannier and Carol in order to keep them updated with the latest developments. From the Airport it was a twenty minute taxi ride to the east of the city. The agent got into a taxi.

"St. Jude's Church please!" The destination was given to the taxi driver. As the taxi reached its' destination and the agent got out. After about ten minutes walking around searching the agent called Major Tannier on the phone. He wasn't easy to get hold of as he was away from the Army H.Q. but eventually the agent managed to get connected to him.

"Major I'm here in Belfast, St. Jude's church to be exact," the agent told him.

"What are you doing there?" He replied.

"Just following up on something."

"I take it you're looking into the problem we discussed." The Major had a sense of excitement in his voice.

"I most certainly am."

"And what have you found." Again the Major couldn't hide his anticipation.

"Your hunch paid off."

"You mean you're in a cemetery." Major Tannier had by now caught on as to exactly where the agent had gone.

"Yes and here it is. Born fifteenth October 1995, died twenty third April 2023, Martin Saunders beloved son of Richard and Emily. Now we know where our stranger is. Can you get Charlie 12 ready to raid this evening?" The agent concluded.

"It's unlikely I can get them to raid this evening but I'll make damn sure that they'll be ready to go for when you return. I'm assuming you'll be returning immediately?"

"Yes as soon as I can but that'll probably have to wait until tomorrow morning now. My job is done here. It would be nice to spend a little time here in Ireland but I have plenty more to do before we can close this case. I'll be back on the first available plane Major."

"Okay then. Contact me as soon as you touch down."

The Major was quite pleased with himself in the fact that he had always thought that Saunders was likely to be a name taken from a death certificate somewhere. It was so easy to get hold of these sort of details nowadays. Most families had lost at least one young member somewhere down the line and it was generally accepted that closure was a good remedy for mourning. Churches were quite keen to help a grieving mother find the last resting place of her beloved and often helped to find out as many details as possible about the circumstances surrounding any tragedy. Even the Ministry of Life lent a sympathetic ear if it believed that the enquirer was a genuine family member and regularly gave out copies of both death and birth certificates without doing too many checks. Also on hand to help were a number of volunteer groups who would do a lot of the work for you if you contacted them. Sometimes the group would ask for some sort of donation but this often worked out cheaper than having to pay to travel around and find out the required details yourself. In addition to all of this, it was quite expected for people to have lost or misplaced their birth certificates whilst moving out of bombed or damaged housing and therefore asking for a copy of a birth certificate was very acceptable. A lot of places were supposed to do some basic checks to confirm that only the actual person made a request for their own birth certificate but this turned out to be very impractical and in the end the authorities had to accept that friends would have to be allowed to pick up or order the certificates so that there weren't too many hold ups.

The Major returned to his office still quite pleased with what the agent had discovered over in Belfast. It was nearly seven o'clock by the time he returned and it had been the Majors intention to clear his desk and pack up for the day. Before he left he would make contact with Unit Charlie 12 before he left and make sure there was someone ready to meet with him and the agent tomorrow morning. He was feeling good and wanted to enjoy the rest of the evening but things weren't going to fall into place for him just like that. As he entered his office there was a note on his desk. He picked it up and read it.

'Please contact Cpl. Leverett at Ops immediately'

The Major picked up the phone. He dialed the extention for Ops.

"Major Tannier here, is Corporal Leverett there please?" The Major was direct. The phone went dead on the other end for a few seconds.

"Leverett here."

"Hello Corporal. Major Tannier here. You left me instructions to ring you." The Major asked.

"Yes thank you major for getting back to me. I have a letter for you from London HQ. I need you to come to Ops and collect it please." The Corporal was firm but as polite as he could be.

"Can't you deliver it to my office?"

"My orders are that you are to collect it and sign for it, Sir." There was a big emphasis put on the word 'Sir' as if replying to an order.

"I'll be straight over." The Major put the phone down. Bang goes my bloody evening he thought. He still cleared his desk and locked away all of his private papers. Some were locked in his desk drawer, agents files were put away and locked into a very strong filing cabinet whilst operational papers were put away in the safe. The Major did this in the hope that once he had picked up the letter he could then go straight home. He made his way over to the Ops office.

On reaching the Ops office, the Major took receipt of the letter and duly signed the large receipt book. This book was intentionally large so that it couldn't be easily carried around so that people could take it to other offices for people to sign. The Major looked at the delivery side of the entry and noticed that it was delivered by a Sergeant who had described himself as a 'Staff Officer'.

"The officer who delivered this letter, is he still on base?" The Major pointed out the delivery details as he spoke to the young Private on the front desk.

"No Sir. He delivered the letter and left immediately. I watched the car turn round and head back to the front gate. Sir!" The Private stood to attention as he gave his answer.

"And did he say that he had come from London HQ?"

"No Sir. He confirmed that you were stationed here at Kentley and then wrote your name on the letter. Sir! He then left." The young

Private felt he was being questioned as to his conduct.

"So why do you say he came from London HQ?" The Major asked again.

"He had London HQ markings Sir, and the letter, Sir!" Again the Private seemed ill at ease.

"What do you mean the letter?" The Major said taking the letter from under his arm. As he said it he looked at the letter which was clearly marked at the top left hand corner 'Pall Mall, London'. "Okay Private, I see." The Major turned and walked back to his office. He tore open the letter and read the brief message that it contained.

'Please ring Major Ives on the Pall Mall exchange, extension 524 as soon as you receive this letter'. The instructions were simple and clear and Major Tannier had no options but to do just as he was asked to do. The Major rang the number and asked for the correct extension.

"Major Ives office." There was a sharp female voice on the other end of the phone.

"Hello. This is Major Tannier from Intelligence at Kentley Base. I've been ordered to contact Major Ives. Is he in?" There was silence from the other end of the phone for a few seconds.

"Ives here, is that Major Tannier?"

"Yes, Tannier here."

"Good. I hear that some of your revolutionaries have been a bit naughty." Major Ives chuckled as he said this.

"We had a little mis-hap the other day."

"Well surprise, surprise, Strasbourg has got to hear about it and don't think it's very funny."

"Well quite major but then we don't think it very funny either. We had some men killed." Tannier made sure that London didn't think that Kentley was taking things easily down here.

"So what are you doing about it?" Major Ives played along for a while.

"We're hoping to arrest a couple of suspects in the next couple of days and we have got a development on another very important case." Tannier couldn't say too much but tried to make it clear that there may be a big revolutionary scalp soon.

"Arresting a couple of suspects eh! And what is the development? What case are you referring to"

"Operation Hunting, Sir! We hope to have a very big catch tomorrow"

"Strasbourg have said that no further action should be taken on Hunting without their knowledge so nothing to be done until you've briefed me please." The Major in London seemed quite definite about this. "And what are you doing about the general misbehaviour of the public?"

"They haven't misbehaved." Tannier found the remark a bit insulting as he knew that most of the market had been as annoyed as The Army were about what the revolutionaries had done.

"So you're quite happy to allow these sort of shootings to go on in your area. You're getting soft Major. Strasbourg have asked me to look into your reaction and I don't think this will read to well on your report." Major Ives was loving every minute of this. He was stirring up one of those little Majors in one of those comfortable bases where he would just love to be stationed himself.

"Of course I haven't gone soft. We will ensure that nothing like this ever happens again." Tannier started to realise he was in danger of carrying the can for this little incident and he wasn't going to let that happen. He liked Kentley and intended to remain here.

"Of course you will. I'll be visiting in two weeks and I want a full report on all the action your boys have taken in response to this. I'll also be sending you a new report every day for the next week listing five deliveries of food destined for traders at the Food Centre. Strasbourg want at least three of these to be turned back each day and on two days, everything must stop. Strasbourg say that the people must pay for the death of the two soldiers. They want action Major and you are the one I've chosen to be responsible for seeing that it is delivered." Major Ives delivered his orders with ease.

"In two weeks you say." Tannier was fuming inside.

"Yes I'll let you know exactly when nearer the time. I also want the brief on Operation Hunting immediately. I'll get back to you with clearance." The phone went dead. Tanniers jaw dropped. Bloody hell, I better get things in motion he thought to himself. Tannier made another call and got through to Major Wooters office. Wooters of course wasn't available. An appointment was made for the next morning.

-

John Silver had been watching Zwolle again this morning. It had been quite a week of hard work. Over the last eight days or so he had watched right through the night twice, done a forty hour continuous stint and spent many a cold night hidden in a tree or tucked away in some bush. He took notes on as many movements he could so that when the time required it, he could refer back to see what his target did in a particular situation. What hand he might use. Could he run? Was he able to lift things? These might all seem strange things to note but they were all important when it came to drawing the bigger picture of his plan.

Having now got some idea of the layout of the grounds, John was happy that his target could only drive out from the front drive and although it wasn't impossible, there was nothing to walk to or from in any other direction. Zwolle had again returned today with a paper bag with the same yellow and green marking on. John guessed that it might be a shop insignia but needed to find out. It was probably only the second time he had seen this insignia. He had also seen Mrs. Zwolle today and a young boy who he guessed was aged about six or seven. He presumed that the lad was a grandson and was happy that these were the only occupants at the house. In John's little note book he had recorded the time that the paper was delivered and the usual time the postman delivered letters. There was also a woman who had turned up a couple of times in the early afternoon. She would be there about an hour and a half but she didn't visit everyday.

John made a visit into Boxmeer on his own and looked around the few shops that were there. He looked on the shelves for any signs of the yellow and green marking he had seen on the bag but nothing seemed to be right. There was a bakers shop but they put bread into white paper bags and there was a general grocer's who packed goods in a brown bag. In between the newsagents and a small bar though, John saw what he was looking for. It was a small shop partly down an alleyway and standing on the floor were a number of the distinctive bags. The shop was a pet shop which sold pet food. So bloody obvious really as Zwolle had a pet, John thought to himself. He had seen a little white dog occasionally during the time that he had been watching. He went back to Zwolle's house and got out to walk around the area of the house which was near to the canal. Sure enough, Mariano Zwolle appeared about an hour later with a little dog. His grandson was with him today and every now and then the boy would run off a little way ahead of his grandfather. They regularly walked down to the canal, stopped there for a few minutes and then returned back to the house. John Silver soon noted that this happened about four thirty every afternoon.

On this afternoon, John Silver had taken up a position in the bushes where he could get a closer look at the two of them as they went on their walk. He was fairly happy that neither of them would see him but just in case he made sure there was a reasonably quick exit in a couple of directions should anything go wrong. There were also a couple of trees he could quickly climb although that would be a very last resort as it would of course put him in a non-exit situation which he was trained not to put himself in.

As they neared John Silver's position, Mariano Zwolle had stopped and he was looking pensively at the canal. The young boy was picking up stones and throwing them into the water. All of a sudden a small dog appeared on the scene yapping at the little boy. John Silver had no idea where it had come from and his worry was that an owner would soon follow. He ducked down a bit more but kept an eye out in case the owner suddenly appeared in the bushes where he was hiding. Whilst all this was going on the dog ran into the bushes with the little boy chasing after it.
"Waar de hond ging, pappy?" The young lad shouted out as he approached John Silver's position at speed. The dog meanwhile had gone out of sight. "Waar de hond ging?" The lad repeated. John Silver considered his next move.

Before he had a chance to decide what to do next the dog had reappeared right in front of him. It yapped loudly and the young boy heard it and started to look into the bushes. John Silver pushed the dog away but it was persistent and continued to bark at him. It caused the boy to start probing into the bushes a bit and this gave John Silver cause for concern. There was no way he wanted to be seen. The dog continued to yap.
"Ik wil de hond vinden." The boy said. This was bad news for John Silver. He looked at the little dog as he quickly picked it up and with one easy move broke the dog's neck. It's head lopped to one side as it lay helpless in John's hand. He climbed a tree and placed the dog down on a big branch in a way that it wouldn't fall. He could hear Mariano's voice calling out.
"Nu teruggekomen, het is tijd voor thee." This was good news to John's ears as he hoped that his grandfather could persuade the young boy not to venture any further into the bushes.

"Ik wil de hond vinden, pappy."

For about a minute it was touch and go as to whether the young boy would come any further but with no more noise from the dog he gave up and returned to Mariano. The two of them returned back towards the big house. John Silver, climbed down from the tree and made his way back to his car. He drove back to his holiday cottage where the agent, he only knew as Jane, was waiting for him. She had arrived a couple of days ago and as requested had made sure she had been seen a few times by the neighbour, Christine.

As John entered the cottage she had a message for him.
"Apparently you need to get back to your home." Jane said.
"Why what has happened?"
"I don't know. All I was told was that there was a message waiting for you but you have to go straightaway."
"When did you receive the message?"
"Came through on the phone here at about seven." Jane pointed to the phone. "Didn't say who he was but he knew who I was and that's good enough for me."
"Okay. What about you?"
"Are you happy for me to take a spare key?"
"Yeah that'll be no problem."
"Then I'll stay for a little while tomorrow. Let your neighbour know you've had to go off on business and then I'll be on my way. Is that alright?"
"Sounds great."

The two agents hugged each other and kissed quickly without showing any real affection. John Silver went upstairs to his bedroom and quickly packed his case. In just under fifteen minutes he was in his car and on his way back to England.

-

Martin Saunders read the details of the message again and cursed under his breath. It was a bit of an occupational hazard of course but still a nuisance when this sort of thing happened. He looked at his watch and tried to calculate what time he had available to him. It was going to be a close thing. As well as this latest situation, he was also working on a special mission for the local revolutionary party in Kentley. It was quite strange for him as he wouldn't normally do anything that might get in the way of a more important task but it was a reasonably simple task for him and being so close to his home it was nice to help out the locals. This local job was a one-off and he was just tidying up the loose ends. He was quite happy that his handler knew about the local job and didn't think it would have given him any cause for concern but it wasn't the real problem at the moment. As soon as he had got back home and sorted out arrangements for moving he would have to make a call to his handler to update them.

      Driving through the night was no real problem if you kept out of the towns. It was generally only in the towns where the Military paid particular attention to the curfew but if you saw another set of lights in the distance it was prudent to turn off the road and wait till they had driven passed just in case they were soldiers. Driving through the tunnel to get to mainland Britain was no real problem as there were a number of people legitimately driving back and forth at all times of the day. Martin Saunders had papers to allow him to travel of course. In the early hours of the morning as the dawn was breaking, the traffic started to move. Again he wanted to avoid any military roadblocks if he could and he knew the best routes to take. As he got back towards his home Martin drove passed his house before parking some distance from it. He then went through his normal routine of turning off the alarms he had set to check and see if anyone had tripped any of them. This would let him know if anyone had been to the place and tried to gain entry or not. This took about fifteen minutes but eventually he was able to enter the cottage and properly and start to getting things packed. As he glanced at the phone in the hall he was interested to see that he had received a couple of messages. Not many people would leave messages for him so he guessed they were important. The first message spoke in an Irish accent and was from an old friend of his who worked with the local priests over there. It was the message he knew was waiting for him. The second was from a car salesman who had found him a car he wanted. Martin wiped the messages immediately. There was no time to get any sleep now he thought.

Chapter 11   -   DINNER

Gary had suffered quite a bit at the hands of the revolutionaries in one way or another. He had eventually worked out that it was the National Revolutionaries who had taken him in the first place and then the local party who had looked after him in the latter stages. Gary was pleased to get home. Gary had been through the wars in recent times and was beginning to pay the price for his adventures. He had a damaged right eye, a broken jaw bone, severe bruising to both of his knees, especially his right knee, the lashes from the whipping his back had received and of course the bullet wound to his ankle which was still giving him a lot of pain. The locals had obviously nursed him back to a condition where at least he was able to be allowed back home but Gary was really not able to do very much.

As Gary was dropped off at the back of his house he remembered what had happened just before he was taken. He had been looking for Sammy who had run out into the back lane. Gary opened the back gate and hobbled into his garden. Sammy wasn't in the garden. Gary listened hard and sure enough he could hear Sammy barking from inside the house. Gary went to the back door but it was locked.
"Bloody marvelous," he cried out to nobody. "What do I do now?" Gary rummaged around in his trouser pockets but he had very little in them. He remembered that when he had come out to search for Sammy he thought he mustn't go too far as he didn't have his keys. He tried the back door again but it was definitely locked. Gary went round slowly to the front door but it was the same situation there. As Gary sat down on the low garden wall he tried to think what he could do next whilst Sammy continued to bark in the knowledge that his master was just outside. 'Sarah should have a key, perhaps I could walk round to hers' Gary said to himself.
"Hello Gary. Have you been away?" It was Gary's next door neighbour. Gary stood up and turned around. "Christ what's happened to your eye?"
"Oh I had a bit of an argument and lost it." Gary replied.
"Have you been in hospital with it then?"
"I had to stay at a friends place whilst it cleared up." Gary hoped his neighbour wouldn't ask much more.
"You should have let us know where you were. We've been worried.

Sammy was left on his own."

"I'm sorry but I tried to get in touch with my sister. She was supposed to come round and look after things." Gary lied.

"Oh she did pop in and see us. She left you a letter." The neighbour went back into his house. Gary wondered what the hell Sarah might have written to him about. The neighbour soon returned with a small but bulky envelope. He handed it to Gary. "Let me know if there's anything we can do for you."

"Will do. Thanks." Gary took the envelope and straightaway realised that it contained a key. He ripped open the envelope and let himself into the house. As he went in the first thing he noticed was that it had been tidied. Washing up done and all the pots and pans put away. Floor hovered and furniture polished. Someone had done a lot of work getting the place in order. Gary sat himself down on the settee and stroked Sammy as he stood up on his hind legs. Sammy ran to the back door to be let out and Gary dutifully unlocked the back door. As Sammy ran around the back garden, Gary made his way slowly upstairs. He visited the bathroom and made his way into one of the girls' bedrooms at the back of the house. He watched Sammy sniff at various items before laying down his territory markers. Gary's eyes moved to the fields on the other side of the lane and the beginnings of the pea crops. Already he noticed a hint of the light green colouring in the plant that he found so calming. It wouldn't be long now before there was a complete blanket of colour in that field. The thought was quite soothing. I think I need a few days rest Gary thought to himself. Not only that, I think the phone needs to be unplugged. No callers. That was the answer. Gary got Sammy back in, locked the house up and went to bed falling asleep quite quickly.

A lot of things were going round in Gary's mind. The local revolutionary sympathizers had got him quite worried especially with the fact that the big boys from The Revolution thought him suspect. It was good to know that the local party still believed him but doubts started to go through Gary's mind. Had he said something out of turn. Perhaps he had said something at work when someone was listening. The thoughts wouldn't subside and he had convinced himself that he was probably the one responsible for the deaths at the Food Centre. Had he left some sort of clue that had given away what he was doing. He went over events in his mind.

He turned his mind to Julie Clark. Was it a coincidence that she had started to take an interest in him just recently or was there a more sinister reason behind it. Perhaps it was because he was now on his own. Part of him hoped that this was the reason why but then again part of him knew he still loved Angela very much and shouldn't even be contemplating any other woman at all. He guessed that he was being most foolish anyway. Gary decided that he needed to get to know Julie Clark a bit better. He had heard Julie mentioned in various conversations as soon as the topic turned to school. In the past he hadn't really paid much attention to it but recently his ears tended to prick up as soon as her name was mentioned. With most people he spoke to it was quite natural to bring Miss Clark into the subject and he was surprised as to how much gossip he got back. The conclusion seemed to be that Julie Clark had not always been a schoolteacher and that she joined the profession quite late. She was as a young girl a very successful runner and swimmer and thought to be able to go on and make a career out of sport. She left the area for a few years but then returned when she took up the teaching post.

There was a knock at the door and Gary got to his feet rather slowly to answer it.
"Hello can I help you?" Gary said as he saw a young man standing at the door.
"I'm from the National Revolutionary Party and you are Mr. Gary Newson." The young man stated the obvious.
"And what about it?" Gary was angry.
"I've come to see if I can help you with anything."
"No you can't. Now fuck off." Gary was so incensed that he swore when he normally would have kept his cool. Gary was about to slam the door in the young mans face when he decided to let his feelings be known. "In fact there is something you can do for me."
"Just tell me and I'll do my best to get it done." The young lad seemed pleased at the thought of actually being able to help.
"Tell your lot that I think that I don't want any help thanks." Gary started to close the door.
"Is that it? Just tell them a message." The young lad was disappointed.
"That's it. Goodbye." Gary shut the door.

Gary came to the conclusion that he wanted to chat to Julie Clark at that very moment. It was ridiculous but that was how he felt. It wasn't the sort of thing he was really any good at doing, talking to members of the opposite sex that is. He would have to come up with some sort of excuse to strike up a conversation with her and gradually get to know her. Gary thought for a while as to what reason he could use to chat to her. There was nothing that sprang to mind immediately. Without further a do, he made his way round to Julie's little house and he knocked on the door. There was no answer.
"I think you'll find she's back at work trying to get the school back on its feet," said the next door neighbour.
"Oh yes. I'd forgotten she said she was going back." Gary replied standing there on his crutch. All of a sudden an idea arrived. He wrote a little note inviting Julie to dinner tomorrow evening as a thank you, which he then posted through the letter box. We'll see if she accepts, Gary thought.

-

Not long after Gary returned home, Sarah called in to see him. "What the hell have you been doing? You're in a bit of a mess. I came round to ask about your ankle but I'm not sure what to say now." Sarah asked as she looked Gary up and down. He was sat in the living room with his ankle bandaged up but his right eye was fully bloodshot and half closed and his right cheek was sewn and full of bruising. Added to that, Gary's right arm was also covered in bruises.
"Yeah the ankle is getting better gradually. I'm having the dressing cleaned regularly so you don't have to worry about it" Gary replied.
"And who have you got to come and change it for you?" Sarah said abruptly as if she should certify anybody who dared to look after her brother.
"Just a friend!" Gary told her nothing.
"Who then? A man or a woman?" Sarah sounded annoyed at Gary's reluctance to actually name the person.
"Just a friend!" Gary said no more. It was obvious that Sarah would not be told who the friend was.
"You don't seem to have been around for a few days and when I hear that you're back you turn up looking as if you've been in a fist fight. Where have you been?" Sarah as always got straight to the point.
"Oh I went off to see an old friend who works at the hospital. He agreed to look at my ankle so I stayed at his for a couple of nights"

Gary told her.

"Is this the same friend who'll be changing your dressing?" Sarah was surprised that Gary had given away that the friend was a male if a little taken aback as to just how easily she had got this out of him. She thought briefly and remembered that it was her brother she was talking about.

"Yes, if you must know. It is." Gary was getting fed up with Sarah's informal questioning and although he usually found it hard to lie to anyone let alone family he found it quite simple on this occasion. Perhaps it was his general annoyance that did it. Gary felt the pressure of her intrusiveness more than anything else with his answers almost being said automatically. Sarah also sensed Gary's annoyance so changed her tack a bit.

"You left Sammy on his own?"

"Well sort of. A neighbour was supposed to come in and feed him which I think they did and he was able to get out in the garden." Gary replied.

"I came round to see you the day before yesterday and Sammy was running around up and down the back lane. I managed to get him back in. The whole house looked a right mess as if someone had been burgling the place. I cleared it up a bit." Sarah informed him.

"Thanks sis. I thought it was my neighbour who had done it." Gary said as sincerely as he could sound. "I was just trying to get some professional help with my ankle."

"So how did you get these other injuries?" Sarah was still not totally convinced.

"I fell over in town the other day and a few kids tried to pinch my wallet." Gary quickly came up with another lie.

"What, and they did this to you?" Sarah was shocked.

"Well I took a blow as they first hit me but I managed to grab on to one of them. His mates came back to get him and gave me a bit of a kicking in the process." Gary tried to laugh as he told his little story.

"Have you reported it to the police?"

"What's the use? You know that unless you can give them name and address they do nothing. Anyway it's what made me make my mind up to go and get some proper treatment for my ankle. You know I needed it."

"Yes I know but next time, bring Sammy round to me first." Sarah told him. "Anyway I've come round to tell you that I spoke to Angela again yesterday and she can remember who you are."

"Is that supposed to make me feel better?" Gary spluttered his reply.

"No seriously. We talked for about an hour and all about you. Not only that but some of it was about how good you were as well." Sarah laughed in an effort to lighten the mood a little.

"Now I don't know if you're telling the truth or not." Gary said, also laughing a little. It caused some pain to his jaw but he tried not to make it noticeable.

"Yes we talked about you. Angela often asks how you are and where you are."

"And do you tell her?"

"Well I sort of tell her what you are doing, not that you tell me or I know everything but she asks me to keep you updated with how you are."

"That's interesting. Is she okay? How are the girls?"

"She's missing you. The kids are missing you. I think the next move is yours." Sarah said emphatically.

"What do you suggest?" Gary said quite bemused.

"Well firstly you might try and tidy yourself up a bit unless you think she'll fall for the sympathy angle. How about calling on Angela to see if you can take the girls out somewhere? Just at the end, suggest that if she wants to, Angela could always come along as well." Sarah had this idea planned out before she came round and suggested it eagerly.

"To do what? To go where?" Gary responded negatively.

"Shopping! Swimming! Pictures! You know the sort of thing." Sarah gave him one or two ideas. "I'm not doing everything for you." Sarah continued. "Most of it has got to come from you or else Angela will know."

"But I'm not very good at doing this sort of thing." Gary pleaded.

"Well you better start getting good and damn quickly." Sarah was adamant. "You've got to find the opportunity to tell her how you feel. Tell her what you want. Don't try and make it sound romantic or anything, just tell her the truth." Gary knew it was up to him and with Sarah helping he knew he would not be able to let things slip. Sarah took out a pen and found a piece of spare paper. She wrote down Angela's address on it and handed it to Gary.

"There. That's where you'll find them. You've got no excuse now." Sarah said.

"Give me a couple of days and I'll go and see her." Gary replied eventually.

"Good. And don't drink before you go and see her," Sarah warned him.

"I know." Gary replied not certain he could guarantee it.

"And if your friend doesn't come and look at your dressings, call me and I'll do it." Sarah shook her finger at Gary as she laid down her orders. A lot of things were going on in Gary's life at the moment and he wasn't quite sure where he stood. At times he wished he could just get away from everything and start all over again but he knew that wasn't possible. He loved Joan and Katy so much and wanted them back. He had a lot of love for Angela and missed her company but then his passions had been stirred recently by Julie Clark. Gary couldn't call it love as he had only just got to know her but he felt a lustful tingle run through his body when he saw her and knew that part of him wanted her. In fact if he was brutally honest he wanted her badly, even if she was working for the Army. Life was complicated.

-

As the sun broke fully through the back window, Martin Saunders was nearly complete. He yawned as he took another quick look around his house to make sure he had cleaned up everything that needed to be made sterile. He didn't have a great deal of furniture as some had already been moved but he put the last bits into the back of the van that was sat on the drive making sure that nobody would see what he was doing unless they were particularly curious.

He would have to try and come back for his car if he was able to but this too had been cleaned just in case he had to leave it. It was most likely to have been compromised anyway, he thought. He looked at his watch and it was just passed five fifteen. He wrote the one word note and then locked the front door before getting into the van and starting the engine.

-

At nine thirty five a call came through to Major Tannier from the agent.

"Have you managed to set anything up for today with Charlie 12?"

"I've been held back by Strasbourg I'm afraid." The Major wasn't pleased giving the agent this news as he knew how much effort had gone into getting this breakthrough.

"What have they said then?"

"Everything has to be cleared by them at the moment before any further action is taken on Operation Hunting. I think this might be after your visit yesterday."
"Damn." The agent just cursed. "So when can we get the go ahead?"
"I've got to brief Major Ives this morning and he'll let me know but in the meantime I'll get things set up with Wooters so we're ready to go as soon as."
"Okay." The agent wasn't happy but would have to accept it.

At ten sharp, Major Tannier knocked on Wooters door.
"Come in." Major Wooters shouted. Tannier opened the door and entered.
"Simon, how are you?"
"Christ almighty you must need something really big." Wooters knew that Tannier had come with the white flag by the way he started the conversation.
"Well it's not really a favour just for me. We're all in trouble."
"What do you mean?" Wooters pointed to a chair and indicated that Major Tannier should bring one near and sit down. It seemed like this was going to be an interesting conversation.

After about nearly forty minutes, Tannier had explained all of the content of his discussion with London HQ and had agreed plans of action with Wooters for various tasks including Operation Hunting. Simon for his part had agreed quite quickly that this was bad for all at Kentley and that something should be done before this HQ Major came down and stuck his nose in. Tannier hadn't quite told Wooters the whole story. Between them though they knew that the Food Centre had to be targeted, and targeted hard. They needed to disrupt right up to the day the HQ Major was due to appear. They would also try and ensure that some sort of press coverage was given to it. Tannier had asked that he be kept up to date with every bit of action that was being planned and when it took place. As per Major Ives instructions, he would keep a full record of everything that happened. Wooters would never know that it would appear like Tannier was planning everything. All went well.

Tannier had agreed the arrangements of getting Unit Charlie 12 briefed. They were due on a late shift that evening so Tannier organised for their night shift to start with a small briefing. Tanniers mobile rang and he answered it. It was the agent just confirming if a meeting had been arranged and at what time. The two would discuss what was going to happen at tonight's briefing.

-

Gary was working hard in the kitchen getting things ready for tonight's meal with Julie. It wasn't that easy as he was still having to get around with the aid of a crutch but at least he was able to get around. Only a few days ago he wouldn't have even been able to stand up let alone walk around. Every now and then Gary would stand up properly and then walk off forgetting his crutch. He was quite able to do so but knew that he should use it as much as he could. Julie had replied to the note Gary had left her by ringing and accepting his invitation. It was a difficult situation for him as he knew he had fallen for her charms and fancied her something rotten but he also had this nagging thought in the back of his head that she may be trying to trap him or get him arrested or some other sinister motive. He never really believed that she could actually fancy him. This meal was going to be a very awkward time and that was without even thinking about Angela. Gary had spent the last couple of days buying and swapping various things in order to be able to get hold of something special for this meal and he was very pleased to have come by a couple of lamb chops. Gary was sure that Julie would be impressed.

Six o'clock on the dot and the door bell rang again. Gary answered the door. He took a long look at Julie standing there. His pulse started to race immediately as he looked her up and down. She looked really sexy.
"Wow you look fantastic," he exclaimed.
"Don't be silly," Julie replied as she started to blush a little. "You've gone to the effort of cooking a meal so it is only right that I should dress up a bit," she continued. "It's surprising what a little bit of make up can do." Julie tried to hide her slight nervousness by playing down how much effort she had actually put into getting herself ready.
"Yeah but you look just gorgeous and you haven't tasted my cooking yet." Gary replied as they both burst into laughter. It helped break the slight tension.
"You're not looking too good though." Julie stroked the side of Gary's face as she spoke. She looked at the bruising on his face and in

particular the state of his bloodshot and half closed eye. She pulled a pained face as she did so.

"I'm okay." Gary replied as he took Julie by the hand and led her into the living room where the table was already set. He kissed her hand as Julie looked even more embarrassed. "A drink?" Gary asked.

"Do you have anything like Gin at all?" Julie asked.

"Yes I think I have a small bottle somewhere." Gary answered as he searched around in the living room cupboard. After a few seconds he had found the remains of a half bottle of Gin. It was a cheap government bottle but at least it was gin. "I think we can get one out of here," he said pouring some into a glass. He then poured himself a Whiskey and turned to Julie. "Here's to new found friendship!" He raised his glass towards hers. The glasses chinked.

"To friendship! Yes I like that." Julie was uncertain as to how she should answer.

"Take a seat. Dinner will be about fifteen minutes." Gary said as he left her and went back into the kitchen. Gary was getting quite good at hiding how much pain he was in. The eye was still giving him some jip but he was able to open his eyes now. He had to agree that the bloodshot look wasn't the most sexy he could have but it got him lots of sympathy.

Gary wasn't too bad a cook and dinner, although not up to restaurant standards perhaps, was quite good. Julie commented on the fact that Gary had been able to get hold of Lamb chops and asked where he obtained them. He didn't let on. A bottle of red wine made the meal just special and Julie was feeling a bit light headed. A lovely meal, cooked by a lovely man and a man she had fancied from the first moment she had laid eyes on him. In the back of her mind was the fact that she knew his wife too well but then as they had split up perhaps that wasn't too much of a problem after all. She wasn't quite sure what the evening would bring but for now she was happy and wishing that the evening could go on forever. Gary soon cleared away the plates and removed the table from the middle of the room. Julie stood in the lounge as Gary cleared things away. She looked around at the various articles that were to be found on shelves. Gary returned. The two of them stood and stared at each other both scared to make the first move.

"Shall I put some music on?" Gary asked eventually.

"Yes please do." Julie replied. Gary put on the nearest thing to something soft and sexy. Gary gestured and they both sat down on the settee. Sammy got on and sat himself down in between the two of them.

"How's it feel to be back at school?" Gary asked.

"Well I'm not back properly yet. I'm just helping out for the rest of this term." Julie told him.

"Did you ever worry that the Army might torture you?" Gary said changing the mood to a somewhat serious one. It started to bring back some of his own recent memories as well.

"There were a couple of times when I was worried." Julie replied. Gary reached across and grabbed her hand.

"I'm glad they didn't hurt you." Gary said rather stupidly. Julie adjusted her position on the settee so that she could sit nearer to Gary.

"You look as if you've been tortured though, what has happened?" Julie stroked his injured face again and Gary lapped it up. She was careful not to actually touch the injured areas and cause him any discomfort. Gary decided to keep to the same story he had used to quench Sarah's curiosity.

"Well I got beaten up by some kids trying to steal my wallet."

"Kids!! How old were they?" Julie sounded surprised that kids could inflict so much damage to a man.

"I would say that the youngest was about fifteen or sixteen but he had a few older ones with him."

"How many were there altogether?" Julie felt sorry for Gary. She knew that this sort of thing was supposed to go on but Gary was the first person she really knew who had actually encountered any real hooliganism.

"There were about five of them. Probably little revolutionaries thinking I'm a pro-government worker."

"So what are your views on the revolution?" Julie asked.

"Bloody hell that's a bit to the point!" Gary looked at her. It was one thing to talk to someone about the revolution but everyone was careful not to give a view as to how they viewed the revolution. Then to actually ask someone outright was very forward indeed.

"Well come on, it sounds like we both support it." Julie continued.

"Yes I know you're pro." Gary confessed.

"And just how do you know that?" Julie quizzed him.

"I have my sources." Gary smiled. Julie returned the smile and then laid her head on Gary's shoulder. They continued to discuss the pros and cons of the revolution for about an hour before Julie asked where the toilet was. This brought a rather abrupt end to the conversation. Both knew that they had probably said too much but neither seemed to be worried.

"Upstairs third door on the right. The light is difficult to put on. I'll show you." Gary led the way upstairs and he opened the toilet door and pulled the string switch to turn the light on. He then went into the main bedroom to wait. Gary wasn't quite sure what he was waiting for exactly. Perhaps it was just to turn the bathroom light off again. Perhaps he was just being the perfect host and making sure his guest was alright before returning back downstairs. The more he pondered over the question of why he was actually waiting in the bedroom, the harder he found it to come up with a sensible answer. Suddenly Julie stood at the door. Gary was sat on the end of the bed.

"What a nice view." Julie said as she pointed to the moon and stars out of the bedroom window. She was standing at the window concentrating on the night sky. The Moon was almost full and very clear in the sky. Julie looked at the face of the Moon and wondered what it might be like to be there. She looked at the twinkling stars as she dreamt about being settled in her own place, two children playing in the garden and a handsome husband there to look after her. Almost as part of a script, Gary walked over and joined her. He placed his arm protectively near to her waist as she stood looking out at the stars. Julie felt safe and happy.

"A Heavenly picture," he said. As he spoke Gary moved his arm and his left hand touched Julies' left hip and followed the contours of her body across the left cheek of her bottom. Julie's heart was beating double time at the mere touch of Gary's hand on her body and the feel of it brushing against her brought a flush to her cheeks. The two of them stared at the bright night sky watching the stars twinkling as Gary caressed and stroked a small area of Julie's body. Almost unnoticeably at first but the motion became more obvious. Gary then suddenly gripped her bare arm and turned her body to face his. As they both gazed into each other's eyes, Gary ran his finger down Julie's cheek and the moment of expectation had arrived. Automatically both felt that they were compelled to kiss and within seconds they were energetically exploring each other with their tongues as well as with their hands. The kiss probably lasted no more than two minutes but it seemed like a lifetime had come and gone for both of them. It had been inevitable from that first moment when they had met at the front door that this would be the outcome and the waiting had only heightened the anticipation leading up to that magical first kiss. The two of them turned and looked at the bed. Another awkward moment had arrived. Gary wasn't quite sure that he was happy to actually cheat on his wife but he knew that he wanted Julie so much. The brief indication of doubt was seen like an amber light changing to red instead of green. In that second the moment had been lost. Gary and Julie looked at each other both knowing that the next step they took would be the point of no return. All of the indicators had to read right.

"Perhaps we should put on some more music." Gary said as he led Julie back down to the living room. They both sat down on the settee again but this time had no worries about sitting right next to one another. Gary started the conversation again and asked about Julie's family. Julie talked about the fact that her parents had split up when she was very young and she had only recently made contact with her Mother again in London.
"I have a sister somewhere nearby as well." Julie continued.
"What's her name?" Gary asked politely.
"Jennifer." Julie replied.
"Does she teach as well?"
"No I don't think so. We were both very good athletes in our younger days although I also preferred swimming. I think my sister would be doing some sort of physical training somewhere. She loved her sport and missed not being outdoors. I have a picture of her." Julie looked through her bag. She produced a photograph and handed it to Gary. "It's only about two years old" Julie told him.
"Do you do any sort of athletics now then?" Gary was quite surprised at the thought of Julie competing in a race. It wasn't that she didn't seem like she was able to run but the competitiveness wasn't very apparent.
"No I haven't done that much exercise at all for a couple of years now." Julie sighed a little at the thought of all the weight she must have put on.
"Well you look very fit. I would have thought you did some sort of sport."
Julie blushed. There was a brief pause again and Gary looked at the photograph and instantly knew who it was. It came as a great shock. He tried not to make it obvious to Julie that he had recognised her

sister but she had spotted his reaction.
"Do you know her then?" Julie asked
"No I don't think we've ever met." Gary said truthfully.
"For a moment there it looked like you knew her. Are you sure?" Gary took a long close look at the photograph and is certain that it is of the blond woman who was shot at the roadblock a couple of weeks ago. She was obviously a lot younger in the photograph but there is no doubting it is her.
"No I'm sorry I don't know her." Gary lied.
"It's a shame as I think you'd get on well with her. When I next catch up with her I'll bring her round and introduce you to her." Julie continued talking, totally oblivious to the fact that Gary had started to turn pale. Gary tried very hard not to show Julie any sort of reaction to her latest comment but guessed that she was too good at picking up body language for it not to go unnoticed. Gary wasn't quite sure what to do in this situation but he knew he was feeling sick. Should he say anything?
"Excuse me a minute, I must visit the bathroom." Gary said apologetically.
"Do you want me to help you with the light?" Julie said in her sexiest voice.
"No I can manage." Gary answered jumping up from the settee and making his way as fast as he could on one leg up the stairs. Julie was a bit surprised at Gary's response and wondered what she had done wrong. Had she come on too strong? She didn't think so especially as she allowed Gary to make the first move. Perhaps he was nervous. Men are funny creatures she thought to herself. Gary soon returned.
"Sorry about that," he said.

    Julie looked at Gary as his silhouette stood out against the background of the lit hall behind him.
"Come back here and keep me warm." Julie pleaded. Gary sat back down on the settee and put his arm around Julie. She laid her head back on his shoulder and then lifted it to give him a big smile. They kissed again. A much smaller kiss but one that said everything. Then another kiss. And finally a big passionate kiss.

    They continued talking about music and life for a little while and then eventually the subject came round to families again. It was a bit embarrassing as they talked about Joan and Katy but managed to leave Angela completely out of the conversation. Quite soon they were back on to the subject of Julie's family and by now Gary had made up his mind that he should tell Julie the truth.

"I think I ought to be honest Julie," Gary looked at her as he said it. Julie felt that now was the time he was going to tell her that he still loved his wife.

"Yes. I believe that honesty is always best in these situations." Gary didn't quite work out what Julie meant but he carried on.

"I have sort of met your sister before." Gary said. Oh God, Julie thought. He's slept with my sister!! Her mind imagined Gary and Jennifer being intimate with each other. Kissing and cuddling each other. "Not that I really know her." Gary continued. Christ it must have been a one night job, Julie's mind was now working overtime as her imagination switched from them making love in a bed to the thought of them groping each other in the back of a car and then to making out on the dining room table.

"We've never even spoken to each other but I sort of saw her the other week." Gary paused whilst trying to work out how to say the next part of his tale.

"So have you or have you not met my sister?" Julie was confused. The visions stopped.

"No not in the full sense of the word." Gary replied. Julie was even more confused. "Look. When was the last time you spoke to your sister?" Gary asked her.

"Ages ago. Well probably two or three months ago."

"I'm not good at telling people these sort of things," Gary said with hesitation.

"What sort of things?" Julie was getting annoyed.

"Your sister was shot at an Army roadblock a couple of weeks or so ago." There, Gary had managed to say it. Julie had gone silent. Her mouth was still open but she couldn't say anything. "I'm sorry to have to be the one to tell you but it was definitely her." Gary felt he had to convince Julie that what he was saying was the truth. Julie just stared into nothingness. Her mouth now closed but her eyes starting to water.

"How do you know it was her?"

"Well it's a bit embarrassing but I saw her body after she had been shot and I keep dreaming about her. She sort of talks to me." Gary was uncertain as to how much he should tell Julie about his dreams.

"She talks to you!!" Julie was finding this very hard to take in. She hoped that it could all be a joke but felt she knew Gary well enough to know that he wouldn't joke about this sort of thing.

"What were you doing at the roadblock?" Julie's voice had changed.

"I was in one of the cars waiting to be searched."

"You're not part of the Army, are you?" Julie moved away from Gary as she asked this question.

"No not at all. I just happened to be in the queue of traffic waiting to be turned out. I was there and I saw her make a run for it as they shot her down. I wasn't the only one who saw it." Gary tried to explain it all. Julie had started to cry. "I'm sorry but you needed to know." Gary gave her a cuddle. Julie cried even more at the thought of her sister being killed that way. Gary held her closer and Julie did the same. Julie cried for about ten minutes before she regained some of her composure.

"I need to tidy myself a little please." Julie said as she got up rather shakily and grabbed for her handbag. It was a strange feeling. She was falling in love with a man she hardly knew and then he tells her the most awful news. Her head was spinning and she was feeling a bit queezy.

      She made her way upstairs and eventually to the bathroom. Gary had hoped that he had done the right thing in telling Julie what he knew. As he thought back to the dreams he had been having he thought that he would be best not telling her anymore. Things that hadn't done so before now also seemed to be making sense. He tried to recall what the blond woman had been saying. 'Look out for her!' Gary had at first assumed that she was talking about Angela but now guessed that all along she knew that Gary and Julie would have this situation and that it was Julie who he had been asked to look after. Gary gave Julie a couple of minutes before he decided that he should follow her upstairs to make sure that she was alright. He felt a bit odd at having to be the one to tell her that her sister had died. Not only that, it had probably killed what at one time had promised to a very electric moment. Gary was also very aroused at the small moment of intimacy they had just shared. He was glad though in a way that he had found the strength to tell her. He knew that Julie was ready to cry and imagined her being in a most tearful state upstairs. He neared the top of the stairs and looked up towards the bathroom. Julie was stood at the door waiting for him.

"I thought you'd never come." Julie said to him as she gave him a small smile. Its' message was deafening. Gary stopped short and looked into her eyes from a small distance before walking over to her. They embraced each other for a few seconds and then kissed like the world was going to end tonight.

The sweet gentleness of love had been shattered by the immense power of lust that took them over. The two of them stumbled towards the bedroom and each started to undress each other until they were completely naked. The whole event had been exhausting for both of them and they took a small rest as the realisation of the occasion dawned upon them. Gary looked at Julie as he admired her body. He slowly moved his hand towards her and gently caressed one of her dark nipples with the lightest of touches from the tips of his fingers. The anticipation of that first touch had practically sent shivers down Julies' spine but the actual feel of his finger exploring her body left her practically paralysed. He stroked each nipple, one at a time until they showed indications of having been properly stimulated. Gary kissed Julies' left breast with little soft gentle lips before continuing to the other breast and from there extending the feeling of pleasure to her nipples with his tongue. He then kissed her stomach and took a few seconds to admire Julies' body. Julie breathed deep and Gary watched as her stomach moved up and down. He looked at every individual hair on her body as they reflected in the low light as her body moved. He liked the look of everything he could see but he was particularly taken by the smoothness of her arms and elbows.

Julie looked into Gary's eyes. Her hands felt the rippling contours of his muscles as she examined his back with them. She slowly moved her gaze over the contours of his face, studying every inch of his frown before she finished by staring at his jaw. She considered just how well formed his features were. Julie then looked at his forehead and hairline. He was a good looking bloke she thought to herself. As Gary turned his head a little, she winced as she looked closer at the injuries he had sustained. She was surprised to find a lot of bruising all over Gary's body. He wasn't exceptionally muscular but his arms were strong. Julie teased him with an attempted kiss pulling away from him so as to prevent him from responding. They cuddled each other tightly, breathing in time. A warm feeling went through her. She stroked Gary's chest and commented on his flat stomach but then she inspected more of his wounds. She already knew about his ankle and had seen his eye and cheek but she looked on aghast at the bruising to his side and his arms. She was amazed at the bruising to his knees and absolutely speechless as she saw the cuts all over his back. It was obvious that he had not received these injuries during a street brawl. Julie wanted to know more but now wasn't the time.

Julie gave him a little peck on his bottom lip but allowing him to do the same this time. Their heads began to move like two magnets, wanting to join but being forced away. The rhythmic motion turned into a type of mating dance, each with mouths open ready to strike like vipers. Gary took control and gave Julie a forceful kiss. They pushed and pulled whilst arranging themselves in the most comfortable position they could manage. They held each others naked bodies tightly as they half pulled a sheet over themselves in some ridiculous attempt to get into bed. It was a night, neither would forget.

-

Sergeant Ed Foulkes interrupted the mumbling conversations from his Unit who were gathering in the 'Briefing Room' ready for the start of another shift. They had all been put on a special assignment so had no idea what was due to be going on tonight. Ed had already been on duty a couple of hours and had had a small briefing of his own.
"I want everyone in top uniform ready to begin briefing in twenty minutes." There were only a handful of the Unit there at the time but both Corporals were in attendance.
"Is there something we should know Sir?" One of the Corporals replied.
"The Major will be at the briefing and I don't want the Unit seen in a bad light."
"We'll round everyone up Sir."
"Is the Major doing the briefing then Sir?" The other Corporal added.
"No, a Field Agent will be doing that tonight." Ed answered as he saluted and went on his way.
"A bloody Field Agent." Rachel Dobbs said out slowly but loud.
"A bloody Field Agent." All the others replied in copycat fashion before bursting out laughing.
"No honestly it's a bit strange for an agent to do a briefing isn't it?" Rachel posed the question generally.

"He probably doesn't trust the Serge to get it right." One of the Privates added.
"Hey will we actually be able to see him?" Another Private joined in.
"You know how secretive they are supposed to be. He'll probably be hiding in a cupboard, or behind a screen." The Unit enjoyed the next twenty minutes getting ready whilst thinking of ridiculous ways that an agent might brief them whilst remaining anonymous.

The briefing carried on as was planned but no action would take place until the go ahead had been given. This meant that all of Charlie 12 were on light duties until further notice but they would have to be ready to move at once as soon as clearance was received. It was a strange situation but one that happened from time to time.

Whilst all this had been going on, Wooters had been to see the Sergeant who was in charge of Unit Oscar 3. This Unit were fairly well experienced and very well drilled when it came to carrying out instructions to the letter. Wooters felt that Oscar 3 were just the right Unit to start the campaign of action against The Food Centre.
"Sergeant, I have some orders that your Unit must carry out to the button."
"No problem, Sir." The Sergeant saluted and clicked her heels as she answered.
"Stand easy Sergeant." The Major took out a manila folder and opened it up on the briefing room desk. The two of them bent over it as they spoke. "First thing tomorrow I want you to shut the place down and clear it completely."
"Do you want me to keep it guarded?"
"No of course not. As soon as you've cleared the last one out your team can return to base. This is purely a disruption exercise."
"And you want all these other things carried out on other days?" She saw the list in front of her and gave the Major a funny look as she ran her finger down the list of events that her Unit were expected to carry out.
"Yes all of these have to be done and within two weeks. I want a full plan from you of dates you intend to carry out the various operations and then I want one day when the Food Centre is disrupted all day." The Major felt confident that the Unit would carry these orders out well. As it turned out it was a number of days before the two Units were allowed to carry out their orders.

The Army was quite active in another part of the area as well. Waydon was being invaded by Army vehicles of all shapes and sizes as they finally moved out all of their equipment from the school. Gary had heard all the noise as the trucks moved in to the school and he hobbled his way down to watch as The Army in usual drill like fashion moved piece of machinery after piece of machinery out of the school. A small crowd of villagers had congregated in front of the shops to watch the exodus and Gary was surprised to see how open the Army were about letting everyone see what sort of equipment they had been using. Drills of various sizes, what looked like some sort of thermo imaging machine, pneumatic supports and lots of other heavy type equipment was brought out in turn and loaded on to trucks. There was even a low loader which had come to takeaway a small earth-digging machine. Gary saw one of the teachers in the crowd and he made his way over to him.
"Are they moving out completely?" Gary asked.
"Seems like it."
"Haven't you been told anything yet?"
"Yes I've just seen the bloke in charge who has said they're moving out but we cannot move in until some repairs have been done. I've just got to lock the place up when I'm given the keys again." The teacher replied giving an empty look as he answered.
Gary had seen enough to satisfy himself that the Army had finished at the school so he made his way back home. As Gary walked down Back Lane he started to think about the girls. He wondered how they had dealt with the situation of moving out. He missed them badly and then realised that he probably missed Angela even more. They were very good together and when they were not having a bad time were probably a model family. Yes, he said to himself, I love Angela. Gary's mind then turned to Julie. He thought back on the other night and how good the sex had been with her. Julie was something really special and everything that Gary wanted at the moment. She believed in him, supported him and looked after him just as Angela used to. Julie made him feel special which was how Angela used to make him feel. He kept thinking back to how things used to be with Angela and that was what he was now feeling when he was with Julie. Perhaps he could feel that again. He owed Angela so much. They had brought up the two girls together and now he had left them to cope on their own.

He guessed that deep down inside that Angela still loved him and he began to feel guilty about how quickly he had disregarded her and fallen in love with Julie. He began to feel very guilty indeed. Yes he decided that he should do everything he could, to try and get Angela back. If there was still a hope it was the right thing to do. Gary got home and poured himself a little drop of whiskey. As he sipped it, he came across the note from Julie. He read its brief contents again quickly before folding it and placing it in his trouser pocket. Angela was his main objective at the moment and he felt he should go round and see how things were. Yes, what a good idea he thought.

Gary had a wash and changed into some smarter clothes. He also fiddled with his hair to try and make that look better but in the end had to leave it as it was. He looked at himself in the mirror and said, yes I'm ready. He poured another small drink into his glass and downed it in one before he set off for Angela's. It didn't take more than twenty minutes to walk to where Angela was now living. Gary knocked on the door.
"Daddy it's you!" Joan cried as she opened the door. "Come in!"
"Is Mummy there?" Gary asked before entering.
"I'll go and get her." Joan said as she ran off to find her Mum.
Angela was soon there and she too opened the door.
"Come in." Angela said. "What have you done to your face?"
Although Gary was able to hide most of his injuries the facial wounds were still very visible.
"Oh I had a bit of an argument with some muggers." Gary kept to the same story.
"What do you want then?"
"I just wondered how you were all getting on." Gary started tentatively.
"As you can see we're alright thank you." Angela replied immediately.
"I also wondered if I could arrange to take the girls out sometime?" Gary added quickly.
"Yes please," Joan said excitedly.
"Hang on a minute." Angela indicated to Joan to sit down and be quiet. "In fact I think your Father and I need to discuss this alone. Here's some money, go down to the shop and find Katy and come back in about ten minutes please." Angela asked.
"Yes Mum." Joan did as she was asked without any fuss. After Joan

had left Angela spoke again.

"And where do you suggest taking the girls?" Angela asked beginning to smell the alcohol on Gary's breath.

"Shopping or swimming or perhaps to the pictures if they'd like to go."

"And would you be driving?" Angela added.

"Well of course I'd be driving." Gary replied thinking it was a stupid question to ask.

"Then the answer is No!" Angela stood up and walked towards the door.

"Why not?"

"You're still drinking and I cannot trust you with the girls if you're drinking." Angela told him.

"I'm not driving today. I won't drink if I'm driving."

"When you can come round here without drinking, then the answer may be yes but not until I can see you without you being drunk." Angela opened the front door as she spoke.

"Look I need you to come home. Please come back."

"I'm not sure that the time is right Gary."

"What do you mean?"

"Just at the moment I think it would be best that we stayed apart. I need some space and need to have some time on my own to think about things."

"What is there to think about?" Gary was demoralised.

"You! I have to think about you." Angela by this time had almost pushed Gary out of the door. "It's nice to see you and the girls want to see more of you but please stop drinking." Angela looked at Gary almost with a tear in her eye. Gary sighed but decided that this was not the time or place to get into an argument and that he should just retire gracefully and not upset the situation any further.

"Oh by the way Julie Clark tried to leave you a message to say that she is back at the school and they should be opening soon." Gary added that last bit as he got up to leave.

"It's good to see you and the girls ask after you all the time but I want them to see you when you're not drunk. Come back when you're a bit more sober please." Angela almost pushed Gary through the door.

Angela thought herself a bit ruthless in the way she had dismissed him especially as he wasn't looking too good. His injuries seemed quite painful she thought but then she went on to guess that they had probably been the result of a drunken session one night. She wasn't sure what she was going to say to Joan and Katy.

-

The members of Unit Charlie 12 were given fifteen minutes for a quick refreshment after having been briefed by who was introduced only as 'Field Agent for Operation Hunting'. It meant very little to most of the Unit but the fact that an agent had briefed them for a special mission was a real talking point.
"I wasn't expecting an Agent to do the briefing were you?" One of the Privates asked as he walked towards the canteen. He had been one of the last ones to arrive and had not been a party to all the previous hilarity.
"No, quite a surprise!"
"Very direct though."
"And well on the ball, knew all the likely pitfalls. I was impressed." The brief discussion was concluded.

"So what did you make of the Field Agent?" A Private asked Rachel Dobbs as they stood perusing the choice of different foods that were available.
"Very impressed," she answered with a sigh.
"You seem disappointed?"
"No not really. No not at all in fact. I was just thinking whether I'd make a good agent."
"I thought they'd have been in civvies, didn't you?"
"True but you forget they are all Army, just like us and quite entitled to wear uniform." Rachel set the record straight.
Unit Charlie 12 were in no doubt as to what was happening tonight, what was expected of them, where each one played their part and what the likely outcome was hoped to be. It was going to be another long night of house searching, interviewing and cross-referencing between the two teams and the agent who was going to keep out of the way.

At 20.30hrs exactly, Unit Charlie 12 loaded into the back of two lorries whilst Sergeant Foulkes, the Agent and both Corporals took two jeeps. The Major didn't come with them. The convoy soon found itself entering the village of Greenfields and making its way to Lavender Lane and the cottage belonging to Martin Saunders. As the

Unit unloaded from the lorries, everyone became quickly aware that the house in question was in complete darkness. Not a single hint of light came from inside the house nor was there any outside lighting to help anyone make their way to the place. Two soldiers were quickly given the job of checking the back of the house, the Privates made their way swiftly down between the side of the house and the garage and checked that the back door was locked. Still no signs of life. They knew their orders were to check the back garden shed to make sure that nobody was hiding in it and they did this easily. The shed was almost completely empty. Two old paint tins and a garden fork stood against the far wall whilst a pile of sacks were bundled in the opposite corner. One stuck his rifle into the sacks to ensure that they were just sacks. The shed was empty. The all clear was passed back to another Private who in turn passed this back to the agent. The signal was given to knock on the front door and then knock it down without waiting for an answer.

Almost as a tradition, Private Rachel Dobbs was given the responsibility of knocking at the front door and being one of the first to enter the house once the door had been knocked down. Being a small sized house the whole place should be checked within about twenty seconds. Rachel waited for the door to fall in but it took two or three attempts by the 'removers' to get the door down and her adrenalin was pumping by the time she finally jumped over the door and into the cottage.
"Army! We are armed. Show yourselves." Rachel shouted as she went into the main room. Right behind her was another Private who went straight for the kitchen whilst two others went straight upstairs. The last soldier to enter the house looked around to see if there were any other rooms to be entered. There were none.
"All clear!" The shout came from upstairs.
"All clear here," shouted one of the soldiers downstairs. The Corporal entered the house and put the lights on.
"Nobody at home Corporal! Completely empty!" Rachel gave him the bad news. The Corporal grimaced and took a long slow look around. No chairs, no furniture. Just a table in the kitchen with a piece of paper on it saying 'Goodbye'. Rachel moved over to the kitchen table and picked up the piece of paper. The table wobbled as she leant on it but it returned to its prior position as she removed her hand. The Corporal said nothing but turned and went back outside to report the

details to the agent and his Sergeant. After receiving the information, the two then walked away a short distance and had a brief discussion.

"Shit and bollocks!" Rachel said to herself. It wasn't said very quietly though.

"He must have known we were coming." One soldier added.

"That's what it looks like." Another answered. Two soldiers then appeared from upstairs.

"What's it like up there?"

"Just completely moved out. Not a bloody thing."

The Corporal came back into the house and turned to Private Dobbs. "I want you to take one other and go over this place looking for anything that might be useful. Old bills. Receipts. Anything you can find".

"Yes Sir." She answered immediately. She took a quick look around. "Private, you stay with me." Her words were said half as a question and half as a command.

"Of course." The Private replied whilst the onlooking Corporal gave a knowing nod to Rachel.

"You know what to do." He turned to the others. "Okay rest of you we have a garage and a shed to look at. This way." The Corporal led the rest out of the house and back out to the front garden where the agent and Sergeant Foulkes were standing. Corporal King had already taken Kenton Bridges and another soldier with the 'opener' to get into the garage. The Sergeant turned to the Corporal and barked out some further orders.

"If you and Matthew can finish up here, I'm taking two with me to a local store."

"Yes Sir," the Corporal replied.

"You have the shed and the garage to complete." The Sergeant continued.

"Yes Sir all is in hand Sir."

"Is Rachel dealing with the house search?"

"Yes Sir."

"Okay that's good. Send half the Unit back to base in one lorry as and when you can and make sure Matthew returns with them. Start working on securing the house but don't leave until I've returned." Sergeant Foulkes finished giving his orders and saluted.

The Corporal returned the salute and got on with his duties. Sergeant Foulkes, the agent and the two Privates all got into a jeep and started on their way to the local General Store right in the middle of

Greenfields.

     Rachel Dobbs moved the one table that was in the room nearer towards the wall and laid her rifle on it. She indicated to Iben to do the same, which he did.
"Have you done many house searches like this before?" Rachel asked as she took a slow look around.
"No not really but surely a house search is a house search isn't it?"
"No it certainly isn't. I'm going to ask you to do the recording so we need to start an entry in your note-book and somewhere here......" as she was saying this, Rachel had removed the backpack she had been carrying and was searching in it. ".....I have some plastic bags in which we place anything that we find. All I need you to do is list everything that I find and note where I found it. Are you happy with that?" Rachel gave clear instructions.
The Private nodded indicating that he knew exactly what he was doing and then got out his note-book. The two of them searched every inch of every room.

     Outside, the others were not having much luck. The shed was empty apart from the few things mentioned before and Private Bridge and his companion were having great problems getting into the garage. It was obvious that they had something behind the doors which would not let them be opened inwards so the best option was to get the 'expander' and wrench the door open outwards. The vital piece of equipment was called for. It took a matter of seconds when they finally used it and inside the garage was a blue Ford Mondeo car, registration number BRO 19 GER. It wasn't good news. Somebody quickly turned the lights on in the garage and straightaway you could see that the car had been cleaned and polished both inside and out. Corporal King opened the car and looked in the glove box but the car was almost like new.
"A professional job eh."
"Yeah! There won't be anything of interest in there." The Corporal replied with a sullen tone. They both knew that they had been beaten here. "Check everything in the garage anyway. Any paperwork, let me know." The Corporal finished as he left the garage and met up with his Corporal. The latter brought Matthew up to date with instructions. They agreed that Rachel should look at the car after she was finished in the house for uniformity.

The agent had taken Sergeant Foulkes to the General Store in Greenfields which is where Martin Saunders was supposed to have been working. The time was nearly a quarter to ten but this was not a problem as far as the Army was concerned. There were lights on in the upstairs part of the shop which suggested that not everyone had gone to bed.

"Knock on the door", Ed Foulkes gave the order. There was a movement of a shadow against the light upstairs and the curtain moved almost immediately.

"Knock again to show we mean business tonight." The light went on in the hallway behind the front door and it opened to show a small man dressed in jeans and jumper.

"What can I do for you?" The man said in a high voice.

"We are Unit Charlie 12 from the European Military Army, we'd like to come in and ask you a few questions." The Sergeant said to him, firmly but politely. If the Army came knocking on your door, it was always advisable to do as they asked and Jim Donald was not looking for any trouble.

"Please come in", he said, opening the door nice and wide. All four of them entered into the hall and after shutting the door, Mr. Donald led them up the stairs and into the lounge where the rest of the Donald family were sitting and talking.

"Sorry to disturb you all at this time of night." The Sergeant said this without raising his voice trying to put everyone at ease.

"Please sit down." Mrs. Donald stood and shooed the two Donald children off of the settee so that there was a bit more room for some of them to sit. It was never going to be possible to allow all four to sit but the Donald's tried to be as accommodating as they could.

"Would you like some tea or coffee?" Mr. Donald asked.

"No thanks we hope to only keep you a few moments" The Sergeant said as reassuringly as he could. He looked at the agent who just looked back at him so he took the lead. "I'm here to ask about your shop assistant Mr. Donald."

"What Mark!!" The reply was said with some surprise. "He seems a nice enough bloke."

"Mark you call him?"

"That's what we know him as, Mark Chambers. You're not going to tell me that he is using an alias are you?" Mr. Donald said with a bit of a chuckle in his throat. To most it might have sounded just a jokey

thing to say but to the Sergeant and the agent it was highly suspicious.
"Do you think he might be using an alias then?" He sat a bit nearer to Mr. Donald as he posed this question.
"No of course not. I've seen papers to say he is Mark Chambers so Mark Chambers he is."
"So why did you say about an alias Mr. Donald?" Sergeant Foulkes could sense that the tension within the room had just gone up quite a bit. Were they hiding something? Had they been expecting their visit? The Sergeant continued, "It's a strange thing to come out with."
"Well yes I suppose it is but after all the trouble I had finding him you never know." Mr. Donald answered but by now seemed so concerned about saying the right thing that he was almost shaking. "My last assistant left at very short notice a few days ago and it wasn't easy to find a replacement you know?"
"The last one?" Sergeant Foulkes asked with anticipation.
"Yes. A David Thomas. Great worker, was one of the best I've ever had but on a couple of occasions people would turn up asking for Mr. Smith or Mr. Brown and just recently Saunders I think but always seeming to want to speak to David. It was strange." Mr. Donald replied.
"Doesn't he still work for you?"
"Know he gave his notice about a week ago." Mr. Donald answered.
"Have you notified the Information Centre?"
"Well sort of. I filled in the forms straightaway. Thomas said he had found another job and needed me to notify the IC immediately. He took the letter himself. I assume they have got it. I was pretty disappointed to lose him." The agent and Sergeant Foulkes looked at each other and shook their heads. They were beginning to realise that they were at another cul-de-sac. They asked a few more questions and then quickly got ready to leave.

Sergeant Foulkes almost rushed to the door to bring the visit to an end before he got asked anymore questions. The agent and Sergeant Foulkes returned to the house where things were coming to a conclusion. Rachel had found two other bits of paper of interest in the house but nothing in the car. She had bagged what she had found. The agent agreed to pick those up at a later date. It was getting late.

-

Whilst all of the activity surrounding the search of the house had been going on, Jeff Hutton was taking it easy in his living room whilst studying some plans of a couple of buildings. As he perused every meticulous detail he drank a nice hot cup of coffee. He took his time working over the plans checking out every angle and possible situation that he could imagine. There was some quiet music playing and the atmosphere was very calming. A real fire was burning and Jeff was very comfortable. He had purchased his little cottage in Bateley about a couple of months ago but hadn't spent any time there really. He had visited on a few days here and there when moving in some furniture and was quite happy that nobody really worried at what times of the day he came and went. He'd got to know one of the neighbours who had often seen him driving his grey Standard car and he felt that the time was right to settle in here a bit more.

There were still a number of things that needed unpacking. His books. The new kitchen table. A box of kitchen utensils. In the end, the move had been a little bit rushed. Jeff had made sure he moved in the tall wooden lamp stand and the old oak writing bureau. There was also that old antique book shelf. There were still a number of other things that Jeff Hutton would need to buy in order to furnish his cottage in the way he wanted it. He took a slow look around the room until his eyes focused on his right hand. He looked at the identity card he held in it and laughed to himself. He walked over to the fire and threw the card on it. He stood there and watched as the card folded and melted and then disappeared completely. He had enjoyed his time as Martin Saunders. He had one more function to perform and then he could relax for a while.

Chapter 12   -   SOUTHWALL ROAD

It wasn't long before Gary got the knock on the door and a member of the local revolutionary party was calling to see what he was up to. Gary had half expected some sort of contact and in fact was slightly pleased to see that they were at least showing some concern for him. A young man in his twenties stood at the door.
"Hello Mr. Newson. I'm from the Kentley group. You know? The revolutionary party!"
"Yes come in."
"I have been sent to see if you are going to attend one of our meetings soon."
"Well as you know I've not really been feeling up to attending any meetings lately and anyway I'm finding it hard to drive at present." Gary lied a little but felt it was a reasonable excuse.
"We can get you a vehicle if you are unable to drive Mr. Newson."
"Thank you very much." Gary knew that he was going to be backed into a corner and felt that it would make sense for him to appear keen and gracious about their offers of help.
"There is a meeting tomorrow night if you can be ready at seven." The young lad played his part well.
"Seven o'clock. I suppose I could be ready then. What is the subject under discussion?" Gary thought he ought to continue to sound interested.
"I don't know." The young lad answered. They shook hands on the agreement and turned to leave. "At seven then!"
"Yes I'll be ready." Gary shut the front door and looked up into the air. How did I agree to that, he thought to himself. He had agreed to attend a revolutionary meeting even though he had no idea what was going to be discussed. He had guessed that after all the torture and pain that the nationals had put him through that the local party felt that they had some sort of obligation to keep in touch. They might even treat him as some sort of special case to start with but in the end they would drop him. He didn't want to get too involved with them anymore. He had seen the bad side of interfering into things that he didn't fully understand but then he still felt that they were fighting for the right cause. And then there were the lists.

The next day seemed to speed through so quickly for Gary. He was moving around the house a lot better than before but was still in very great pain. Getting upstairs was still very difficult and of course painful but he was able to move from the lounge to the kitchen if he needed to. Sammy still expected to be taken out for his regular walk but eventually caught on to the fact that he would have to make do with the garden. Eventually the afternoon turned into early evening and Gary had noticed that the clock was indicating that it had gone passed six. He decided that he ought to start getting ready, not that he had much to do. Just before seven, Gary looked out the front window and saw a car with a person sat in the driver's seat, parked outside. It had to be the car he was waiting for. Gary gathered his coat and left the house. As he appeared from the front door, the driver got out and walked towards Gary in a very subservient manner. Gary waved him away.

"Mr. Newson?" The driver said it in a 'can I help you' type way but it also served both as an indication that the car was in fact for him and as a question to ask that the driver had indeed got the right man.

"Yes." Gary answered as he slowly made his way down the path. He wasn't sure what sort of answer the driver was actually expecting but 'Yes' was all he was going to get. The driver went to the back door and opened it, gesturing Gary to get in.

"Let me take your stick, Sir." The driver was polite, efficient and very helpful. Gary wondered what he did normally.

Gary got to the meeting in good time to allow him to take one of the special seats situated a bit to the side and in front of the main crowd. He was beginning to feel very important indeed, even though he knew he wasn't. It was very difficult not to get carried away by all the service and hospitality. He was brought a cup of coffee and continually asked if he was alright which after a while started to get annoying. Gary thought he should show some sort of gratitude for the way that he was being treated but then began to think that the revolutionary party might have felt that he was going to turn against them. Was this the reason he was being waited on? Did they fear that he would go to The Army and let them know everything he knew? Then Gary realised that he didn't actually know that much. Apart from the lists of course.

The meeting was one of those usual affairs, full of reported wrong doings by the authorities and of course The Army and a call for everyone to stand together and refuse to buy certain items identified as government fund raisers. The crowd who had gathered were also the usual motley crowd who probably had nothing better to do and were quite pleased to find some others to talk to. Gary looked at each and every one of them. It wasn't something he had really done before but sitting in his new position in the important seats, he was able to look to his side a bit and stare at all the faces. Where were the young pretenders like his brother David. Years ago there were a number of lads like David wanting to do what was right. Where were the potential political activists that Gary remembers seeing at those meetings. Women like Angela who were full of anger and ready to change the world. Gary couldn't see anyone like this at all. He knew that they were still about but they obviously didn't come to these sort of meetings. All we had gathered here in this decrepit Odeon were a sad bunch of old men who wanted to hear some shocking revelations. The speakers didn't disappoint them of course and the tin would always go round. Not everybody could afford to donate. The tine found its way to Gary, and normally he would fumble around and then pass the tin on to the next person without putting any money in but he realised that tonight he couldn't do that. Everyone was watching to see how much he put in the tin. Gary hadn't prepared himself for this and he searched his left trouser pocket to find he only had a fifty penny piece. This wouldn't look good. Gary knew he had to put a couple of E's in at the very least and he would probably have to donate some paper money instead. Gary took out his wallet and took a gulp on noting that the smallest bank note he had was a 20 E note. Almost with the precision of a hospital operation, Gary pulled just one 20 E note from his wallet and folded it before sliding it gently into the donation tin. Gary wanted to swear. The meeting came to a close and the crowd slowly dispersed.

One of the local leaders made his way over to Gary. He smiled.
"Hello Mr. Newson. It's very good to see you here at one of our meetings. What did you think of it?"
"It was good." Gary nodded his head in some sort of approval whilst lying.
"You surprise me." The leader replied.
"In what way?"
"Well I found most of the speeches repetitive and full of lots of useless information. For the older ones amongst us it must have seemed quite

boring." The local leader seemed to keep his inane smile whilst talking and Gary found it very un-nerving but he realized he would have to be a bit more honest if he was going to get through this situation.

"Well I didn't want to be rude but have to agree you do have a point." Gary was going to leave his answer at that but then decided to just add a little bit more. "In fact I was thinking where were all the younger people?"

"Good you have noticed. We do have younger members but they are not prepared to come to these sort of meetings just to hear stories of what our beloved government is doing wrong." The local leader clenched his fist as he said this. "They want action, not words Mr. Newson. Don't you think that is a good thing?"

"Very commendable! Are we talking about small little actions though?" Gary had started to speak his mind.

"Yes most of the time. We do not have enough trusted and respected organizers to create any big actions." The local leader paused for a moments' thought and then changed the topic. "We are looking for people who have been there and fought for the cause before."

"I can guess you are." Gary replied.

"A man like your self would be a useful addition to our management staff."

"I'm not sure I'm up to doing very much at the moment." Gary tried to back out of a little corner.

"Don't be silly Gary. You can do so much just sitting in that chair. We need new ideas. New people! We need you Mr. Newson." Gary was stuck. He couldn't say no yet he didn't want to say yes.

"I can't really devote much time to you as I have a full time job and a family." Gary started to make excuses.

"But your family have left you, haven't they?" The local leader obviously knew a lot more than Gary had given him credit for. There was also another man, rather better dressed than most but still very sinister looking who was listening to the conversation rather intently whilst trying not to make it noticeable that he was. Gary wondered if he was from the National Party.

"You're right. I should perhaps do more but I honestly don't know what I can do to help." Gary hoped the reply would be acceptable.

"Mr. Newson. It is late. We should sleep soon and think about what has been said." The man gave out his hand for Gary to shake. He then clicked his fingers and the driver appeared ready to return Gary back home.

    As Gary sat himself down back on his settee, he opened the whiskey bottle and poured a drink into a small glass. He downed this in one swallow and then poured another one before putting the top back on the bottle. He thought over his current predicament. It wasn't good. In fact it was a real pain in the arse as far as Gary was concerned. Why the hell did the local revolutionary party want him to be a full time member? They obviously were still working on the instructions of the Nationals. Gary drank a bit more and soon nearly half the bottle had gone. Sammy lay on the carpet looking up at him. Gary began to fall asleep in the chair.

    Gary awoke suddenly and for a minute couldn't quite work out where he was. He was of course laying on the settee and it was half past three in the morning. Gary pulled himself from the settee and made his way up to bed. His ankle still hurt as did other parts of his body but it was his head giving him the biggest pain at the moment. For no particular reason, Gary then remembered what the driver had said as he had dropped him off. He said he'd be back at ten tomorrow morning for him. They wanted him to attend another meeting. Gary wasn't looking forward to it. Gary set his alarm and amazingly it woke him up at nine o'clock. Gary tried to stretch but with great pain. His head was thumping and his throat felt as dry as bath towel. A quick wash helped a little bit but the drop of whiskey perked him up even more. As he expected, at ten, the car was waiting for him outside.
"Hello Mr. Newson. Do you want any help?" It was the same driver from the night before.
"No I can manage thank you." Gary stumbled but got into the car.
"You don't look too good. Are you coming down with something?" The driver spoke to him via the rearview mirror.
"This is me on a good day at the moment."
"Perhaps a little bit of the real stuff sir?" The driver handed Gary a half bottle of proper malt whisky. Gary took a swig and it warmed his throat as it went down.
"That's better." Gary agreed.
"I've got some mints if you would like one sir?" The driver was for some reason trying to help Gary.
"Very kind of you." Gary took the pack of sweets from the driver and

proceeded to extract the next mint in line from the packet. It wasn't that easy but he eventually succeeded. There was a few minutes when the journey continued without any conversation but Gary hoped that this new found friend might be able to help him further. "So where exactly are we going?"

"Just a house in Chale." The driver seemed to have no qualms about telling him that.

"Whose house is it?" Gary continued.

"Nobody's really I suppose. It's one that is used as a safe house or for meetings like this."

"Yes. Just exactly what sort of meeting is this?" Gary was on a roll.

"Well I understand you are being interviewed to be one of the Kentley organisers." The driver replied in a manner that suggested that Gary should have known this already.

"Oh am I."

"What did you think the meeting was about then?" The driver was surprised at Gary's reply.

"I hadn't got a clue." Gary brought the conversation to a close.

The car arrived at an ordinary terraced house in Bright Avenue on the outskirts of Chale. Gary was assisted from the car and to the front door which opened as he walked up the path. The local leader he had spoken to at yesterdays meeting was the first one to greet him.

"Mr. Newson, come in."

"Thank you." Gary looked around and saw two others sat behind a table. One seemed to be better dressed than the rest and Gary assumed this was the National representative. The other man stood and gestured Gary to sit in the empty chair on the near side of the table whilst the local leader came and took his place behind the table. All three were unshaven and had greasy black hair. It seemed to be a compulsory requirement. The better dressed of the three said nothing at all and left all of the talking up to the others. The local leader stood up, shuffled some papers and then coughed to clear his voice.

"We convene this meeting of the Kentley Revolutionary Party in order to clarify the qualities of our trusted colleague here today, Gary Peter Newson. He is to be judged about his abilities to perform the role of local party organiser and the panel gathered here today shall be fair and honest in their judgement. So beg we continue." The local leader sat back down and looked at the person sat to his right. It was a look that was more of a signal to tell the man that it was his turn to play his part. Gary assumed from his dress that this person was also a local chap. He hadn't seen him before but the way he was dressed indicated that he was a revo of only small significance. Gary was still bemused by all of this and slowly taking in what had been said. Before Gary could say very much the other local chap stood up to say his bit.

"Gary Peter Newson has been associated to the Kentley party for the last twenty years. He has attended numerous rallies and has always shown the utmost support for all of our revolutionary policies. He led a successful assault on the Kentley Army Armoury and more recently been singled out as the one person who could be entrusted to retrieve the most important of documents from the hands of the local government." The chap paused briefly. Gary was beginning to guess what was coming and was a little annoyed that it had been taken for granted that he would agree to join the group. The thought of interrupting this little façade and telling everyone in the room what he thought of them passed through his mind but just as quickly he realised that that wouldn't be a very clever thing to do. He was determined to make sure that the local leader knew how he felt though. The chap continued. "We are pleased to be able to consider such a valued member of our local community for a position as local party organiser." The chap stopped and looked at Gary. Gary wondered what came next. The main local party leader intervened to help matters.

"Gary this where we need to know if you would like to become an organiser?"

"Oh er! Yes." Without even thinking, Gary had given the answer they wanted.

"Good. Then if you just allow us to consider our verdict. Please give us a few moments." The leader gestured Gary to leave the room. He got up and the driver opened the front door so that Gary would go into the front garden of the house. Gary hobbled around a bit as he waited. His only thought was that he could do with a drink. In fact more than just one drink. The driver stood next to the front door of the house as if on guard. Gary wondered what he'd let himself in for but then considered that he didn't really have much option. If the local party come calling on your door asking for you to join them you either do or they consider you a government sympathiser. Gary certainly felt his beliefs were more on the side of the revolution but then he was no activist. There was still this nagging feeling about the threat of the national party taking him for torture again. Perhaps that was why he had been invited to join. So they could just grab him anytime they wanted. Perhaps the locals did believe him and they wanted to be able to protect him a bit more and that was why he was being invited to join. Gary wasn't really sure what to think.

"Mr. Newson." The local leader invited him back into the house. Gary entered the room again. "Please sit down." The local leader said. "We, the panel have considered your application and agree that you have the required talents needed to perform the tasks of the post. Congratulations Gary, you are one of us." The local leader shook Garys hand.

"Thank you."

"There will of course be a small probation period but after that you will be fully installed as a local party organiser." The local leader spoke with some excitement.

"Yes of course. A probation period!" Gary replied. The better dressed of the panel got up and left the room without speaking or even looking at Gary. He went into the house and obviously into another room.

"So you'll probably want to know what you do next?" The local leader said.

"I suppose I do."

"We have another meeting on Friday. We will discuss current issues, plans and policies and you will need to be at that meeting. We'll drop you off a note to confirm it and again we can have a car pick you up."

"Yes good." Gary was just wanting to be away from the place.

"The driver will take you back."

Once again, as soon as Gary returned back home he took to the bottle. He only had a half a bottle of whiskey left so he had to walk down to the local shop to buy some more. Already a little the worse for drink, and of course struggling on his crutch, it was quite a journey. Gary felt like everyone was watching him as he made his way to the local general store. He had enough money to buy a couple of cheap government bottles which he did. Both whiskey. Gary spent the rest of the day thinking about what might take place at the next revolutionary meeting. Gary had hoped that Angela might have actually called round to see him after his visit the other day but it would seem that she had no intentions of doing so. She knew he wasn't able to get around as easily as he would have liked and had hoped that she might bring the girls round. He missed Angela. He missed the girls. The only comfort he could take to help him through the current bad times was whiskey. I say that whiskey was the only thing that helped Gary forget his problems but in fact I'm wrong. Vodka and wine worked quite well as well. Gary was starting to drink a bit more than he used to. In fact he was drinking a lot more than he used to. In fact, Whiskey, Vodka and wine was all he was drinking at the moment.

Friday came and Gary was picked up as usual and taken to the meeting. He wasn't treated like a celebrity for once and this suited him. He was introduced to the other organizers and then the meeting got down to business. A number of subjects were discussed and Gary listened just in case he was asked anything. He wasn't really that interested. Then another subject was started. Subject five on the agenda, 'National matters' it was entitled. Things took a sudden change as far as Gary was concerned. The meeting Chairman spoke. "So we turn to National Matters and of course there is still just the one." The Chairman looked at some notes he had to his side before continuing. "Alan Harris. I feel you should carry on from here."
"Yes Mr. Chairman. Well you all know what we are talking about. The National Committee still feel that we are responsible for the loss of these so called lists and we are being blamed. Mr. Newson, can you help us at all?" Alan Harris turned in the direction of Gary and all eyes turned with him. Gary started to sweat.
"The lists! Ah, the lists. I didn't think that the local party was supposed to know about the lists." Gary needed time to think.
"Well we don't Mr. Newson. That's why we turn to you." Alan Harris replied.
"Well I know very little about them either. I'm not quite sure what I'm allowed to tell you about my involvement I'm afraid so I'd rather not say anything." Gary felt that taking just a general stance of being unable to discuss anything would be enough to stop this casual interrogation. The local leader who had initiated Gary's acceptance as an organiser stood up.
"Gary. We just need to know if you can provide the National Party with any information. They are not completely happy that you say you can give them nothing and they will no doubt ask you again and again until they are convinced otherwise. It's just that until they are convinced, we get as much hassle as you do. So we just ask, if you

can let them have anything then please tell them sooner rather than later."

"Honestly, I wish I could but although it may seem to them that I should know something, I don't." Gary said no more. The meeting went on to subject 6. Gary was hoping that he had done enough to convince some of the local organizers. If any of them had been around long enough they might have had some sympathy for him as most knew how unbelieving the Nationals could be. Very soon they were on to the last listed subject. 'The Southwall Road riot'.

"Okay, we now have to plan for a planned demonstration next week. We have been given our instructions and leaflets will be handed out. Our targets are three houses on Southwall Road where serving Army Officers live. We must give them a piece of their own medicine my friends." On this statement the whole of the table grunted in agreement and approval.

"So who are these Army Officers?" One of the organisers asked.

"No and we don't need to know. There will be a guest speaker and I want a couple of rousing speeches from our own committee as well." The Chairman banged his fist on the table.

"Are you organising the details then?" Alan Harris asked the Chairman. Before he was given the chance to answer the local leader spoke.

"I think this is an ideal event for Gary to run." There were a few murmurings.

"But I don't know what is required." Gary started to make his excuses straightaway.

"Don't worry, I'll guide you. It will be easy for you." The leader replied.

"But Jeff, are you sure. He doesn't want to do it and we're not sure he can either." One of the other organisers seemed to be voicing the opinion of all of them. The local leader just turned his head towards the doubter and glared at him. "But then if you're sure he can handle it." The poor chap bowed his head in shame at being brave enough to cast any sort of doubt on the local leader's decision.

"So that's agreed then." The leader spoke with an air of certainty.

"I'm not sure. I'd rather watch one first." Gary guessed his plea would be in vain.

"We'll talk afterwards. Mr. Chairman." The leader handed things back.

"If there's no other business, I declare this meeting closed." The committee all rose and quickly filed away from the premises. The local leader walked over to Gary.
"I'm hope you will agree to organise this event. I think it will show the Nationals whose side you're on."
"I'll think about it." Gary replied.
"I'll contact you tomorrow. I need to know by then." The leader left his comments fresh in Garys mind as he too departed from the premises. Gary was taken back home, to his house and his whiskey.

It wasn't long though before Gary was being called on again. A delegation from the local leadership visited him at his house and they were very direct in their manner.
"We have started to make some plans for the rally at Southwall Road." One of the delegation said.
"Oh have you." Gary replied.
"We expect you to continue with the organization and we will be back in a couple of days to go over your ideas."
"I said before, I don't really know what I need to do." Gary put it bluntly. The Leader of the delegation looked around and picked out an empty chair which he walked over to and sat down on. He then slowly removed his leather gloves. The room was silent as all of this was going on. When both gloves were laying in his lap the man pulled out a cigarette from a packet he had in his coat pocket and then calmly lit it. He took a draw and then blew it out though his nose. He then leant forward and looked over to Gary.
"Frankly Mr. Newson I think your attitude needs a little bit of adjustment. I'll also be honest with you and tell you that if I had my way the Nationals would still be holding you. I don't fully agree with their methods but I don't like you. I don't believe you and I certainly don't want you organising this bloody rally but I'm a democratic man and have been outvoted." All of this was said in a slow deep calm voice. It sent shivers up Gary's spine. "Now I think you have been given an opportunity here that you don't deserve and I'd be over the moon to see you chuck it back at us. I'm sure a word with the Nationals and they'll have you sorted." The Leader sat back and started to put his gloves back on. Again there was silence.
"Yes I think it would be good for me to organise this rally." Gary said. The delegation leader got up and made his way back towards the front door. He stopped and turned.

"Unfortunately I think you have made the right decision Mr. Newson. John here will let you know what we expect." On saying this he left the house and everyone looked at Gary.

"Well then John, you'd better tell me hadn't you."

"I suppose I had." John replied.

"Look I have never organised anything quite like this before so what do I do?" Gary felt he ought to start listening.

"It's quite easy really. In this file are the addresses of some serving Army personnel who all have homes on Southwall Road. You need to memorise the actual numbers and the ranks of the soldiers. There are no names. You will then need to write a little speech based on the subject of the rally and make sure you read it through as you'll be addressing a few hundred on the day." John explained as briefly but as comprehensively as possible.

"So all I've got to do is give a speech?" Gary found that quite easy.

"No that's not all you've got to do."

"So what else?"

"You will also see in the file details of the subject on which our guest speaker is going to talk. You must touch on that subject but not cover it in your speech. You need to remember the man's name so you can introduce him on the day. Got it?"

"I think so. Seems quite simple." Gary knew he could do this without too much trouble.

"Then you need to know exactly where the soldiers houses are as you will be stepping down from the rostrum at the end of the guests speech and leading the crowd down Southwall Road, pointing out those houses on the way. Don't get it wrong."

"And that's it?"

"Apart from handing out the leaflets before the rally." John had finished.

"What leaflets?"

"We'll be bringing them round to you. Make sure you know where the houses are."

"I will."

"Okay Mr. Newson. We'll see you later." The delegation left.

Gary wiped his brow and poured himself a large whiskey. He downed it in one and poured himself another. After a couple of hours the bottle was half empty.

-

Unit Oscar 3 were on a very early start this morning and the Sergeant had planned a briefing for them at 03:00hrs. It was too early for most of the Unit but they were all in the briefing room at the required time. Sergeant Bailey explained their task for the day and then split her Unit into teams of 4. By 04:00, the whole Unit were in lorries and on their way to the Food Centre. As they approached, the order was to park up and keep an eye on what was going on.
"Are we just going to lock the place up then Serge?" One of the Unit asked.
"No. We will watch the traders setting up their stalls and then we'll be going in about sixish to close everything down." She knew what she had to do. She may not have agreed with it but she still did it. The traders had seen The Army parked outside and most were pleased to see them. There was still a feeling of some insecurity after the shooting the other week and a few traders had been chatting about how close they had got to being shot themselves. It took most of the traders about two hours to set up their stalls. Fish, vegetables were the first stalls to be set up closely followed by the meat traders. By six o'clock, all of the traders had at least made a start to setting up if they hadn't all finished and as you looked around the Food Centre, there was quite a large array of food available for sale. Unit Oscar 3 kept a watch.
"Sergeant, what are we waiting for?"
"I need to see at least three people shopping and buying some food." The Sergeant knew what was required. After about ten minutes, the first customer had turned up. A little old lady was checking out the vegetables. She had her trusted old shopping bag with her and after a brief haggle with the trader she purchased what looked like a mixture of apples and carrots and one big cauliflower.
"I want two of you to detain that woman as she leaves." The Sergeant had issued the orders and two of the Unit duly carried them out. The old lady was bemused as the two uniformed soldiers came up to her. She was less than ten metres from the exit as they performed the arrest.
"What am I being arrested for? What are you doing?"
"You'll find out." The Private answered her. The two looked in her bag and confirmed that it was full of fruit and vegetables as they took the poor old lady back to the lorry where the Sergeant was waiting.
"Have you checked the produce at all Private?"
"Er..er.. no Serge." The Private answered a bit confused.
"Well get it out of her bag and let's have a look at it. Corporal." She shouted for the Corporal to attend whilst she put her hand in the bag

and pulled out a carrot. The Corporal was at her side almost immediately. "Corporal, do you see how poor quality this carrot is?" "I think I see what you mean Serge." The Corporal took the carrot and broke it in two. "It just breaks in your hands Serge. Not up to proper quality I'm afraid." The Corporal played along as he grabbed for another vegetable and tried to break it. He was unable to. The Sergeant grabbed the carrot from him and threw it on the ground and stamped on it crushing it to mush.
"See Corporal. That one too wasn't up to standard."

By now the two Privates were also beginning to understand what they had to do and they emptied the woman's bag and either stamped on it or broke it up somehow. The old woman was in tears as all of this was going on whilst one of the traders looked on in amazement.
"Private. I think I can see someone buying what looks suspiciously like poor quality fish over there. Go and sort it out." Two Privates immediately picked on the next poor shopper and performed similar type antics. The old woman was given her shopping bag back and told in no uncertain terms to go home. She didn't.
"Look Lady. Go home now or else you will be arrested for loitering and buying substandard food." The Sergeant tried to make it as clear as she could to help the old lady out. "Okay Oscar 3, we now need to take this investigation further and we need to inspect some of the food being sold at the Food Centre." The Sergeant led the Unit in and took two Privates aside for some private orders. They immediately went up to the fish stall and lifted their boots up and trod on some of the fish on the stall
"What the bloody hell do you think you're doing?" The fish trader complained as he grabbed at the soldier to stop him.
"Arrest that man for assault." Instructions were issued and the man was arrested. Two other market traders had started to make their way over to intervene but on seeing the arrest stopped and thought twice about getting involved.
"What do we do now Serge?"
"Check this fish for any signs of dirt." She said this as she picked up a few fish and dropped them on to the ground before stamping on them and then picking them up and putting them back on the stall. "If you find any dirt anywhere, record it in your notebook and confiscate all the wares." The two traders looked at each other and guessed that the

fish trader must have spoken out of turn or complained and that he was being taught a lesson the Army way. They were wrong.

By nine, the whole of the Food Centre had had its wares confiscated and it was in the process of being burnt by the Army. Some of the smarter traders had packed away what they could and gone back home but Unit Oscar 3 had achieved their goal.
"Any trader found trading in this Food Centre until it has been given the 'all clear' by Army Regulations will be arrested. All public should be warned to keep out of the Food Centre or run the risk of being taken into quarantine." She shouted out her proclamation. The Food Centre was effectively shut. The public watched as what looked like perfectly good food was burnt.

-

Today's riot had been chosen so that it took place very close to the houses of serving European Army personnel. Gary had been very busy during the day giving out the required leaflets but then had to wait a couple of hours before the riot was ready to be started. It was due to start at 17.30hrs on the junction of Southwall Road and Templegate. By 17.15hrs a few people had already started to congregate and it was supposed to be Gary's job to stand up in front of them and tell them who it was that was going to speak to them tonight but Gary was nowhere to be seen. He wasn't far away. Just a few hundred yards in fact nut he was having trouble getting away from his current drinking friends who he had spent the last hour and a half with. Eventually, loaded up with two half bottles, one in each pocket of his raincoat, Gary made his way to the point of tonights riot. Obviously when he got there he was surprised to see around a hundred people stood about chatting to each other. The revolutionary top dogs quickly found him out and pushed him to an open space where Gary became visible to all. The crowd hushed.
"Ladies and Gentlemen! May I thank you for coming along tonight on such a wonderful evening". Gary gesticulated with his arms as he said this.
"Get on with it," a shout came from the crowd.
"I will, I will" Gary shouted back scratching his head. "To speak to you tonight about Army tactics of the day is Rodney Himpleton, I mean Humpleton. Rodney Humpleton" Gary said as he walked back holding out his left arm to introduce his speaker. A very average man

walked forward and the crowd clapped a little.

"My name is Rodney Humpton but the name is unimportant. What I am about to tell you is what is important and you should all know what you have so far been kept in the dark from". The man continued his speech which would tell of how the Army are about to introduce new instructions including shoot to kill at meetings like these. Heavier enforcement of the curfew laws! Less food in everyday shops so that the Army can eat better! The planned speech would last about thirty minutes when it was Gary's job to point out to the crowd that Army personnel lived nearby. Gary waited in the background. His revolutionary colleagues were less than impressed with him so far. He was late. Drunk! Not at all what was required on a night like this. They knew that there would be Army amongst the crowd. Armed soldiers would appear before the night was over. One of the Revo bosses walked over to Gary.

"Are you drunk my friend?" He said in a sinister manner.

"No, I needed a little one to steady my nerves that's all."

"I would guess you've had more than one. Perhaps you should go home now." The Revo said to Gary in a friendly but positive manner. Gary nodded but had no intention of going anywhere.

Our agent was amongst the early crowd. Looking around to see who was there. Gary standing up to start things off came as a bit of a surprise. He wouldn't have been the usual choice of Revolutionary to start off this type of meeting and then be trusted to run things but then there had to be new people at sometime. The old and trusted revolutionaries were not always available and younger blood had to be introduced. By now the guest speaker was getting into his stride. He had been very well briefed and was able to mention the incident that had taken place at the Food Centre earlier that morning where the Army had destroyed perfectly good food for know reason what so ever. The crowd was growing and seemed to be applauding the speaker. He continued to say how the Army had closed down the Food Centre and prevented the good people of Kentley from buying food for their families whilst the Army still ate in their big canteens. The crowd was getting more and more worked up. It wasn't until Rodney Humpton reached the end of his speech that the crowd had grown to nearly a thousand and the agent spotted another familiar face. It was Martin Saunders. Well in fact he was now known as Jeff Hutton of course but as far as our agent was concerned it was Martin

Saunders.

"Martin 'bloody' Saunders." The agent said a little out loud forgetting the exact situation they were in. A few people turned and stared at the agent but more in the way of saying 'be quiet' than anything else. The agent was actually alone at this time although there were the usual two soldiers from out of the area, very close by waiting to be called in if and when the riot began just in case it got out of control. The agent did have a mobile phone but there was no way it could be used in this crowd to call for Army back up so the agent was left to follow Saunders. Saunders was on the move but the agent was following behind. At this moment, the agent was sure that Saunders was unaware that he had been spotted and wanted to keep it that way but Saunders would keep looking around in case he saw anyone he didn't want to see him. Saunders weaved in and out of the crowd but was obviously making his way to the far side of the junction where he vantage point would be much better.

It was around this time that the speeches were coming to an end and Gary was expected to do his next duty. Whilst Humpton had been talking, Gary had been drinking and he was slow to respond as usual but by now he was being replaced by last minute stand-ins who had been recruited or requested to help during the speech. Another Revolutionary got to the small rostrum and started to shout his support for the guest speaker. The crowd responded with a big cheer and this was what sprung Gary into action. He pushed his way to the rostrum but met against two big guys who were not going to let Gary take the stand anymore. He pushed again but realised it was a useless waste of energy so he put his hands up in the air and started to back away. The two big men relaxed knowing that they had done their job when Gary made a quick dash for the rostrum this time getting one foot on to the top. He pushed the previous speaker down the other side and started to address the crowd immediately.

"Well comrades what a great speech." Gary said holding his fist in triumph. The crowd gave a big cheer and a grin covered Gary's face. The look of triumph was more one of beating the two heavies though.

"Are we going to show the Army what we think of them?" He continued. The crowd gave another big cheer. The Revolutionary local leaders looked at each other and let Gary have his moment. They could not get him down from the rostrum at this very moment without it looking bad.

"Friends and colleagues, it is time we moved on." Gary continued addressing the crowd. A lot of this was in fact as was planned by the leaders they just weren't sure if Gary would carry it out properly.

"As we make our way down Southwall Road, we will shout for fair treatment and free speech". The crowd reacted positively but by now a number of other actions were being put into motion. Firstly the revolutionary leaders were preparing to vacate the area, the idea being not to be caught on camera by any press, not to be in a position to be arrested by the Army and to leave the main demonstrating to the people. Gary had been partly briefed on this. He was told to identify just two houses on Southwall Road that belonged or housed Army personnel and then to get right out of the area. Not surprisingly, Gary had forgotten this element of the plan. The agent was also busy trying to make contact with the two armed soldiers who had been appointed to help in order to get back and arrest Martin Saunders. Lastly the plain clothed Army personnel who were there to keep an eye on developments were hurriedly reporting the latest back to HQ so that Units on standby could get into the right positions to operate and break up the riot if it got out of hand.

Gary had got down from the rostrum and started to push his way through the crowd that had congregated in Southwall Road. He was getting a bit carried away with all the buzz of the crowd and the feeling of being able to lead them where he wanted to. As he pushed through to the other side of the crowd he was in effect leading the riot. He had been told that number 36 was the first house to point out but alas, by the time he had broken through the crowd the other side, he was already up to number 40, Southwall Road. Pointing slightly in the direction of number 36 Gary shouted that this was a house where one of the Army lived.

"That house should be shamed. A member of the Army lives there" he shouted but without mentioning the number or making it fully clear which house he meant.

"Tell them what you think." Gary slurred this sentence aloud.

The crowd roared at about three houses around the area of number 36 and unfortunately the only sort of response came from Mrs. Skinner at number 38. Hearing the noise outside she pulled her curtains closer together so that nobody could look into her house.

"There's a soldier up there now." One of the demonstrators shouted.

"They've probably got a gun," shouted another.

"Let's show them." Two or three said in unison. A brick went through the bedroom window of number 38. A few smaller stones followed to break more windows and the front door was battered by passing fists. Seeing that the crowd was getting a bit out of hand, Gary tried to divert their attention away from what he felt was the wrong house.

"There's another Army person lives down here at number 59." Gary shouted as he ran further down Southwall Road.

Whilst this was going on, messages were getting through to Army HQ as to what exactly was happening at the riot. Within two minutes, two Army land-rovers were approaching the crowd from the far end of Templegate and this was another signal for the crowd to start rushing down Southwall Road. The Army plan was to disperse the crowd out of Southwall Road and push them into the town via Templegate but although Unit Delta 5 had made their move there was a delay on the vital piece of transport getting into Southwall Road. A water cannon had been dispatched to make its way into the other end of Southwall Road but had some trouble getting passed some parked vehicles and so was late. Nevertheless it was soon to turn into Southwall Road and the rushing crowd would have nowhere to go. The agent meanwhile had made contact with the two armed soldiers. They were told exactly where this Martin Saunders was supposed to be but getting to him might prove a little tricky because of the crowd. The main plan was for the Army to try and push demonstrators or rioters out of Southwall Road where certain individuals could be picked out for arrest. The normal Army would not have Martin Saunders down as a target so the agent wanted to get the two armed soldiers in a similar position to the regular Army ready to pick Saunders off when he came through. They found their position quite quickly whilst the agent went back off in search of Saunders. The agent would indicate exactly who to arrest.

Gary by now had realised that his job was done. He was confused as to exactly how he felt. He found himself shouting outside number 59 with the rest of the crowd even though he hadn't previously felt that strong about freedom or justice. It was a bit like he had taken drugs, felt the high of all the emotion but was now coming down to recall that he didn't really feel at home rioting. What if the bosses at the Post Office could see him. He was supposed to be off sick recovering but there was always a chance that his photo might appear in the paper. It was just about this moment when the crowd started to change. The water-cannon vehicle turned into Southwall Road and drove towards the crowd. The targets of the Army houses soon became a forgotten theme and the crowd turned their attentions on the Army soldiers and vehicles that had come to break up the riot. A large proportion of the crowd took very little time to decide that it was time to get out of the way. They ran passed armed soldiers and into Templegate and to the relative safety of the Town Centre. Some made it as far as a small side road off of Southwall Road to run to the south of the town but a core stayed to stand up for their rights. Somebody lit a petrol bomb and threw it towards the water-cannon. Being armoured it had little effect on the vehicle itself but the fact that a bomb had been thrown meant that the Army stepped up their operations. The Lieutenant in charge of this operation asked for immediate back up of Units for both the roadblock on the south part of Templegate and another to back up the water-cannon. The Units were already on their way, just waiting for instructions as to where to go. The Lieutenant also gave instructions to shoot if necessary. Shoot to wound if possible. As some more of the crowd ran to the junction of Southwall Road and Templegate a mass of them turned right before realising they had run slap bang into the Army road-block. The front runners stopped but from behind a number of rocks and stones came hurtling towards the soldiers. A number of shots fired out above their heads and the crowd turned to run up the north part of Templegate. During this, some shots were fired at the Army themselves. It wasn't clear where they had come from but they were accurate shots and two soldiers received wounds. New instructions were about to be issued.

The agent meanwhile had got back onto Southwall Road and fortunately located Martin Saunders again. He was standing at the back watching everything that was going on around him but not looking like being in a position to make a move himself. It was almost as if he was enjoying seeing all the demonstrating and wanted to get a full portion of it all. The agent was careful enough to act like one of the crowd but with panic setting in this was getting harder to do. One minute the crowd was rushing one way and next the opposite way. In an effort to avoid the pushing of the crowd the agent made it to the opposite side of the street to Martin Saunders. Standing against the wall the agent turned to see if Saunders was still there only to meet his glare from across the street. Almost immediately, Jeff Hutton knew he had to get out of the way. Whilst the agent was watching, Saunders took out his gun and checked that it was loaded and then put it back into another pocket. He was on the move. He moved down Southwall Road to start with and the agent followed from the other side of the road. Both kept out of the rushing crowd knowing that it would be difficult to tread one's own path if they ventured in. Having moved about fifty yards from the junction, Saunders looked up at where the water-cannon had got to. Already it was firing on to some of the crowd and knocking them off their feet. This was the last thing he wanted and the time had come to get into the crowd. He jumped in about three body widths and the crowd took him back towards the junction of Southwall Road and Templegate. The agent stayed out of the crowd and ran as much as possible along the far wall to keep up with Saunders. A number of the crowd had also taken refuge against the wall which made running difficult and keeping an eye on Saunders whilst doing so even more difficult. As the crowd approached Templegate, the automatic push had ceased and there was a mixture people standing still, facing the Army and running left up Templegate. The agent got to the two armed soldiers and indicated that Saunders had almost definitely turned left. The three of them went a little way to look for him but no sign could be seen.

Jeff Hutton breathed a sigh of relief as he watched the passing crowd from his position of relative safety, looking out through the upstairs bedroom window of a safe house on Templegate. That was a close one, he thought to himself.

Gary by now had been knocked over by the water-cannon. He had knocked his head against the brick wall of a nearby house as he had done so and was feeling rather groggy at the moment. Despite the wet, he had slumped himself down against the wall in an effort to try and recover. Not only was Gary feeling the effects of his drunkenness but also the pains of his ankle, jaw and back were killing him at the moment. A number of others were also laying on the floor, unable to get up again after being forced down by the water-cannon. There were still a number of demonstrators running about though.

The Lieutenant gave his instructions to advance nearer to

Southwall Road. They had been happy to just be a deterrent in forcing the crowd away but having been shot at they were content no longer. As the Army moved forward slowly, another few shots rang out and another soldier went down. The response was almost immediate as the Army opened fire on the crowd. They were shooting at no targets in particular as nobody could see where the shots had come from but three of the crowd went down from this first volley. All wounds were at leg level. The Army inched nearer to the junction of Southwall Road. As they passed the building line of Southwall Road, another couple of shots were fired at the Army. A second volley was returned and another couple of the crowd fell.

"Cease fire!" The Lieutenant shouted.

"We have four down Sir." One of the Sergeants shouted.

"Can anyone see exactly where the shots have come from?" The Lieutenant continued.

"No idea here Sir," came the reply. It was what the Lieutenant had feared. Sniper shooting and a number of the general public shot in retaliation.

"No more shooting until we identify targets," was his final order. The crowd by now had almost dispersed completely. There were still the odd few trying to throw stones at the water-cannon and a number of demonstrators down injured on the ground but the basic riot was at and end. The people left on the streets stood and waited to see what the Army would do next. The Lieutenant had his instructions to get things cleared up and back to normal as soon as possible so he arranged for two lorries to be on stand-by to take arrested civilians back to HQ. The agent turned up with the two armed soldiers and approached the Lieutenant. He was a little confused to see a civilian approach him like this but as soon as the 'I' badge had been flashed he understood the situation.

"Firstly get one of your men to arrest that dark haired man over there in the blue checked coat." The agent pointed to a man trying to sneak around the corner and into Templegate who the agent recognised as one of the organisers.

"Will do Sergeant," the Lieutenant replied. "Is there anything else?"

"Yes. Permission to take one of your jeeps Lieutenant," the agent said.

"We can get you out of here in a lorry." He replied.

"No you don't understand. I'm looking to arrest a suspect and I need to move quickly," the agent replied.

"Yes okay Sergeant. Take that one there." He pointed to a free jeep. The agent and the two soldiers got in it and drove down Southwall Road towards the water-cannon which had stopped its firing by now. The two armed soldiers were under the impression that they were still looking for Saunders but the agent called a halt as the jeep approached the water-cannon. Pointing to a slumped body on the side the agent ordered,

"Get that man in the jeep."

"Is this Saunders?" One of the soldiers asked.

"Of course not, just get him in," the agent replied. Once Gary had been put in the back, the jeep continued on its way. Both the soldiers recognised the man immediately as the man from the Food Centre. They were both impressed as to how quickly the agent had seen this man in Southwall Road. They weren't quite as impressed though when after just a couple of minutes they were ordered to offload him into the doorway of a deserted and shut down shop but then they are trained to follow orders and not ask questions of senior staff. Gary was by now in a bit of a mess.

"We'll have another quick run round the area to see if I can see Saunders," the agent said to the two soldiers as they drove away from the shop. Gary was now safely out of the way left to sleep it off. The agent and the two soldiers spent another twenty minutes driving around but no sign could be seen of Saunders. They all returned to Army HQ. The Lieutenant waited until things had calmed down a little bit and then went around arresting the remaining demonstrators who were laying about on the road in Southwall Road. Those still walking and trying to get to the relative safety of the Town Centre were searched for weapons, identities noted but then allowed to proceed home. The demonstration is finally at an end. The clearing up process has started.

-

Meanwhile, back in the safety of his new little cottage in Bateley, Jeff Hutton is at home sat in front of his fire enjoying a little sip of brandy and taking it nice and easy. Just in case he had set a temporary alarm system up around the house so that if anyone were to break in whilst he was asleep, he would know. In the next few days, he would be preparing a number of safety devices all around the cottage, both inside and out but he was happy to make do with the makeshift one for now. Looking back on the events of his day he concludes that it was a close one today. I'll have to be more careful in future he thinks to himself.

-

Gary wasn't quite sure where he was. He could hear no noise but felt that he was crouched down as if he was hiding or taking cover from something. He tried to open his eyes, the right one in particular giving him trouble. He couldn't make much out and it was difficult to work out whether it was because he couldn't use his right eye properly or if it was the effects of the alcohol he had consumed that day. Probably a bit of both he thought. His head was spinning and he felt the bump and cut on the top of his head which he must have received when he hit the wall. Gary tried again to look around but all he could make out were some parked cars and a few people in uniform moving around. Gary started to lose consciousness. The cars seemed to be parked in a line and the soldiers seemed to be running after someone. It was the blond woman again. Gary could see her trying to climb over the fence. She turned and looked at Gary but said nothing this time, she just looked at him. Gary heard some gunfire and the blond woman convulsed in front of the fence like a disco dancer with St. Vitus' dance. There were no wounds but she moved and jerked to every shot that Gary heard. Eventually there was the final shot from the soldier right in front of her and the wound ripped through her stomach. All the while that this was going on she never took her eyes off of Gary. Nothing was said and the scene was disappearing bit by bit. Gary collapsed.

It was a number of hours later that Gary started to regain his senses. The first rays of sunlight were starting to take a grip on the receding night sky and dawn was swiftly upon us. Gary felt the cold as he began to get some feeling in his body. It wasn't the coldest of nights but the alcohol had done its work and brought his body temperature down to well below normal body heat and he felt every bit of cold like it was kicking him in the ribs. Gary shivered and then pulled his arms around himself a lot harder to try and warm up. This only hurt more as the aches and pains in his body took their turn in causing problems. Gary tried to recall exactly what had happened to him in the last few hours. He remembered leaving home and getting a bus into town. He remembered walking the streets and handing out leaflets. He remembered going to the pub. He remembered standing up on the rostrum looking at the large crowd gathering for the rally. He couldn't remember much else. There was a vague recollection of people rioting in the streets but Gary wasn't really sure if this was fact or fiction. Gary didn't know where he was let alone how he'd got there. He was cold, tired and dirty. For some reason that he couldn't figure out, his clothes seemed to be fairly damp. Perhaps it was the early morning dew. Perhaps there was a leaking gutter he had slept under. Gary had no idea really. He got up and walked around surveying the area he had found himself to sleep in last night. He was impressed with his choice as it was apparently unused, quiet and hidden from general sight. It looked a little familiar though. The building had a doorway that was permanently open but Gary still thought he should know exactly where he was. He tried hard to work it out. He guessed that he would eventually have to get up and walk round the place to see exactly where he was but at this precise moment, walking was the last thing he wanted to do. He thought some more. It was no good. He was going to have to get up. This wasn't as easy as first believed but after a few attempts he made it to his feet. The effort or the rush of blood sent Gary spinning but he kept on his feet with the aid of some wooden crates. Gary took a few steps and it came to him where he had spent the night. He was at the back of Paiges, the shop where he first gone to revolutionary meetings. The place where he had searched for his brother David! The place where he had first met Angela! The place where he had fallen in love! Gary started to think about Angela. More memories of the people throwing stones and rocks at the houses were beginning to come back to him. He could also remember soldiers in the streets. He looked around at the old shop.

    Gary wasn't quite sure how long he'd been in the shop but guessed he'd made his way there after the riot and sat down to have a sleep. As he got himself back on his feet he felt the large bump on the back of his head and wondered how he'd got that. He couldn't remember. At that moment his only thought was that he wanted to have another drink so he walked to a little place he knew that made its' own vodka. It was a little house on Reed Street where two brothers had mastered the art of making very strong vodka out of potatoes and grain. It was a very strong concoction but Gary had tried some before and knew what to expect. He paid his money and walked off with his lemonade bottle full of the home-made vodka. As he walked back to the town centre he swigged at the bottle and it was almost half empty by the time he made it down to King's Bridge. Gary was actually beginning to feel a bit sick so he bent over the river wall and gave an almighty wretch which caused a pain that he could feel all the way back to his stomach. Gary didn't bring up very much apart from some small quantity of colourless bile. Gary hadn't eaten for a while so there wasn't really anything for him to bring up but it didn't stop him from going through the motions of being sick another two or three times. The force of his involuntary action had left him with a feeling like he had pulled a muscle in his stomach. It was another five minutes before he was able to sit back down properly as he clung on to the railings. When he finally made it safely to the ground, he found himself with that awful sickly taste in his mouth and throat and the feeling of having been beaten up in his stomach. Gary took another swig of the vodka to try and get rid of the taste in his mouth but it only made him feel sick again and Gary went through the same routine again until he passed out altogether and dropped to the floor.

Perhaps fortunately, but perhaps not, two soldiers had been watching Gary from the other side of the river and they drove round to see what had become of him.
"He is totally out of it," said the first soldier.
"Stick him in the back," the second suggested. They put Gary into the back of the jeep and took him to the Army prison. Throughout all of this, Gary had lost consciousness and it was the next day before he came round. It took a while for Gary to start taking notice of exactly where he was. The immediate thing was the coldness of his surroundings and his urgent need for some vodka. His eyes were having trouble focusing but this was not a great concern. Gary knew that in time he would be able to see exactly where he was but his immediate concern was for some sort of drink. Vodka, Whiskey anything would have done. As he sat up a little he searched his pockets for the small bottle of vodka he was sure was there but he found absolutely nothing. Inside pockets, outside pockets, the area around him were all searched meticulously with his hands but to no avail. He just couldn't find that bottle. His next move meant that Gary needed to get his eyes working. They were tired and throbbing. The feeling was like the veins on the back of his eyes were hitting his actual eyeballs and giving him great pain. Fortunately the place he was in was dark and there was no brightness to cause him even further

pain as he got his eyes open. He struggled to his feet and looked around.

He was in a small cell. He guessed it was a cell like the one the revolutionary leaders had put him in before but this time there were a few more luxuries in it, like a little bit of light from a dim light bulb some ten feet above his head, a bench that he could sit on and a bowl with some water in it. Gary crawled over to the bowl to give it a closer look and was pleased to find that it seemed to contain proper water. He knelt down at the bowl and cupped his hands so he could refresh his face a little. The water was freezing cold but it was refreshing and brought him round a little bit more. He cupped his hands a second time but the cold water made him feel even colder than he was before so twice was enough. There was a noise. Clink. A shutter in the cell door drew back and a pair of eyes looked in. A larger clanking sound suggested that the door was being unlocked and indeed it opened to allow in a bit more light and Gary could see two uniformed soldiers outside the cell door.
"Come on then you old git," one of the soldiers said as he stood holding the cell door open. The other soldier just laughed. Gary got to his feet slowly and walked towards the door. "Come on we ain't got all day." The second soldier pulled Gary through the door and kicked him hard on the left cheek of his bum. Gary stumbled but kept on his feet.
"You bloody tramps ought to be taken out and shot." The second soldier shouted into Gary's ear.
"Leave him Mikey. Let's just get him down there." The first soldier locked the cell door as he spoke to his colleague and the three of them walked down a corridor to another room where Gary was pushed into. This room was quite bright and the pain of the reflection from a number of white and silver items around the room caused more pain on Gary's eyes. The two soldiers left him there and within seconds a man in a white coat entered the room.
"Sit down." The order was short, sharp and to the point. Gary sat on the only chair in the room whilst the man put down the clipboard he had been holding on the desk and took a pen from his top pocket.

Gary guessed he was a doctor as he had a stethoscope around his neck and the normal abruptness of a doctor. "What is your name?" The doctor asked as he studied the sheet on his clipboard.

"I don't know?" Gary replied almost without thinking. He knew fair well who he was but in the position he was in, all he wanted to do was get out of the place and back home without anyone in authority finding out he had ever been there. Gary started to think of some of his happier days with Angela. Days when they would spend warm summer afternoons in the garden. It gave Gary a warm feeling inside.
"Where do you live?" The sudden nature of this next question caught Gary unprepared.
"Waydon." He answered quickly.
"Where in Waydon?" The doctor followed up immediately. Gary took a bit more time.
"I don't know where. Just Waydon." The doctor wrote a couple of things on his sheet whilst Gary thought about where he could get some drink. Hospitals had made him think of the smell of alcohol and it reminded him that he badly needed a drink. His stomach was crying out almost. Gary started to think back to his garden. The flowers and the vegetables.
"Open your mouth." Gary opened his mouth and the doctor examined his teeth and tongue. He looked in his ears and then turned on a lamp that was on the desk and looked in his eyes. "Open your shirt". The whole examination was done with military precision. The doctor listened to Gary breathing and then wrote some more things on the sheet.
"Am I ill?" Gary asked. The doctor looked at him out of the corner of his eye but continued writing. He never answered. A soldier entered the room.
"Yes, he can go." The doctor said without any real acknowledgement of either the soldier or Gary. He handed the clipboard to the soldier and the soldier took Gary by the arm and led him further down the corridor. Gary was a bit surprised that the doctor had not given him a better examination. His ankle was still bandaged and giving him a little bit of pain and he thought that the doctor would have seen him limp and taken a look. He didn't.

    At the bottom the corridor turned to the left and Gary could hear the far off murmuring of voices. The corridor led into a large square area where there was a sort of desk with another uniformed soldier sat behind it. The soldier who had led Gary to the desk pushed him to the opposite side of the desk and handed the clipboard to the soldier behind the desk.

"Number 475109, sir." The soldier clicked his heels as he said the last word.

"And the doctor has said?"

"He's okay, sir." The soldier gave a salute, turned and clicked his heels again and then marched off down another corridor. Gary looked around to see another three men sitting on chairs against a wall.

"Right 475109, go and sit down over there." The soldier indicated slightly towards the other three men and Gary went over to them and sat down. They were all quite smelly and looked like they should have died a few years ago. It never really dawned on him that Gary might also be smelling a bit. As he thought about it he remembered that he hadn't actually washed for a few days. His mind wandered back to his garden and this time thoughts of Sammy Playing about with a ball. It suddenly struck him that Sammy might be locked in the house. He hoped that Sarah might have looked in and fed him and with that thought his mind turned to drink again. He looked at the bloke next to him who seemed to have a bottle poking out of his pocket.

"Any chance of a swig of your bottle friend?" Gary said quietly.

"Fuck off!" The man said in a slurred style. Gary couldn't actually hear the words exactly but he got the message.

"Go on. Just a little drop." Gary was desperate.

"Kiss my arse," was the reply, this time a little clearer.

"Listen up 475109." The soldier behind the desk barked. Gary wasn't sure if that was his number or not but he listened just in case. "You have refused to give us your name and address. You are not obliged to but if you refuse you will be given the customary two weeks imprisonment for vagrancy. 475109 do you hear me." The soldier looked over to all of the men sitting against the wall.

"Give him your name if you can remember it." The man sat next to Gary said in a croaky old voice. "You won't get no vodka in there." He continued. Gary was in a quandary. He didn't want his identification known to the authorities but he didn't want to spend two weeks in this place.

"I take that as a no. Sergeant Russell, take him away please." A young looking lad came and grabbed at Gary's arm again and led him to the top of a small flight of steps. At the bottom of the steps there was a wooden locked door and a mop and bucket. The soldier unlocked the door and behind it was darkness.

"Mind the steps," he said as he pushed Gary into the dark. The smell was overwhelming and he started to gag. It stank of shit and urine in the main but there was a lot more to it than that. Gary was at the top of what looked like four small steps. He couldn't make them out properly firstly because of his poor eyesight and also the lack of light inside the place he was now in. The motion of retching forced Gary forward and his immediate reaction was to reach out and grab hold of something to steady himself before taking any further steps forward but his right hand grabbed at fresh air and his left hand just brushed against something cold and wet. It was in fact a wall which was sweating or at least covered in an oily grease. Gary automatically smelt his hand and he was nearly sick. The heaving felled Gary to his knees but he was unable to stay in that position as the floor he was on was also covered in a sodden type film.

    Gary slowly went down the four steps to a small flat landing at the top of a sloped walkway where he stopped. It was very dark but not completely dark. There was evidence of some sort of light coming in from the outside over in the distance about thirty yards away. You could just about make out the overall shape of the room Gary now found himself in. The smell was dreadful and Gary wondered if he would suffocate because of the apparent lack of fresh air. He held his stomach as he went through the usual vomiting motion but of course nothing ever spewed out. It was painful.

    Gary decided he would have to make his way further into the room as he was faintly aware that other people were looking at him. He couldn't see them looking but he sensed it. The sloped path had a railing that forced you to turn left and walk down it. There was a bundle of cloths on the pathway which turned out to be a couple of other prisoners who were laying down trying to sleep. As Gary kicked the first one, it moved and hit out at him, catching him just under the knee. Gary stumbled and slipped down the slippery slope as other bundles kicked and punched at him forcing him further down the slope. Gary wanted to get to the bottom and out of the way but as he reached it, he was in for a shock. The floor was not just damp but covered in a sort of thin film of liquid. Every step was on a moist texture. The smell was even worse. Gary looked and saw that this floor was apparently the lowest level of the prison. There were various ledges at different heights but most were occupied by bundles, Gary assumed they were people, some alive, some not quite so alive. The walls were still damp and drips were dropping from various points of the roof. As Gary slowly picked his way across the floor, his feet stuck to the floor because of the thickening quality of the liquid that could be found on the floor. Gary could only guess what it consisted of. The sound of breathing could be heard from all over the prison and it gave the room a terrifying sort of atmosphere. Gary imagined it to be the resting place of dead people on their way to hell.

     The stench was getting worse and Gary was alarmed to find he had just walked into another prisoner who was in the process of emptying his bowels right there on the prison floor. A lump fell on Gary's boot. Gary quickened his step as the prisoner behind him pulled up his trousers again but it wasn't easy to move that quickly. His eyes were gradually adjusting to the dark and Gary saw a small place up on a high ledge that seemed empty. He clambered up and sat down trying to make himself a little more comfortable. A prisoner came over to him.
"Have you got any drink then?"
"No I haven't." Gary said.
"No I haven't." The prisoner repeated taking the micky out of Garys' somewhat posh accent. He shook his head as he said it and two other prisoners came over to see what was going on.
"I bet you've got some in those pockets of yours." The prisoner said to him in a very aggressive way.
"Honest, I haven't."
"Honest I haven't." Again his reply was mocked. "We don't bloody believe you do we?"
"No." The reply came from the other two prisoners who moved in to search Gary. He used all the strength he could muster to hold off the first prisoner but was soon overcome by the other two. The first prisoner grabbed hold of Gary's throat. His hands were covered in filth and slime and smelt of the same general stench.
"I've been here nearly a month and I know when someone has drink with 'em." One of the others kicked Gary in the side and soon all three had been through all of his pockets. They soon departed, satisfied Gary had no drink on him.
Gary sat again for a while, keeping his eyes peeled in case anyone wanted to come and attack him again. He would make sure he got in first next time. After a few hours, everyone seemed to have quietened down a bit and all were asleep or trying to rest. Gary was in great pain. On top of everything else his ribs were beginning to feel sore

from the periodic retching he had been forced to do. He wanted fresh air. He wanted a drink. He was tired. He fell asleep.

Gary was woken by the sound of the loud clunk which turned out to be the unlocking of the door. For a while Gary had almost been able to relax in his new surroundings but having woken again the smell caused him further pain.
"Come and get it," was the shout as two large wooden containers were dumped at the bottom of the small flight of steps. There was a scramble for the contents of the containers but Gary was in two minds whether or not to go and have a look and see what there was. The prisoners who had positioned them selves on the slope were the first to the containers and got first pickings. A voice talked to Gary.
"You need to eat my friend if you're going to survive in here. There isn't much but there is some bread and meat and some water. Take what you can and bring it back. Don't drink the alcohol." The voice spoke softly as he went on his way towards the slope. There was a small fight breaking out at the bottom of the slope as two prisoners fought over a piece of meat that had been dropped on the floor. Gary followed the softly spoken prisoner towards the slope. The liquid on the floor had risen a bit since Gary last traversed it and he could feel his trousers soaking up the residue as he walked through it. The friendly prisoner walked to the top of the slope and quickly picked out some bread and meat and then grabbed a container that seemed to contain water. He turned and although he wore a dark cloak that covered almost the whole of his body he sensed Gary right behind him and he indicated towards the containers inviting Gary to pick from them. There were about a dozen pieces of roughly broken bread and some small pieces of meat. The meat didn't smell that good and it wasn't possible to tell exactly what sort of animal it had come from. Gary took a piece of bread. It was hard and seemingly stale. He then reached for the other container which held bottles of water. There were only about three left. Gary grabbed one. There was a movement to Gary's left and it seemed like the prisoner who had accosted him the night before who knocked the bottle from his hand.
"You don't deserve any water. You haven't been here long enough. Get in line." The prisoner said in his croaky voice. The bottle was knocked from Gary's hand and back into the large container. The prisoner took hold of it knocking Gary back in the process. Almost immediately and swiftly but without rushing, the dark cloaked prisoner

moved towards the croaky voiced prisoner and with a show of strength his hand appeared from under his cloak. He took hold of the croaky prisoners arm and it was as if the whole of the prison knew that they were being told off. The hand was strong. The arm was firm. Above all, both hand and arm were clean. Gary stared at what was happening before him. It was as if this prisoner had just stepped out of the bath. "That water is for you." The voice was again soft but forceful. Gary knew he should take the water. He did and scurried back down the slope and back to his place on the ledge.

Some of the prisoners had also managed to get themselves some bottles of alcohol. One of the tramps who had earlier been on the lower part of the slope had moved to the ledge next to where Gary had previously settled. As Gary returned the prisoner looked up at him through his bearded face. A pair of eyes stared into space. There was a hint of death in the look for a second before he spoke.
"I will look after you. Here have a drink." The prisoner offered Gary a swig from his bottle. Gary drank a drop and it burnt his throat as it went down. It was more like methylated spirit than anything else and had a greasy texture as it swam down Gary's throat.
"I suggest you don't drink anymore my friend. It will cause you more pain later if you do drink it." The man with the dark cloak spoke to Gary as he drifted back passed him and away into a dark corner. Gary handed the bottle back to his new companion and then settled himself back onto the ledge. He ate the bread slowly and then drank the water. His new colleague just drank the bottle of meths before coughing and then finally being sick all over Gary's coat. Gary turned his head away as the smell was more like the devils breath than anything else that Gary had ever smelly before. The new companion grabbed at Gary's arm and Gary turned to face him but the smell of his breath was too much for Gary to bear. His eyes watered and he began to feel his own body get ready to be sick. He fought against it for a few seconds but was unable to prevent himself from bringing up some newly eaten bread.

The doors opened again and two uniformed soldiers stood at the door whilst two others in boiler suits came in and removed the two large containers. They were gone a matter of seconds before they were back with a large torch. They ventured down the slope, kicking at the bundles on the way. They shone the torch around and Gary shielded his eyes as they shone it on him. The beam was strong and it hurt his eyes. The torch had remained on a bundle in the far corner. The two men in boiler suits went over and kicked the bundle. It just tipped over. They kicked it again. The prisoner was obviously dead. They just picked the bundle up with their heavily gloved hands and carried it out through the door. They were back again after a few minutes with a hose pipe. The floor of the prison was hosed down and some of the prisoners took the opportunity of using the clean floor to urinate on or squat and shit in a cosy corner. Within an hour or so, the floor was again covered in most areas. The soldiers used the mop and bucket to disinfect the steps and the landing before shutting the door and locking it again. This routine was followed for the next couple of days.

      Gary did not eat the next day but tried to sleep through most of it. On the third day he made sure he got to the top of the slope first and grabbed two bottles of water. There was again a small scuffle over the containers but all stepped aside as the prisoner in the dark cloak approached. Gary waited for him to return to the other side of the prison and spoke to him.
"How long have you been in here?"
"I'm near the end of my last week. I will be called in a couple of days. You will have to keep strong. Nobody leaves for a couple of weeks unless they are carried out. When I go, you must eat and drink to keep yourself strong and then get out of here and don't return." The soft voice spoke as if he knew Gary.
"Why are you here?"
"A number of reasons my friend. Why are you here?" He turned the question on Gary. Gary thought before replying.
"Yes I suppose also a number of reasons but I can't really remember why now."
"No, none of us can." The voice was gone. Gary slept again.

      It was probably a couple of days later that Gary woke and all of a sudden realised that he hadn't noticed the acrid smell anymore. Had the smell gone he wondered. It hadn't. After the mornings routine the door opened again and a uniformed soldier entered and walked down to the top landing. He looked at his piece of paper and started to hail his message.

"Prisoner 3258......" the message faltered and finally stopped as the prisoner in the dark cloak walked towards the slope. It was as if even the soldiers were in awe of this man. He was elegant in his walking and seemed as strong as anyone as he swept passed the soldier and out through the door.
"Er prisoner 325887 is called forward..." The soldier tried to carry on with his message but he was having difficulty. Gary watched the prisoner in the dark cloak as he stopped momentarily at the prison door. It was almost in some sort of farewell gesture but a very brief one. The prisoner was gone.
"...is called forward for release." The soldier finished his message, turned and went back out of the door slamming the bolts behind him. Gary's soul sank in the thought that he had over a week to spend in this place. He had not drunk anything else other than water after that first day. He had found that the meths burnt and he had also been offered some other liquid which may well have been urine for all Gary knew. The smell of meths mixed with the sick, the shit and the urine was hard to suffer but Gary just had to. Gary's thoughts were interrupted by the sound of the prison door opening again. The same soldier came to the landing and started to read out his next message.
"Prisoner 475...." Gary thought how lucky it was for some other bastard to be getting out. "...109 is called forward for release." The soldier read his message but nothing seemed to happen. Gary guessed that the prisoner in question might not have been as lucky as he'd first thought as he may well be laying dead on the day of his release. "Prisoner 475109 is called forward for release." The soldier repeated his message. Gary suddenly realised he recognised the number. "Prisoner 475109......" Again the soldier started to repeat his message. Gary jumped to his feet. "I'm here, I'm coming." Gary couldn't understand.

Gary was taken to the registration desk where the same soldier was again sat behind the desk. He handed Gary a form.
"You have been given an early release order. You are very lucky." The soldier pointed to a door which another soldier opened and Gary was free.

Gary had no money. He guessed that it had been taken from him or stolen but the result was he had no way of getting home except to walk. It would take a few hours but that didn't put Gary off and he started out to make his way to the Bateley Road. He searched around in his coat pockets to find that he still had his identification card and his residents' card on him. That was a bonus he thought to himself. Even better still, he felt in his trouser pocket to find that he actually had his house key as well. He seemed to have lost a few days and he was trying hard to think back to what had happened to him since the riot in Southwall Road. In fact he was trying to work out how he had got out of Southwall Road. There was quite a lot that Gary couldn't remember but unfortunately what he couldn't forget was the terrible place he had just left, the prison.

Gary had his coat on as he set out but it stank of sick and alcohol amongst other things. It was quite strange for Gary but although he could breath the fresh air if he breathed in the fumes of his coat too much he started to feel sick again. He took his coat off and looked at it. It was covered in stains of various shades and colours. Gary went through the pockets and kept all the papers and things he needed before rolling the coat up in a ball and hiding it behind a fence. Someone will find it and burn it for me, Gary thought to himself. The next problem was his trousers. They were not only covered in old sick but were wet from the urine in which Gary had been forced to lie around in. He found a wire fence with a loose wire and ripped the legs of his trousers so that they turned into shorts. He might have looked a bit strange but at least he smelt a bit better. A shower was just what Gary needed but he had a long way to go yet before that was possible. Another four and a half miles in fact until he got home to Waydon.

As Gary started to eat up the miles the light began to fall. Gary had calculated that he had about two more hours of daylight left which should have been enough for him to finish his long trek. His ankle was still not completely correct and as he went on it gave him more and more pain. Gary couldn't run the risk of sitting down and resting. He was certain that if he did he would not be able to get up again and continue so he persevered without stopping. The Waydon turn-off was now in sight. This gave Gary a new option which he took. The main road had just fields to either side of it so he could walk across a field and possibly save himself a quarter of a mile. It made the walking a lot harder but he did it. Now the Waydon village sign was in view. He was almost home. He's made it.

Gary got to his front door almost ready to drop. His ankle had started to bleed again and was giving him a lot of pain but his whole body was in such a state that it all ached and helped him to forget how painful his ankle really was. As he unlocked the front door Gary had a bit of a surprise as Angela was there waiting for him. He almost fell in through the door.
"Are you alright?" Angela said anxiously.
"Now I'm home I am." Gary replied. "What are you doing here?"
"I've come back to ask to move back in." Angela said.
"Oh." Gary was dumbfounded.
"That's if it's okay to move back in?" Angela said waiting for Gary to respond.
"Of course it's okay. This is your home." Angela ran up to him and gave him a hug. She stepped back and looked him up and down and gave him a big kiss. "Phoar!!! What is that stink?" Angela finally asked.
"It's a long story. I'll tell you if you want to know but not now. I need a wash or a bath." Gary replied as the girls came out to see him.
"Hello Daddy." Katy was the first to say something.
"Hello Katy darling. It's good to see you back home." Gary replied. Katy smiled and went back into the living room. Joan then appeared.
"Hello Dad," she said. "You're not drunk are you?"
"No I'm not drunk." Gary said as he shook his head and gave a little smile.
"And is your eye better?" Joan continued.
"Yes it's a lot better thank you but I still have to be very careful." He turned to Angela, "Are you back to stay?"
"Probably," she replied. "A lot of it is up to you. We need to talk but have your bath first." Angela said. Gary went up and had his bath but instead of coming straight back down sat and then lay down on the bed. Within a couple of minutes he was asleep. Angela came up to see what he was doing and smiled as she saw him sleeping on top of the bed. Talking can wait she thought as she tucked him in.

-

Back at Army H.Q. the small detail of Unit Tango 7 soldiers were just returning from a special tour down to the south coast. There were four of them altogether in the group. Private William Taylor started to sign off his forms hoping that he could leave straightaway for home.

"Private Taylor." His Corporal barked out.

"Yes Sir."

"Attendance form!"

"Here we are Sir. All completed." Private Taylor looked hopeful. "Is everything okay, Sir?"

"Yes. Dismissed." The Corporal saluted the Private and it was returned. "Taylor, you live on Southwall Road don't you?"

"Yes Sir." The Private replied wondering why he was being asked such a question.

"Please report to the Comms room before you go." The Corporal clicked his heels. Turned and marched off out of the locker room. Private Taylor had all of his bags ready and as he now had a few days off was keen to get away. He made for the Comms room, knocked and entered. As he went in there was a Major waiting for him.

"Hello. Taylor isn't it?" The Major looked briefly at the sheet of paper in his hand.

"Yes Sir."

"I'm afraid I have to tell you that there has been a little bit of trouble in town and there was a riot on Southwall Road." The Major paused.

"Oh bloody hell!!" Private William Taylor wondered what was going to come next.

"No real great problems but your house was one of the targets and it has been bombarded by rocks and stones but everyone would seem to be alright." The Major moved over to the Private and laid his hand on his shoulder as he said it.

"My Mum!"

"Yes she's alright. A bit shaken but okay. We have an armed Unit on duty in the street whilst the windows are being fixed." The Major gave him the news.

"Broken windows!" William didn't know what to say.

"Just wanted you to know before you got back home. Now be on your way. Give your Mother my apologies." The Major coughed. William Taylor picked up his bag and made his way hurriedly down to the gate. One of the Army chef's came out to see him.

"Billy. I've heard about your house. Here, take this lot and let your Mum have it." The chef gave him a big black plastic bag. It was full of fresh steaks, joints of meat and a couple of separately wrapped cooked chickens. On top was a big box of chocolates.

Chapter 13 - AS IT USED TO BE

Angela and the girls had been back three days now and Gary had at last managed to catch up on some of the sleep he had lost. Angela did still have that one worry but she had purposely placed a bottle of vodka and a bottle of whiskey in the living room and not a drop had been touched in the three days. She hadn't just placed them slap bang in the middle so that they could be seen as this would only make things worse. She knew where they were and Gary would have been able to find them without too much trouble if he had really wanted to have a drink. She was reasonably happy that Gary was trying to give it up.
"I'm very pleased with you." Angela said as she came into the living room to see Gary.
"Why what have I done?" Gary replied.
"You haven't had anything to drink, alcoholic wise, since you've been back and that's very good." Angela congratulated him. Gary smiled and gave a little laugh.
"There's a lot more to it than that." Gary sighed and sat forward. "You just don't have a clue what sort of things I've been up to in the last few weeks." Angela sat down next to him on the settee. She placed her hand over Gary's mouth.
"I don't need to know anything about what happened to you, that's all in the past now. What matters is what you are going to do from now on," she said with the authority of a teacher.
"Don't worry. I won't be drinking for a long while." Angela bent forward and gave Gary a big kiss. He put his arms around her and responded appropriately.
"I love you Gary Newson." Angela said.
"I love you too." Gary replied.
"I know you do." Angela laughed before giving Gary another kiss.

Gary was surprised what difference a couple of days in a hell hole could make but it had helped him turn the corner. He recalled when he first got there he felt that he was made to drink until he felt sick but then perhaps that was just his imagination. Gary tried to remember as much as he could but everytime he did all that would happen would be the thought of drinking the horrible meths type liquid he was offered and this started to make him feel sick almost immediately. Whatever happened he seemed to have been cured. He didn't want to drink again at the moment. After everything that had happened to him in the last few weeks he was very pleased to be back to his normal self and tomorrow he would be returning to work to take on his old duties. Looking back on the last couple of months, he was very annoyed at the way he had got so deeply involved with the revolutionaries of Kentley. He might have even handled the old PM bloke a bit differently had he been thinking straight but he promised himself that there was no way he would ever go down that path again. Angela had been right, he had put her and the family at risk and he could see that now. So much had happened, and all at the same time. All at the wrong time. He hadn't been strong enough to cope with it all. He felt compelled to let Angela know some of what had been going on.

"Aren't you the slightest bit interested in what got me into the state I was in?" Gary asked Angela.

"Yes I'm interested but don't think that now is the time to be told." She replied.

"How do you mean."

"Let's enjoy each others' company again for a while." Angela said.

"You mean like we're dating again?"

"Yes, and getting to know one another. We've both changed since those days long ago and we've grown up slightly differently. I need to get to know the new you." Angela said seriously. Gary scratched his head trying to get his mind round the idea but then thought that it could be quite exciting. It would be a bit like going out with someone completely new.

"And I've got to get to know the new you?" Gary finally replied.

"Yes that's right. The only bit of cheating is that eventually we find out that we both share a lot of the same history. Have the same happy memories and even better, are both related to the same lovely two children." Angela finished.

"We can't go wrong then can we?" Gary said quietly.

"Well let's not push our luck. No hopefully not. As we get stronger, you can then tell me some of your horrible experiences of the recent past."

"Okay!" Gary agreed. The two kissed again and the girls gave both of their parents a great big hug.

"It's good to be a family again Mum." Joan whispered in her ear.

"Yes I know what you mean darling." Angela replied.

Sammy the dog was not going to be left out and he ran around the living room jumping up and down and wagging his tail whilst barking. It was almost as if he had understood every word of what had been said over the last few minutes and he was agreeing with them all.

"I suppose you want to go for a walk?" Gary said to Sammy.

Sammy barked again almost as if he was answering.

"I'll tell you what." Angela said. "We'll all take Sammy for a walk." Everyone was happy with that solution.

-

The next morning was a very important one for Gary. He was up at his usual time of six fifteen but this morning Angela was up with him to help him get dressed properly, pick out just the right tie and to set him off with as much confidence as was needed by a new boy starting work for the very first time. Gary hadn't actually been off that long but both Gary and Angela guessed that people at work had also noticed that Gary had not been himself for a few weeks and that today signified the beginning of a brand new era for him.

"You don't need to get up." Gary said.

"Oh yes I do." Angela replied. "I need to make sure that my man goes to work showing them all what he can do. Now what tie are you intending to put on today?"

"What would you suggest?" Gary allowed Angela to take over.

"Something bold and bright that says, hey I'm here and I'm here to stay," she told him.

"I have that red one, is that what you mean?" Gary suggested.

"It certainly might be." Angela searched in the wardrobe and found the tie in question. "It is bright isn't it?" Angela held it up but was rather negative with her tone. "No I think a different colour but one just as bright." Angela said as she carried on looking at Gary's tie collection. "This will do!"

Angela pulled out a patterned tie which was predominantly light blue but had bits of dark blue and purple in the pattern. It was quite a bright tie with the light blue having a sort of sheen effect. What do you think?" Angela said as she showed Gary.

"Yeah I like that one." He replied. Angela continued to help Gary get dressed and then gave him a little kiss before he set off for work. "Go get 'em boy!" Angela said as she waved him goodbye.

"See you later." Gary replied.

Gary drove to work with a strange feeling in his stomach. He wasn't sure if it was because of all the fuss that Angela had shown to make him feel special, the fear of what he might encounter when he got to work or the remains of stomach strain from his experiences of last week. Whatever it was, it stayed with him till he got to work.
"Hello everyone!" Gary shouted as he entered the Sorting Office.
"Hello Gary." The team replied, almost in unison.
"Nice to have you back again boss," another added.
"I suppose you had to come back sometime." One of the staff walked over to shake Gary's hand to greet him back.
"Have you been running things for me whilst I've been off?" Gary asked.
"Yes and enjoying every minute of it. Now it's back to bloody sorting again." Micky laughed.
"Come up and see me in a few minutes just to go over what has been happening please."
"Yeah, no problem. I'll see you in a minute."

Gary went into his office and gave it the once over. Nothing seemed to have changed much. Quite often when someone else has been doing your job for you you'll expect to find various things out of place but it looked to Gary as if Micky had changed nothing. Only a couple of minutes later and Micky was in the office.
"Alright Gary how are you feeling?"
"Feeling absolutely great."
"Obviously I heard you were not well but nobody seems to know what's been wrong with you. What was it?" Micky got straight to the point.
"Difficult to answer that one. A cross between depression, stress and something close to a breakdown is the best way of describing it. Basically I needed a break."
"Oh. I thought it was going to be some normal illness."
"Well it's a lesson that we should all take heed of. Don't work yourself into the ground. Take a break now and then. Nobody will let you know if you're heading for a breakdown." Gary was serious.
"Right I'll take that on board." Micky replied looking at him strangely.
"No I mean it. It is something that I intend to look at when I'm back as well and you're the right bloke to help me implement it."
"Me. What do you want me to do?"

"We'll be looking at when the staff last had time off and make sure that they get a decent enough break regularly. Right what's been happening since I've been gone?"
"Not a lot really. I've just worked on files in order as they've come in. Finished some but some are only partly done. Everything is in order." Micky told him.
"Oh the AP said he would be in late this morning but would pop down to make sure you were okay as soon as he got in. About ten I think."
"I'll look forward to it." Gary replied.

    Micky returned to the Sorting area and Gary flicked through the files. None gave him any jitters as they all seemed pretty genuine files. Gary got stuck into them straightaway and felt as if he had never been away. The time flew by and nine thirty came quite quickly. There was a knock on Gary's office door and Andrea was stood there. She was doing public counter duties again this morning.
"Come in."
"Gary it's great to see you back at work." Andrea said. She then produced a white envelope from behind her back which she handed to Gary. "Here's one bit of post that hasn't got a file to go with it. It's just to say we've missed you." Andrea thought about stopping to give Gary a hug but then thought better of it. She left Gary on his own opening the 'Welcome Back' card which had been signed by all of the staff. Gary stared at the envelope for a few seconds and then set about opening it. He just wasn't expecting anything from them. He was almost in tears.

    Gary had been overwhelmed by the card he had received and feeling slightly emotional about it all he felt he needed to get some air. Nobody would really miss him for ten or fifteen minutes so he went for a walk around the town and found himself walking along Eastbank. The place was pretty well deserted at this time of the morning and Gary looked up at the various buildings and in particular the different types of architecture that each building portrayed. On some of them it was almost possible to make out the old names showing what the original buildings were used for. Some were painted on now half broken boards that had faded away in the years of weather that had beaten and washed at the paintwork. Others were half carved. Gary tried to make sense of what he could still see but gave up after a few minutes.

He looked up and down the street to see if there was any other activity. There was an Army lorry ahead of him and he could see some soldiers moving around but it wasn't clear exactly what they were doing. He walked a little bit nearer and tried to get a closer look. Parked behind the Army lorry was yet another lorry but this was a civilian marked one. It actually looked like one of those 'Honey & Blake' lorries that delivered to a lot of the small general stores. Gary looked again and it seemed that the soldiers were unloading this other lorry. It looked like it was carrying boxes of tinned goods and jars of food like beans, spaghetti and jam. It was obvious from the way the soldiers were holding the boxes that they were heavy so Gary assumed they must have been full boxes. The soldiers though were just taking the cartons out of the lorry and throwing them into the river. What on Earth were they doing, Gary thought to himself and then he thought back to recent events around the Food Centre. It was probably more ways in which the Army was preventing food from getting through to the people. More ridiculous orders that were being meticulously carried out.

    He noticed that there was another man with the soldiers who was not in uniform. Probably the driver of the first lorry He stopped and watched briefly as the lorry driver took a couple of punches from a couple of the soldiers who had arrested him. The driver was likely to get a lot worse from his boss when he returned with an empty lorry. For a split second he considered going to the drivers' aid. He then gave it a second thought. Gary turned and walked away fairly quickly. He made his way back to work and by the time he had returned, everyone had returned to their usual duties and everything seemed like normal.

    There was some more good news when Gary got home that night. Joan and Katy were waiting to tell their Dad the news as soon as he came into the house and they were jumping up and down impatiently as he walked through the door.
"Okay girls calm down," Gary said.
"But Dad we've got some news to tell you." Katy was the first one to talk.
"Yes and you're going to like it." Joan added.
"So let me get in and sit down and then you can both tell me." Gary pushed his way through passed the girls and Angela popped out from

the kitchen to give him a little kiss. "I hope there's more of those later you sexy little woman." Gary said. He was feeling back to normal as he gave Angela a cuddle and just squeezed her bum a little before giving it a friendly pat.
"Ooh. What's got into you?" Angela replied with a grin. She returned to the kitchen whilst Joan and Katy grabbed at Gary's hands and pulled him into the living room.
"Now sit down Daddy." Joan ordered. Gary sat.
"So what is this news?"
"We're going back to school tomorrow." Joan and Katy tried to tell him together but Joan was the louder of the two.
"That's great news. Back to your old school again?"
"Yes. Miss Clark came round to tell us this afternoon." Joan said.
"Miss Clark eh! Miss Clark." Gary let his mind wander for a few seconds. He then slapped his hands on his knees and jumped up to walk into the kitchen. The girls ran off to carry on getting their bags ready for tomorrow. Gary walked up behind Angela and kissed the back of her neck whilst running his fingers through her hair. "The girls seem happy to go back to school."
"Yes they've been bored."

-

The next morning Gary tried to get on with his usual work duties but he needed a break. He went down to see Micky Mercer.
"Micky."
"What is it boss?"
"I'm just going out for another walk."
"Yeah no problem. We can cope with anything here." Micky turned to the others who all nodded in agreement.
"Good. I won't be too long." Gary went for a quick walk round town again. It would take him a few days to get back into the swing of doing a full days work but he knew he would get there eventually. It was just that at the moment he needed to take time out to clear his head.

Gary walked around the town again and looked in a few shop windows, not that there was ever much to see, and found himself walking along Wall Street. In the near distance, Gary spotted one of the revolutionary leaders and it seemed that he had also spotted Gary. It was not a moment that he was looking forward to but an inevitable one. Gary was dreading the time when the group would make contact with him and get him back to the meetings. He had hoped that this would happen later rather than sooner but fate had its own plans.

"Mr. Newson, how are you?" The leader had crossed over the road to talk to Gary.

"Much better I think."

"I gather you are back at work." The leader spoke as if Gary had been back at work for weeks rather than days and that it had been broadcast on the national news.

"How did you know?" Gary was annoyed as well as surprised.

"You know how it is. We have members everywhere and I get to hear what is going on. Anyway, I have a special interest in you Gary. I wanted to know when you were going to go back to work."

"I forgot. You have someone else working in the Sorting Office don't you?" Gary said in a resigned manner.

"Gary, we have people working everywhere." The leader put his arm around Gary's shoulders as he said this last bit. "We've been waiting for you to get back on to your feet. I gather the family is back and you are almost back to where you were before the lists came into your life." The leader seemed genuinely concerned for Gary.

"Yes. The lists! Those bloody lists!" Gary pondered.

"You know we never really found out what happened to the lists Gary." The leader wasn't going to let the subject drop.

"Well I've told you time and again, I don't remember anything about the lists."

"Don't worry. We believe that you don't."

"Sorry. It just seems that every time the subject comes up, everyone seems to think that I know what was written on the lists and I don't." Gary said in a pleading sort of voice.

"We believe you Gary. You don't have to convince me. As for the Nationals, well that's a different matter."

"So what are they going to do about it?" Gary was concerned that he might be taken in for questioning by the National Revolutionaries again. Kidnapped when he was least expecting it. That a group of blokes would just bundle him into a car and take him off. He would have to leave Angela and the girls behind not knowing what had come of him. It wasn't a pleasant thought.

"As far as I can tell they won't be doing anything about it." The leader tried to say this as sincerely as possible. He had a few doubts but guessed that they wouldn't try anything else like they had done. At least not without having other evidence.

"I suppose that's some relief." Gary took a deep breath. "I know they don't believe me."

"At the end of the day they've got to deal with the situation as it is."

"What do you mean?"

"Well the whole point is, is that you did have the lists." The leader thought before continuing.

"I know that. I took them to the Food Centre."

"Right. To hand them over to us."

"Yes to hand them over to you." Gary repeated the revos words.

"But we never got them."

"Well I handed them to my old boss, you know, your agent as agreed." Gary held his arms out to his side in an 'honest' gesture.

"Did you see what he did with them?" The leader was keen to get to the bottom of the problem but needed a break.

"No. Just as I gave them to him, I heard what I later realised must have been a bullet passing by my ear and then I saw Billy and then there was just panic and pandemonium." Gary tried to recollect in his own mind what happened.

"So the Army shot at you."

"To be honest I couldn't tell if it was Army or not." Gary was uncertain.

"So who was it shot at you?"

"Well I saw the uniformed soldiers and it wasn't any of them and it wasn't until after the first shot had been fired that I saw the two plain clothed soldiers produce their guns. After that I just froze before getting the hell out. It could have been anyone firing at me. I don't really know." Gary started to sweat a little as he remembered how near he must have come to dying that day.

"Well anyway, the revolution party has lost the lists. The Army may have them. They may have the false ones we intended to swap or they might have both."

"Oh I see". Gary didn't see.

"It puts our people at risk but hopefully not too much risk as surely the Army would have reacted straightaway if the lists were accurate and nearly a month down the line, still nothing has happened. It just means that we have to stop certain operations, re-plan others and move some of our important people."

"There's a lot to do then." Gary tried to sound interested.

"Yes well whatever we do we must ensure that the senior members and those sympathizers who are in government positions are not put at any risk. Locally we have already made some plans that we can put into operation as and when we are told to." The leader seemed to be sad as he explained the situation.

"So what should I do to try and clear my name?" Gary was more concerned about himself.

"There's nothing you can do Mr. Newson."

"Nothing?"

"No. I would suggest that you try and forget all about the lists. Put them to the back of your mind and get on with living your life."

"Just that!"

"Unless you remember some of the names and addresses in which case you must contact me immediately." The leader's eyes lit up at the thought but it was for only a brief second.

"I'll let you know at one of the meetings." Gary said.

"Are you going to come along to some then?" The leader sounded surprised.

"Well I thought I had to. Technically I'm still on the committee aren't I?" Gary wasn't quite sure how to put this last statement as all of his dreams would come true if he wasn't on the committee but he didn't think he should sound that keen to not be included.

"Put it like this Gary. Your heart isn't really in it anymore is it?"

"If you put it like that I suppose not but don't think I side with the Government." Gary wanted to make sure that his sentiments weren't given the wrong labeling.

"No we know that it's just that you're not really what we are looking for on the committee at the moment."

"Oh what a shame!" Gary worked hard to stop himself from punching the air in celebration.

"We know we can call on you if things get really tough but we feel you are not quite right for committee material." The leader looked at Gary as he told him this news. He took hold of his hand and shook it.

"Thank you friend for what you have done. Just live your family life from now on."

"Thank you. I will."

"We may call on you one day. Don't be too surprised."

"Until then!" Gary started to leave and go on his way. He had taken no more than a couple of steps when the Leader remembered something.

"By the way I forgot to tell you."
"What?" Gary wondered what it was that he needed to be told.
"The National Party has accepted our proposal to start up a new section of the revolutionaries. I can't tell you what they'll be doing of course."
"Naturally."
"But I can tell you what they are going to be named."
"What they are going to be named?" Gary repeated the sentence.
"The new group will be called The Newson Section." The Leader seemed most proud on making his announcement.
"The Newson Section!" Gary was stunned.
"Yes named after one of our most highly praised members." As Gary heard these words his first thoughts were 'why did they name a revolutionary group after me?'. Then it dawned on him.
"You mean David?"
"Of course! Who else would I mean?" The Leader gave Gary a big smile, waved his hand in a sort of salute and then turned and went on his way. Gary started to make his way back to work. It then hit him that there was still a sympathizer or a revolutionary who was working at the Postal Section or maybe even in the Sorting Office itself. He went through the staff one by one trying to work out who it might be. Gary never found out.

It is quite amazing really, Gary thought to himself how he, Angela and the kids are all back to living their lives normally again. The family home is like nothing was ever different. Angela and Gary still didn't see eye to eye on everything but now discussed things rather than argued about them and Gary didn't worry about what was going on at the school anymore. He knew exactly what was going on at the school now.

At this very moment, Angela was waiting outside the school for Joan and Katy to be allowed out from lessons and come home. A lot of the Mothers were there waiting for their children to be let out and many of them had formed into little groups chatting away about absolutely trivial things. Nobody trusted anyone enough to discuss any serious subjects so the topic of conversation would always be about the weather, the colour of flowers and of course the latest episode of Teamball. There was a renewed unity amongst most of the parents waiting outside as it was a great feeling to see all the old teachers back at Waydon School. Julie Clark appeared from the throng of children now spurting forth through the front doors. She held the hands of both Joan and Katy as she accompanied them to the front gate.

"Hello Angela how are you?" Julie shouted from a little way away.

"I'm okay thanks. Is it good to be back?"

"Oh you better believe it. And I have vowed not to argue with any authorities again but concentrate on teaching" Julie seemed excited.

"Yes it feels like a chapter in my life has come to a close and now I have some blank sheets in front of me on which I can write a new future." Angela also said quite excitedly.

"A new beginning for us all." Julie said.

"Yes. I'm sorry to hear about your sister." Angela said as sympathetically as she could.

"Well we've all had some bad times just recently. I hear that you and Gary are back. The girls are pleased to have their Daddy back home again. I'm pleased for you both as you are both lovely people." Julie said.

"Yes I suppose I'm lucky to have him." Angela said thoughtfully.

"But don't tell him that," she continued as they both laughed.

"No you keep a good hold of him." Julie warned her. "You don't know how lucky you are to have a decent man."

"I will and yes I do," she replied. The two girls grabbed hold of Angela's hands waiting to make their way home. Angela didn't respond immediately so the two girls pulled at their Mum to try and will her away. Angela tried to hold her ground. "It's good to see you back at school."

"Yes thanks I'm glad to be back, and you know, I think that the future for us may just be a lot better." Julie concluded.

Angela was pulled by Joan and Katy all the way back home and they did it in quick time. It wasn't too long before Gary was home as well. Angela busied herself in the kitchen whilst Gary tinkered around in his work room. By six o'clock, dinner was being served. After having dinner, the whole family sat down in the living room and decided to watch television. The girls sat on Gary for a while and then made them selves comfortable sat on the floor but still leaning on either Gary or Angela. The television was turned on and after a few seconds a picture appeared. There was a news reader dressed very smartly. She held her sheets of paper and looked at the camera.

'And the government announced today that there had been a confirmed breach of the food regulations at a local Food Centre today' The newsreader spoke most clearly and then turned to the video screen as pictures of Kentley Food Centre were shown. *'Food Inspectors have found food to contain traces of salmonella and have declared the Food Centre closed until it can be properly cleaned and checked again. The local traders are being prosecuted for failing to keep an orderly market. It is hoped that the Food Centre will be open again in a few days'*

Gary knew it was all rubbish and that the Army had planted whatever germs might have been found. Was it all because of him, he wondered.
"That's all a load of rubbish." Gary said to Angela.
"I know darling but let them report it how they want. We know the probable truth."
"Yes but will the children, the people of tomorrow know?"
"We'll have to do our best to make sure that the children do know." Angela sighed.

-

Gary's first couple of days back at work had gone reasonably well and he felt that after this weekend he would be able to make a better effort at tackling some of the files which had started to pile up in his tray. The staff had been brilliant and helped him to slip back into his duties without too much trouble. What was more, Angela and the kids had moved back in and family life was good. Gary felt he was a very lucky man to have all these wonderful people around him and he guessed it had been a very close call to Angela leaving him for good. As he sat there on the settee next to her he leant across and gave her a little kiss on the cheek.
"What was that for?" Angela turned to face him as she said it. She was glad to have Gary back. She had missed him terribly. He was a dependable man. In lots of ways a very sexy man. She kissed him on the lips. They kissed each other momentarily. It had been a long time since they had last kissed anything like this.
"I just love you." Gary eventually replied.
"And I love you too." Angela smiled as she felt complete again. Gary looked at her and saw just what a sexy woman he was married to. The two of them looked at each other for a few more moments until that familiar music sounded on the television and grabbed their attention.

It was the music from 'Teamball' and this meant that the whole family would be sat in front of the television glued to it like hypnotized robots. Angela prepared to shout out for Katy and Joan to come and join them but they had already found their way into the lounge.
"Have you two been kissing?" Katy asked with a disgusted tone.
"Urgh!!" Joan added whilst pulling a funny face.
"It's what grown ups do." Gary answered.
"I hope I never grow up." Joan concluded.

The four of them settled down on and next to the settee so that they could all watch the television.
The voiceover on the theme music introduced the show as usual.
"I hope you are all sitting in your seats now as you won't be for long. It's time for another challenge of Teamball, with your host, Johnny Johnson." The voice delivered the opening message with the usual excitable voice as the camera zoomed in from above a green field to the host and Compere Johnny Johnson who was there waiting on the green. Today he was decked out in an all white suit which was of the usual design with thick pointed shoulders and a very thin cut into his waist. His trousers, which were unusually also white, were extremely thin and still clinging to his very skinny legs but today Johnny Johnson was wearing what looked like cut down red Wellington boots. They were big, extended at the front to give him the strangest of looks and to finish off his look, Johnny had his hair dyed in two colours, red and bright yellow which were split into four sections. His hair looked as if it could have been a hat he was wearing but it was definitely hair. Johnny was wearing thick framed red glasses today with a yellow light on the corner of each glass. The lights would flash every now and then.

The weather looked reasonable and the conditions fairly good as the camera on the ground panned round to bring Johnny Johnson into frame. The Compere was holding a big microphone in one hand and a large cane with a sort of glass ball on the top. The cane was spiraled red and yellow to match his hair and the glass ball would show yellow snowflakes if he shook it about. He wore a badge showing the programmes logo on his left lapel and as the camera got nearer to him he started to jump up and down and wave his hands and legs about in no particular fashion.

"Hiya folks. I hope you're ready to be entertained." Johnny Johnson started off with a slightly different version of his usual opening line. *"It's the country's most popular event and it's nearly time to start."* Johnny said the final line in his usual strange voice whilst continuing to jump around like a maniac. *"On this Dominical day, the weather seems to have been very good to us with a little bit of sunshine. We might get a little bit of rain later but we don't care do we as we'll all be having a great time."* Johnny stopped to allow the camera to pan round and take in the surrounding area. The camera pulled out to take in not only the green where the event was taking place but both of the competing teams, who were waiting to be called, the crowd and the referees. The camera snapped straight back to the Compere. *"Don't forget though, tonight is a very special night. It's a special night because it's Teamball but it's a very special night because one of the teams is playing for a holiday."* Like normal, Johnny Johnsons' voice was excitable all the way through and he did little jumps and waves of his arms whilst he spoke. *"Yes tonight our reigning champions could be winning a family holiday of a lifetime and that hasn't been won for a long while now."* It had actually been over a year since a family had won three games in a row. Gary couldn't actually remember when this had last happened.
"Darling can you remember the last time a family actually won a holiday?" Gary asked Angela. She thought for a couple of seconds.
"No I don't think I can."
"Someone has won it before haven't they?"
"Oh I remember someone going to some far off island somewhere I think." To be honest, Gary and Angela were both uncertain whether or not anyone had ever won a holiday. They were both hoping that the Howley-Smythes did it.
"And can you remember who our reigning family are? Yes it's that posh lot from Swindon, the Howley-Smythes." Johnny continued in his high pitched silly voice whilst jumping up every now and then.
Having delivered his last line he waited for the Howley-Smythes to be the next camera shot so he continued to nod his head excessively and pulled one or two silly faces whilst he waited for the camera to do its bit. After a brief pause, the camera panned out and moved to the left until the Howley-Smythes came into shot. Behind them you could just see the side of the stand in which the crowd were sitting and the noise that the crowd of supporters were making was starting to be heard. Once again the Howley-Smythe team were all wearing the same sports

gear that they had before. Each player had his or her name on their back. Within seconds, Johnny Johnson came back into shot and he walked towards the Howley-Smythe team. Because he was wearing Wellington boots, he walked a silly style so that his legs sort of kicked out to the front and at an angle after each step. The camera caught just two or three of his steps before he started to speak again.

"So here they are, our reigning champions, the Howley-Smythes. Come and chat Mother." Johnny Johnson spoke with a northern accent for this last line. He grabbed Marilyn firmly but gently by the arm with the hand that was holding the cane and he turned her towards the camera. "Hello Marilyn how are we today?"

"Feeling good Johnny." Marilyn answered with a happy big smile.

"Feeling good." Johnny repeated this little bit and did another jump.

"And are the team ready for their challenge today?"

"Oh I think we are."

"And is everyone excited about possibly winning the holiday of a lifetime?" Again Johnny nodded his head ferociously as he said this line whilst pulling a funny face for the camera at the end of it.

"We're just looking forward to the game Johnny." Marilyn quite rightly didn't want to sound over confident. She knew that her team were pretty good but also knew that the show would have found worthy opponents for them for this third game. As it happened, the opponents who had been chosen were a very fit team and had been on stand-by just in case a family were going for their third win.

"And have you got some new tricks up your sleeves for us today? Perhaps we might see some more acrobatics from you?" Johnny asked again.

"We're not quite sure what we're going to do today. You'll have to wait and see." Marilyn was not going to give anything away even though the family had naturally been planning like mad.

"And once again fellas." Johnny gave a funny face to the camera.

"We have the incredibly sexy Geraldine with us." Johnny moved straight over next to Geraldine and as before, put his arm round her waist and gave it a little squeeze. Geraldine was lapping up her moment. She had traces of some make up on today, not that she really needed it. She was acting as coy as she possibly could and the television company was loving it.

"I believe you've had lots of mail this week Geraldine."

"Yes just a few." Geraldine smiled at the camera as she said this and was getting right into all of this fame. She kept a constant smile on her

face all the time the camera was on her and Johnny was beginning to feel a little bit out done. Having a sexy contestant was okay but he was the star and made sure that everyone knew.
"I think you've had a few offers of marriage?" Johnny tried to break Geraldine's composure by asking her this.
"I have and all I can say to all those lovely men out there is hello." Geraldine curtseyed and gave a big wave to the camera. *"I just haven't made up my mind yet."* Once again, the television company thought that this was brilliant. Company executives were over the moon with her response as they knew that this would have all the men tuning in. Johnny was taken aback at her reply and not very pleased at all. He wasn't going to have this girl taking all the limelight. He was being given his instructions through his ear microphone and he could hear the director saying 'keep the camera on Geraldine a while longer' which started to annoy him. He interrupted.
"I think you have actually had some different sorts of offers in some of the letters Geraldine. What would you like to say to those men out there?" Johnny had seen some of the letters that Geraldine had received and as always they contained a mixture of kind comments, horrible comments, nice offers and darn right disgusting suggestions. He also knew that she and her family had been rather upset by some of the contents and hoped that making her think of this would put her off. He was wrong.
"Well I just have to say to all of you out there, thank you for all of your letters, I loved them all but some better than others." She was just beautiful and the viewing figures must have been shooting through the roof. Johnny wasn't very happy but had to admit defeat and he turned his attentions to the father Harry. The director wasn't pleased but had to go with it.
"So Harry, how do you think your family will do today?"
"We'll do our best. I want to win for my other two daughters, Victoria and Jane." Harry tried to indicate over to his other two daughters but Johnny was having none of it.
"So let's see what sort of holiday you could win." Johnny got back to jumping up and down a bit more as he waited for the video of the holiday prizes to be shown.

Gary sat glued to the television.
"Hope you're not drooling over Geraldine my dear." Angela said to him in a sarcastic manner.

"Of course not, I'm just very interested in the programme." They both knew he was lying.

Johnny Johnson finished off with his normal little bit of interviewing and allowed the tapes of the two families to be shown as usual. Today's opponents for the Howley-Smythes were the Chumbra family who came from Nottingham. They were obviously handpicked to be difficult opponents for this third run and when you saw the taped introduction of the family they came across very subdued and not at all keen. As the cameras went live, the Chumbras were nearly all dressed in traditional saris and long silk coats. All of this was designed to give the Howley-Smythes a false sense of security but they weren't going to be fooled. They knew that they would be up against a tough fit family for this event and they had various plans to try out depending on what their opponents were capable of.

"So here we are today in York. The referee has indicated that we are ready for the countdown so let's get ready." Johnny Johnson had done his opening bit and he now allowed today's match referee, Pauline Mills to take control. She started the countdown clock and made sure that both teams went to their places behind their respective lines. The Howley-Smythes went into a huddle and talked over their opening plan whilst the Chumbra family started to remove their traditional Indian dress to reveal a more sporting type attire underneath. As they did it became obvious that nearly all of the Chumbra team were pretty fit and they started to do some stretching exercises in order to warm up those muscles that on some of the team were also very evident.

The crowd started to join in with the countdown.

"Sixty, fifty-nine, fifty-eight." Both teams now took up their positions ready for the rocket to fire. Johnny Johnson was working hard getting the crowd into a frenzy. The crowd was actually a lot bigger than expected. It was of course nowhere near to either familys home but as it was a third run it had attracted a very large independent crowd, most of whom it has to be said were shouting for the Howley-Smythes and Geraldine in particular.

"Ten, nine, eight." All of the crowd were shouting out. The rocket went off and the game begun.

As before the whole of the Howley-Smythe family got behind the ball and started it rolling up the course. Harry and James did the on hands pushing with the other four members of the family either pushing them or getting a small hand on the ball. Quite quickly the ball was in motion and after a few seconds the four members of the family broke away and formed a defensive barrier in front of the ball. The last time, the Howley-Smythes waited for the right moment and then charged the opponents further down the field but this time the Chumbras were a lot swifter over the surface and reached the Howley-Smythes a bit quicker than they had expected them to. The fact that the ground was also a lot firmer helped the Chumbras and very soon the two families had clashed. Having the advantage in numbers it didn't take long for one of the Chumbra men to get to the two ball pushers and they were able to bring the ball to a halt having only travelled about 12 yards down the course. There was a lot of pushing and shoving and the Howley-Smythes managed to push one or two of the lighter members of the Chumbras to the ground and push the ball about another couple of yards before calling for their first 'time-out'. The Howley-Smythes were exhausted. The ball had got passed the quarter way stage and less than fifteen minutes had gone. It was a tight call but the Howley-Smythes were reasonably happy with their progress so far. Time-out meant that the Chumbras had to return back down the course further than the Howley-Smythes and it gave the reigning champions a slight advantage when the next start took place.

    The Howley-Smythes went through a very similar start again and managed to push the ball another 6 yards before coming to a stop. Mark and Jennifer were quite accomplished at putting their opponents on to the ground but the Chumbras were no push overs. They were all very fit and Ali and Vitali were particularly strong. They both used some form of martial art to throw off their attackers and in certain cases their feet tripped the Howley-Smythes with such precision that the scene resembled an old 1970's kung-fu movie. There was a small inquest during the time-out in case the tripping was perceived by the referees as kicking. The latter was of course not allowed but Pauline Mills was happy that the Chumbras had not broken any rules and she allowed them to continue. The next few minutes was a hard battle for both sides with a lot of fighting going on, some un-noticed punching but also some very obvious karate chopping. The Howley-Smythes called for their second time-out after 25 minutes had lapsed to find that they had pushed the ball just over the half way mark. This was not a brilliant position for them and what was worse, Harry had found it very hard to push with his left arm having taken a karate blow just above his wrist. He was later to find that the bone had broken in his lower arm but for now he just played through the pain. Geraldine had also been injured and was finding it hard to put much weight on her right leg. She wasn't going to give in though and showed that she also had a great fighting spirit. During the first half, the cameras had done a lot of close-ups on Geraldine and her strength had shown through just as much as her beauty. She was becoming a superstar. Unfortunately things weren't going the way the Howley-Smythes had hoped and despite gallant efforts from all of the family the Chumbras had limited them to pushing the ball just another 3 yards in the next 5 minutes and with time running out it was looking like the Howley-Smythes would fail on their third attempt. This wasn't unusual in the show as most teams were almost completely unable to even run on their second game let alone able to survive enough injuries to be fit for a third game. It was all getting a bit too much for Geraldine as she thought that her own inability to be able to provide much strength was the reason for their failure. She was beginning to cry but didn't give in completely and the cameras picked up on this as much as they could. The sexy Geraldine in distress was superb television. Another 'time-out' was called.

    The Howley-Smythes had a big huddle. Geraldine was comforted and some bandaging put on Harry's arm but they knew it was all over for them. They remained positive and decided that they would have to go out fighting. The game restarted and quite quickly the same stalemate situation had appeared. All of the Howley-Smythes were pushing at the ball and the Chumbras just picked them off one at a time. The ball was moving but very slowly and nowhere near quick enough for the champions. The Chumbras were beginning to start to taste success and you could see that with just 5 minutes left, they were ready to celebrate. One of the Chumbra family, Avind was so excited that he started to work even harder at removing the Howley-Smythe family from the ball. Harry was again there pushing at it as Avind grabbed at him but Harry wasn't going to be moved easily. Avind had stopped him from pushing the ball but not happy with that he tried to force him away from the ball altogether. He pulled at his bandaged arm and then started to bang it with his clenched fist. Harry was in terrific pain and he let out a howl that could be felt right through the television. Marilyn felt it more than most and she leapt at

Avind grabbing at his neck as she did so. She was so incensed with him trying to damage Harry's arm she had lost control. Avind and Marilyn were scrapping on the floor both punching each other. Avind connected with one of his punches and hit Marilyn straight on the nose. She was knocked back by this blow and the pain took a couple of seconds to kick in but then it did. She felt the pain and then felt the blood start to trickle from it. At this, she ran at Avind again like a mad woman. He was unable to get away and Marilyn was on top of him and had him in a position where she could have been able to break his arm if she'd wanted to. The Chumbras weren't quite sure what to make of all this and stopped to watch what was happening to Avind. Avinds cousin Jusinda reacted first and landed a knee into Marilyns side to try and force her off of Avind but Marilyn found a new strength and brought her elbow down on to Jusinda, giving her a dead leg. This caused her to hop on to her other leg but Marilyn wasn't finished with her and she landed another blow with her arm right into Jusinda's stomach which winded her. Avind, by this time had broken free from Marilyn and instead had got hold of her by the neck. The two of them continued their fight with blood flying from Marilyn's nose all over the place. The Chumbras were stunned at the scenes. Harry wasn't so stunned and got his family to give the ball one great big push. They were pushing towards the line but James had other ideas and got the family to push the ball at a different direction. Straight at the winded Jusinda who was now laying on the ground less than a yard away. She didn't notice what was happening until the ball was almost right on top of her and she held her hand out to stop it from crushing her. Jusinda pushed to try and stop the ball from falling on top of her but it just kept coming. She gave out a scream as her arm got trapped and she pushed hard with the other hand to prevent further injury. The pushing family felt the resistance and moved into a position to see what was causing it.

    Almost without thinking, three of the Howley-Smythes jumped towards the referee and she blew the whistle to bring a pause to the game. The crowd wasn't exactly sure what was happening and Johnny Johnson couldn't shed any light onto the situation either but James knew what he was doing. It was against the rules for any member of the challenging team to place their hand on the ball whilst it was in motion and that meant a penalty had been committed.

Pauline Mills went back to her other referees and they had a little discussion. They consulted the book of rules before walking over to Johnny Johnson.

"So ref. What is going on?" Johnny was right in there keeping the audience up to date with the game. *"Are you penalizing someone?"*
"Yes I'm afraid that a foul has been committed by the challenging side." The crowd gave out a gasp whilst Johnny pulled another funny face. *"A hand was placed on the ball whilst it was moving."* The crowd hissed whilst Johnny waved around his cane in a rebuking manner. *"This will mean that the player has to serve a two minute penalty and the pushing side are allowed to move the ball 5 yards in any direction they would like."*

"Oooh that's a bit harsh ref." Johnny tried to get the crowd going again but most were quite pleased to see the penalty being awarded and didn't respond so he quickly changed his tack. *"But that's good news for the pushers isn't it."* He turned to the crowd and a big cheer went up. The crowd was really going for it. There were shouts for the 'Howley-Smythes' and shouts for 'Geraldine' all emanating from the grandstand. Whilst all this was going on the referees, under the guidance of Pauline Mills were measuring the penalty distance of 5 yards. The Howley-Smythes couldn't believe their luck. By the time the ball had been moved they were less than a yard from the line and with 2 minutes still to go they had a great chance of getting the ball over the line. Jusinda had by this time got back to her feet but she was clearly shaken by all the events that had surrounded her. Avind wasn't exactly ready to get back to the job in hand but he knew he had to. Marilyn was in a right state. Her nose was pretty bent and the blood hadn't quite stopped dripping from it yet. She went a little bit dizzy but the break had given the family time to bring her round a bit and she was prepared to continue. Harry spoke to the team.

"Come on now. One big last push and the game is ours." Harry had forgotten one thing. When the game restarted the Howley-Smythes had to start from the top of the pitch again. They would have an almost 50 yard run before they could actually start to push the ball but they weren't put off. As the game restarted, the Chumbras started to walk up the pitch towards the on rushing Howley-Smythes. Ali and Vitali were the first to reach them and they encountered James and Mark to start with but James had managed to push Ali on to his own brother-in-law which freed Mark who made straight for the ball. There was a lot going on and the crowd was reaching a climax so nobody really watched Ali as he fell. Vitali had positioned himself so that he could use what strength he had in his legs to try and keep the ball from the line but Ali fell on Vitalis leg. The sound of the leg breaking seemed to drown the noise of a thousand voices and all viewers must have grimaced as they heard the deafening crack. Everyone that is but Vitali who found that the pain drowned out every sound. Marilyn flinched for a split second but continued to take out Avind and Sinitta quite easily and Geraldine did the same with Parminder. Jusinda tried in vain to run at any Howley-Smythe she could but her task seemed to be impossible. Mark and Jennifer got to the ball with a minute left but found it hard to get the ball going. Time was running out but Harry joined them and helped by using the one arm he could use and the ball started moving. It rolled once and then a second time and on the third roll it was over the line. The Howley-Smythes had won. The crowd went mad.

    Gary, Angela, Katy and Joan all jumped for joy almost celebrating as if they had won the holiday. They all came together in a big hug in the middle of the lounge and jumped around with glee. Gary struggled a bit with his injured ankle but he managed somehow.
"That was brilliant." Katy said.
"They won." Joan added.
"So where do you think they are going to go on holiday?" Gary asked. It wasn't to anyone in particular but to anyone who was prepared to answer. Nobody did. Holidays were not really that common and only the really lucky people, the rich, the government leaders or prize winners ever really went on them. Gary and Angela had never been abroad on a holiday and had only been to stay away a couple of times when they had managed to visit some distant relation who had a house big enough to take them. It was unlikely that the Howley-Smythes had much idea where they would choose to go for their prize holiday. It didn't really matter at this moment. They had won and that was all that counted. Johnny Johnson left the Howley-Smythes to their celebrating as he wound up the show.
"Next time we'll have two new families trying to win a holiday of a lifetime. We'll see the Howley-Smythes, yes that posh lot from Swindon again when they'll be telling us where they want to go for their holiday. Till then, bysee bye." Johnny Johnson jumped and waved as the camera pulled away and the music started. Another Teamball game was over. The country felt good.

The next day Gary was back at work as usual. Things were getting back to normal and Gary was back at his desk doing the reports he had been doing for most of his career. Reports about wrongly addressed post. Gary tried to immerse himself in work for a while but he still needed a bit more time to get right back into the old routine. Andy came into the office, knocking as he did.

"Alright boss?"

"Yes Andy. Problem?"

"No just checking to see if you need anything."

"Like what?" Gary wasn't quite sure where this was leading.

"Nothing really. We just heard that you were trying not to drink anymore and I just knew that around this time you used to have a little one." Andy was genuinely concerned. Gary was a bit surprised. Not only was he shocked as to how up front Andy was about his concerns but the fact also that he was right, it was around this time that he used to drink. Gary pulled open his bottom drawer. A half bottle of vodka slid into view. Gary grabbed it and placed it on the desk.

"Shall we open it?" Gary said gripping the top.

"I don't want one boss."

"Nor do I." Gary answered. He handed the bottle out to Andy.

"Here, get rid of this for me please." Andy took the bottle and winked.

The day went quite slowly but it was time for Gary to pack up. He put all his files away and locked up as usual. He decided that he would have a quick walk round to the library before he went home. Gary closed his briefcase and placed it in his car before he took the small walk across the market place to the library. Almost as if planned, walking the other way across the market place was Julie Clark. They saw each other immediately and automatically stopped. Gary stood where he was as Julie walked over to him.

"Are you okay?" She asked.

"Everyone seems to be asking me that at the moment." Gary tried not to sound annoyed about the question but Julie guessed he was anyway.

"Sorry, I'm just worried about you."

"Well you don't need to be. I'm doing fine thank you." Gary looked at Julie and some of the passionate feelings started to flood back. She was very attractive, he thought to himself. There was an obvious pause. Julie broke the silence.

"I'm glad to hear the you and Angela are back together."
"Er yeah." Gary was a little embarrassed.
"No I mean it's good to hear that Katy and Joan have their parents both living together again." Julie forced a smile in his direction as she said this and tried to sound as genuine as she could. Gary wasn't quite sure what to say. He took hold of her hand.
"I'm sorry."
"No need to be. We both knew what we were doing." Julie pressed her lips together tighter so as to keep the smile on her face.
"Well I must be going. See you again soon." Gary continued on his way over to the library. Julie turned and watched him as he strode across the market place. She looked at his forceful stride and she recalled how strong he was. She remembered how gentle he could be. She wiped a tear from her cheek and then turned and went on her way.

-

    Almost as an after thought the Major on duty for the afternoon asks for Unit Mike 10, who are the duty Unit, to be in the briefing room at 15.00hrs that afternoon. The Sergeant in charge of the Unit makes sure that his team are there on time.
"Unit Mike 10, attention!" The Sergeant shouted as the Major entered the room.
"Thank you Sergeant."
"Unit Mike 10, at ease!"
"Okay Unit Mike 10, as you know there have been a number of reports flying around of revolutionary agents moving in and around Kentley just recently and so far we have not had much luck in arresting many of them," the Major started his talk. The members of Mike 10 were quite pleased to be getting this sort of talk as up till now they felt a little bit on the outside of things. Charlie 12 always seemed to be involved and Delta 5 always seemed to be back up but at last they were being given something to do themselves.
"For the next few nights, I want thirty minute roadblocks set up at varying exits from the town. The choice is yours. The list of wanted names is available for you. Go out and find." The Major concluded. He turned to the Sergeant and saluted before leaving the room.
"Well there it is. We're doing some road-blocks as well," the Sergeant smiled as he said it. All of Unit Mike 10 let out a cheer. As most Units know, road-blocks are usually only effective for about ten to

fifteen minutes at the most and the first one more effective than following ones.

The Unit was being given the chance to make their own decisions as to where they should operate so they had a team discussion to chat over the forthcoming exercise. They chatted and swapped views and eventually decided that they wanted to set up a road-block on the Bateley Road first. The element of surprise was paramount and they planned it down to the final detail. The road-block would happen at point 'A' but armed soldiers would wait until a line of traffic had stopped before showing themselves about a hundred and fifty yards further down the road. This would be so as to catch any vehicles turning round, stopping as soon as the road-block was in sight or trying to slip off another way. Unit Mike 10 sprang their trap, so to speak, and about six cars were caught inside the area where they had no option but to go through the road-block. Third in line was a grey MFV Standard car driven by Martin Saunders. As he approached the interrogation point he looked closely at all the soldiers before concluding that he didn't recognise any of them. It put him at ease as he was called over.
"Hello Sir, can I see your papers please?" The soldier asked. Saunders handed him his papers.
"Another road-block? This is getting to be normal practice." Martin Saunders said to the soldier.
"On your way home Sir?"
"Yes."
"And where have you been today?"
"To the Job Centre! Is that a problem?"
"No Sir. I won't keep you a minute." The Private took the papers over to where the list of suspects was. There were about eleven names on the list and the Private checked against it to see if this mans name was on it. It was all in alphabetical order so he fingered his way down the list to the H's. Nothing was on the list. He walked slowly back to Saunders and handed him his papers back.
"Thank you Mr. Hutton, you can continue on your way." The Private saluted.

So was it Martin Saunders or was it Jeff Hutton? Or was it John Silver? Maybe even David Thomas. Who knew? The occupant of the grey car laughed as he continued on his way home to Bateley, with all his papers in perfect order. That would also be the last time he had to drive into Kentley for quite a while. 'Yes', he thought to himself, Jeff Hutton needs to get to know one or two things about the area of Bateley.

As he approached his little cottage he pulled his car into the roadside in front of the driveway. His neighbour was stood outside in his own front garden gently pulling up the odd weed here and there. He had nodded slightly to Jeff as he looked over at the car. Jeff got out and locked the car door behind him before opening the front gate and walking up the path.
"Hello there. Didn't see you go out in the car today. Thought you had walked."
"Yes I went for a walk this morning but then came back for my car."
"Oh right." The neighbour couldn't think of an occasion when he might have missed him coming back for the car but didn't question it. Jeff went indoors and hung his jacket on the peg in the hall. Picking up the post he quickly looked at each letter and was happy that none of it was of any consequence before placing it down on the shelf.

He looked at his watch and worked out it would be about another hour before it was dark. He went into the sitting room and sat down on his settee. It was quite a comfortable settee but not really the colour he wanted. He would get it changed fairly soon. He picked up an old newspaper and continued to read the articles briefly. None of them captured his attention fully. He looked over at his oak writing desk and spotted the box situated next to it. It was the box of books that he still hadn't fully emptied.

As the light began to fade outside, Jeff got up and prepared to drive his car into the garage. He started up the motor and reversed the car a little before swinging into the drive. Jeff left the engine running as he got out of the car and he looked all around. Happy that nobody was watching, he opened the garage doors before steadily but swiftly driving his grey MFV Standard car into the garage. Although he had increased the size of the garage, there wasn't a great deal of room to park two grey Standard cars. He would spend the next week or so making sure each one looked identical to the other.

After that, Jeff Hutton would take the next few months easy he decided. He would take a bit of a break and settle down in Bateley, become just one of the community, grow some vegetables in his garden, grow a beard perhaps, keep himself to himself and disappear into the background until called upon. It would be quite an easy life in fact.

Chapter 14   -   LOOKING BACK

The long awaited meeting between Major Wooters and Major Tannier was at last taking place in Tanniers office. There had been a number of reports going backwards and forwards between the two but as they had fallen out recently, Wooters was playing his hand as long as he could to make Tannier squirm. There had of late been a pretty strong rivalry between the two and although it never turned bitter, both parties were very competitive and enjoyed scoring points at the others expense. Any opportunity to rub the others nose in any sort of glory was not going to be missed by either. The reports in question mentioned not just 'a list' of names and addresses that had been retrieved from the operation at the Food Centre but in fact two lists and of course Tannier was desperate to get to see the lists to find out exactly what they contained. Wooters knowing this, held on to the lists as long as he could and long enough to do a few checks on them of his own. He knew that he would have to hand them over fairly soon so he arranged for the meeting at Tanniers office.

Major Wooters knocked at the door.
"Come in," Major Tannier barked. The door opened and in walked Major Wooters.
"Hello Jacques. How are you today?" Major Wooters asked.
"Not too bad Simon." Jacques replied. He rubbed his brow as he indicated for Simon to sit down in the chair. "And have you brought all the reports today?"
"Yes and the lists."
"Well then I suppose I better say thank you and congratulate you on a job well done Simon." Jacques said reluctantly.
"Don't thank me yet. You haven't seen the lists". Major Wooters opened his briefcase and started to search around for the lists.
"You might as well know that we have been looking for these lists in the local school at Waydon. We were certain from other information received that one of the teachers there had hidden them in the school building" Jacques started to explain to Simon. "All of our efforts seemed to have been wasted."
"I take it you've shut down your operations there now?" Simon asked as he continued to look for the lists.
"Yes. We've shut down operations and should be out in another couple of days. What a waste of time and energy it was." Jacques

considered as he spoke.

"Oh here they are." Simon said with some relief. He produced two envelopes from his briefcase and waved them in front of Jacques. "We've had most of the names checked out of course and as far as possible some of the addresses." Simon added as he handed the lists over. Jacques shook his head in annoyance rather than anything else but he knew that the regular Army would want to have their little go at the lists first.

"Tut tut." Jacques continued. "You regular boys trying to be what you never will be."

"We have as much right as you to check these lists out." Simon said confidently.

"Yes but you don't know what you're looking at do you?" Jacques concluded. "For instance you say there are two lists. Why do you think that was?"

"We have assumed British or local revolutionaries and then some foreign ones. The second list is pretty much full of addresses all in and around the Strasbourg area. We've had some of those addresses checked out as well." Simon didn't really care that he had trodden all over the Intelligence's precious lists.

"And what did you find?"

"None of the people on the Strasbourg list seem to live at any of the addresses given. Some people we cannot even find at all. Not only that, one or two of the addresses don't seem to exist anymore." Simon told him.

"What do you mean?" Jacques enquired.

"Well we made some enquiries and found that there were three addresses that were knocked down at least ten years ago. Not quite sure what those addresses were. One I'm told quoted a number that had never existed. As far as the local list is concerned, all of the people on it have moved on or disappeared at least two years ago. The lists are useless".

"Is that why you're now giving them to us?" Jacques asked.

"No they were always yours Jacques." Simon told him with a smirk.

Major Tannier put the lists back in the envelopes and slipped them into his inside pocket. "Send the reports to me through the post please Simon. I'll give them the once over but no doubt your teams have worked to the best of their abilities again."

Major Wooters wasn't sure if that was meant as an insult or not but he didn't respond.

Major Tannier had already made an appointment to see the agent from Operation Hunting. He had been given some strict instructions from Strasbourg which he had to put in motion but he knew first and foremost that the agent would want to have a look at the lists. The meeting was arranged so that the Major would be picked up by the agent in a car and as always both parties were on time.

"Get in Major" the agent said opening the passenger door.

"Excellent timing," the Major said as he popped into the car. They drove off to a quiet part of town and then pulled into a lay-by for a chat.

"Did you get the lists?" The agent was straight to the point.

"Yes I have them here" the Major pulled them from his inside pocket and handed them to the agent.

"Have you looked at them?" The agent asked.

"No but I've been told of their contents". The agent took out the first lists and perused the list of names and addresses all of which came from the Kentley area. The second list contained a list of foreign names and some addresses in Strasbourg. This was a strange list as some of the addresses seemed a bit incomplete to the agent. After about five minutes the agent spoke.

"Well I don't recognize any of the names on either list. I take it that the regulars have checked them out a bit?"

"Yes and they've come up with zero." Major Tannier said with some feeling. "Major Wooters has said that most of the local names have moved on in the past couple of years. None live at the addresses they are down to. Seems a bit fishy to me"

"You mean like we have been given a false list of names" the agent questioned.

"Well don't you think it a bit funny?"

"But Andrew Longhurst came back to get these lists. He knew we were after him and he put his life on the line for false lists? I don't think so," the agent concluded.

"I take it Longhurst has always been the one we were after?" Major Tannier asked.

"Yes he was in charge of Postal operations for the revolutionaries until we ran him underground. It then came to light that he had left behind this list that he desperately needed. And lo and behold he came back for it. I cannot believe he would come back for a list more than a year out of date. But he did." The agent was confused.

"We'll work on the lists a bit more and see if we can get anything else," the Major added.

"Yeah okay," the agent said very quietly.

"You can drop me off just outside HQ can't you?" The Major asked.

"Yes that'll be no problem. Oh one more thing. I saw Martin Saunders or whoever he might be during the Southwall Road riot. He is obviously still about. May keep his head down a bit for a while but ask your Units to keep an eye out for him. You know the description."

"I'll tell Unit Charlie 12. They'll catch him if anyone can," the Major concluded. "I'll just need to see you again briefly tomorrow if that's alright?"

"Yes of course."

-

Kenton Walwright Haydon Bridge was off duty today but Trisha had been asked to do some extra work on base so he decided that it was the right day to take a stroll around Kentley and look at how life was in the small town. Trisha wasn't particularly that interested in what was going on in the town like he was so he was quite pleased to be on his own. He could also go to places that he probably wouldn't have been able to with Trisha. Reed Street for instance! Kenton was quite able to go into the rougher areas of Kentley. It was very much like how things were in his younger days. Being of Jamaican origin he was quite aware of the gang culture and able to look after himself if necessary.

As he walked down Reed Street he turned right and walked along a back street to make his way towards Spencer Road. This would easily bring him back into the main area of the town. Kenton looked at the boarded up houses as he slowly made his way to the corner. A couple of shabbily dressed men were stood on the opposite corner and they watched as he got nearer to them. Kenton was in fact on the wrong side of the road and knew he would have to cross over to continue around the bend into Spencer Road. As he started to cross one of the two men looked at him more intently.

"Hey man. You looking to score?"

"No thanks, I'm cool." Kenton decided to be polite and get away as quickly as he could but the man grabbed his arm and pulled him a bit closer.

"You selling then?" The man said. Kenton stood tall and strong and looked down at the man's hand grabbing his arm.

"I don't think you want to do that."

"Hey Mark, we have a tough one here." The two men laughed as the first man gripped Kenton's arm even stronger. Kenton stared down at the man's hand again and almost immediately the tension heightened as all parties realised that nobody was going to back down that easily. Kenton quickly wrenched his arm from the man's grip and took up a defensive stance.

"He looks like a man who might have some money Joe." The second man spoke as he drew a flick knife from out of his jacket pocket and clicked it open. Kenton watched both men as they moved either side of him. It was a classic mugging move but Kenton knew what they were thinking probably better than they did. He had done it all before many years ago. The tension remained.

As the three of them moved slowly into different positions each trying to gain some tactical advantage it looked as if the situation was heading towards either a stand off or a dramatic conclusion a third man appeared from one of the house doorways.

"What we got here Joe?" The man asked assessing the situation quite quickly. Kenton kept his eyes fixed firmly on the man with the knife but was aware of where the other two were.

"A rich boy taking a stroll in the back yards Jimmy."

"You here for some pleasure son?" Jimmy said to Kenton. Kenton knew what he was asking.

"No I'm just minding me own business and your boys have got a bit shirty."

"Maybe you have come here to see how business is. You one of Marky's boys?"

"No. I'm just on my way through. No trouble. No seeing." Kenton kept his eyes trained. He knew that if he was identified as a serving Army soldier things might get a bit more difficult but with luck he'd get through this.

"Hey it's Kenton ain't it?" Jimmy asked. Kenton twitched. Who the hell would know him around here? He must have been recognised as a soldier.

"Maybe! Who's asking?"
"It is. It's bloody Kenton. Hey man you must remember me?" Jimmy asked. The tension lowered somewhat as Joe and Tabs felt that Jimmy genuinely knew the man. Kenton looked at Jimmy.
"It's Jimmy. Jimmy Stone. From the Knox Club!" Jimmy replied. Kenton knew the name. The Knox Club was a Snooker Hall where a number of the old gangs used to meet in his old days in Camden Town but the name Jimmy Stone didn't mean anything.
"How do you know the Knox Club boy?" Kenton looked at Jimmy.
"Hey I worked in there when I was off school. You used to play the reggae man hey?" Jimmy replied. Kenton half remembered a young lad who would dish out the balls at the snooker club. It could quite easily be this man.
"So if you's know the Knox Club, what be the name of the owner?" Kenton asked him as he slipped back into the old style of speaking.
"Hey man, that easy. Ollie used to run the club." Jimmy held out his hand ready for a high five slap. Kenton was absolutely gob smacked and he looked Jimmy in the eye before slapping his hand down on Jimmy's. He shook has head violently.
"Can't believe it man! You live round here?" Kenton relaxed. Joe and Tabs relaxed. Everyone was happy that the incident had passed.

    Jimmy and Kenton walked away from Joe and Tabs and chatted a bit.
"I do some business ya know." Jimmy declared in a proud tone. "I can do you a deal."
"No man, I kicked all that years ago." Kenton put his arm around Jimmy.
"You not selling it either?"
"No not selling." Kenton laughed as he replied. "I changed man."
"You still with that gorgeous woman?"
"What Trisha?" Kenton said it without really thinking. "Oh no you mean Malitia."
"Yeah she was gorgeous. You with her?"
"No she died."
"Died!" Jimmy did a little step back as he remarked. "She died man." He wasn't sure whether to be sorry or embarrassed. "Hey man I'm sorry."
"No problem man. She was killed in a car accident. You know on Haverstock Hill." Kenton thought back again to the accident. Jimmy

stood with his mouth wide open. "Some stupid little runt smashed into us."

"Yeah, it was a bad day all round." Jimmy spoke quietly.

"I'd say it was a bad day all round." Kenton smacked his fist into his palm. "I wish that kid had died in the accident as well though."

"He didn't die in the crash?" Jimmy held out his hands and arms in a questioning motion and looked at Kenton as he asked. Kenton looked up to the heavens.

"No. He never died in the accident but I made sure he got what he deserved. He took my Malitia from me. He got what was coming to him man." Kenton waited for a reply but none came. Kenton started to turn to see where Jimmy was when he felt the pain in his side. Kenton felt a cold shiver move through his body. He wasn't quite sure what had happened.

"That was my big bro man. You killed my bro." Jimmy removed the long blade from Kenton's side and allowed his victim to drop to the floor. Blood came from the wound fairly quickly. Kenton died two hours later.

-

It was midway through the afternoon and Gary had been working hard as the AP was seen to leave for home. The PM had not been in at all today so Gary was left in sole charge, not that it meant he had to do very much. Gary sat back in his chair and started to think back over the events of the past few weeks. Although he could come across as a very insecure person at times, inwardly Gary was very confident and always felt fairly happy with the major decisions that he made in his life. Not all decisions were the same. Some were fairly easy to make whilst others needed a lot of deliberation. Some brought with them more problems than he might have preferred but when he looked back he always seemed to come to the same conclusion that at the time he made that decision, it was the right one to make. Gary got up and walked over to his big cupboard that contained mainly old files and index books. Down on the bottom shelf to the right, Gary pulled out what looked like an old suitcase. It was very big but was obviously old and had seen better days. You wouldn't have noticed it really as you looked at all the files in the cupboard but Gary knew it was there. He placed it on his desk and then came back round and sat down. As he continued to think back, Gary opened the case to reveal an old travelling typewriter. It was one that Gary had purchased from an old junk shop in Chale a number of years ago. He repaired it and it worked almost perfectly. It hadn't been used very much in fact only once in the last few months but Gary had need to use it just once more. Gary retrieved some papers from his inside jacket pocket and opened them up on his desk by the side of the typewriter and started to copy them.

At that very moment, Gary's mind went back to the meeting at the Food Centre. That point when he handed the old PM those very important lists. Those lists that the PM had told him he had drawn up himself. Those lists that Gary assured the old PM were the ones he had retrieved from the safe and then Gary thought particularly about how his stomach churned as the old PM looked into the envelope that Gary was handing him. At that moment Gary was uncertain as to how the PM was going to react but to not react at all was not what Gary had expected. The original lists were on both blue and off white pieces of paper and anyone who had seen the originals would have straightaway described them as being handwritten on old notepaper. The lists that Gary gave to the old PM were not only on new white foolscap but they were typed. Typed on this very typewriter as well. When Gary allowed the old PM to have a look at the contents of the envelope he was convinced that he would probably refuse to accept them. He might have just walked away or he might have questioned exactly what Gary was handing him but no, he grabbed for them like they were gold dust. It was obvious that the old PM had never seen the original lists before in his life. Not that that came as any great surprise to Gary who was beginning to trust absolutely nobody. Gary had guessed that somebody within the revolutionaries had seen the original lists before and that they would have eventually discovered that the ones Andrew Longhurst had picked up were false. Certainly Longhurst himself couldn't tell if the lists were the originals so why did he lie. Why did he bother to go to the lengths of telling Gary that he had written the original lists when in fact he hadn't?

Gary was checking out all sorts of people and Andrew Longhurst was no exception. Of course there was the file on the wrongly addressed letter but Gary had gone much further than the file. He had worked well with Gloria over at the Information Centre and eventually she had found an Andrew Longhurst that used to live in Kentley. He had sort of disappeared about six years previously in a way that undercover agents sort of disappear. According to the MOI he had put in a report that he was moving to Leicester. Gloria was brilliant and she had gone back to some old files to find a copy of a letter from Andrew Longhurst stating that he was moving to Leicester. She then found that the official moving form had been returned from the Leicester MOI stating that nobody of that name had moved into their area. Gary was guessing that Andrew Longhurst was not who he said he was and wasn't surprised to find that going back six years, Longhursts details of employment had him down as a market trader assistant. Not only that but according to history on Andrew Longhurst, he used to live in Leicester which was where he was born and grew up and didn't move to Kentley until the early twenty first century. He certainly wouldn't have known about the children's playground at Kentley station. What Gary couldn't figure out was how he survived working at the Sorting Office for as long as he did. If he was going under the name of Andrew Longhurst he certainly didn't register under that name but that was the name all the staff knew him by. It was possible that higher management knew him as someone else altogether. It would have been quite easy to do that. Gary didn't have access to that sort of information so he would never be able to know. His last check was one that not many people think about doing and often overlook. He had gone back and done further checks on Mrs. Susan Jennifer Hobbs. Maiden name Barrett, not Longhurst. Gary felt that under these circumstances that he had probably done the right thing in changing the lists. Gary may not have been the bravest but he had some sense.

It had been quite time consuming but Gary had thought it would have been worth it. Going through all those old files to come up with enough different names of people that he knew couldn't be traced. One's who due to certain bits of mail were classed as 'unknowns'. Most of them came with addresses that had their own history of uncertainty so even if the revo's or the Army checked them out they would get absolutely nowhere. A stroke of genius he thought as Gary praised himself. Obviously getting addresses for the foreign list was a bit harder but the old map he had found at the bookshop came in useful. Gary finished typing out a copy of those original lists and then he shredded the former. He even took care to burn some of the shredded strips and place some in other bins. He wasn't quite sure what he was going to do with his copy of the original lists but he felt he should keep it for some possible problem that might raise its ugly head in the future. He folded the new lists up and put them back into his jacket pocket. He wouldn't tell Angela about them but just put them somewhere safe. He wasn't quite sure yet where he would put them exactly and he pushed them further down inside the pocket. Then he felt into his trouser pocket and pulled out the note. It was the one from Julie. He read it again.

Gary, I'm back teaching at Waydon. Hope you feel better. Julie x

He folded it back up and put it with the lists. His trusted little typewriter had finished its immediate usefulness as well so that was closed up ready to be taken home. This was certainly the end of an episode in Gary's life.

The time was nearly four o'clock and Gary felt that he had done enough work for today. It was time to go home. Gary packed away his files and trays and locked up. He quickly got into his car and started off for Waydon. Gary drove to the outskirts of Waydon but parked up by the side of the road where the pea fields were. He sat there for a few minutes watching the light green fields and it made him feel happy. The rest of the journey was eventless and within five minutes he was indoors being greeted by Joan and Katy.
"Hello Daddy." Katy cried out as she ran down the hall.
"Hello dad," Joan shouted from upstairs. "I'm busy writing a letter, I'll be down a bit later."
Gary was pleased to see the way his girls had got through the recent difficult times. They must have been affected in some way by the split but they didn't show any signs of it.
"Hello darling. What sort of day have you had today?" Angela greeted Gary from the kitchen door.
"Another very normal one." Gary replied as he took his coat off and walked towards Angela.
"Which is just what I'd expect." Angela said as they both broke into a laugh. They gave each other a big cuddle and a little kiss and both realised just how happy they were again. The girls had got back to where they were before without any problems in fact they had more or less treated the break up as a bit of a holiday.
"Are you cooking dinner?" Gary asked as he sniffed at the wafting aroma that was coming from the kitchen.

"Yes. I managed to get some leeks and even a little bit of cheese to make a sauce." Angela advised.
"I don't know how you do it." Gary said as he smacked Angela on her bum with a friendly pat. It was obvious that the Newson's were a very happy family again. The family sat down to a lovely meal after which, Gary felt full up. "I think I'm going to go for a little walk."
"Are you taking Sammy out again?" Angela asked with some surprise at Gary's statement.
"No I'm not taking Sammy." Gary replied as Angela gave him one of those 'what are you up to looks'. "I want to go for a walk with my wife." Angela smiled as she got up and grabbed her cardigan.

    The two walked slowly along Church Lane with Angela's arm in Gary's. They didn't really say a lot except some meaningless mutterings about the weather or the village. Angela gave Gary a small kiss and they stopped to look over the fields. The crop was like an ebbing tide of pale green with little crests of white as the peas swished and swayed to the call of the wind.
"I feel happy." Gary said.
"And so do I."

    As they returned back to the house after their short walk, Gary sat down in his most comfortable chair and started to doze. He was very content now. Everything seemed to have got back to normal. He had had his little adventure and now he was back where he belonged. Back with Angela! He turned to see Angela sitting in the car seat next to him as he placed his hands on the steering wheel. The car was stationary in a line of traffic. Gary looked out through the window to see some activity up ahead and all of a sudden he was flying again. He moved up to where the military road-block was in progress. It was a scene he knew so well but he didn't know. It was like he knew he had been here before but couldn't quite remember until it happened just what was going to happen. He found himself watching the blond woman running from the car she had left towards the fence. She had been waiting in the queue of traffic and had just got out and run. She was running in slow motion. Everything was in slow motion. The woman's blond hair was starting to flow as she ran with such majestic style towards the fence. Soldiers were also running. They were running to try and stop the blond woman. Gary was right there in the middle of it all but he was invisible to nearly everyone. Everyone

except the blond woman who had now reached the fence and seemed to be trying to climb it. The picture was confusing as she had also turned to face Gary and seemed to be talking to him.
"Watch out for her." The blond woman said very clearly. Gary looked at the blond woman's face. It was definitely Jenny Tetridge. Definitely Julies' sister. "Watch her." "Watch her." Gary then heard the shots of a machine gun and he watched as once again Jenny's stomach was ruptured and blood and flesh flew in all directions. She dropped slowly to her knees. There was just one soldier stood there firing at Jenny. Gary looked at the soldier's boots and then started to see how the soldier was standing. He couldn't make out who the soldier was or see any sort of face but all of a sudden it struck him that the soldier who had fired was in fact a woman. He looked back to where Jenny was still on her knees. Her hair was covered in blood but she was still talking to him. "You know who she is." Jenny pointed towards the soldier as she finally fell due to some further shots. Gary looked again at the soldier who this time turned towards him as if to shoot. He tried to make out the soldiers face. He was convinced she was female but he couldn't make out her face and then the soldier spoke in a woman's voice. It was a familiar voice but not one he could straightaway put a name to. He just knew he had heard the voice before.
"I won't hurt you Gary. You don't have to worry about me." The soldier let her gun drop to an easy position so that it wasn't aimed at anyone. The soldier then turned and walked away. This was all done in slow motion but the soldier seemed to leave the scene very quickly. Gary turned his head as he watched the soldier go and he noticed that Julie was sat in the back of the car. She was crying. Gary said nothing as Julie got out of the car and also walked away. He looked once more at Jenny's dead body.

     He woke with a start. Angela was there trying to wake him. "You were talking in your sleep." Angela seemed to find it funny.
"What." Gary took a couple of seconds to remember where he was. "What was I saying then?" Gary wasn't quite sure if he wanted Angela to know what he had been dreaming.
"I don't know really. Something about your watch I think." Angela kissed him. She got up and walked into the kitchen. "Do you want some tea?"
"Yes please." Gary answered.

Gary couldn't stop thinking about what his dream meant. What was the woman in his dream trying to tell him? When Gary was younger, his sister had often sat down with him and talked about how he was feeling. Sarah was really more like a Mother to him than a sister. If anyone could help him understand what was going on in his mind it would be her. He wondered if he should go and see Sarah and tell her about the dream to see what she thought but then he thought perhaps not. What was this woman's involvement in all this? Was it someone at work he knew? Could it have been Julie? Was she involved or was she still prominent in his thoughts. That could well be the answer. In the end he could not resist the urge to go and see Sarah and try and discuss the dreams.

"Actually darling I think I'll just skip tea for the moment." Gary got up off his chair and stretched. He walked into the kitchen and gave Angela a big cuddle from behind. "Darling you don't mind, do you? I'm just popping round to see Sarah for a while. Is there anything we need whilst I'm out?" Gary asked Angela. Angela turned to face him. "No nothing I can think of. You're not going to be long are you? Can you afford some cake? The shop next to Sarah's sometimes has some cake at a reasonable price but always try and get the price down." Angela told him.

"Okay, I'll see what I can do." Gary said in between kissing Angela and opening the front door. Gary made his way to Sarah's house quite quickly and knocked on the door as he walked in. Sarah was cleaning and looking like she was packing as well.

"Hello Gary. Would you like a coffee?" Sarah asked.

"I'd love one" he replied. Sarah walked off into the kitchen and Gary followed. Again it looked like Sarah was either spring cleaning or packing some things away.

"What are you doing?" Gary asked, indicating all the boxes around.

"Just packing away some things." Sarah gave a non-committal answer. She continued to make a couple of cups of coffee.

"How do you get hold of coffee so easily?" Gary asked impressed at the fact that Sarah was always able to offer coffee to guests whilst most families hadn't seen coffee for years. Not only was coffee not that easy to buy but it was also very expensive if you wanted the real stuff.

"I have to pay but I know someone who steals it from a big warehouse outside of Chale somewhere I think. I don't ask too many questions."

Sarah replied shrugging her shoulders. Gary waited for the right moment to talk about his dream and confront Sarah with his fears about her possibly being involved with the revolutionaries but it never really came. Gary was certain that everything was well with the world. They drank coffee and chatted about how good it was to see everything back to normal and then Sarah gave Gary her latest news.
"I'm going to spend a few weeks away up north, a little bit of a holiday." Sarah said.
"Oh are you. When are you going?"
"As soon as I can get away. Hopefully tomorrow or possibly the next day. I have one or two things I need to do first but then I'll just get in the car and go." Sarah explained a bit.
"How long exactly?" Gary asked.
"I don't know but probably a month or so. I'm going to see George's family." Sarah shed a single tear as she mentioned her intentions. Gary knew that getting him and Angela back together again had probably reminded her of George and as a consequence wasn't surprised to find her wanting to go off and visit his relations. "I was going to pop round to ask but as you're here it's saved me the trip. Would you and Angela be able to look after the place for me whilst I'm away?" Sarah knew they would but knew it was only polite to ask.
"We'll keep an eye on the house." Gary assured her.
"Thanks. I'm glad to see you and Angela back again." Gary and Sarah gave each other a big hug.
"Thanks Sis." Gary said very quietly.
"Thanks for what?"
"You know very well what."
Gary was also very lucky to have a sister like Sarah. She had really been the main party in getting Angela and him back together. He owed her a lot. Gary returned home. He had forgotten to get some cake but Angela wasn't that concerned. She had managed to get hold of some muffins and in fact four of them so that the whole family could have one each. Katy and Joan had never eaten muffins before and were very excited when Angela was cooking them. She had also managed to get hold of some jam, home made but still jam and Gary was again impressed at the sort of swaps that his wife was able to achieve.
"How on Earth did you get hold of some jam?" Gary asked.

"I have my contacts you know." Angela gave him a little smirk as she replied.
"You are just fantastic."
"And don't you forget it Gary Newson."

All four of the family sat down at the dinner table and licked their lips in anticipation of the small luxury that was about to come their way. The dinner had been very filling and this did seem a bit greedy to also have a supper but then the Newson family deserved to have something special. Gary was pleased he had forgotten to get cake as nowadays, cake was often hard and stale and nothing like as tasty as muffins. After they had all finished, Angela got the girls ready for bed. Joan was already dressed in her pyjamas and quite willing to go but Katy wanted to sit with her Dad.
"Do I have to go to bed Mummy?" Katy said in that sympathetic style.
"Yes you do darling."
"Daddy can't I stay up for a while with you?" Katy just tried her luck.
"Come on now. It's time for bed." Gary gave Katy a hug and stood her down on the floor. Katy knew she had to go to bed now. Gary and Angela were working together again.

Angela got the girls to bed and then came back down to have a relaxing evening with Gary. By the time she got back downstairs, he had turned on the television but wasn't really paying much attention to it. Angela came brushed herself down and sat down next to him on the settee. They cuddled each other and Gary kissed her. The television was turned on to Channel 1 and there was the local news on at the moment. As always, nothing really exciting had happened and the reports were mainly about the weather in different parts of the country so Gary turned it over to Channel 2. On this side there was an interview with a Government Minister who was trying his hardest to explain why the cost of bread had risen so much this week. The interviewer was giving him a real hard time but The Minister stuck to his guns and tried to convince the watching public that they were still much better off than they were a month ago. Gary and Angela were fed up with that so they truned to Channel 3 but there were no programmes being shown at all at the moment. Back to Channel 1 and the news had turned to things happening in other countries. The newsreader talked about a tragic accident that had happened yesterday

where one of Hollands elderly retired residents had fallen into and drowned in a local canal. He must have hit his head when he fell in as he obviously made no attempts to try and save himself. The alarm was only raised when neighbours heard his little dog barking.
"Just another unfortunate incident." Gary said out loud.
"I suppose so. I guess that as it was an ex-minister it was a bit more important." Angela replied not really concerned at all.
"Happens all the time." They both agreed. The television was soon turned off and they both went to bed early that night.

-

It was likely to be for the last time but another meeting had been called that took place in The Library. Sat at one of the reading tables was the agent who was soon joined by Major Wooters. He was in his civilian clothes so that nobody would think of him as military. The two had very little to discuss as things were coming to an end as far as Operation Hunting was concerned. There were just a few things to close first. Their chat lasted no more than ten minutes and it was time to leave. Only one of them had brought a car so the agent and Major Wooters drove back towards the Army HQ after yet another hurriedly arranged meeting. They chatted about various things but the Major wanted the opportunity to bring this latest chapter in Operation Hunting to a close.
"I take it that I just wait now until you contact me with an update?" The agent said.
"Yes we'll check out the lists and I'll send you some reports. Usual address?"
"Yes usual address," the agent confirmed.
"I have the authority to tell you that you have done an excellent job. This has come direct from Strasbourg and probably direct from Martin Busch who was well impressed with you, you know?" The Major said with a smile.
"Does he want to see the lists?" The agent added a quick question.
"Yes he wants full copies of all reports. He has been keeping up with everything you've been doing," the Major added.
"Bloody Hell that's a bit frightening."
"You may not have realised but thanks to you telling us about the events in Southwall Road, we also arrested a local organiser, Bob Dawson. He's singing like a bird and we may get a few more things

from him as yet. I am also told to tell you that you should consider taking a break. You'll get the reports to read and return but we want you to have a break and to concentrate on getting back into local life. It's the 1st. of June today. Perhaps a trip to a relax centre. Is that understood?" The Major barked the last sentence like an order.

"Yes Sir," the agent replied. "Funnily enough I was intending to take a break. I'm going to get away from this place for a while."

"I can say that as long as you get that first report in, the others can wait a little while. There have been one or two regrettable deaths and of course the lists do not seem to be as interesting as we would have liked but for now Operation Hunting will be temporarily closed for now." The Major said sternly. The car came towards the gates of Army HQ and it slowed down and pulled in about ten yards from the entrance.

"Hope this is near enough for you," the agent said to the Major.

"Oh yes I nearly forgot. I could never get used to calling you Sergeant could I?"

"No you do seem to have a bit of a mental block there," the agent replied.

"Well I don't have to worry anymore as I have the great pleasure in telling you that I can now call you Lieutenant." The Major beamed as he said this last bit.

"Lieutenant?" The agent said back in some disbelief.

"Does it sound good? I hope so as I can now call you Lieutenant Newson," the Major said as he opened the door to get out of the car.

"Thank you Major." Sarah replied as she shut the car door and drove off back to her little cottage in Waydon.

Lightning Source UK Ltd.
Milton Keynes UK
UKOW05f2340050913

216501UK00006B/68/P